RUTABAGA
THE ADVENTURE CHEF

ERIC COLOSSAL

AMULET BOOKS
NEW YORK

PUBLISHER'S NOTE

This is a work of fiction. Names, characters, places, and incidents are either the product of the author's imagination or are used fictitiously, and any resemblance to actual persons, living or dead, business establishments, events, or locales is entirely coincidental.

Cataloging-in-Publication Data has been applied for and may be obtained from the Library of Congress.

Hardcover ISBN: 978-1-4197-1380-4
Paperback ISBN: 978-1-4197-1597-6

Text and illustrations copyright © 2015 Eric Colossal

Printed and bound in China
12 11 10 9 8 7 6 5

Amulet Books are available at special discounts when purchased in quantity for premiums and promotions as well as fundraising or educational use. For details, contact specialmarkets@abramsbooks.com, or the address below.

ABRAMS The Art of Books
195 Broadway, New York, NY 10007
abramsbooks.com

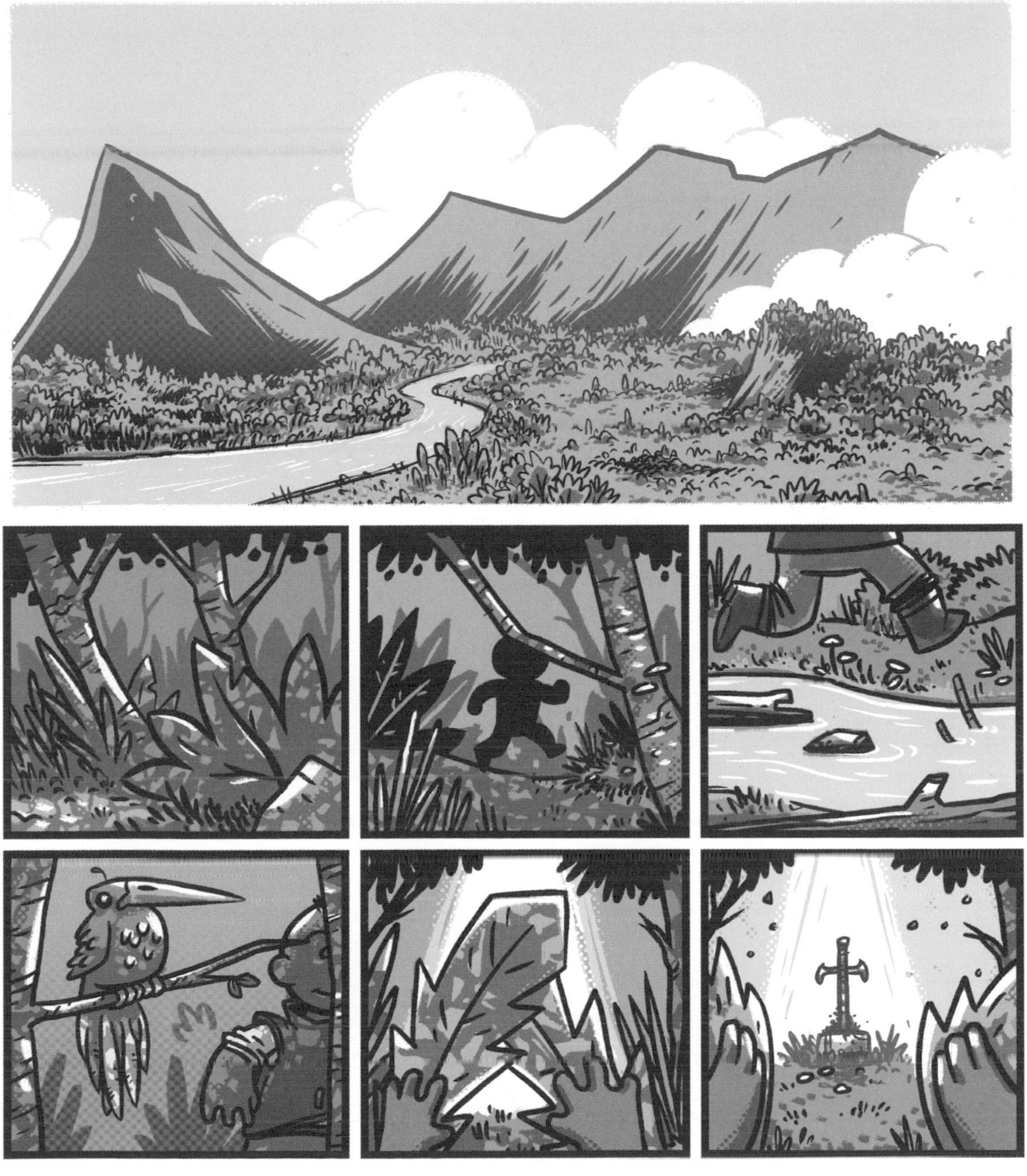

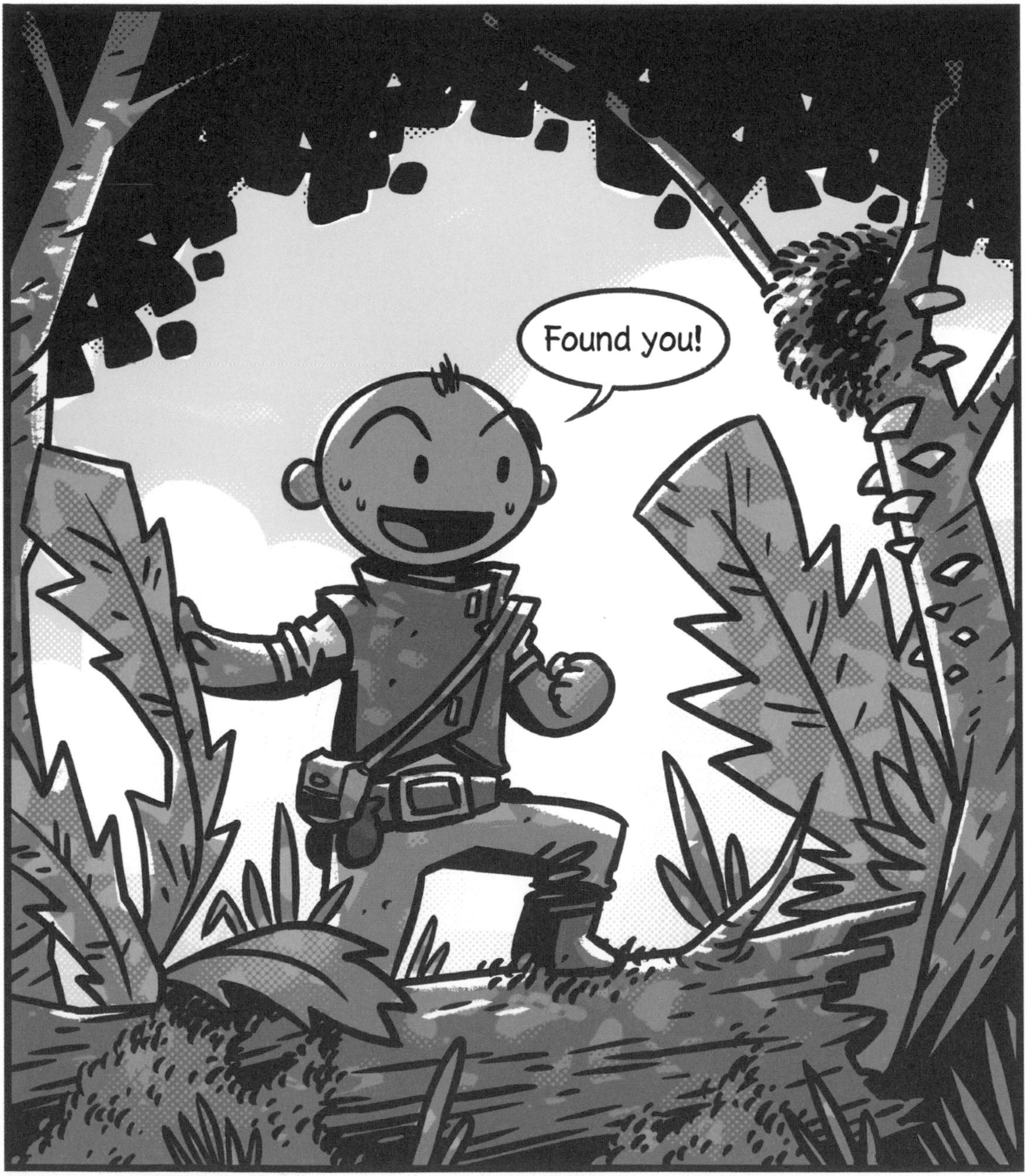
Found you!

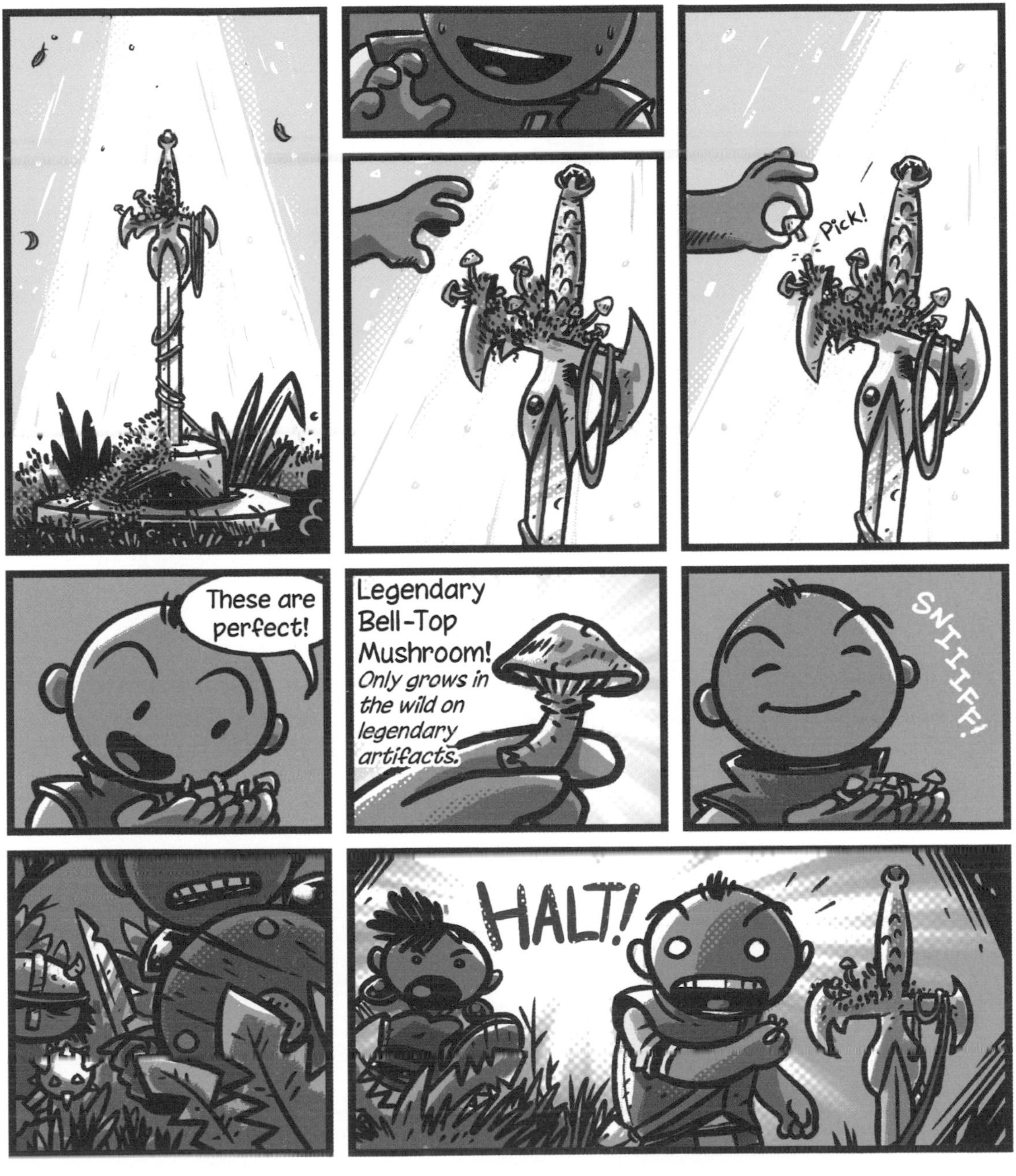
PICK!
These are perfect!
Legendary Bell-Top Mushroom!
Only grows in the wild on legendary artifacts.
SNIIIFF!
HALT!

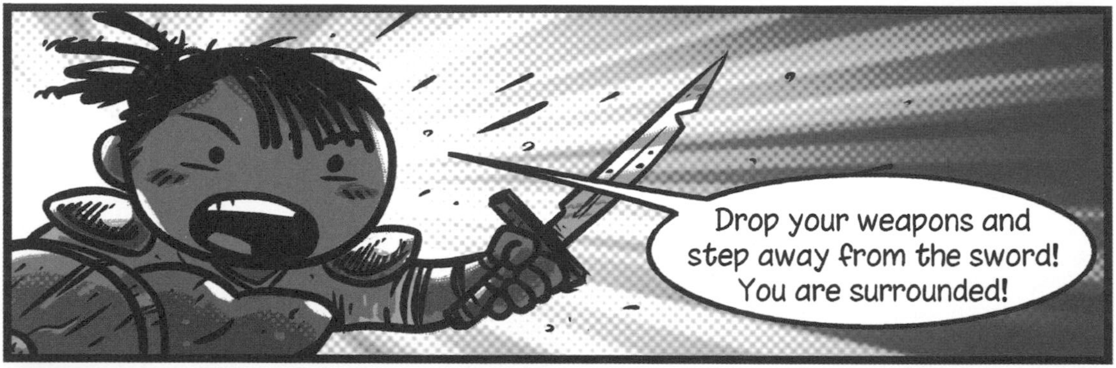
Drop your weapons and
step away from the sword!
You are surrounded!

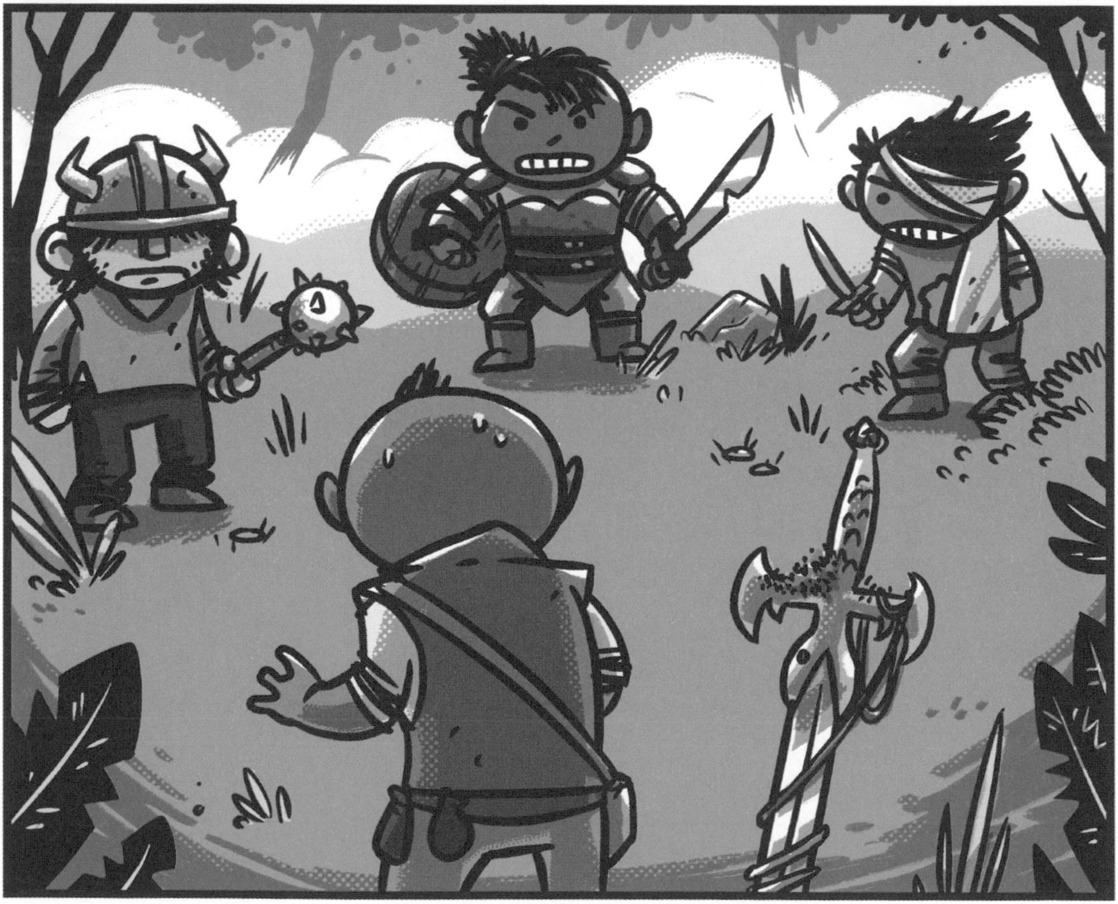

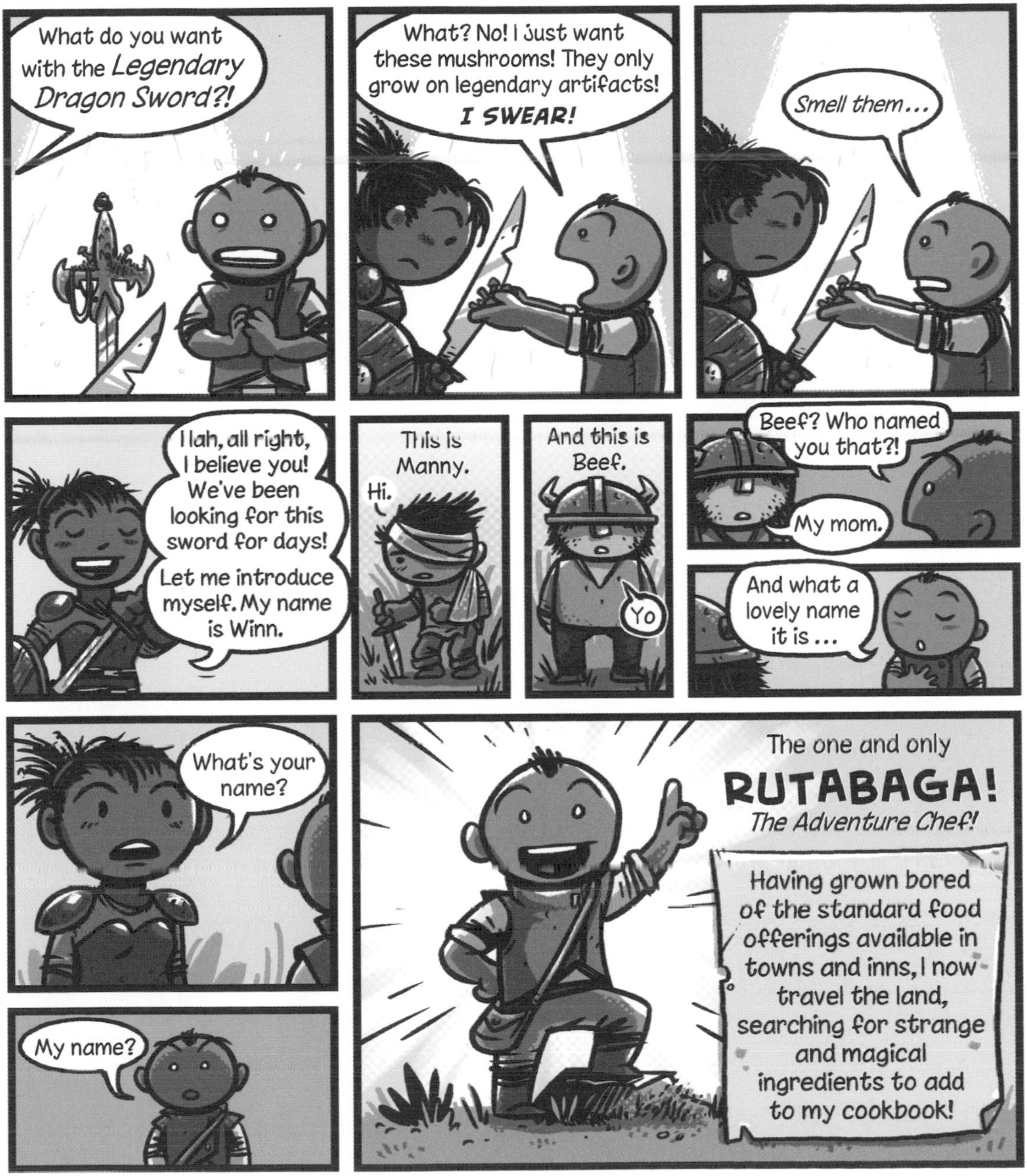
What do you want with the *Legendary Dragon Sword?!*
What? No! I just want these mushrooms! They only grow on legendary artifacts!
I SWEAR!
Smell them...
Hah, all right, I believe you! We've been looking for this sword for days!
Let me introduce myself. My name is Winn.
This is Manny.
Hi.
And this is Beef.
Yo
Beef? Who named you that?!
My mom.
And what a lovely name it is...
What's your name?
My name?
The one and only
RUTABAGA!
The Adventure Chef!
Having grown bored of the standard food offerings available in towns and inns, I now travel the land, searching for strange and magical ingredients to add to my cookbook!

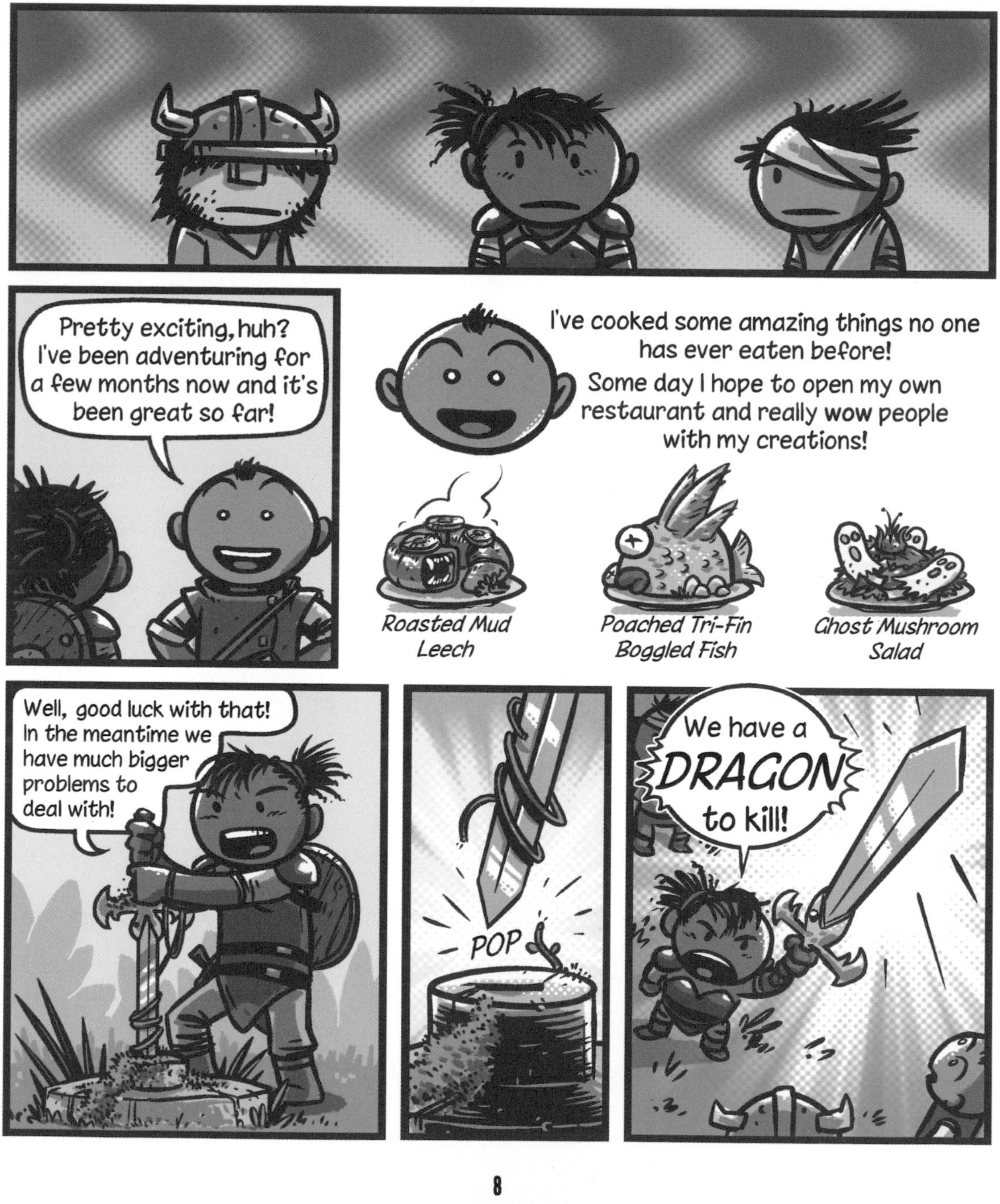
Pretty exciting, huh? I've been adventuring for a few months now and it's been great so far!
I've cooked some amazing things no one has ever eaten before!
Some day I hope to open my own restaurant and really wow people with my creations!
Roasted Mud Leech
Poached Tri-Fin Boggled Fish
Ghost Mushroom Salad
Well, good luck with that! In the meantime we have much bigger problems to deal with!
POP
We have a DRAGON to kill!

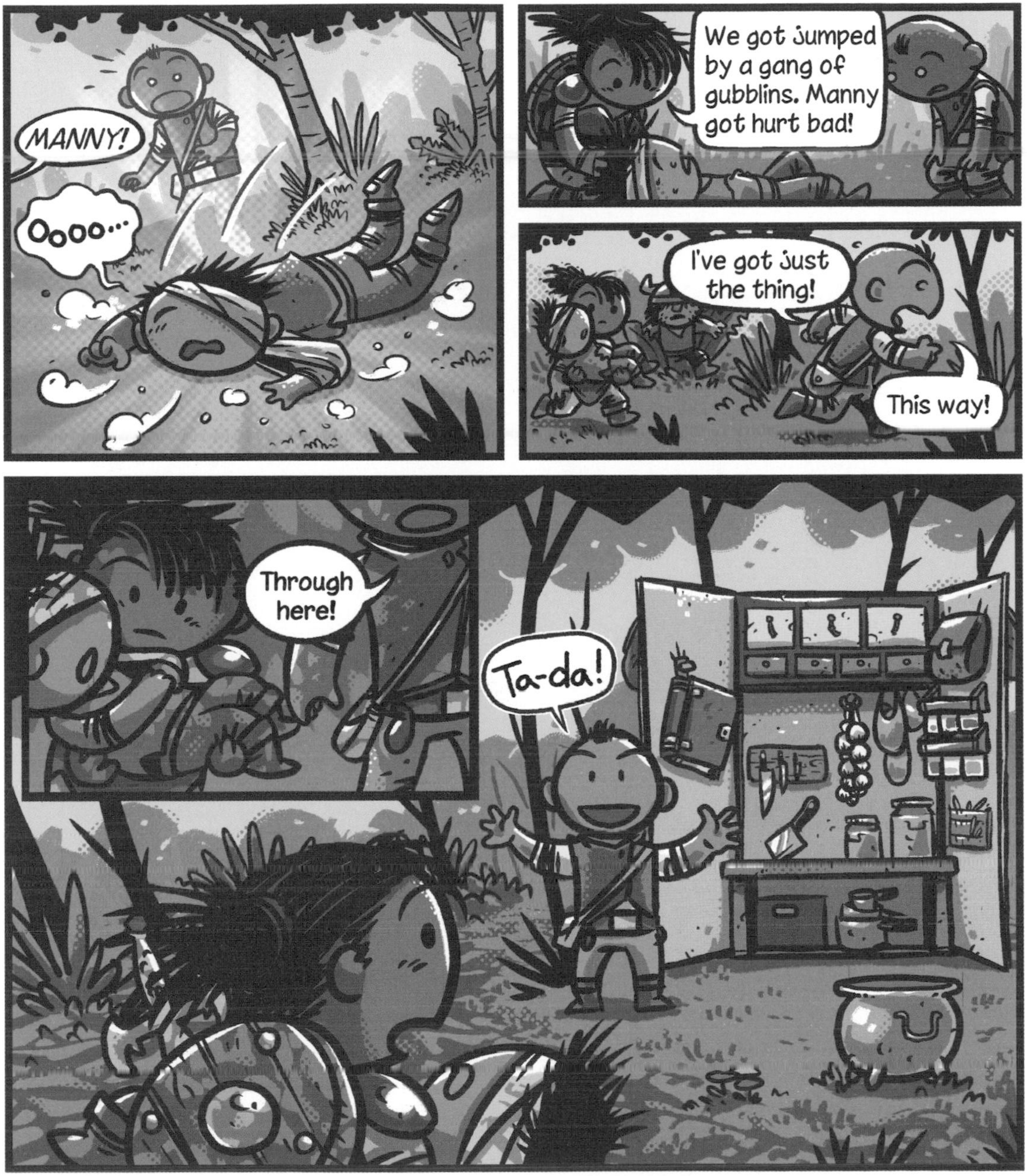
MANNY!
Oooo...
We got jumped by a gang of gubblins. Manny got hurt bad!
I've got just the thing!
This way!
Through here!
Ta-da!

Lay him down here.

LET'S GET COOKING!

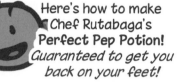

Here's how to make Chef Rutabaga's **Perfect Pep Potion!** *Guaranteed to get you back on your feet!*

Ingredients

One White-Tipped Honey Spice Root

Corkscrew Juicer

Sweetened Blood Berries

Parasol Stem

Slice Honey Spice Root into fours and place in juicer.

JUICE IT! Add Blood Berries to taste. **SHAKE IT!**

Add Parasol Stem for a garnish and serve!

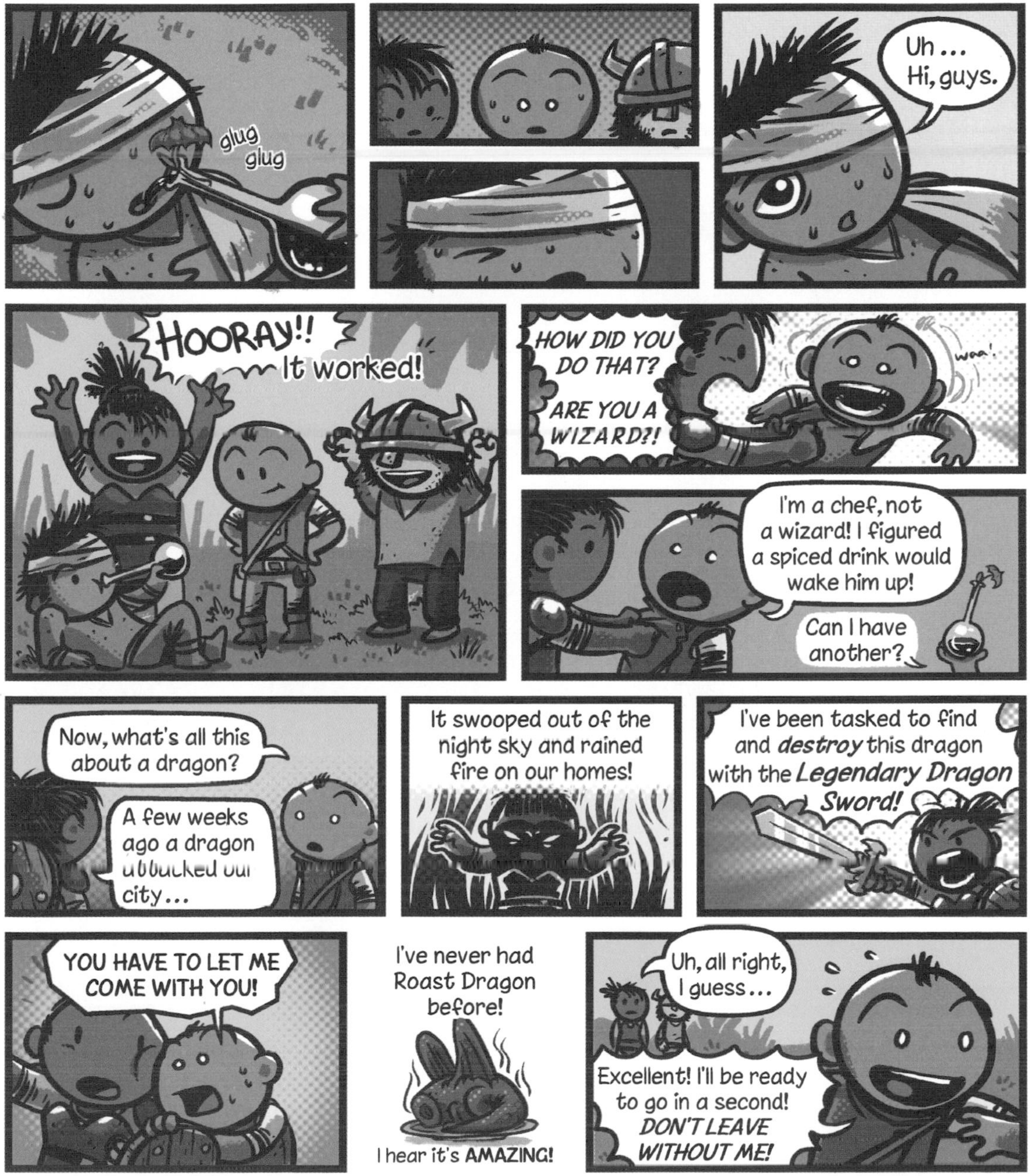
glug
glug
Uh... Hi, guys.
HOORAY!!
It worked!
HOW DID YOU DO THAT?
ARE YOU A WIZARD?!
I'm a chef, not a wizard! I figured a spiced drink would wake him up!
Can I have another?
Now, what's all this about a dragon?
A few weeks ago a dragon
city...
It swooped out of the night sky and rained fire on our homes!
I've been tasked to find and *destroy* this dragon with the ***Legendary Dragon Sword!***
YOU HAVE TO LET ME COME WITH YOU!
I've never had Roast Dragon before!
I hear it's **AMAZING!**
Uh, all right, I guess...
Excellent! I'll be ready to go in a second! *DON'T LEAVE WITHOUT ME!*

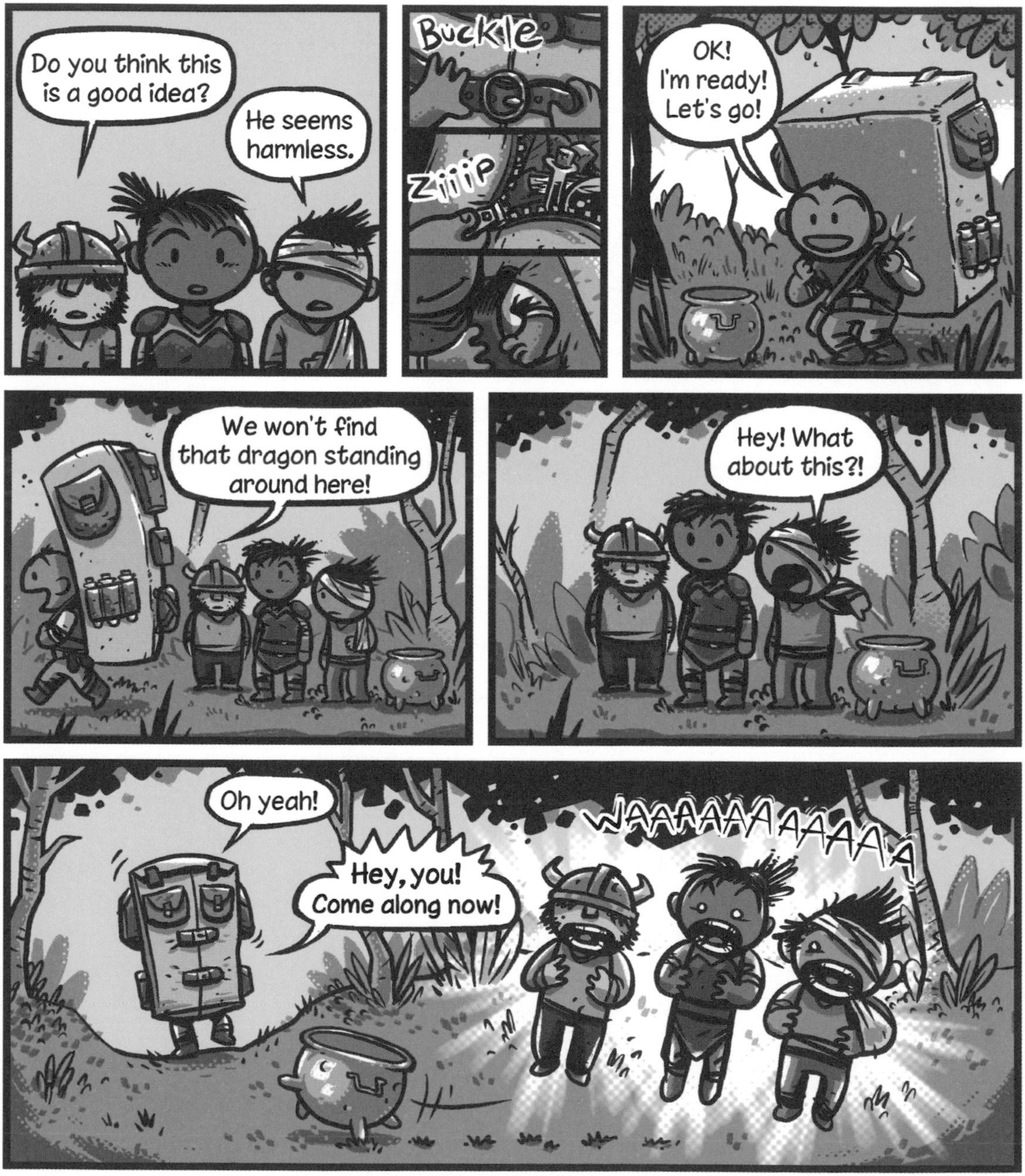
Do you think this is a good idea?
He seems harmless.
Buckle
Ziiip
OK! I'm ready! Let's go!
We won't find that dragon standing around here!
Hey! What about this?!
Oh yeah!
Hey, you! Come along now!
WAAAAAAAAAAAA

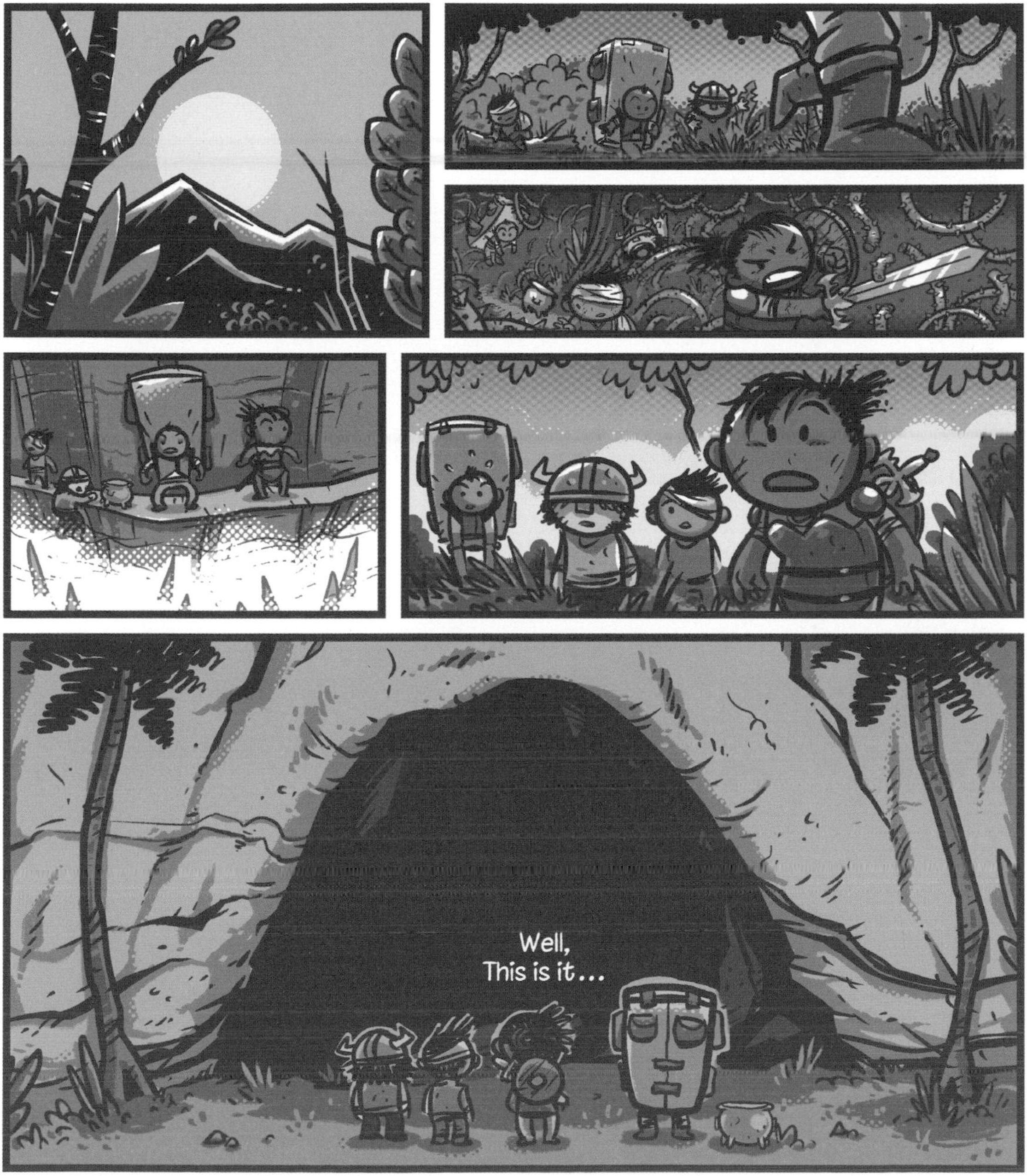
Well,
This is it...

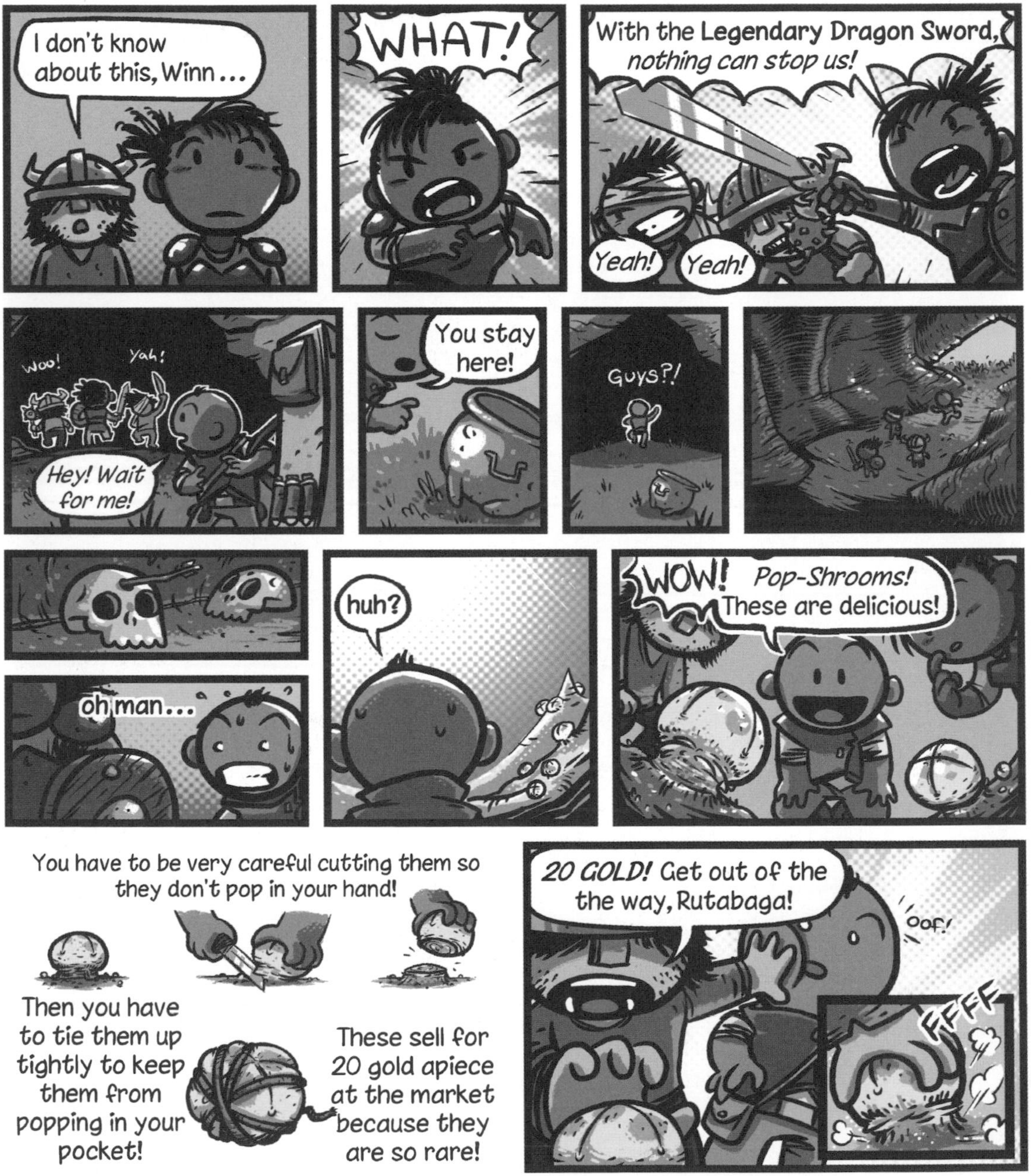
I don't know about this, Winn...
WHAT!
With the Legendary Dragon Sword, nothing can stop us!
Yeah!
Yeah!
Woo!
Yah!
Hey! Wait for me!
You stay here!
Guys?!
huh?
oh man...
WOW! Pop-Shrooms! These are delicious!
You have to be very careful cutting them so they don't pop in your hand!
Then you have to tie them up tightly to keep them from popping in your pocket!
These sell for 20 gold apiece at the market because they are so rare!
20 GOLD! Get out of the the way, Rutabaga!
Oof!
FFFF

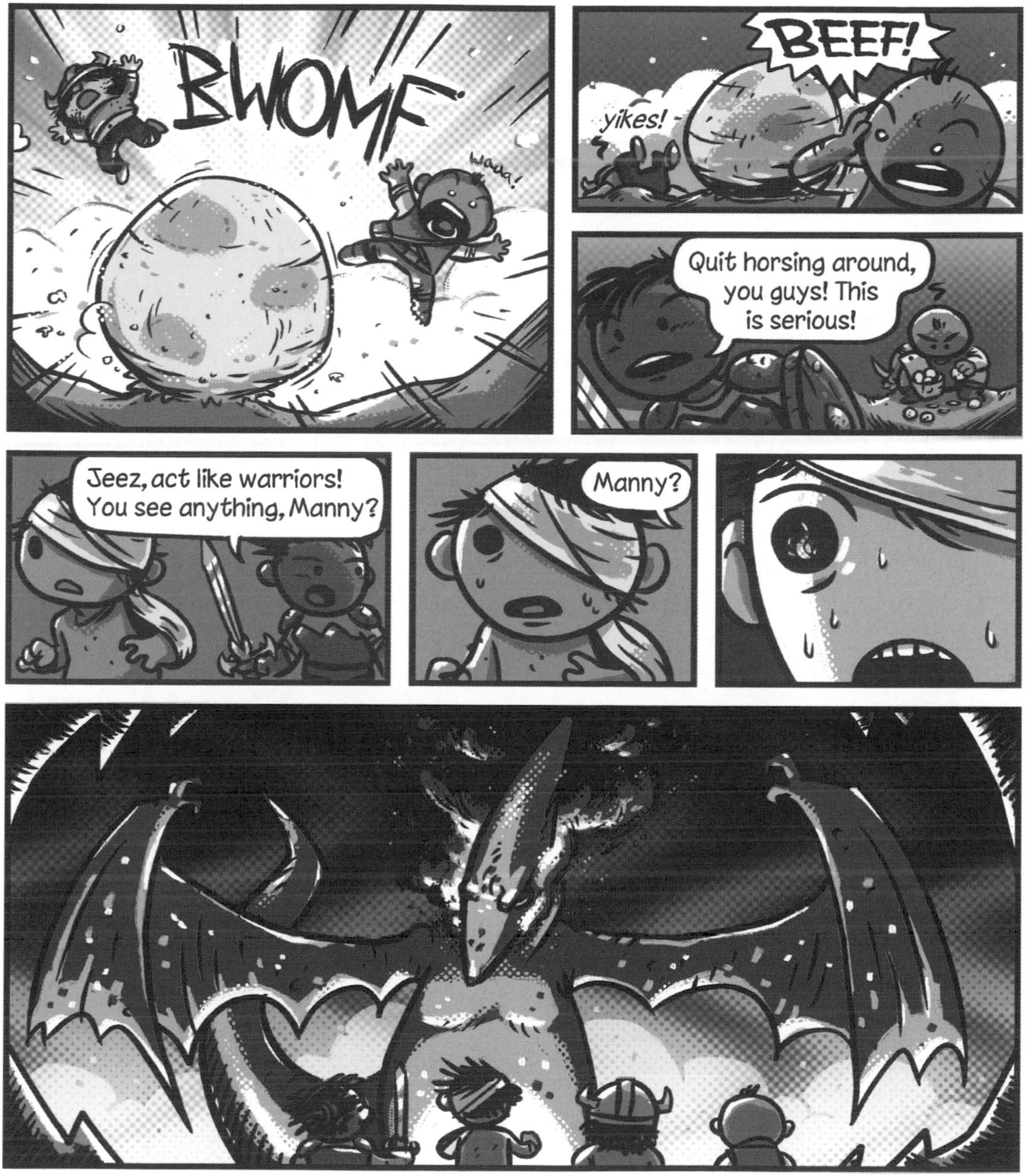
BWOMF
wawa!
BEEF!
yikes!
Quit horsing around, you guys! This is serious!
Jeez, act like warriors! You see anything, Manny?
Manny?

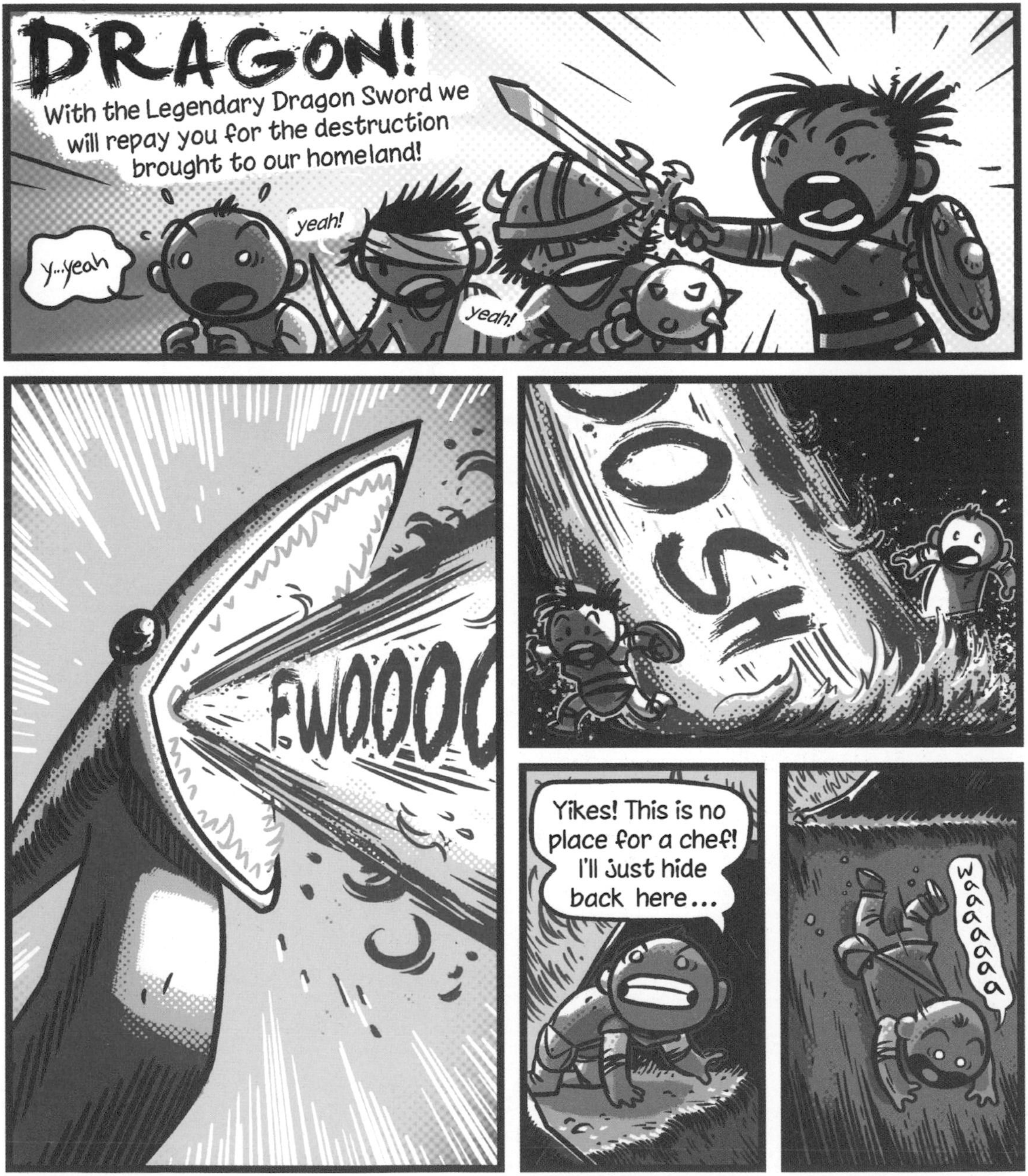
DRAGON!
With the Legendary Dragon Sword we will repay you for the destruction brought to our homeland!
y...yeah
yeah!
yeah!
FWOOOO
OOSH
Yikes! This is no place for a chef! I'll just hide back here...
waaaaaaa

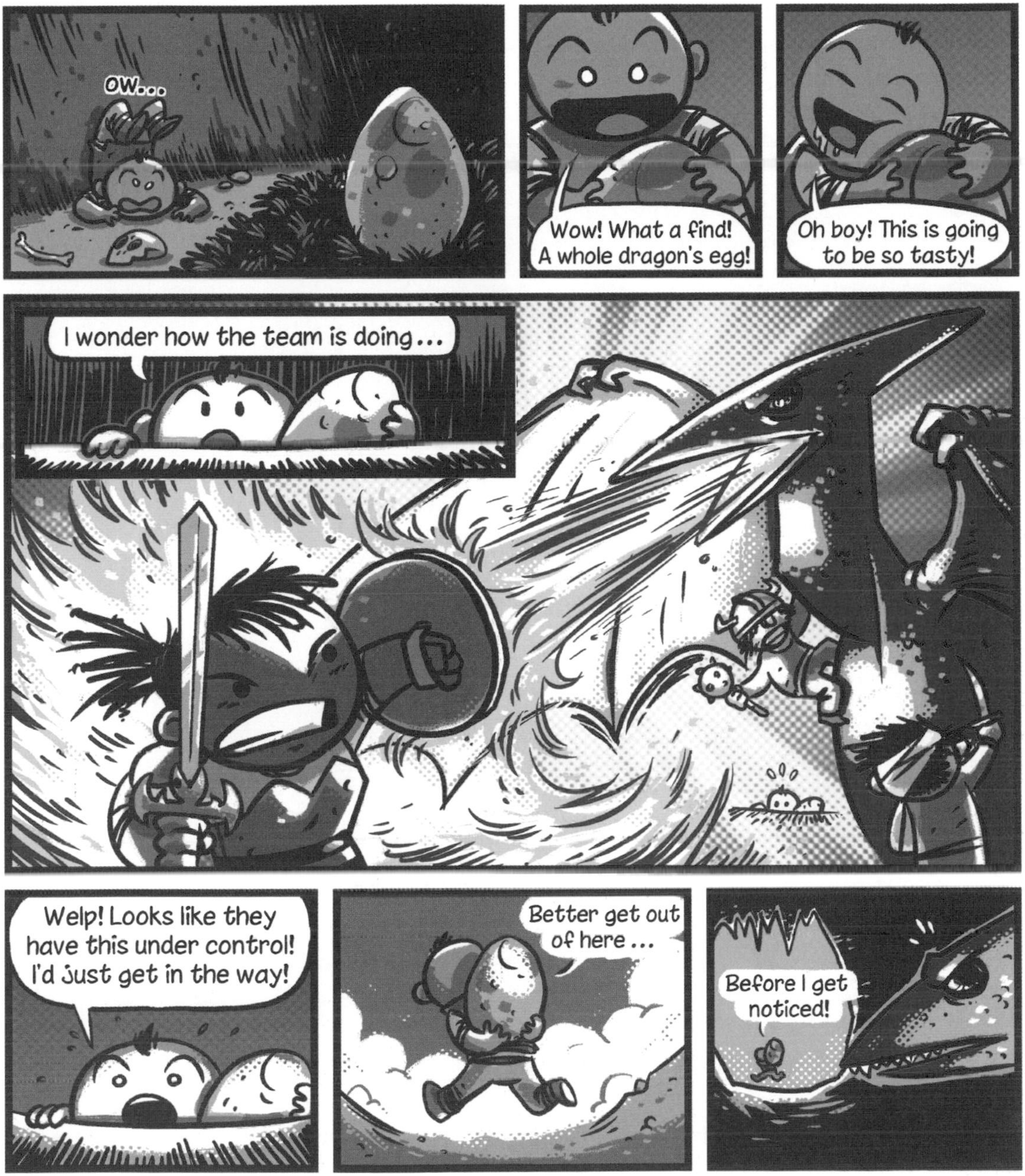
OW...
Wow! What a find! A whole dragon's egg!
Oh boy! This is going to be so tasty!
I wonder how the team is doing...
Welp! Looks like they have this under control! I'd just get in the way!
Better get out of here...
Before I get noticed!

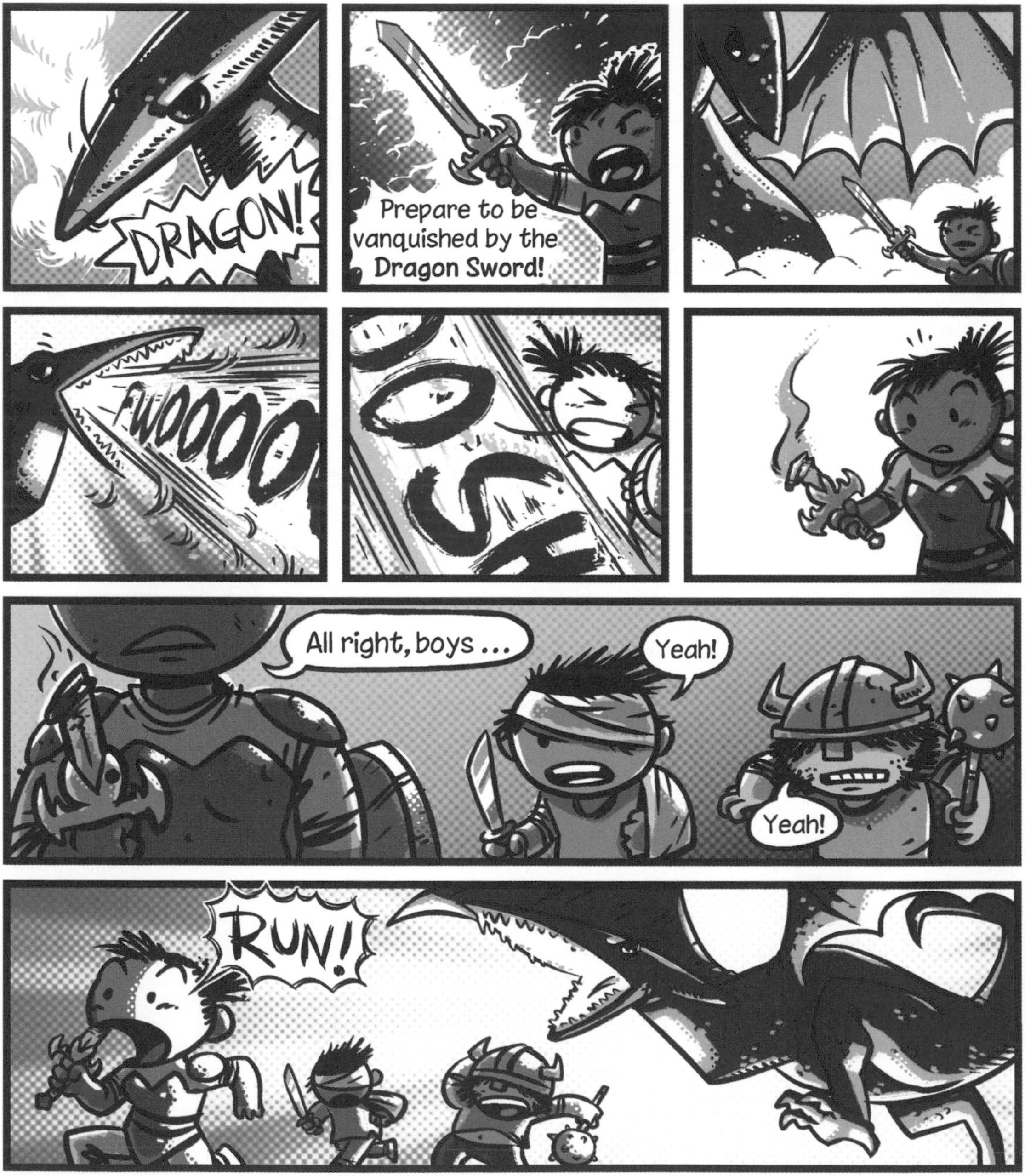
DRAGON!
Prepare to be vanquished by the Dragon Sword!
FWOOOO
OOSH
All right, boys ...
Yeah!
Yeah!
RUN!

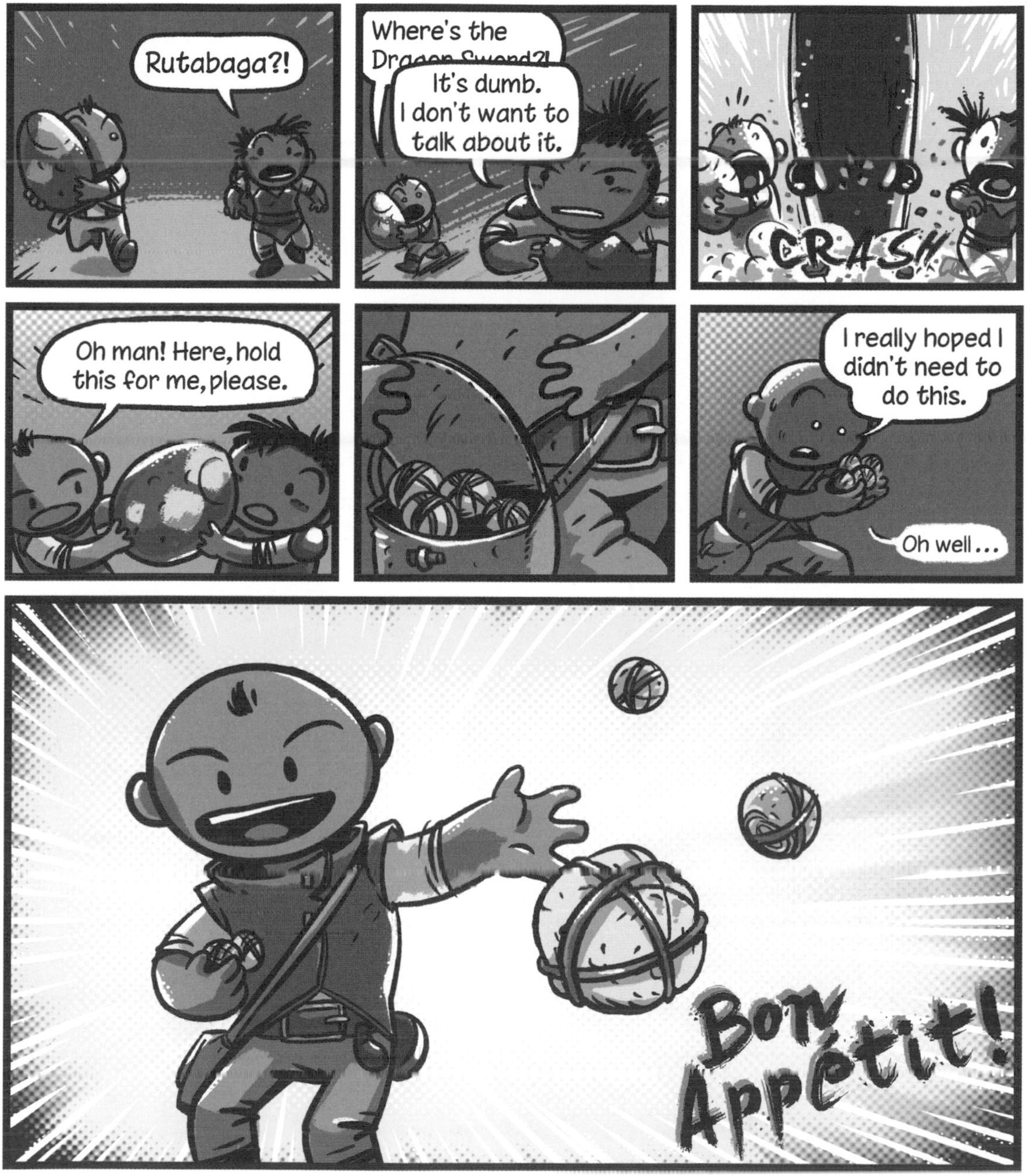
Rutabaga?!
Where's the Dragon Sword?!
It's dumb. I don't want to talk about it.
CRASH
Oh man! Here, hold this for me, please.
I really hoped I didn't need to do this.
Oh well...
Bon Appétit!

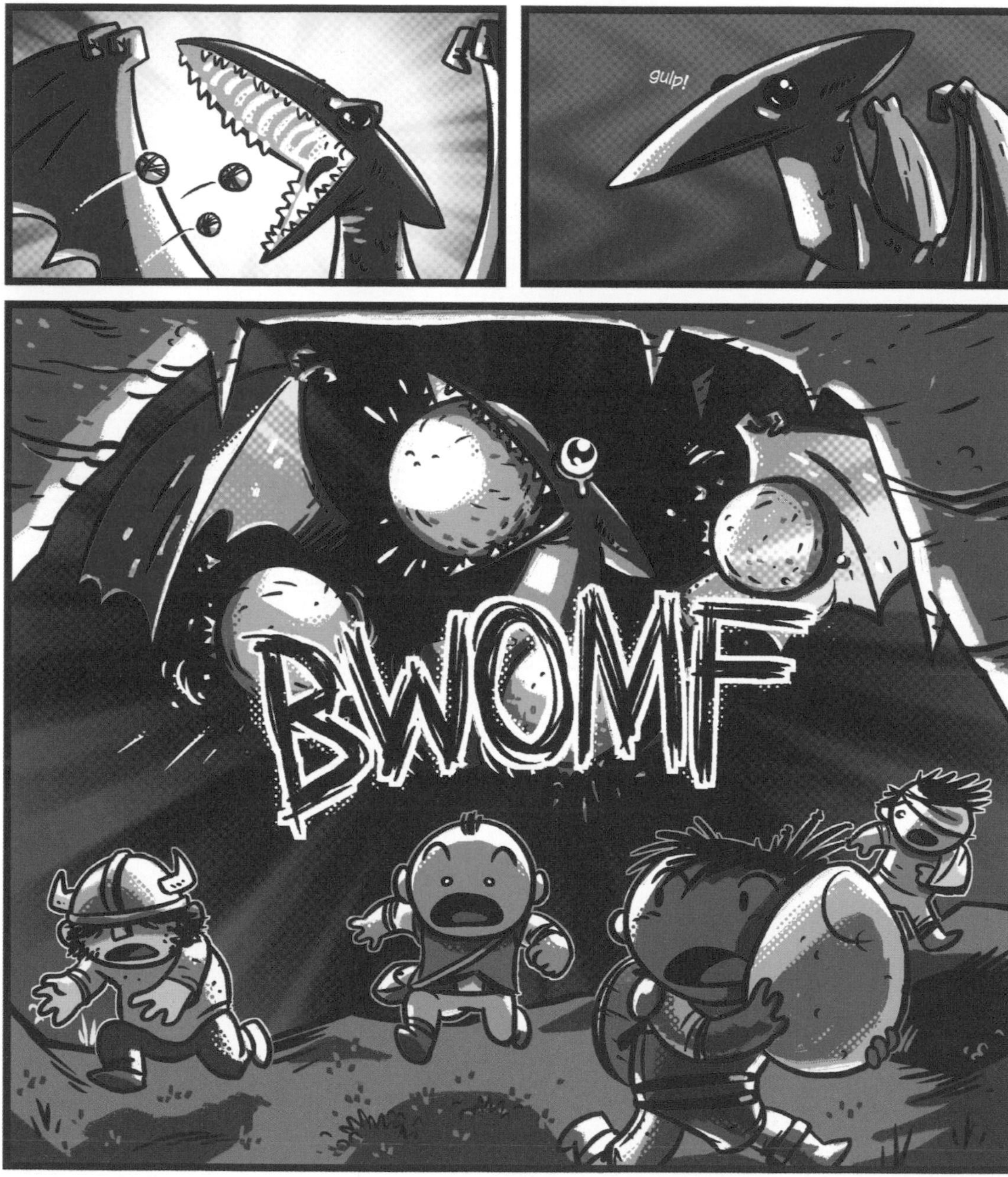
gulp!
BWOMF

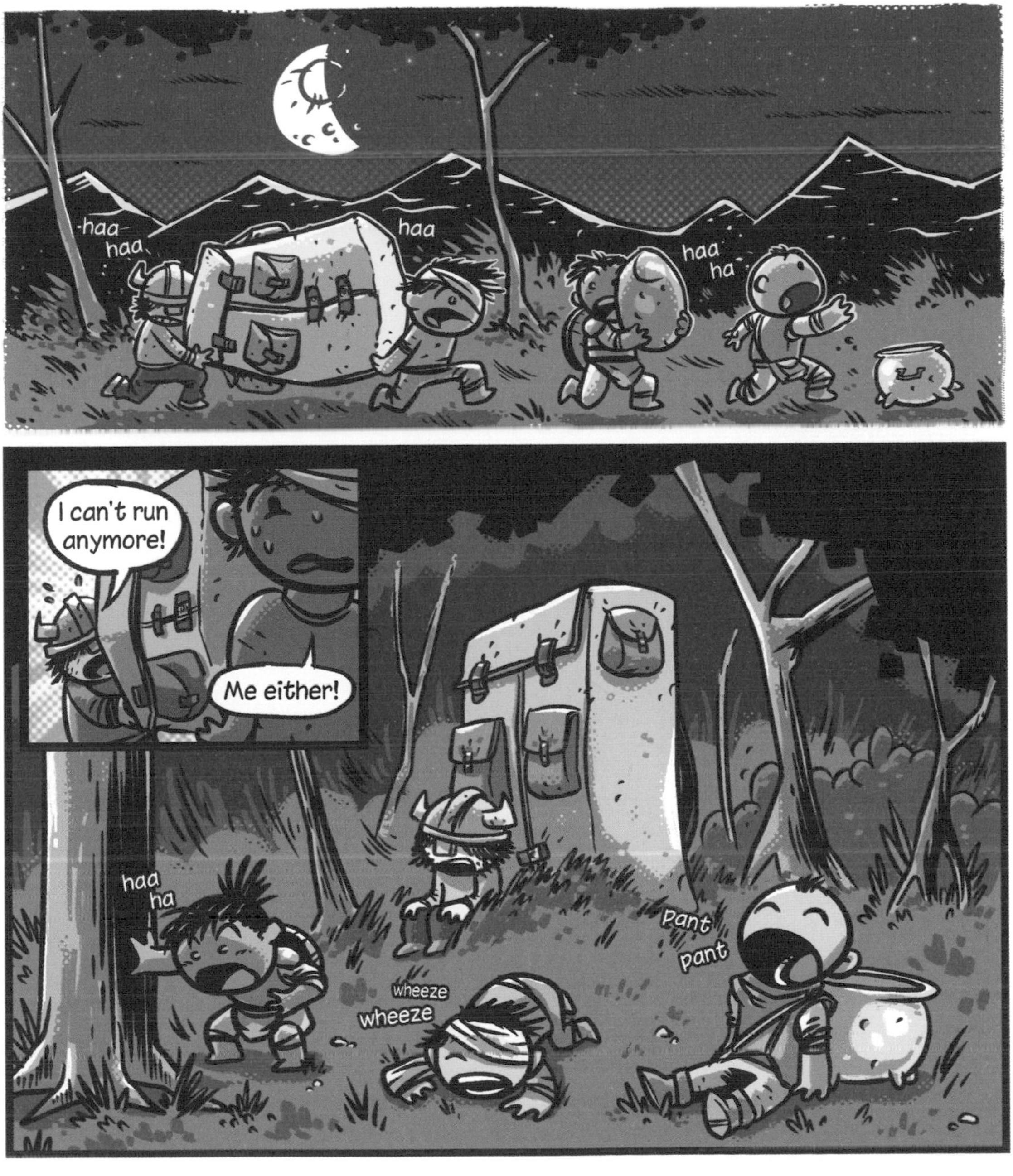
haa
haa
haa
haa
ha
I can't run anymore!
Me either!
haa
ha
wheeze
wheeze
pant
pant

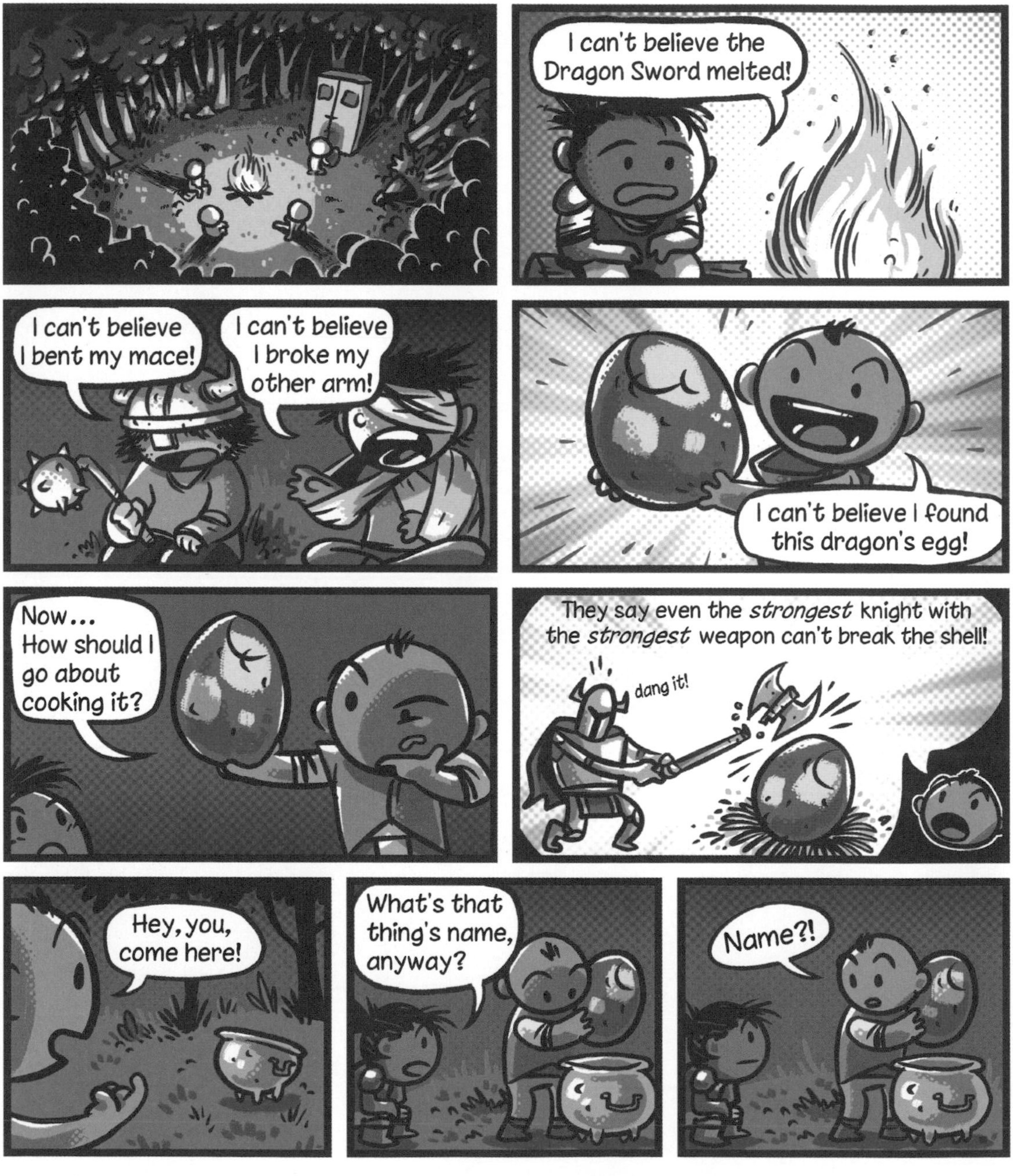
I can't believe the Dragon Sword melted!
I can't believe I bent my mace!
I can't believe I broke my other arm!
I can't believe I found this dragon's egg!
Now... How should I go about cooking it?
They say even the *strongest* knight with the *strongest* weapon can't break the shell!
dang it!
Hey, you, come here!
What's that thing's name, anyway?
Name?!

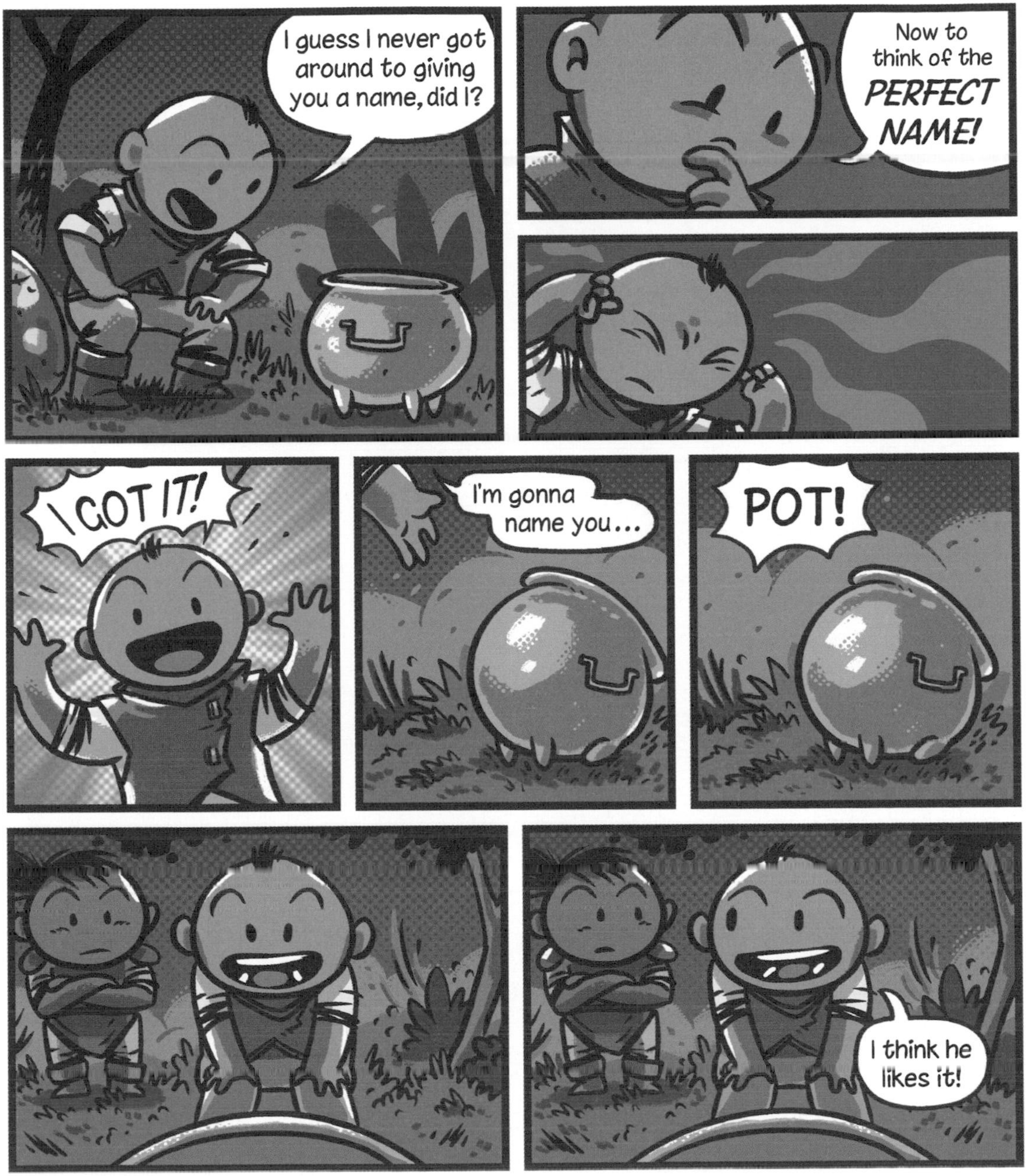
I guess I never got around to giving you a name, did I?
Now to think of the PERFECT NAME!
I GOT IT!
I'm gonna name you...
POT!
I think he likes it!

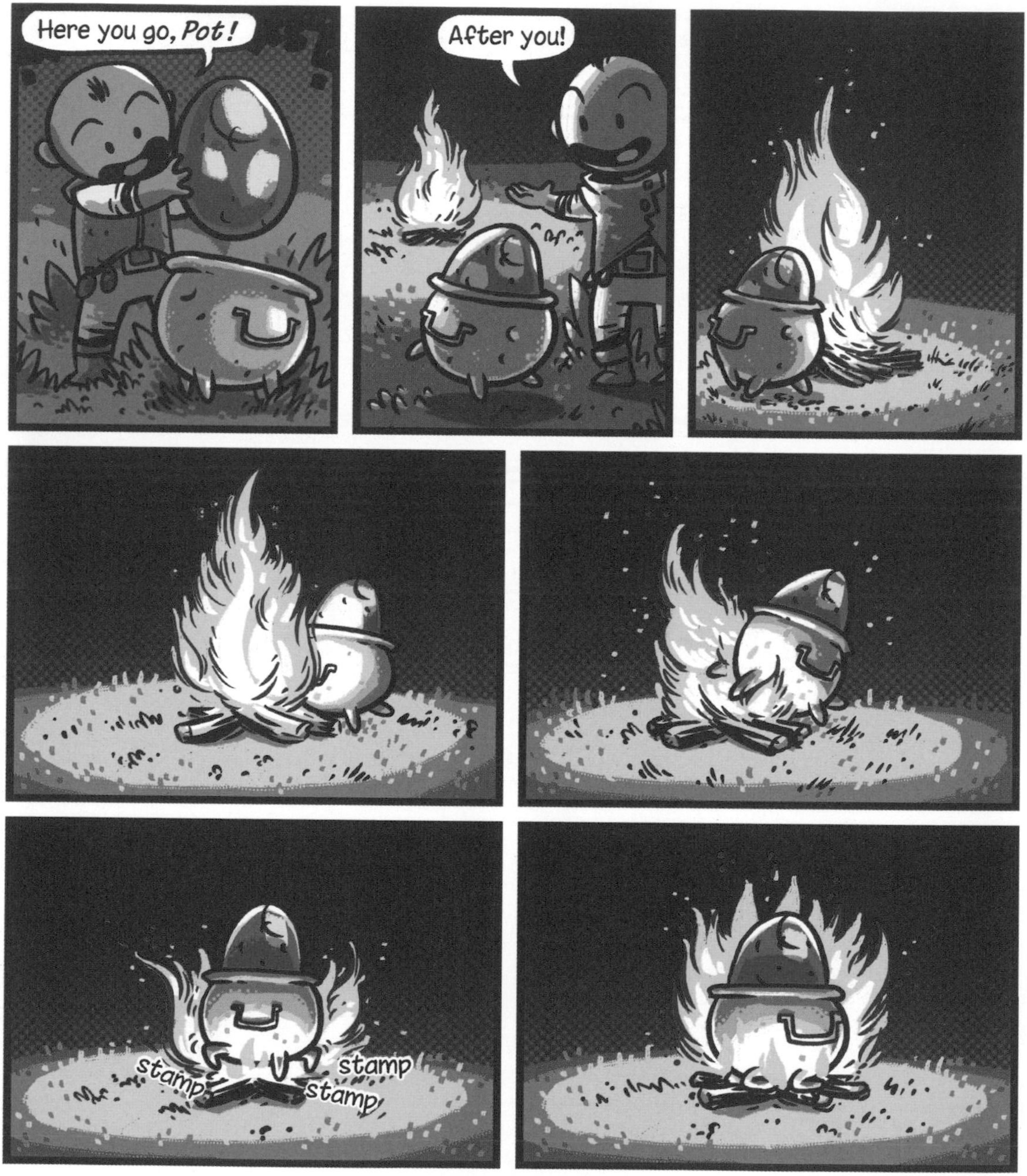
Here you go, Pot!
After you!
stamp
stamp
stamp

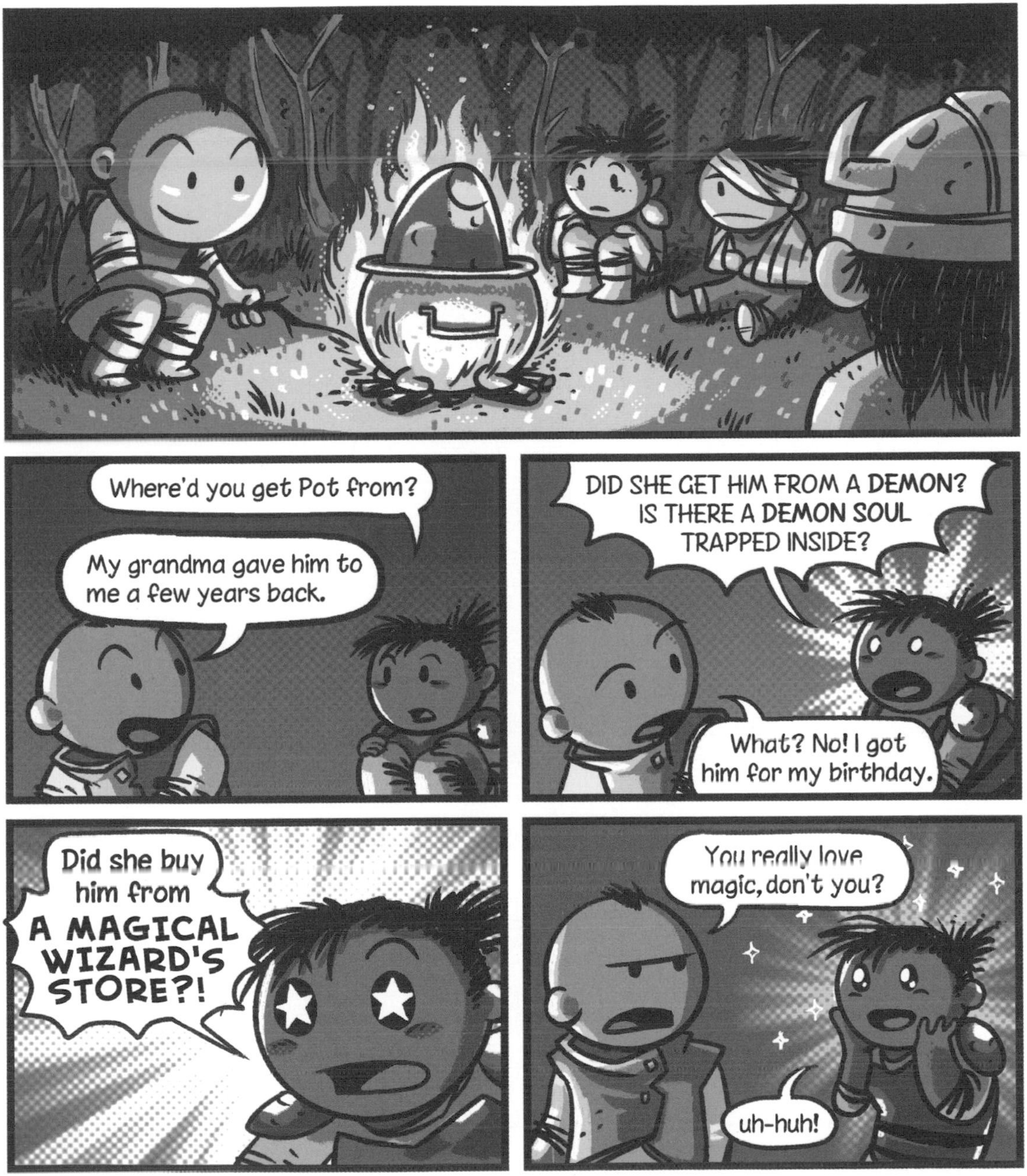
Where'd you get Pot from?
My grandma gave him to me a few years back.
DID SHE GET HIM FROM A DEMON? IS THERE A DEMON SOUL TRAPPED INSIDE?
What? No! I got him for my birthday.
Did she buy him from A MAGICAL WIZARD'S STORE?!
You really love magic, don't you?
uh-huh!

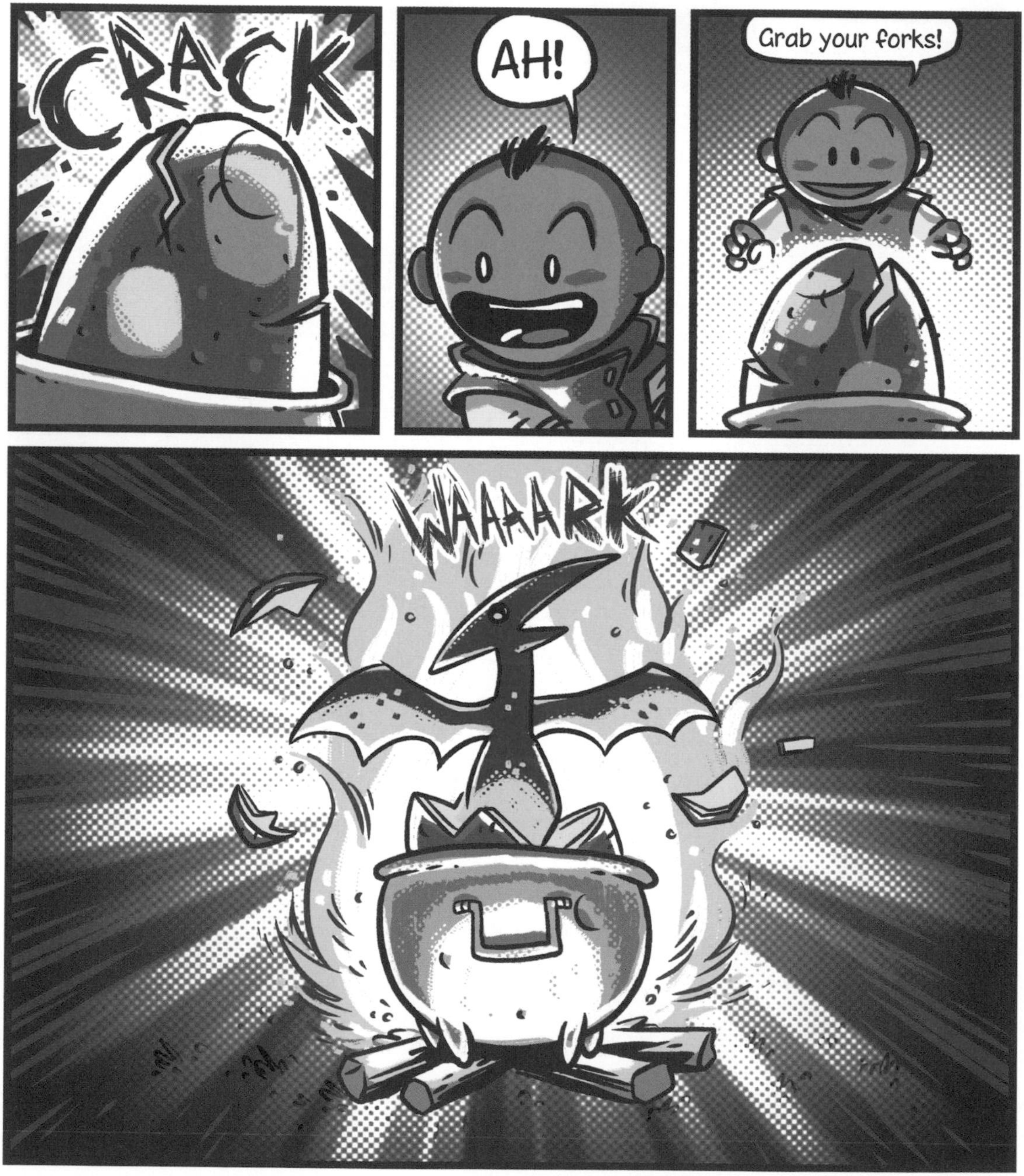
CRACK
AH!
Grab your forks!
WAAAARK

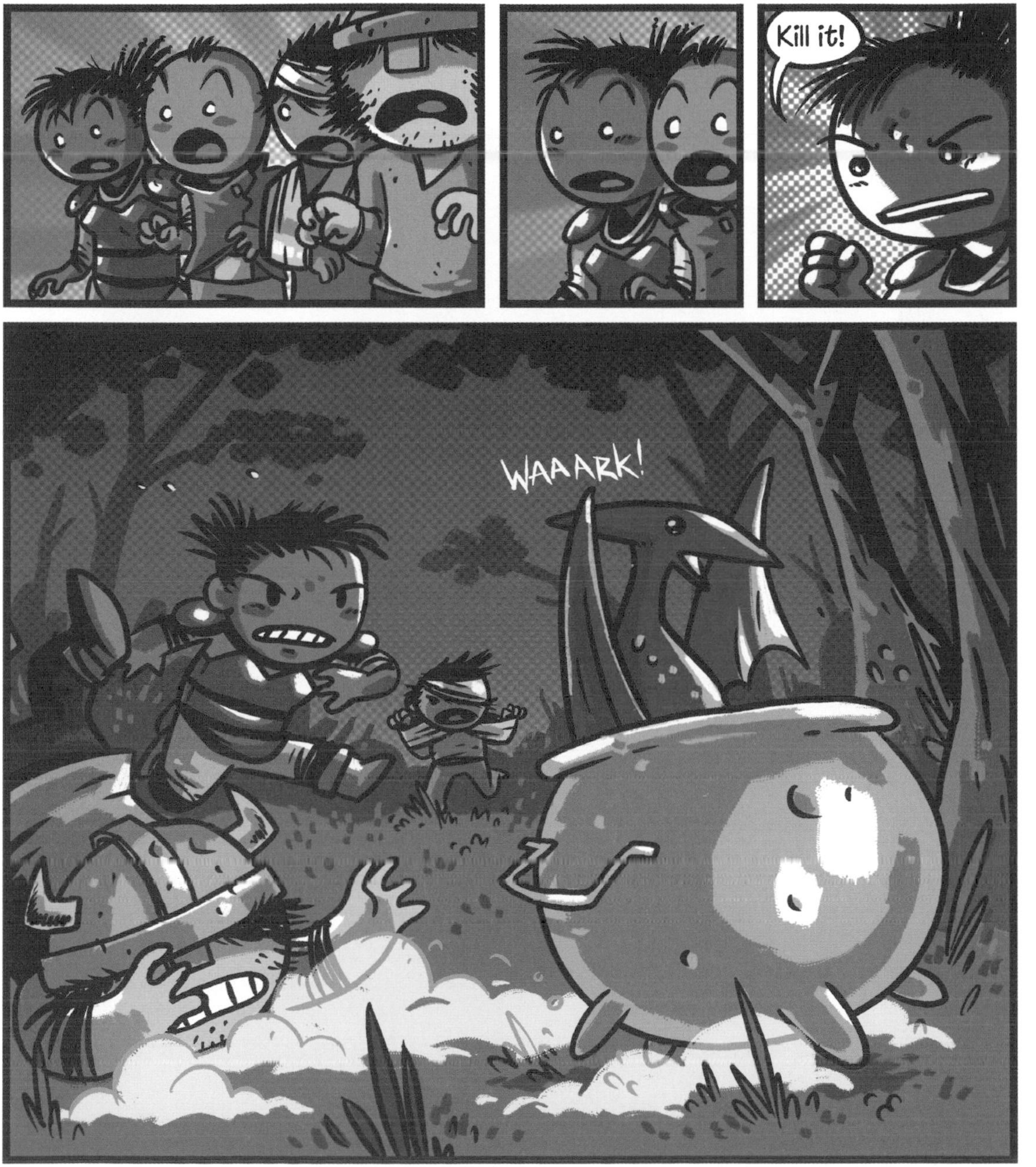
Kill it!
WAAARK!

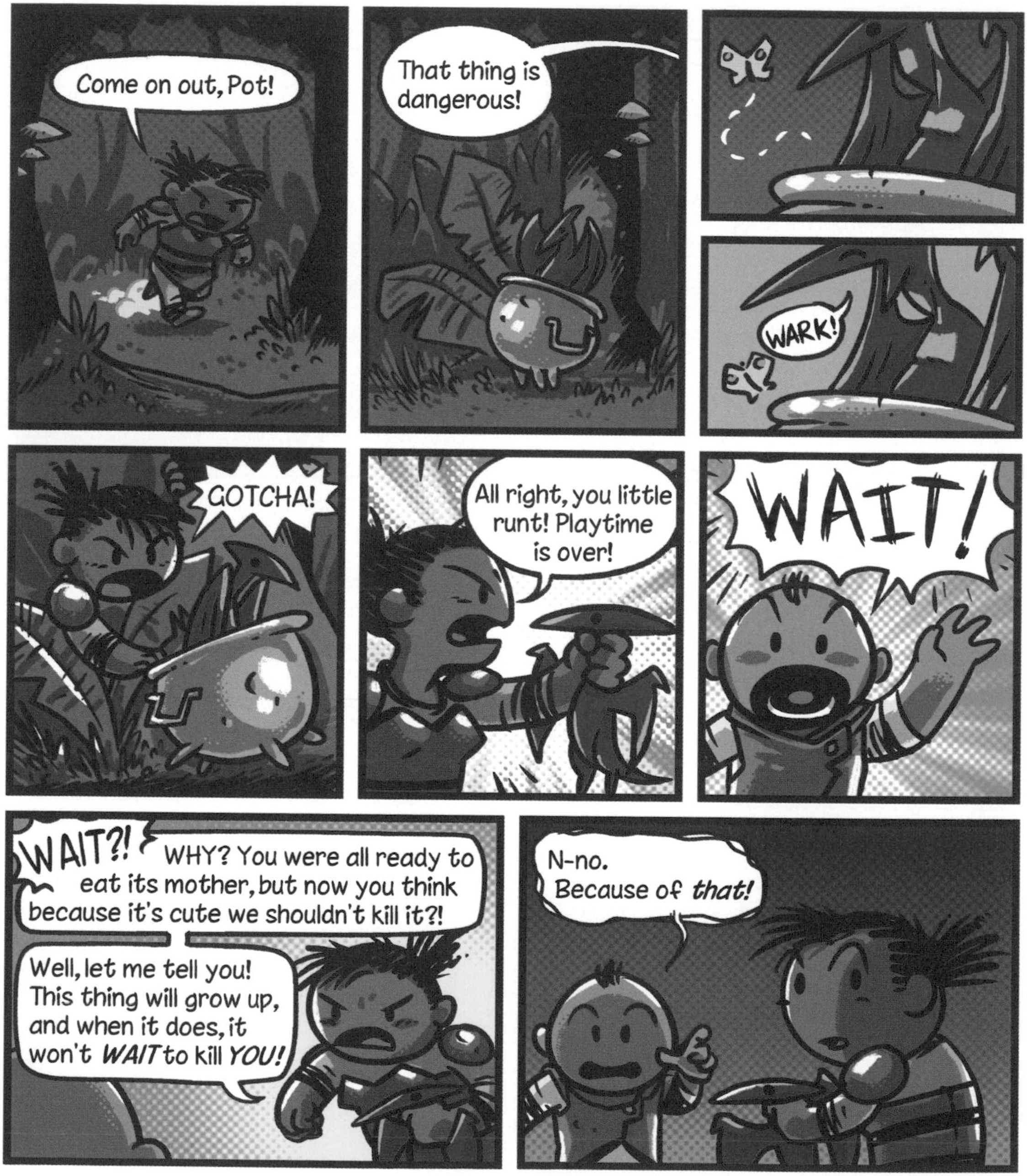
Come on out, Pot!
That thing is dangerous!
WARK!
GOTCHA!
All right, you little runt! Playtime is over!
WAIT!
WAIT?!
WHY? You were all ready to eat its mother, but now you think because it's cute we shouldn't kill it?!
Well, let me tell you! This thing will grow up, and when it does, it won't WAIT to kill YOU!
N-no. Because of that!

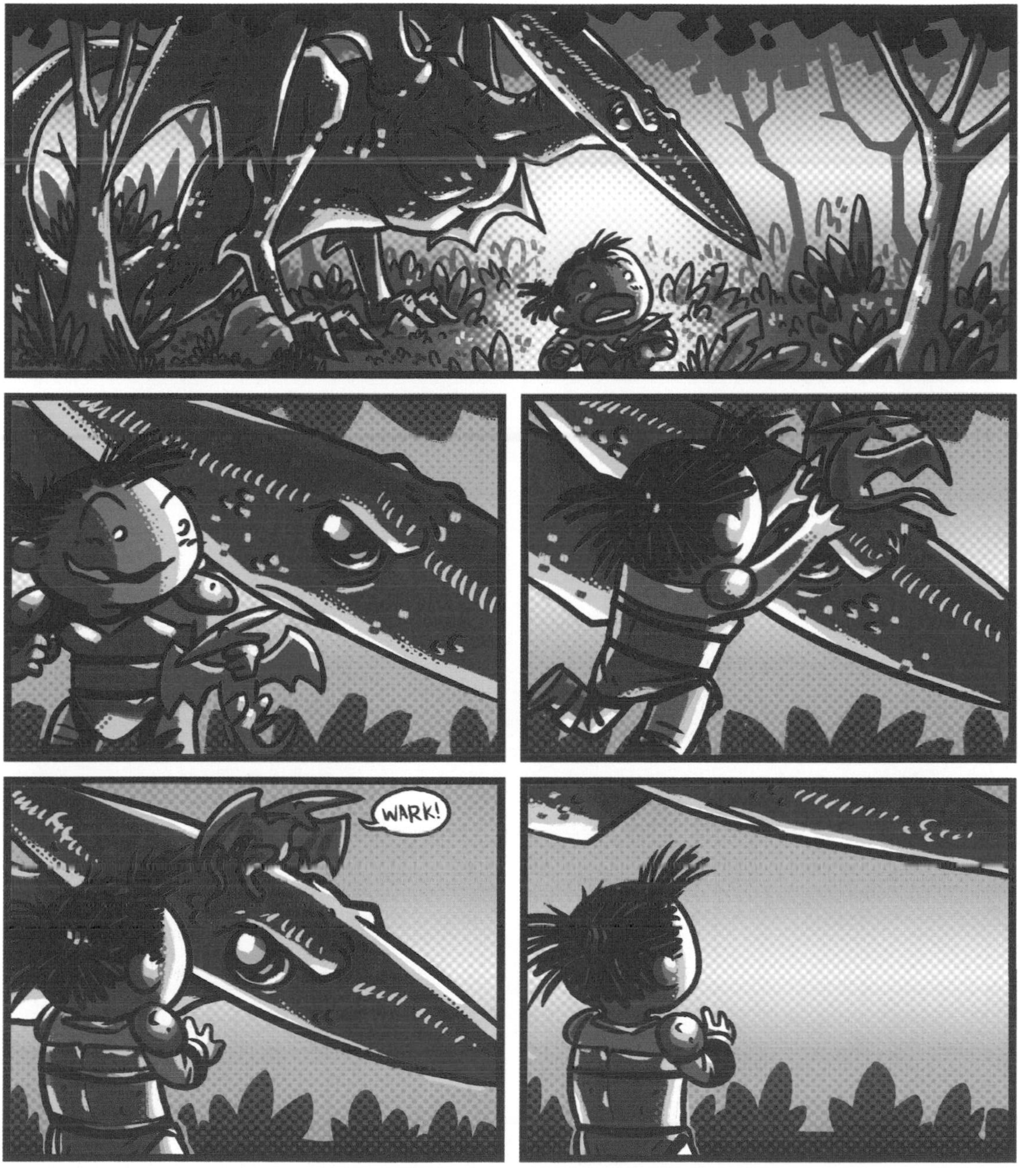
WARK!

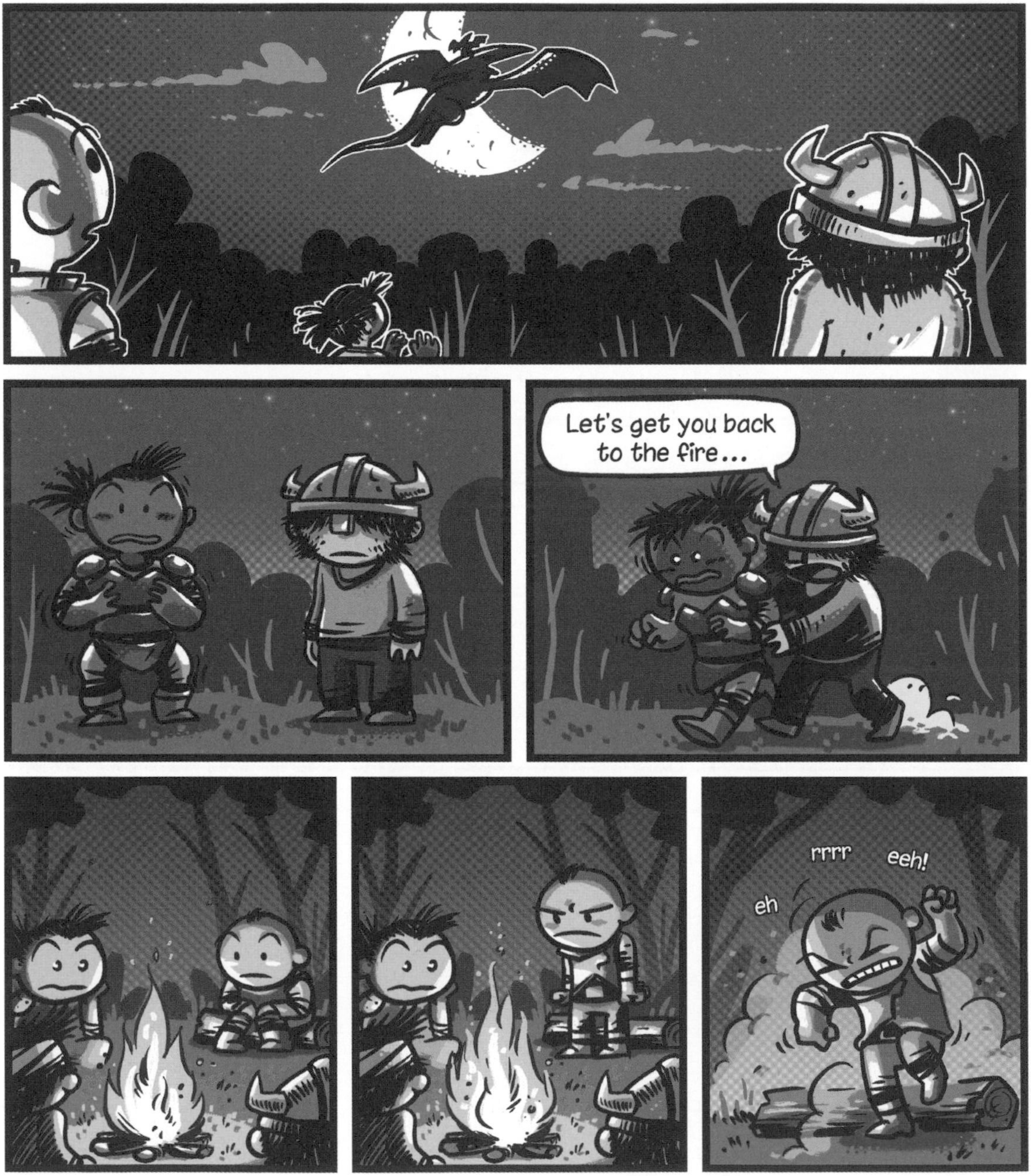
Let's get you back to the fire...
eh
rrrr
eeh!

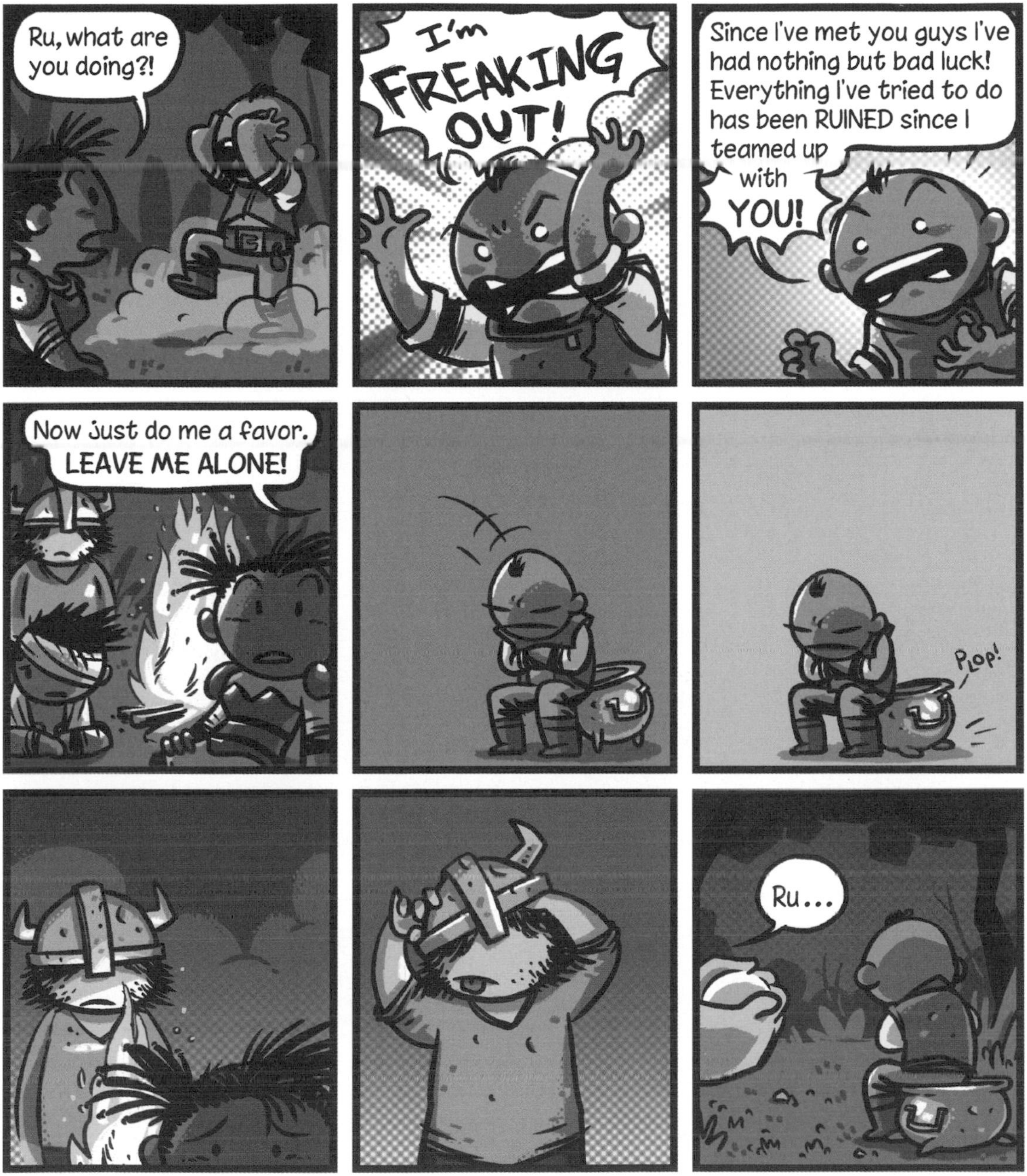
Ru, what are you doing?!
I'm FREAKING OUT!
Since I've met you guys I've had nothing but bad luck! Everything I've tried to do has been RUINED since I teamed up with YOU!
Now just do me a favor. LEAVE ME ALONE!
PLOP!
Ru...

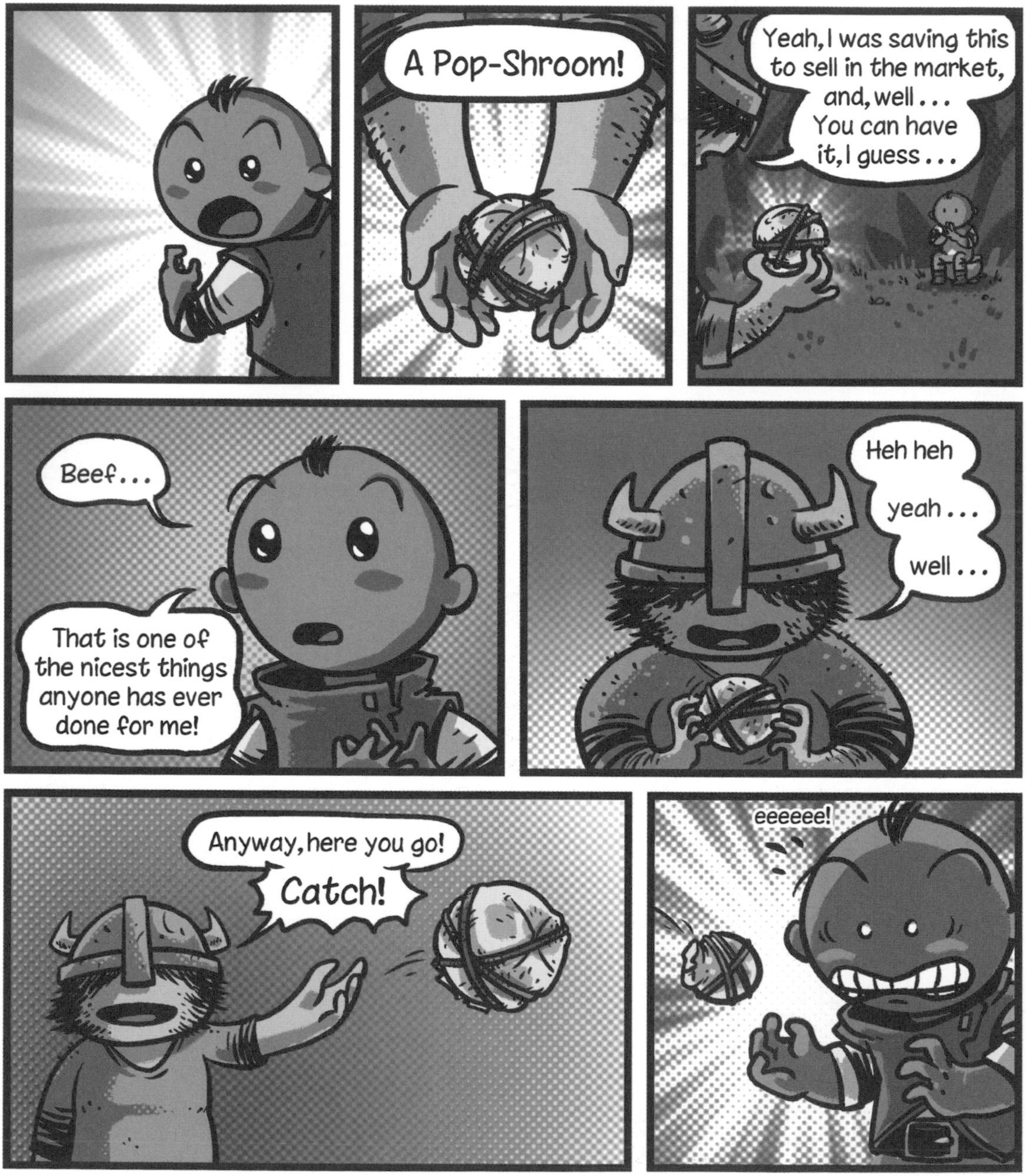
A Pop-Shroom!
Yeah, I was saving this to sell in the market, and, well . . . You can have it, I guess . . .
Beef . . .
That is one of the nicest things anyone has ever done for me!
Heh heh
yeah . . .
well . . .
Anyway, here you go!
Catch!
eeeeee!

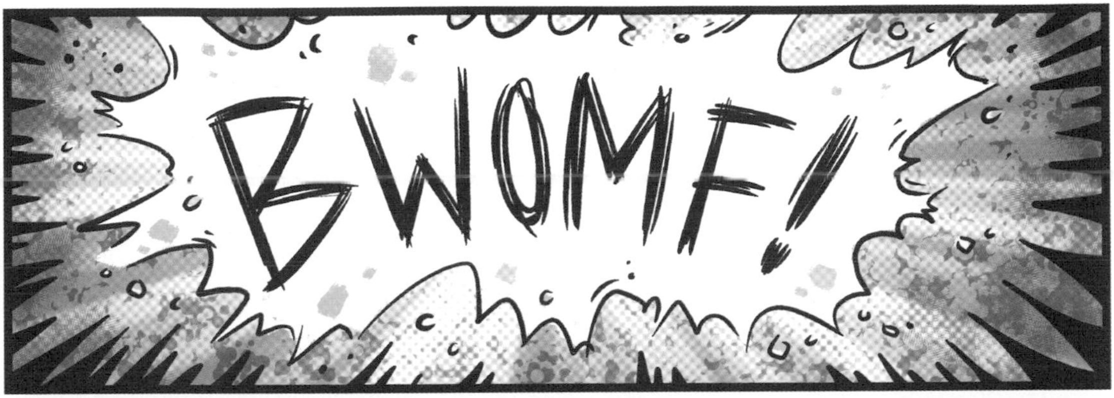
BWOMF!

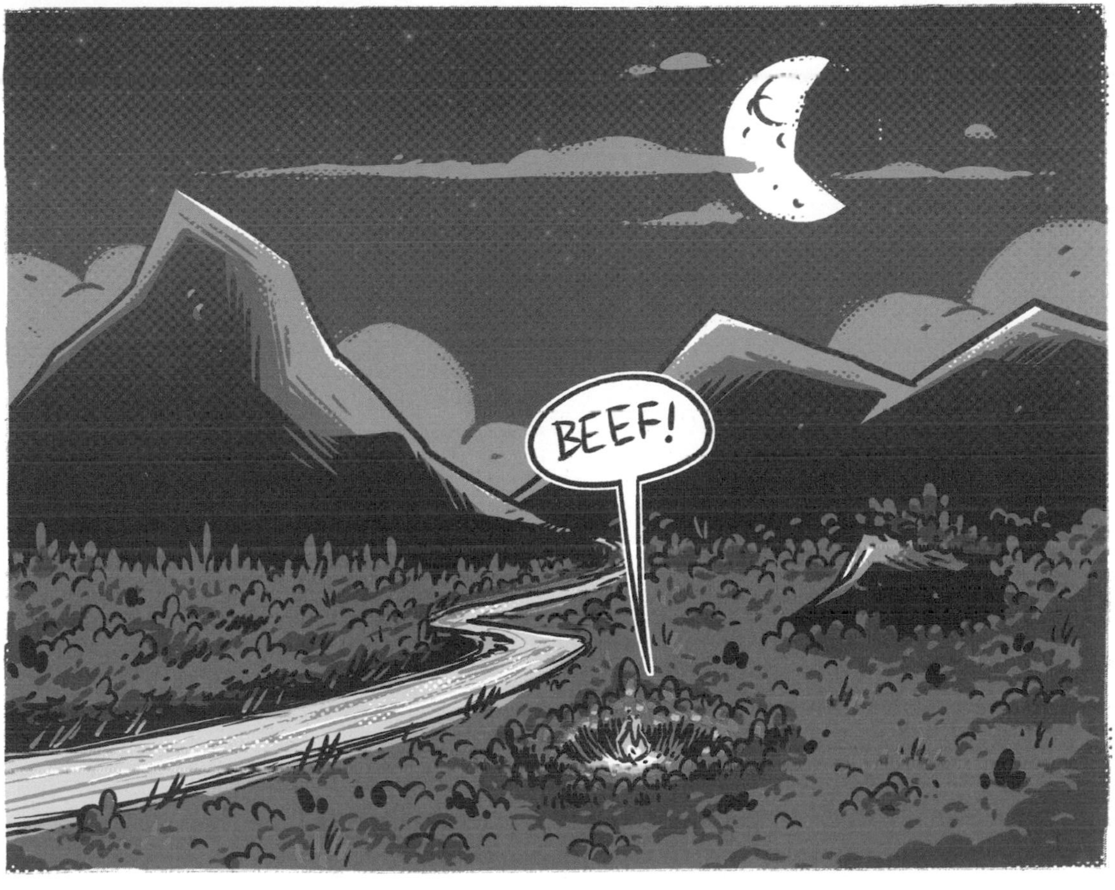
BEEF!

END OF
CHAPTER ONE

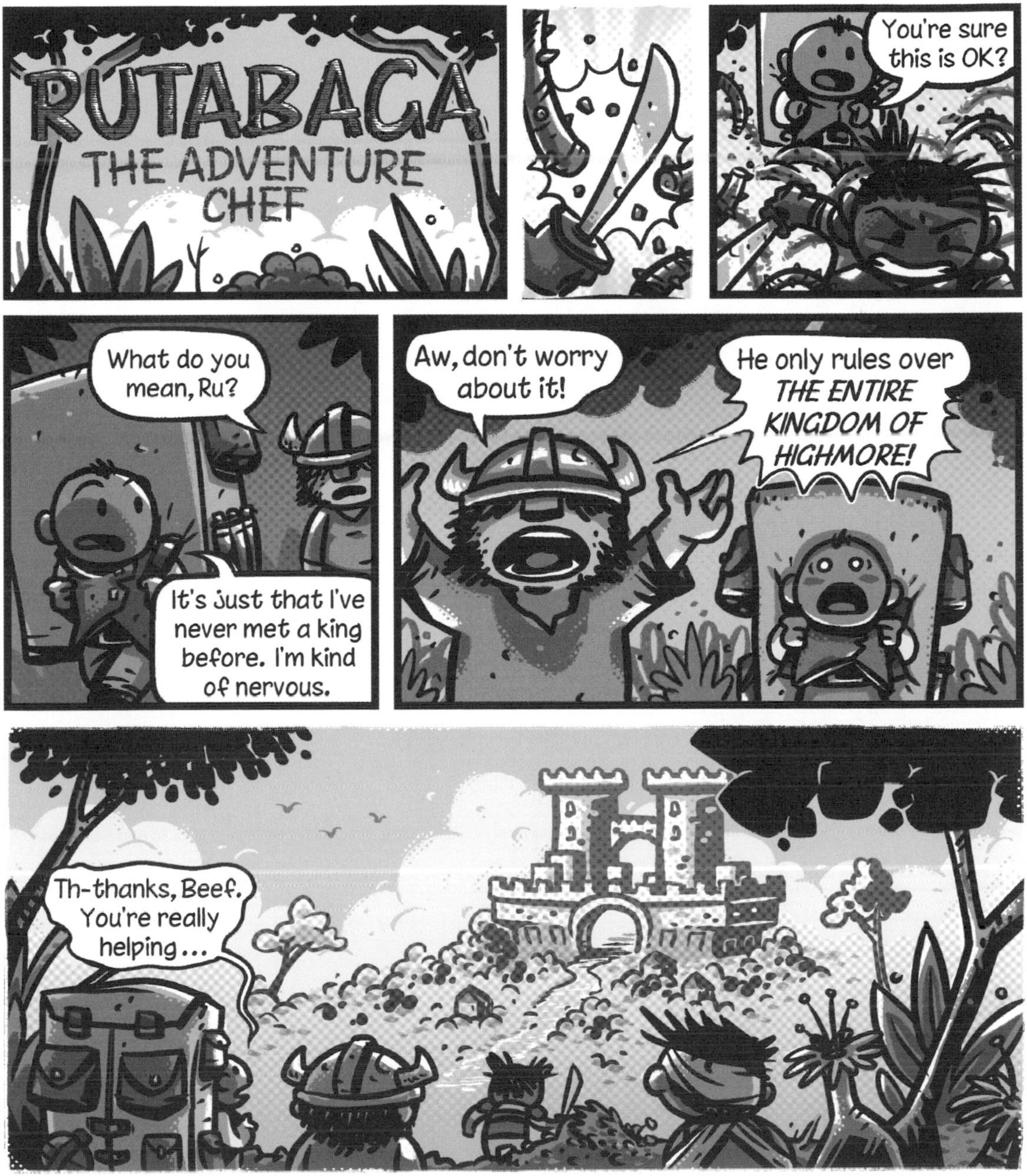
RUTABAGA
THE ADVENTURE CHEF
You're sure this is OK?
What do you mean, Ru?
It's just that I've never met a king before. I'm kind of nervous.
Aw, don't worry about it!
He only rules over THE ENTIRE KINGDOM OF HIGHMORE!
Th-thanks, Beef. You're really helping...

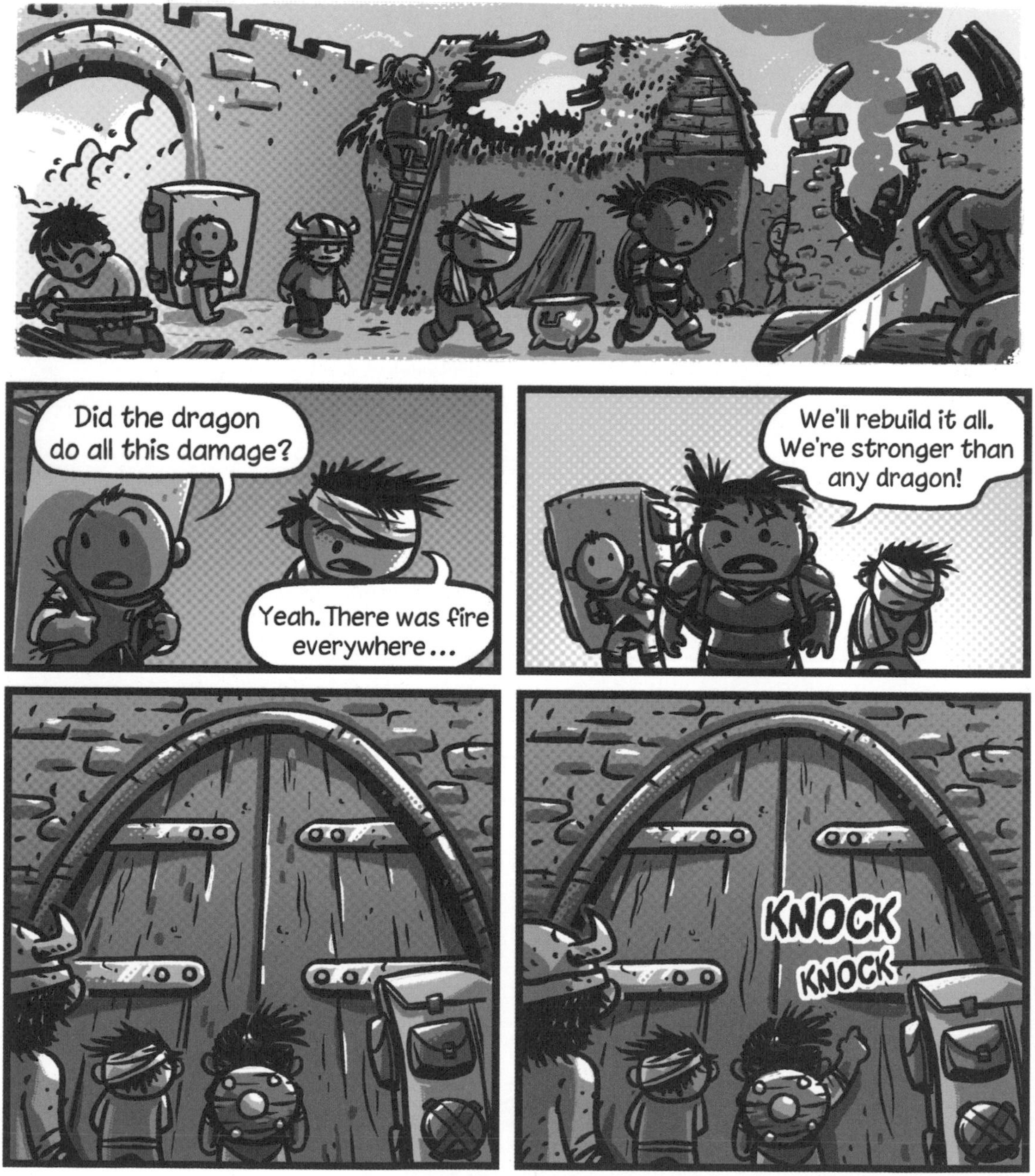
Did the dragon do all this damage?
Yeah. There was fire everywhere...
We'll rebuild it all. We're stronger than any dragon!
KNOCK
KNOCK

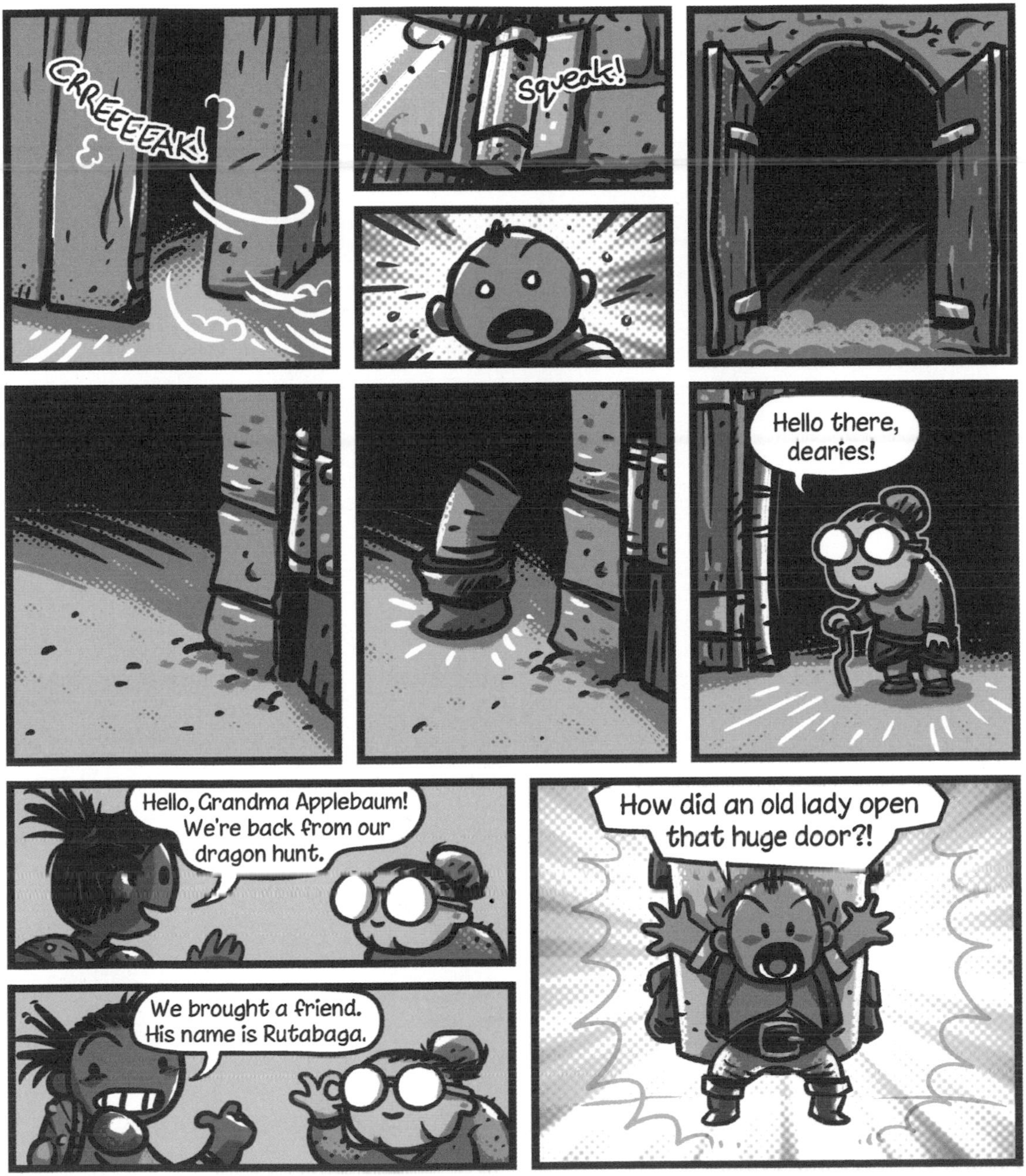
CRREEEEAK!
Squeak!
Hello there, dearies!
Hello, Grandma Applebaum! We're back from our dragon hunt.
We brought a friend. His name is Rutabaga.
How did an old lady open that huge door?!

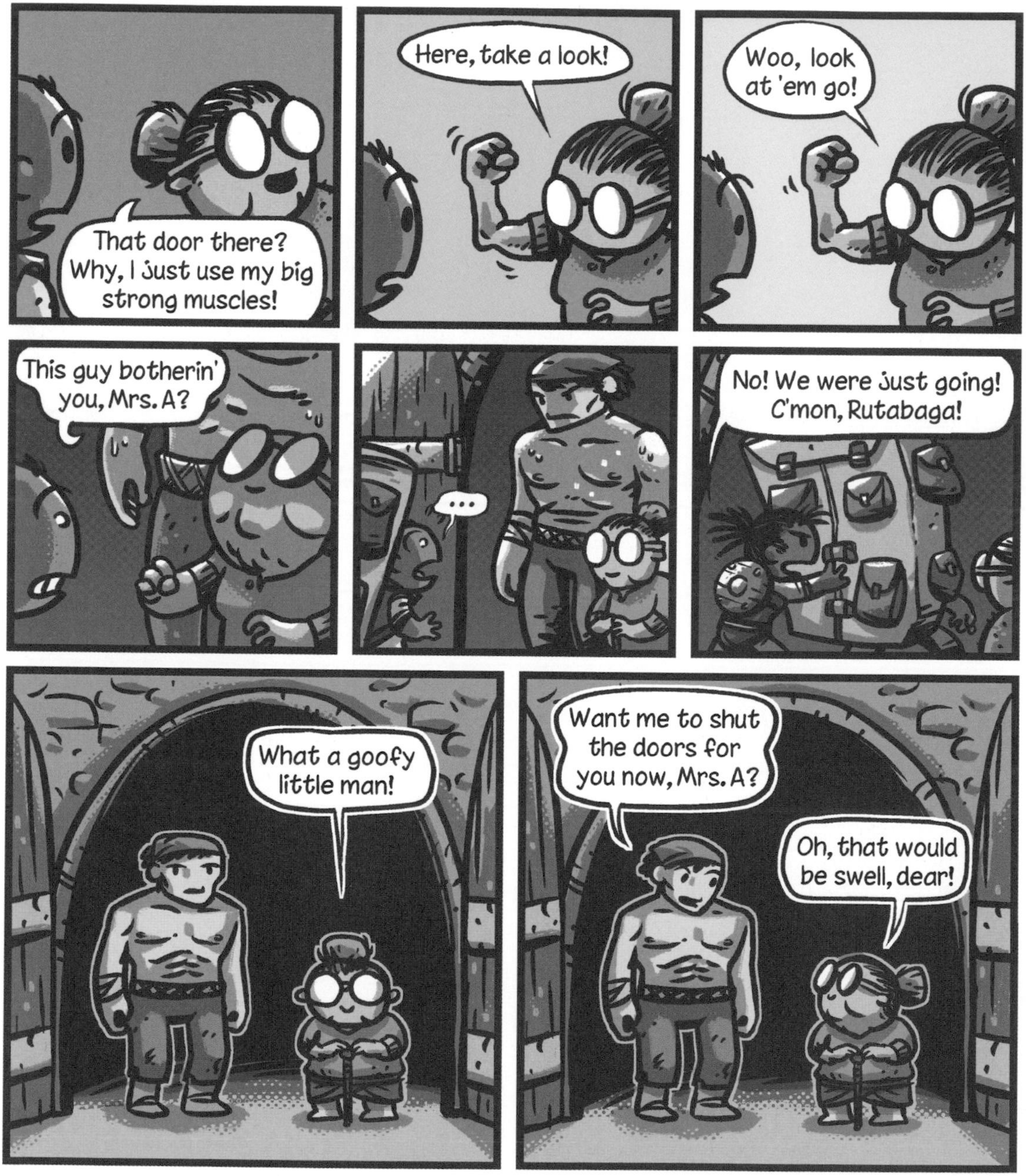
That door there? Why, I just use my big strong muscles!
Here, take a look!
Woo, look at 'em go!
This guy botherin' you, Mrs. A?
...
No! We were just going! C'mon, Rutabaga!
What a goofy little man!
Want me to shut the doors for you now, Mrs. A?
Oh, that would be swell, dear!

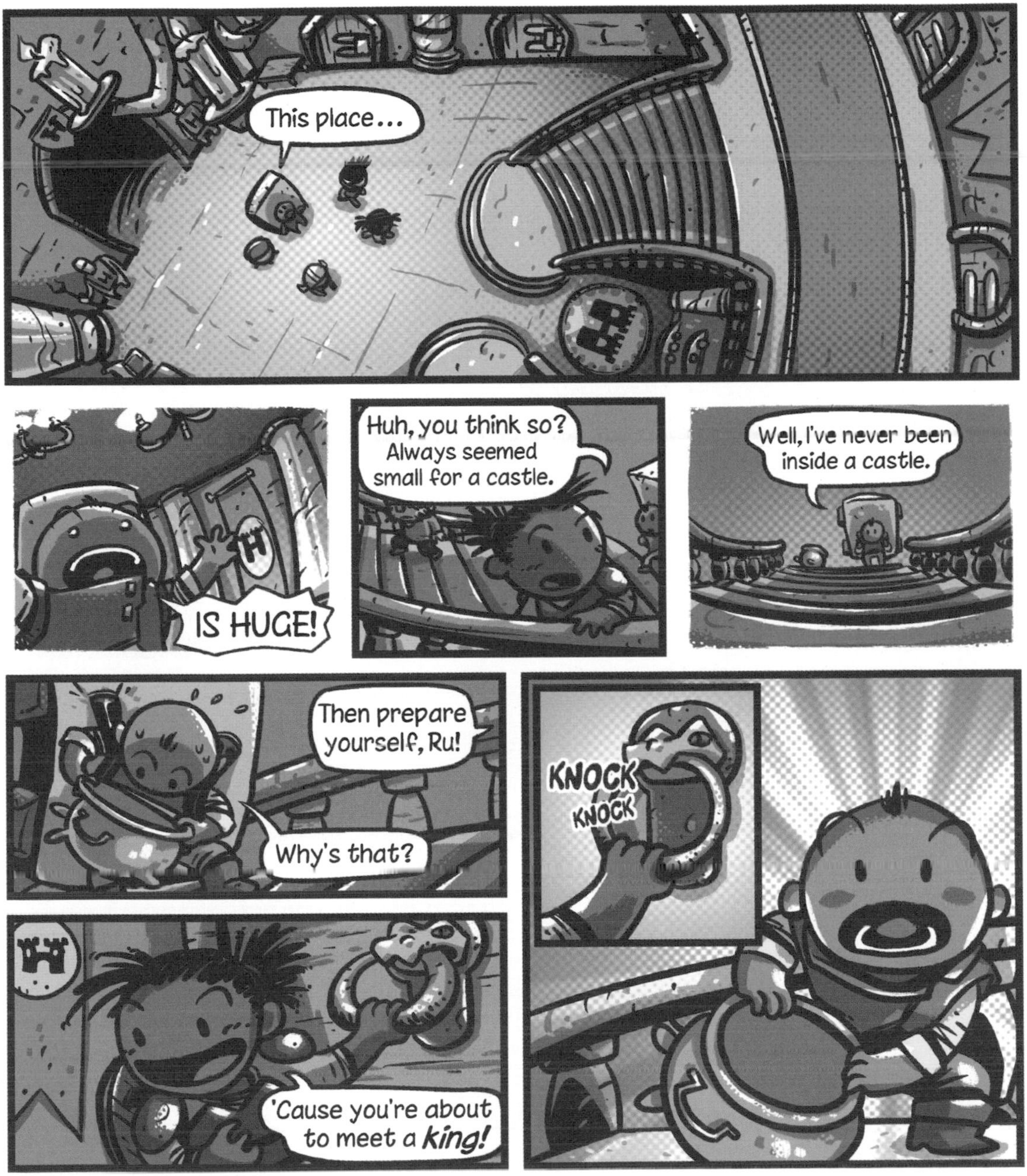
This place...
IS HUGE!
Huh, you think so? Always seemed small for a castle.
Well, I've never been inside a castle.
Then prepare yourself, Ru!
Why's that?
'Cause you're about to meet a *king!*
KNOCK
KNOCK

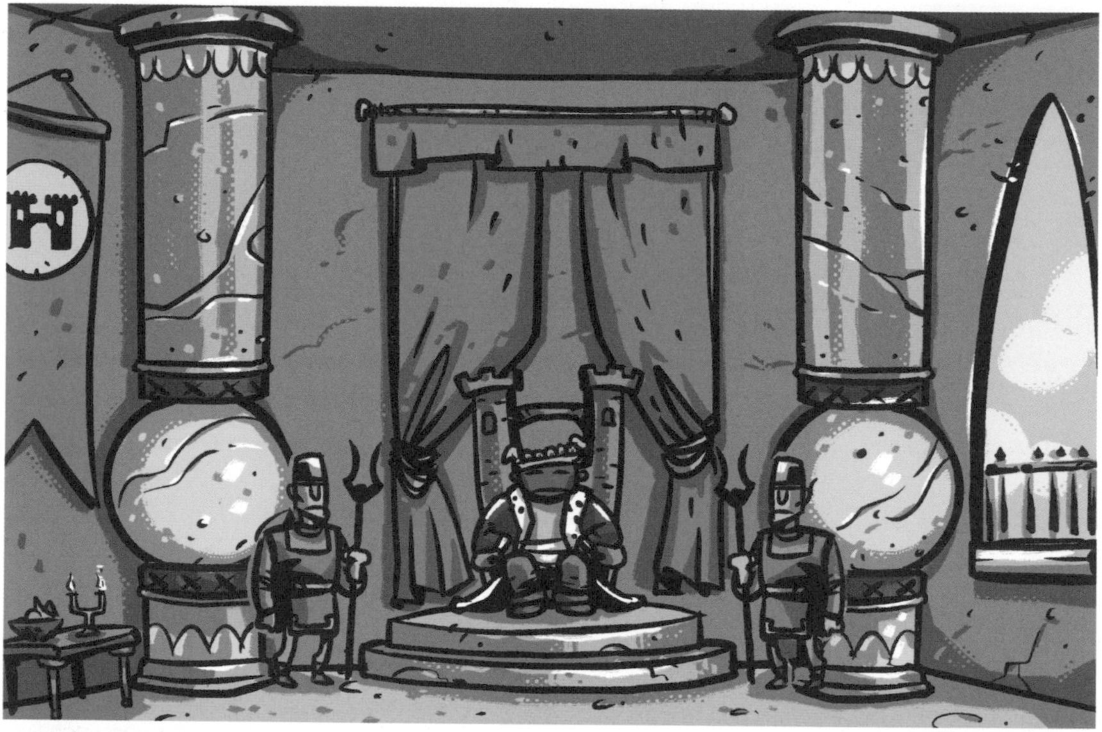

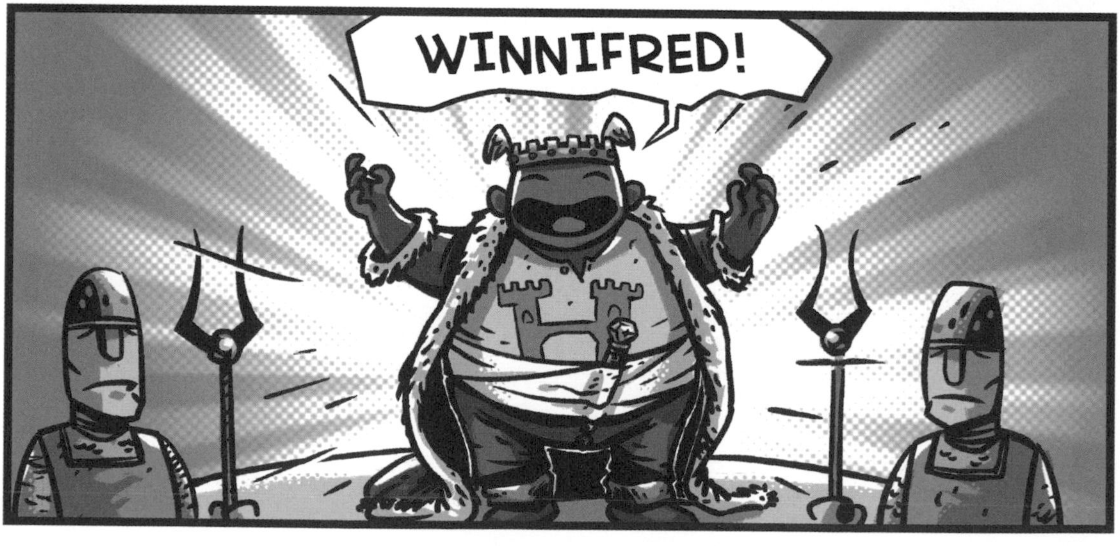
WINNIFRED!

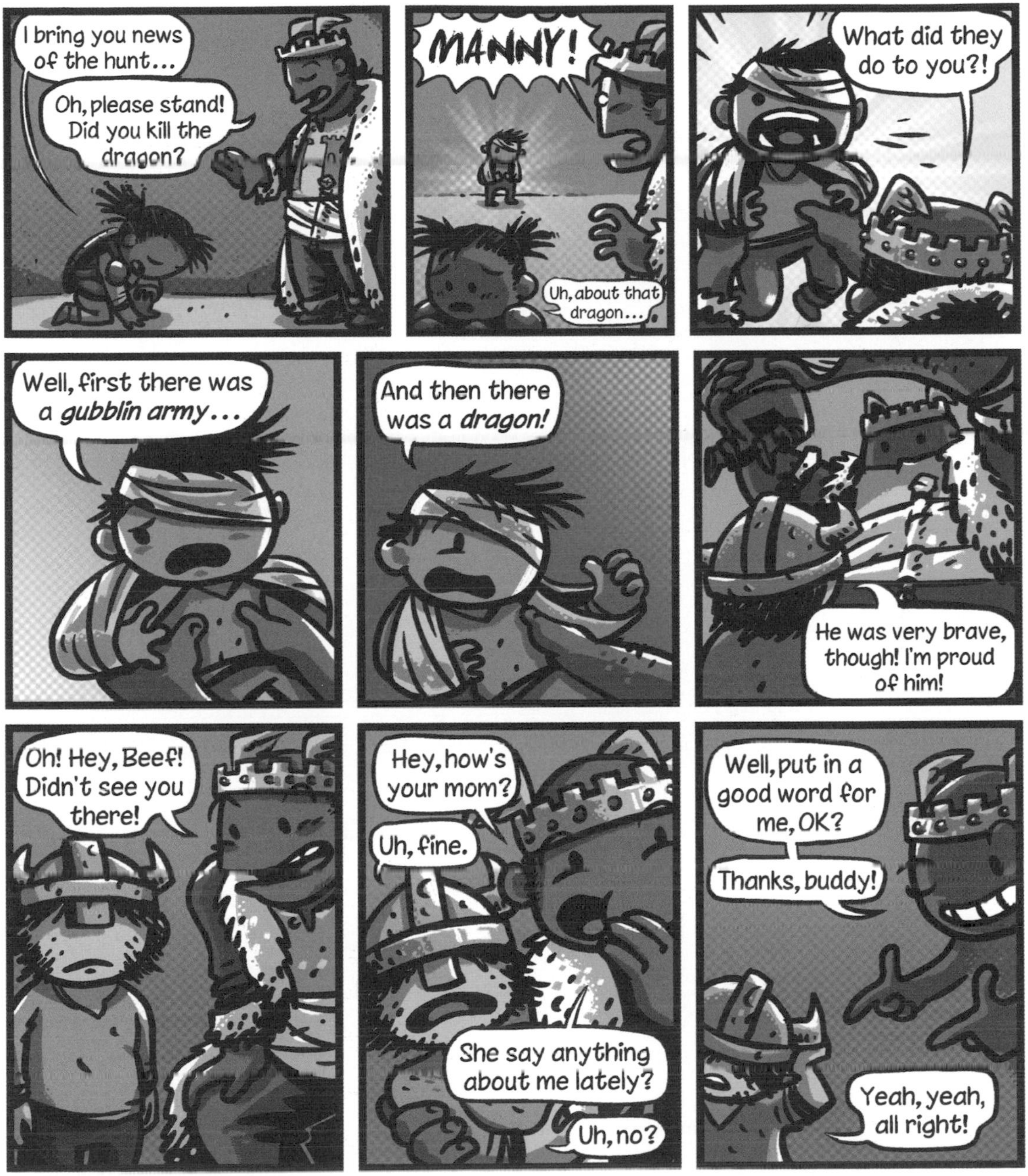
I bring you news of the hunt...
Oh, please stand! Did you kill the dragon?
MANNY!
Uh, about that dragon...
What did they do to you?!
Well, first there was a *gubblin army*...
And then there was a *dragon!*
He was very brave, though! I'm proud of him!
Oh! Hey, Beef! Didn't see you there!
Hey, how's your mom?
Uh, fine.
She say anything about me lately?
Uh, no?
Well, put in a good word for me, OK?
Thanks, buddy!
Yeah, yeah, all right!

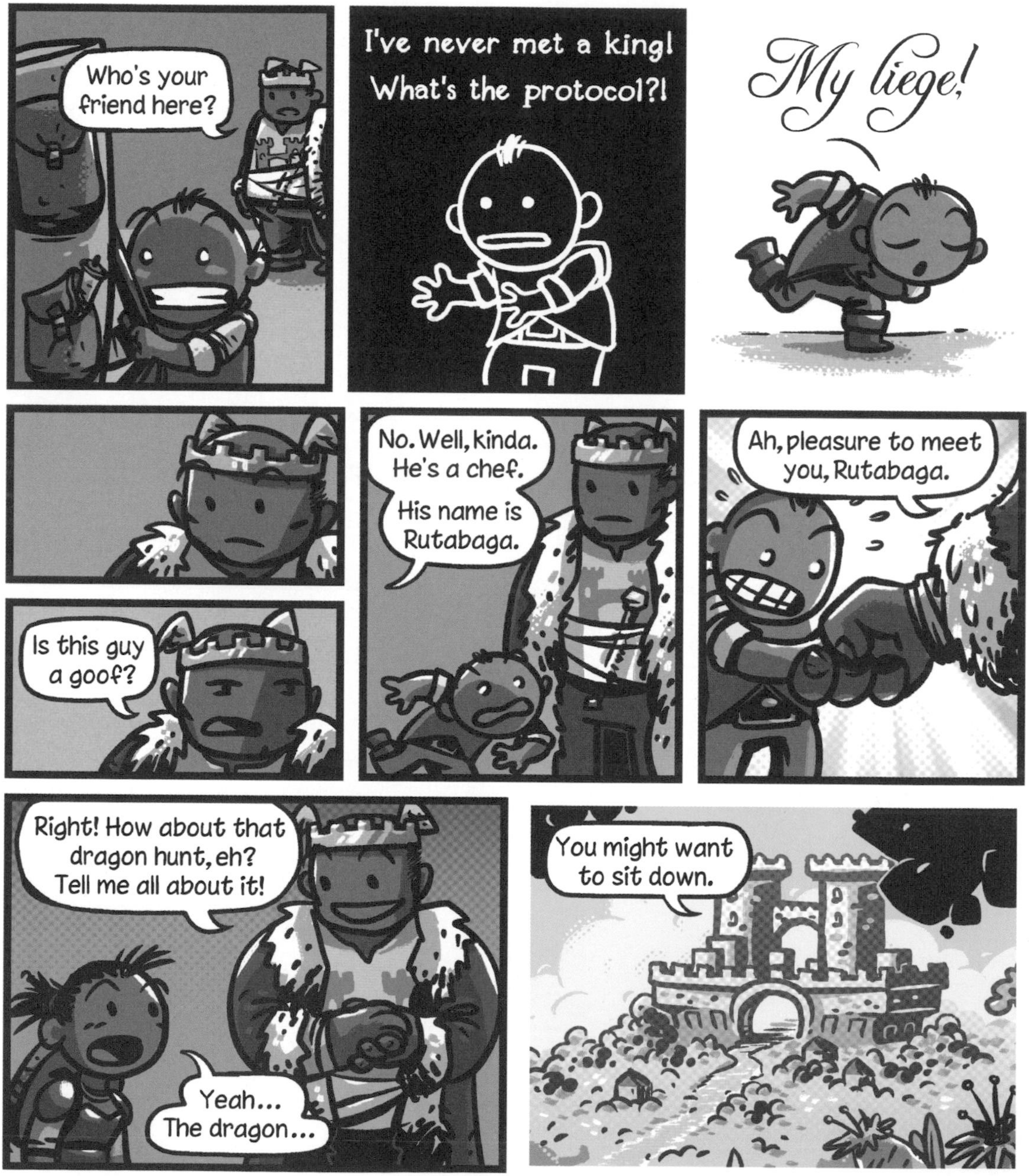

Who's your friend here?
I've never met a king! What's the protocol?!
My liege!
No. Well, kinda. He's a chef.
His name is Rutabaga.
Is this guy a goof?
Ah, pleasure to meet you, Rutabaga.
Right! How about that dragon hunt, eh? Tell me all about it!
Yeah... The dragon...
You might want to sit down.

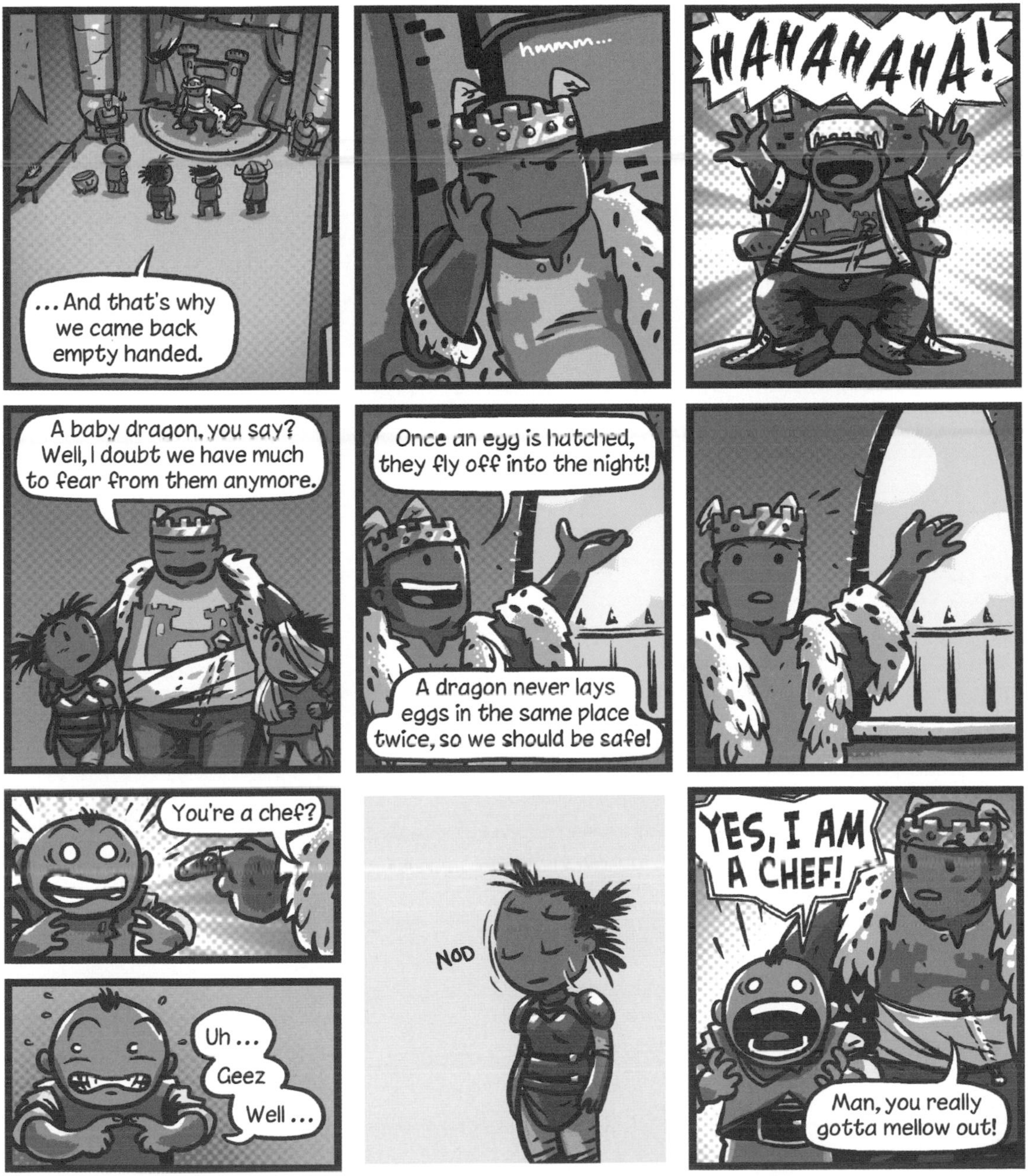
...And that's why we came back empty handed.
hmmm...
HAHAHAHA!
A baby dragon, you say? Well, I doubt we have much to fear from them anymore.
Once an egg is hatched, they fly off into the night!
A dragon never lays eggs in the same place twice, so we should be safe!
You're a chef?
Uh...
Geez
Well...
NOD
YES, I AM A CHEF!
Man, you really gotta mellow out!

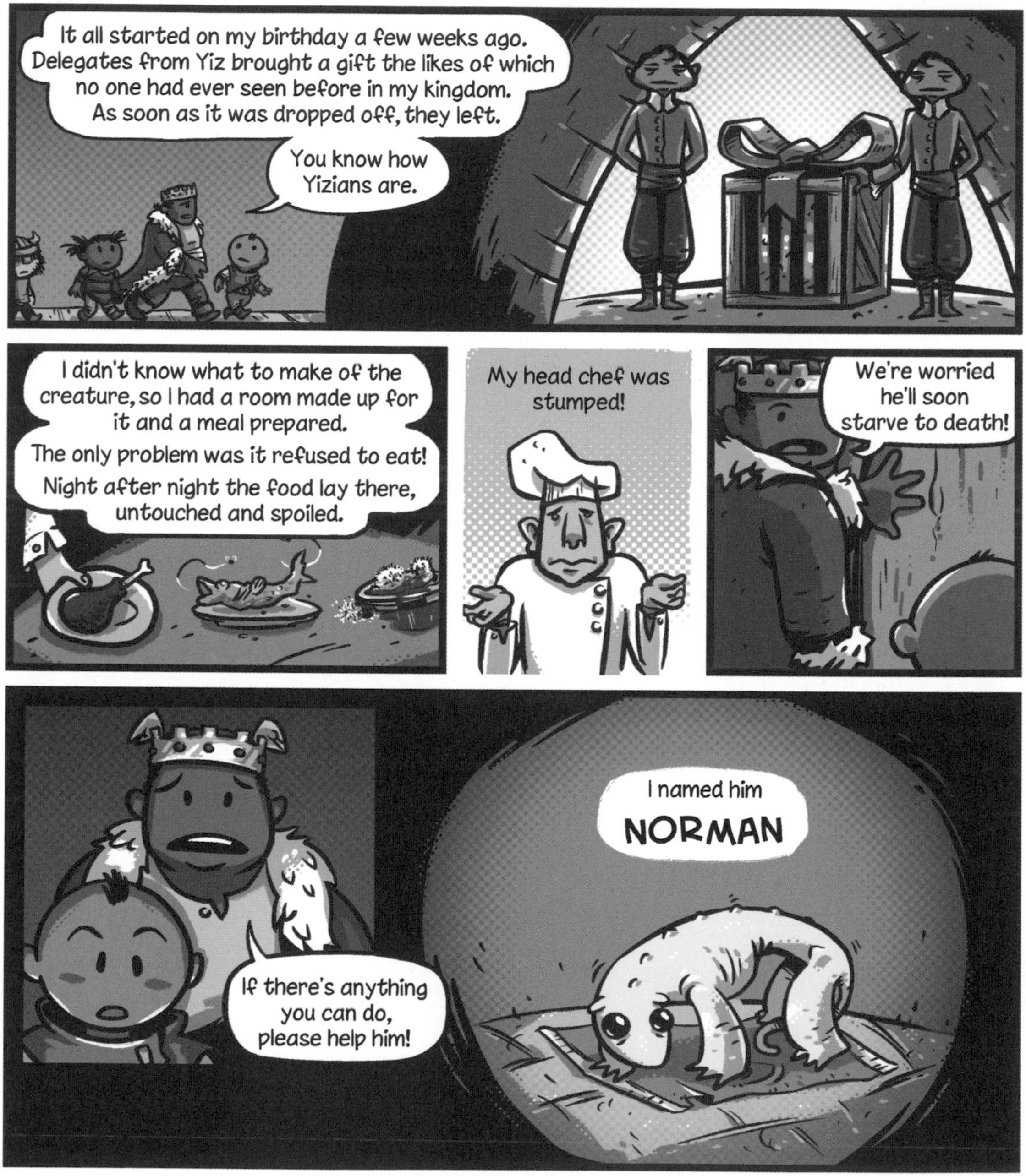
It all started on my birthday a few weeks ago. Delegates from Yiz brought a gift the likes of which no one had ever seen before in my kingdom. As soon as it was dropped off, they left.
You know how Yizians are.
I didn't know what to make of the creature, so I had a room made up for it and a meal prepared.
The only problem was it refused to eat!
Night after night the food lay there, untouched and spoiled.
My head chef was stumped!
We're worried he'll soon starve to death!
If there's anything you can do, please help him!
I named him NORMAN

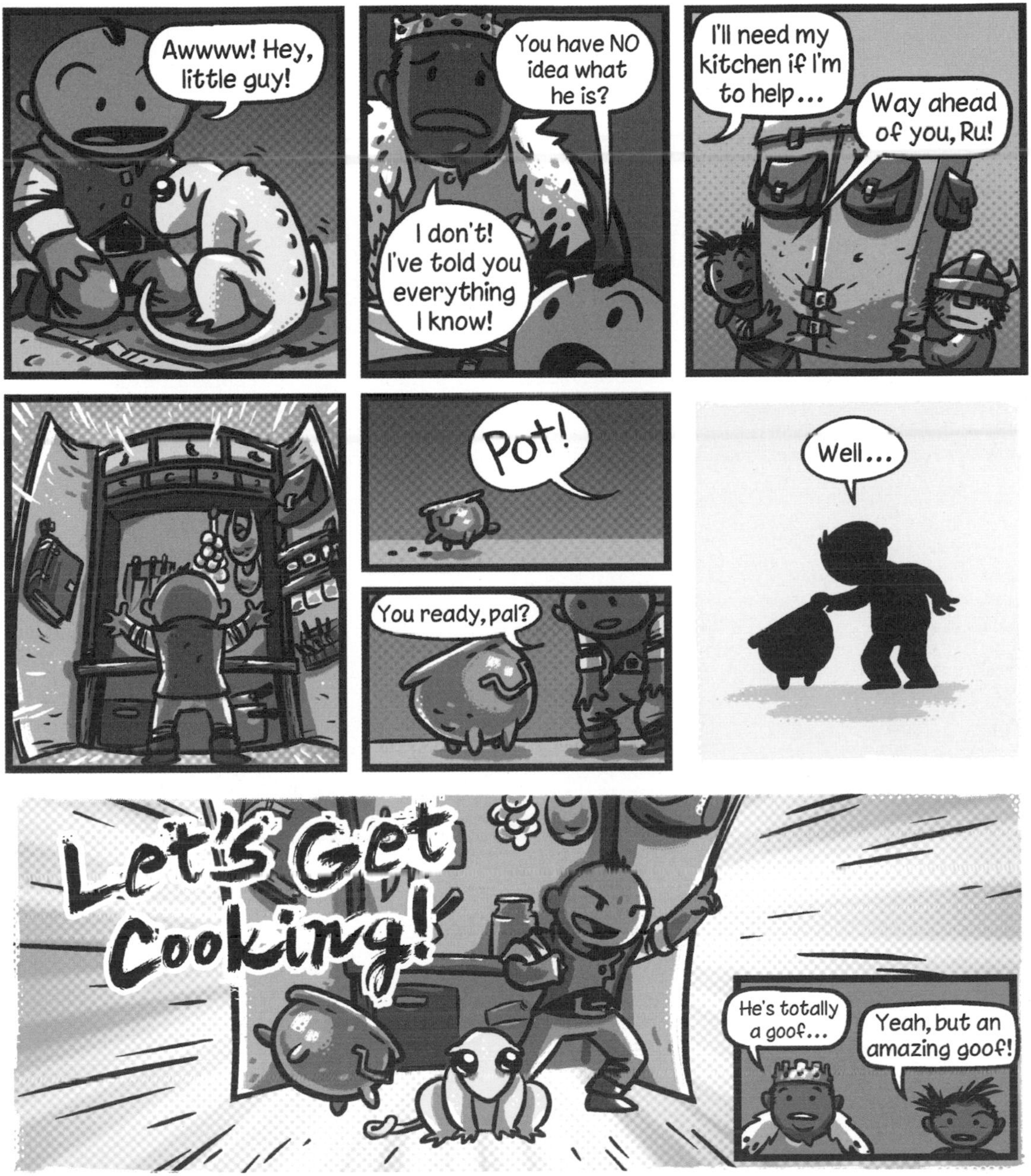

Awwww! Hey, little guy!
You have NO idea what he is?
I don't! I've told you everything I know!
I'll need my kitchen if I'm to help...
Way ahead of you, Ru!
Pot!
You ready, pal?
Well...
Let's Get Cooking!
He's totally a goof...
Yeah, but an amazing goof!

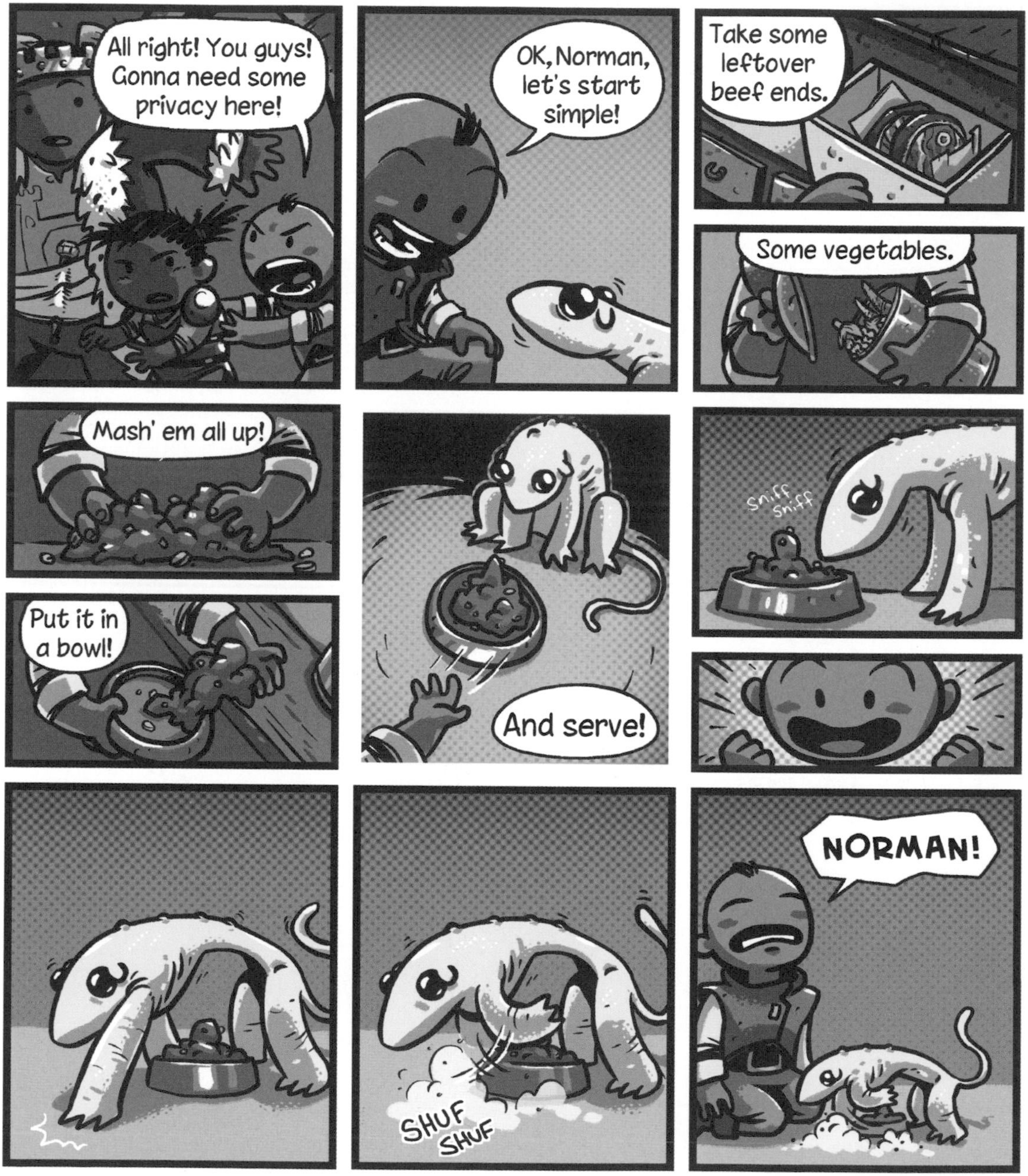
All right! You guys! Gonna need some privacy here!
OK, Norman, let's start simple!
Take some leftover beef ends.
Some vegetables.
Mash' em all up!
Put it in a bowl!
And serve!
Sniff Sniff
SHUF SHUF
NORMAN!

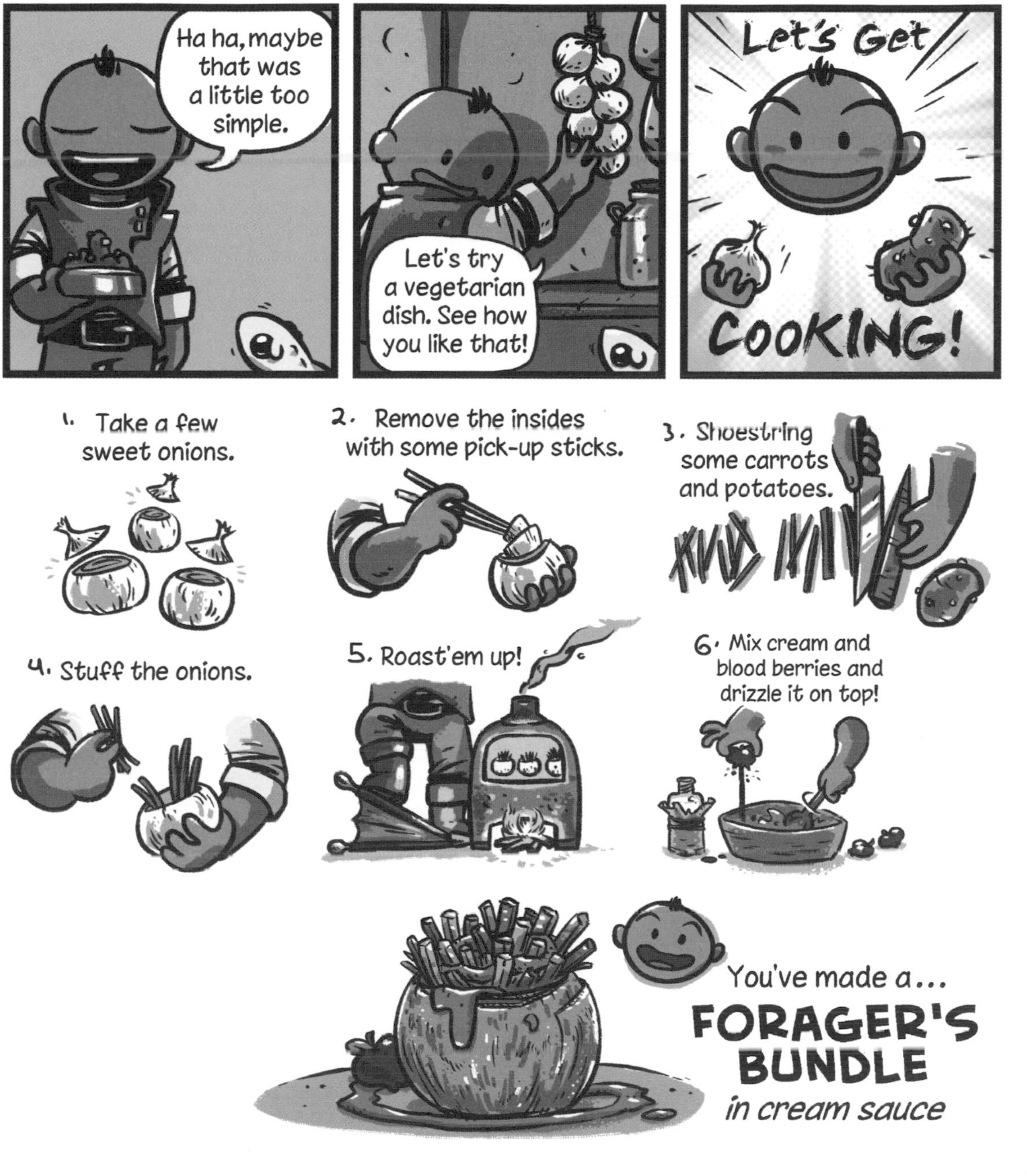
Ha ha, maybe that was a little too simple.
Let's try a vegetarian dish. See how you like that!
Let's Get
COOKING!
1. Take a few sweet onions.
2. Remove the insides with some pick-up sticks.
3. Shoestring some carrots and potatoes.
4. Stuff the onions.
5. Roast'em up!
6. Mix cream and blood berries and drizzle it on top!
You've made a...
FORAGER'S BUNDLE
in cream sauce

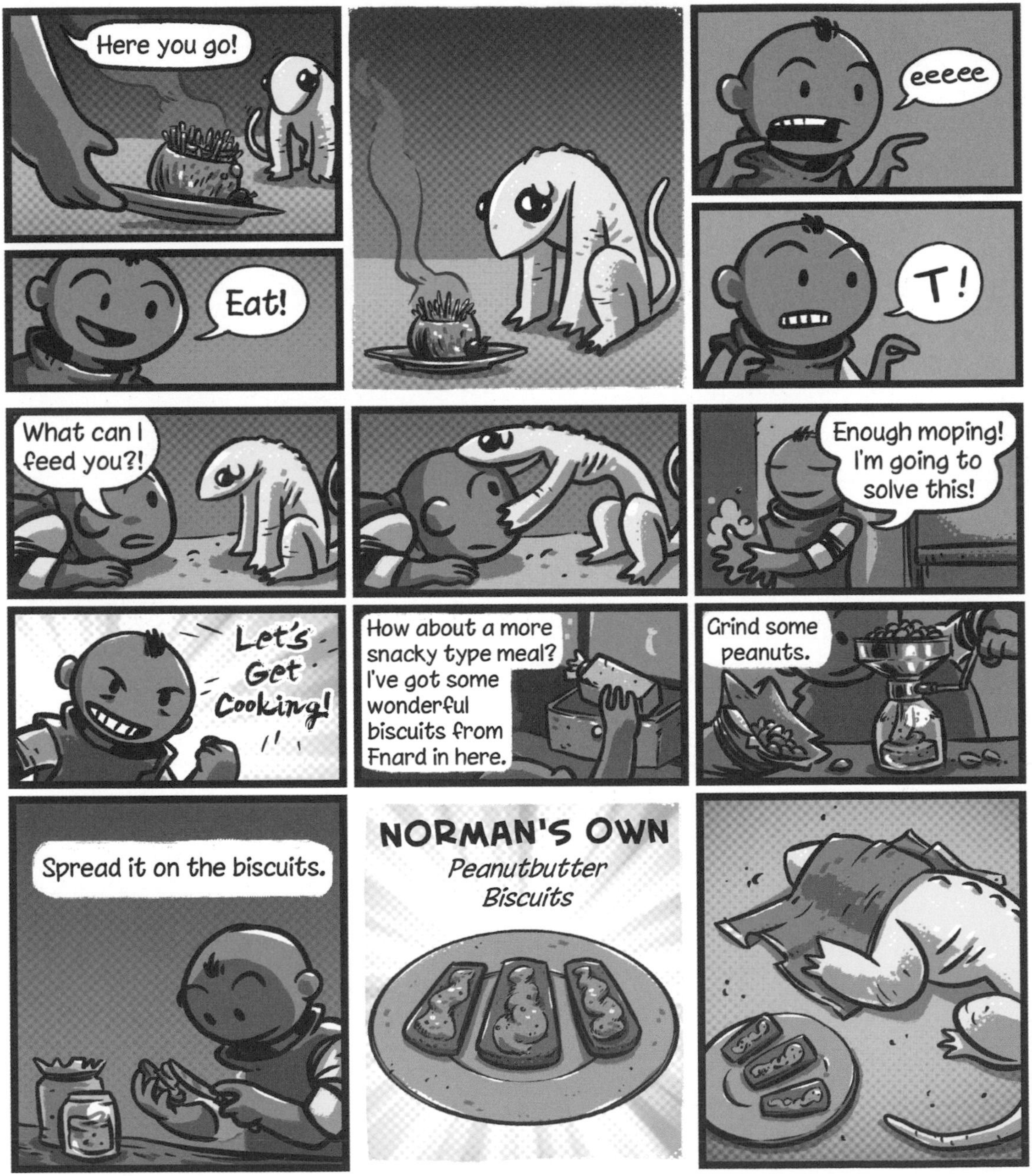
Here you go!
Eat!
eeeee
T!
What can I feed you?!
Enough moping! I'm going to solve this!
Let's Get Cooking!
How about a more snacky type meal? I've got some wonderful biscuits from Fnard in here.
Grind some peanuts.
Spread it on the biscuits.
NORMAN'S OWN
Peanutbutter Biscuits

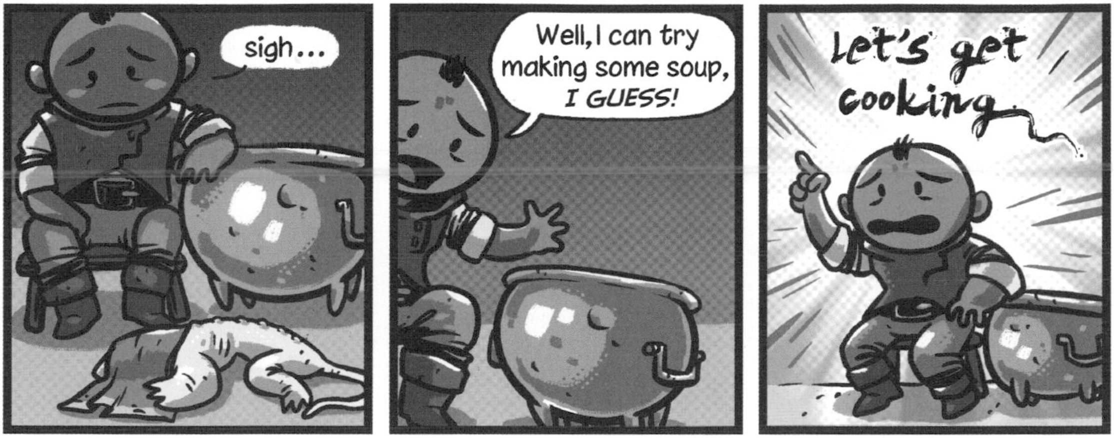
sigh...
Well, I can try making some soup, I GUESS!
Let's get cooking

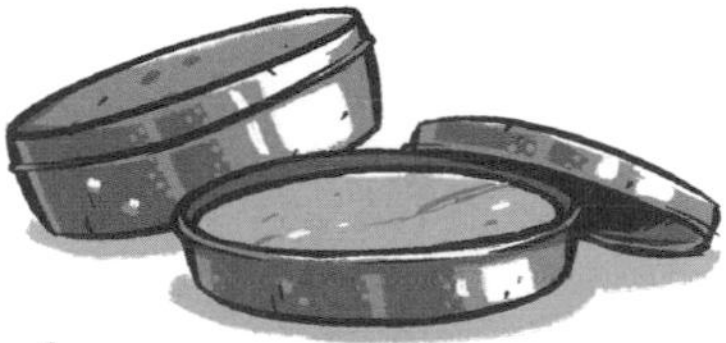

1. One puck of dehydrated portable chicken stock.

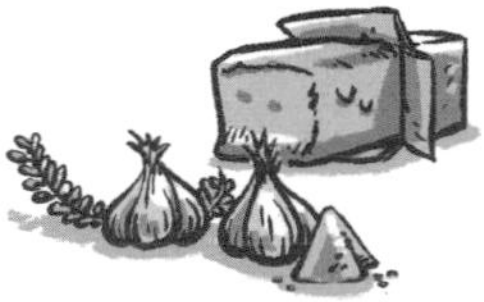

2. Your favorite herbs and seasonings and PLENTY of butter!

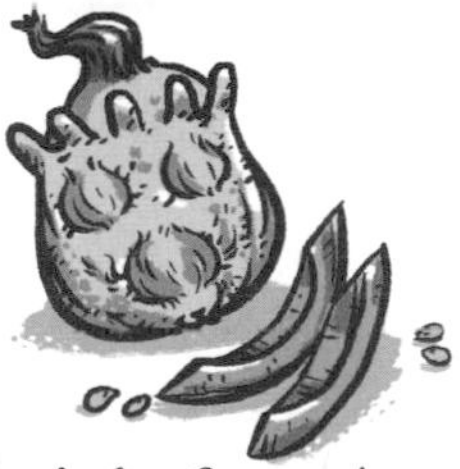

3. A nice 2-pound King's Head Squash, cleaned and cut.

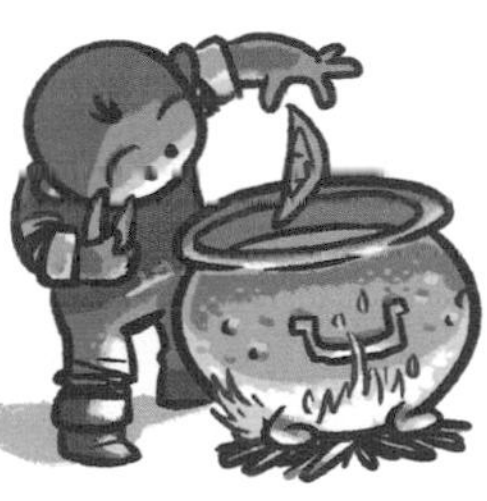

4. Prepare the stock as normal and add all ingredients.

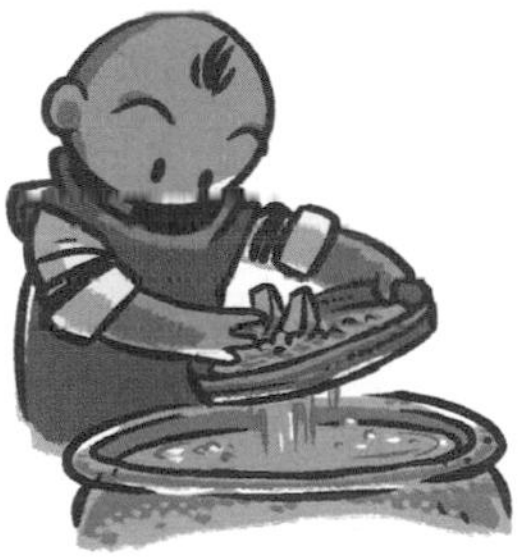

5. When the squash is tender, puree it through a drum sieve.

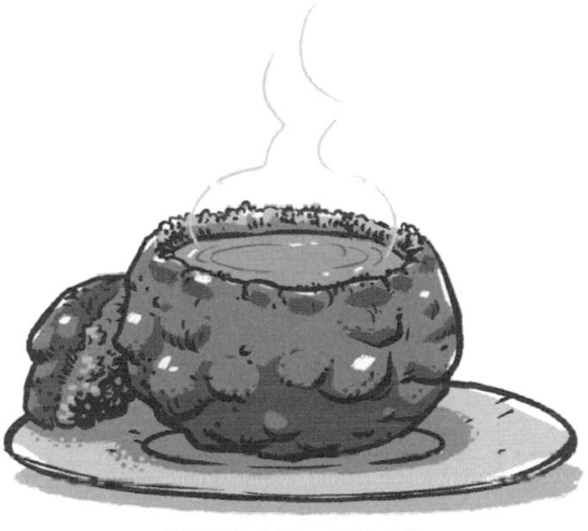

KING'S HEAD SQUASH SOUP

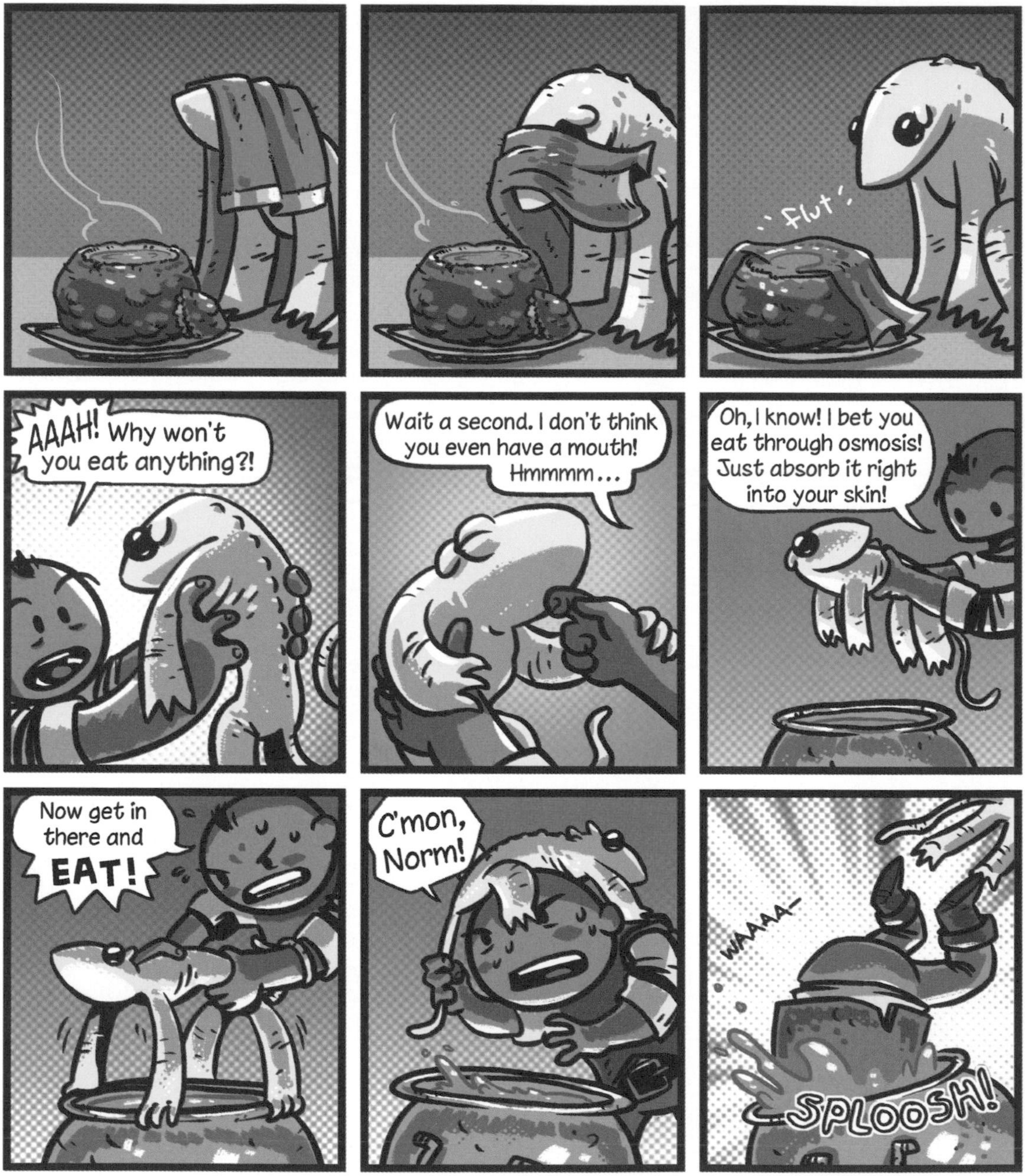
flut
AAAH! Why won't you eat anything?!
Wait a second. I don't think you even have a mouth! Hmmmm...
Oh, I know! I bet you eat through osmosis! Just absorb it right into your skin!
Now get in there and EAT!
C'mon, Norm!
WAAAA—
SPLOOSH!

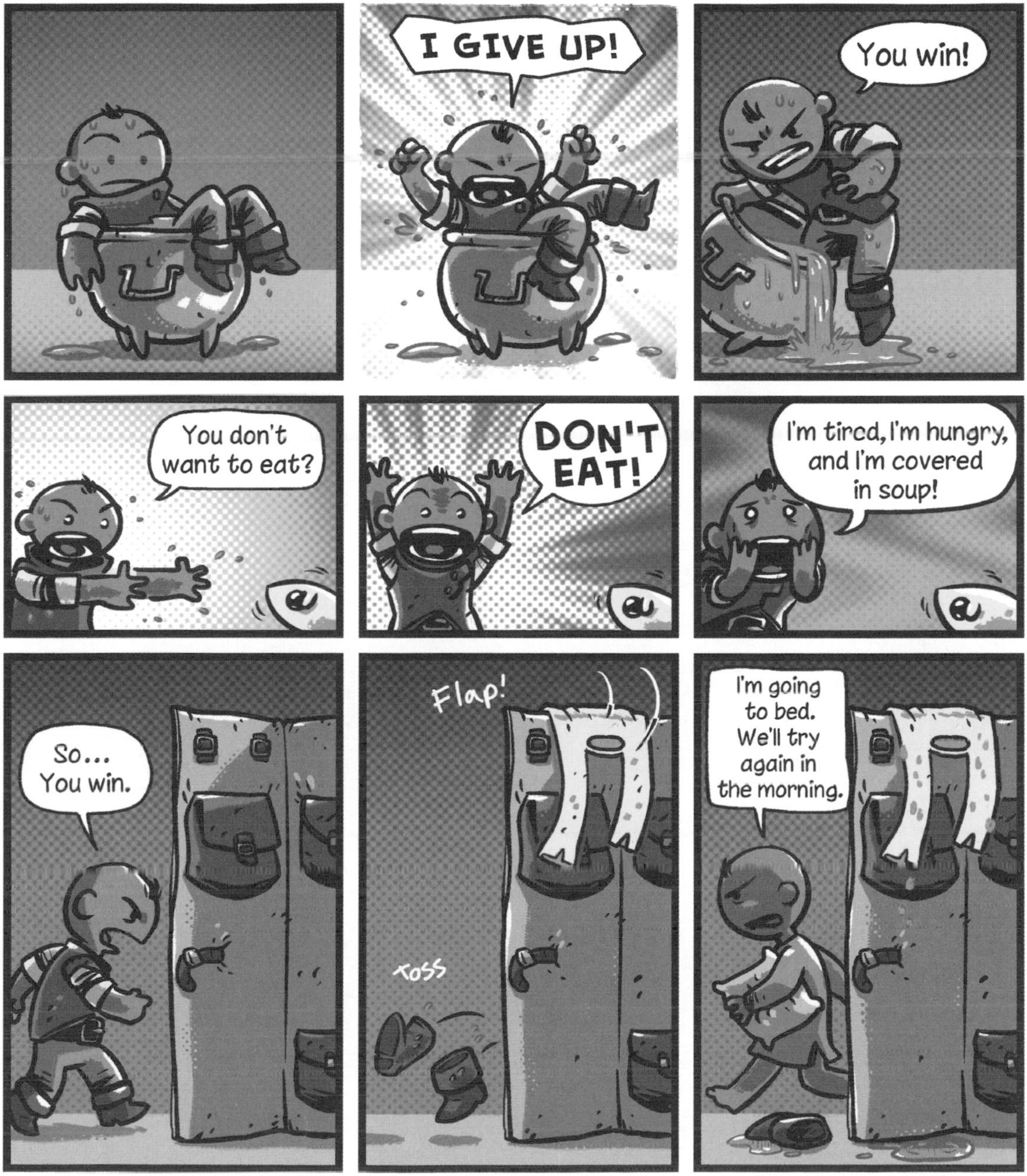
I GIVE UP!
You win!
You don't want to eat?
DON'T EAT!
I'm tired, I'm hungry, and I'm covered in soup!
So... You win.
Flap!
TOSS
I'm going to bed. We'll try again in the morning.

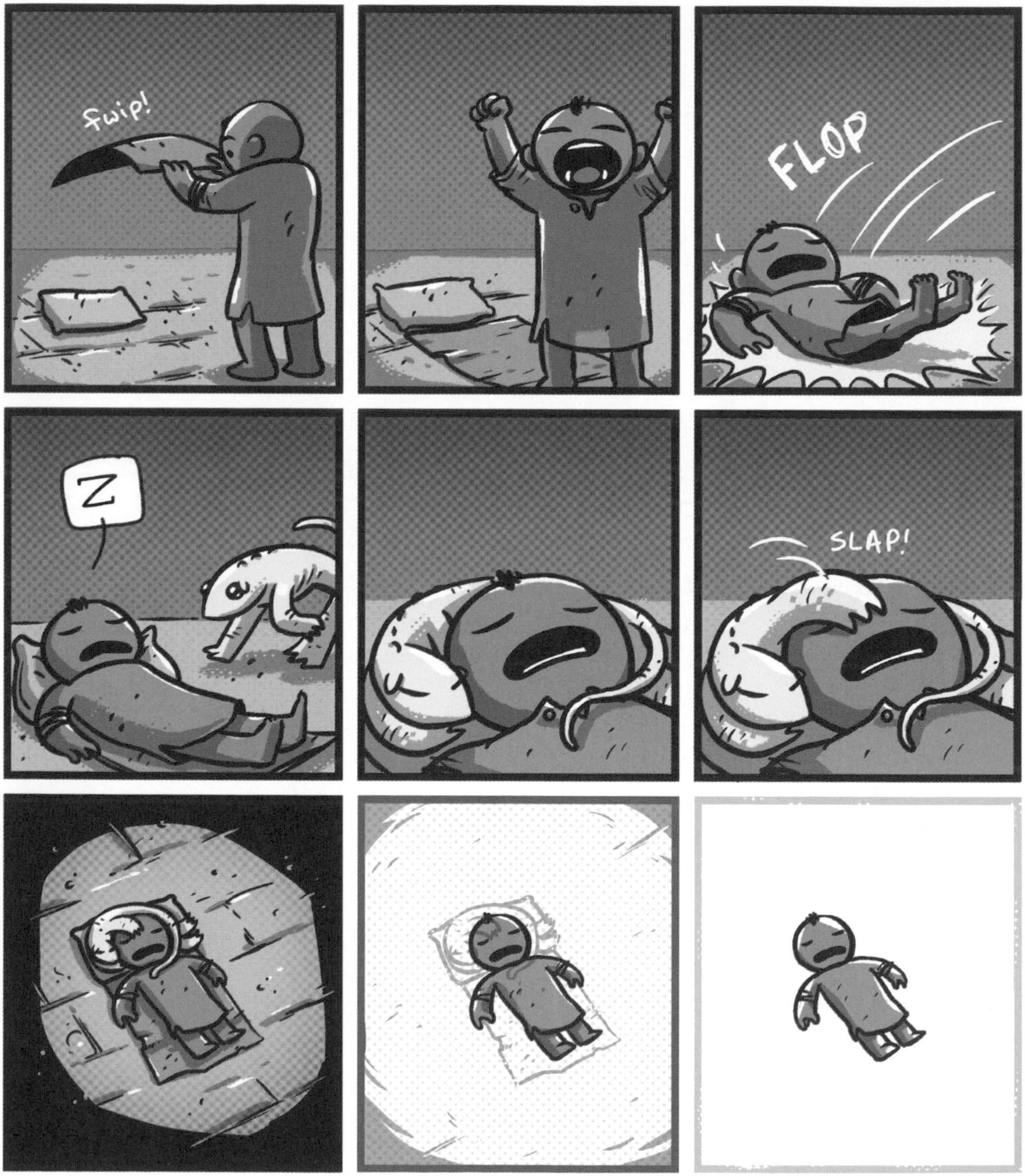
fwip!
FLOP
Z
SLAP!

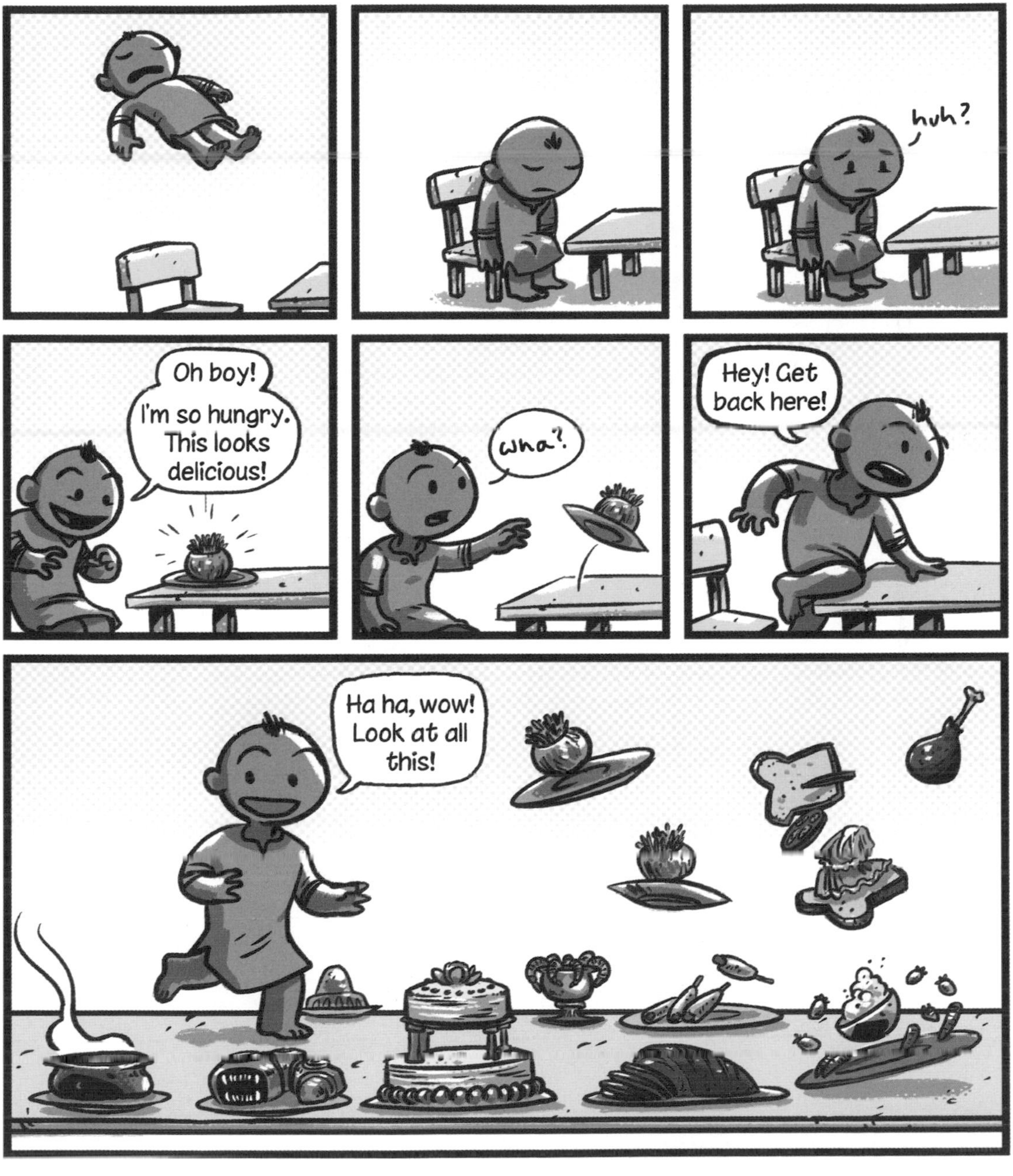
huh?
Oh boy!
I'm so hungry. This looks delicious!
wha?
Hey! Get back here!
Ha ha, wow! Look at all this!

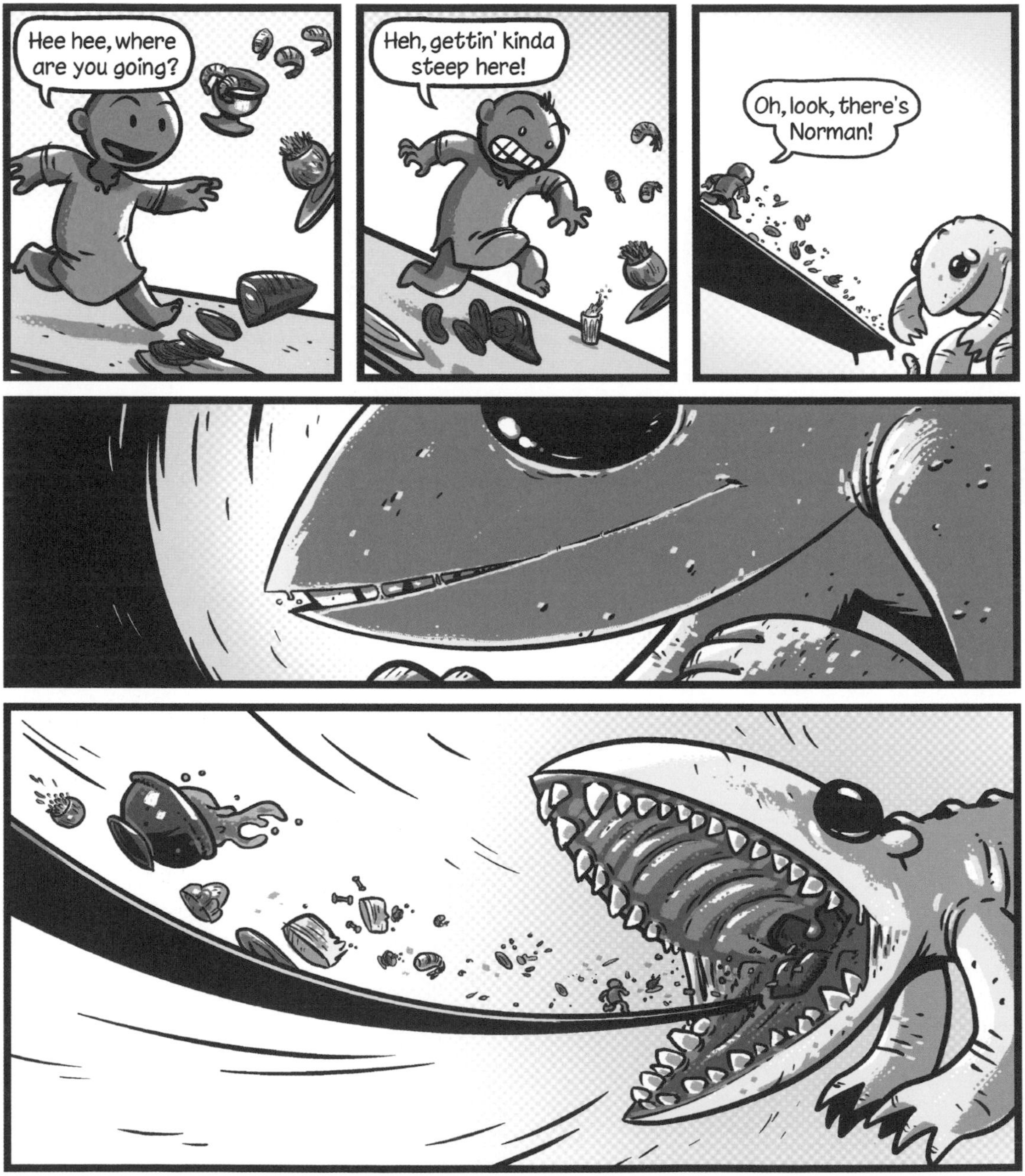
Hee hee, where are you going?
Heh, gettin' kinda steep here!
Oh, look, there's Norman!

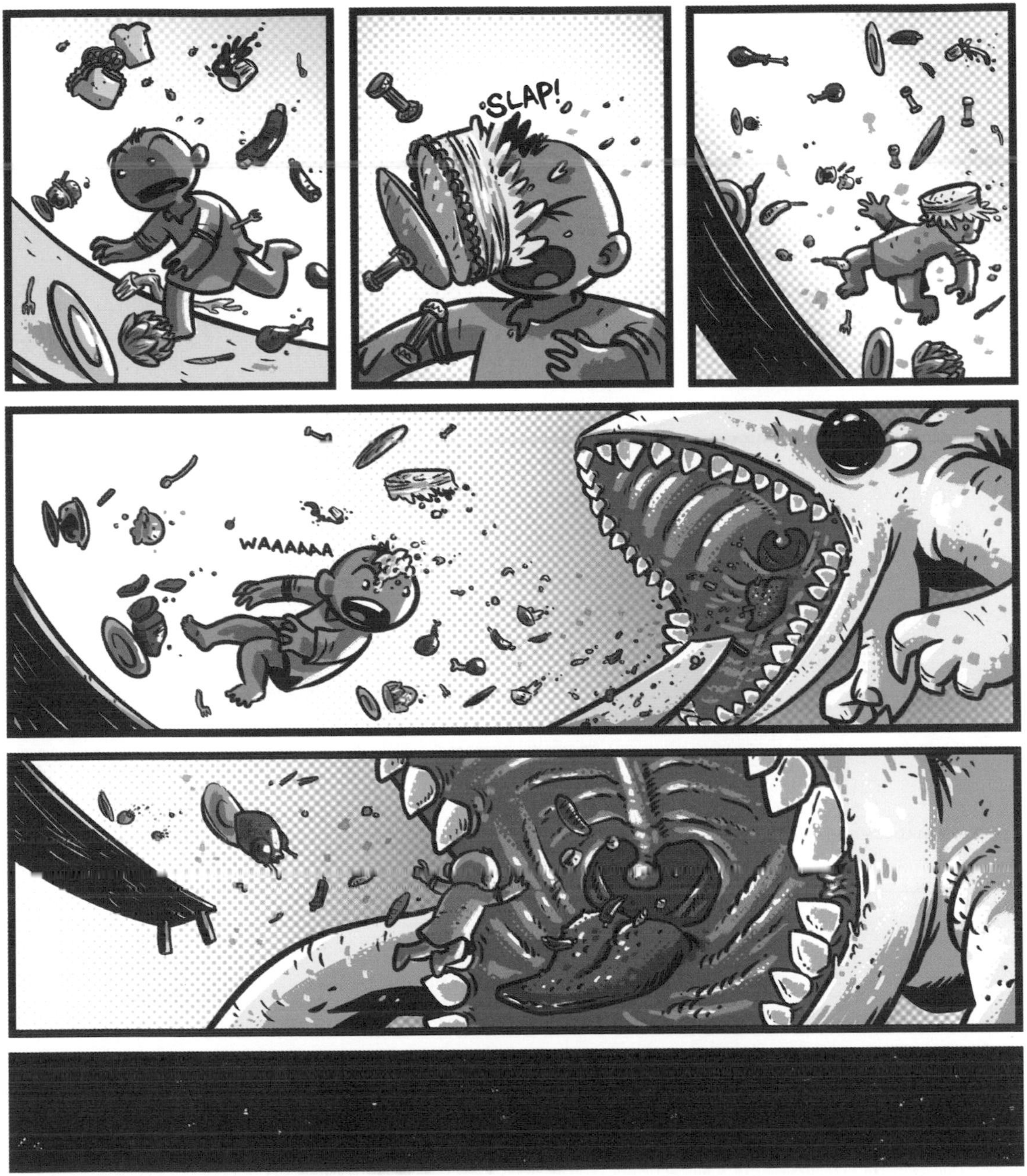
SLAP!
WAAAAAA

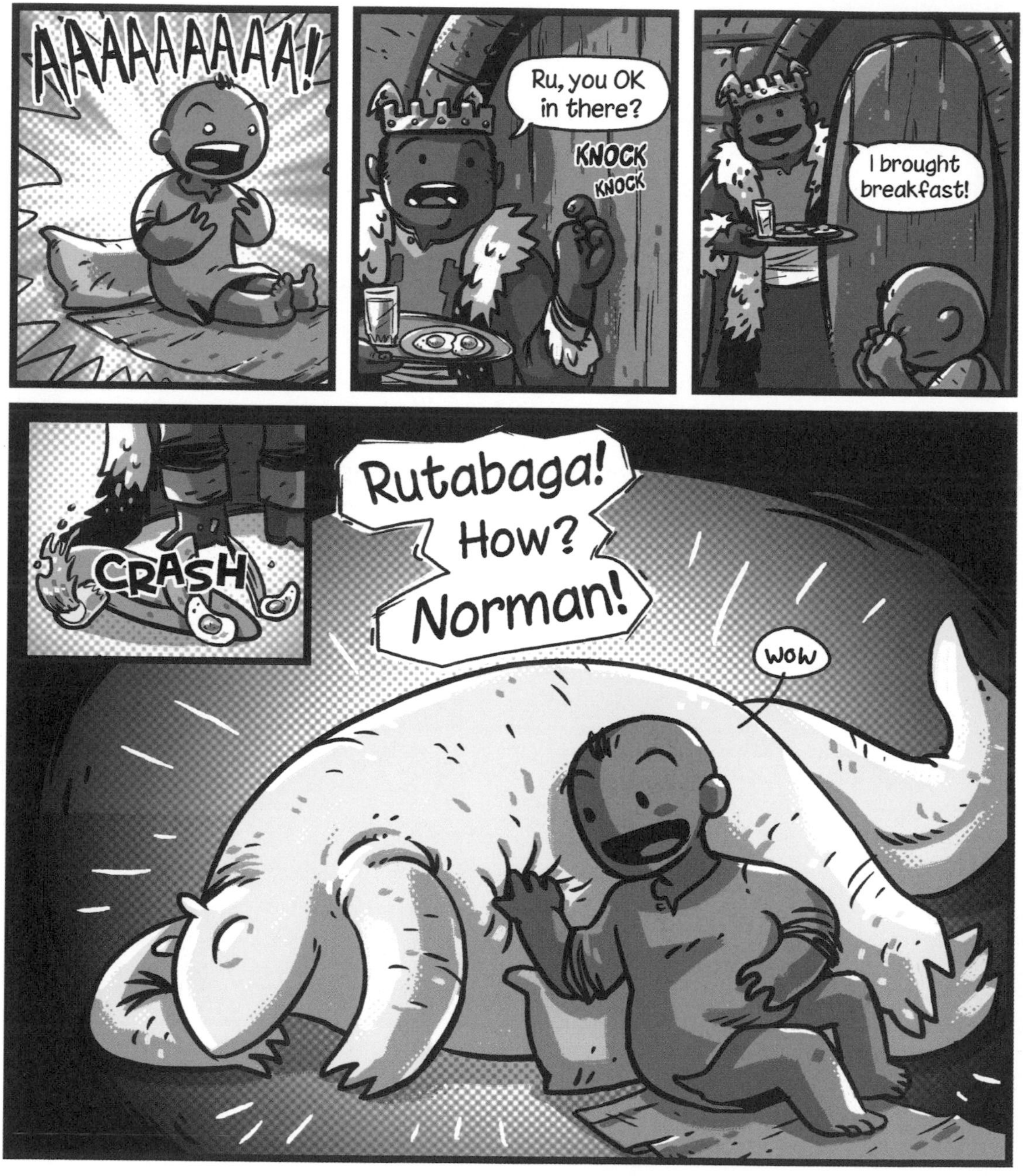
AAAAAAAAA!
Ru, you OK in there?
KNOCK KNOCK
I brought breakfast!
CRASH
Rutabaga! How? Norman!
WOW

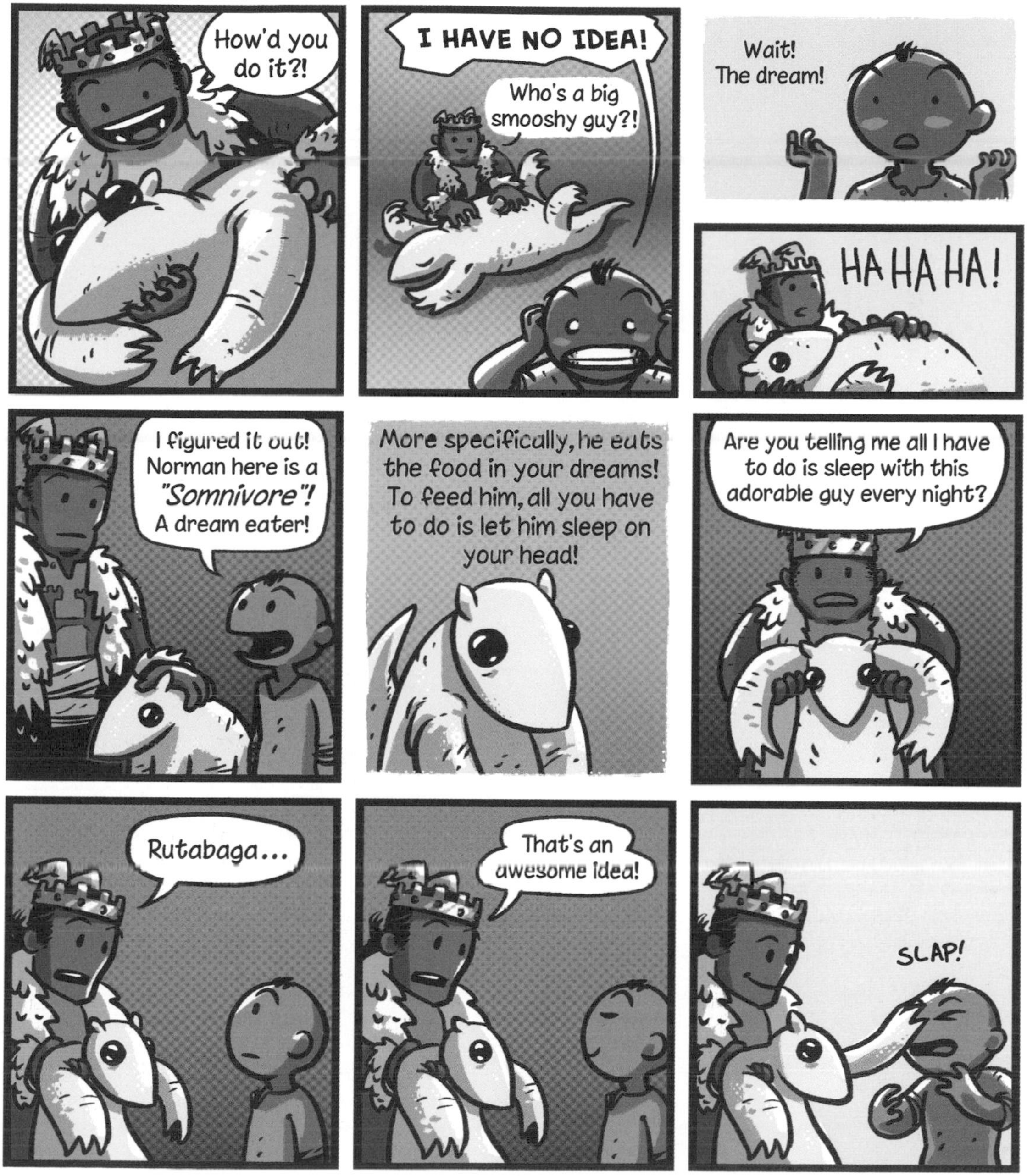
How'd you do it?!
I HAVE NO IDEA!
Who's a big smooshy guy?!
Wait! The dream!
HA HA HA!
I figured it out! Norman here is a "Somnivore"! A dream eater!
More specifically, he eats the food in your dreams! To feed him, all you have to do is let him sleep on your head!
Are you telling me all I have to do is sleep with this adorable guy every night?
Rutabaga...
That's an awesome idea!
SLAP!

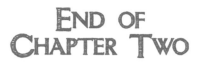

END OF CHAPTER TWO

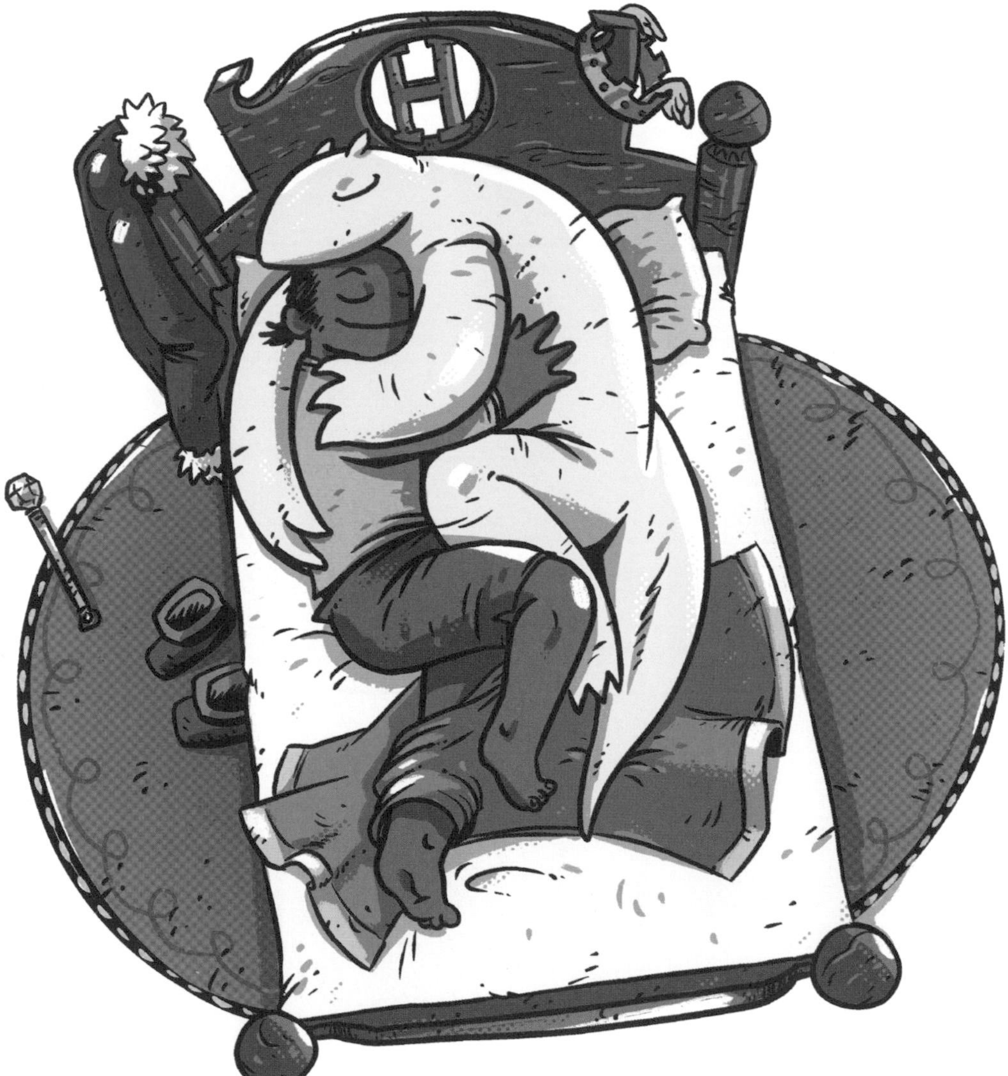

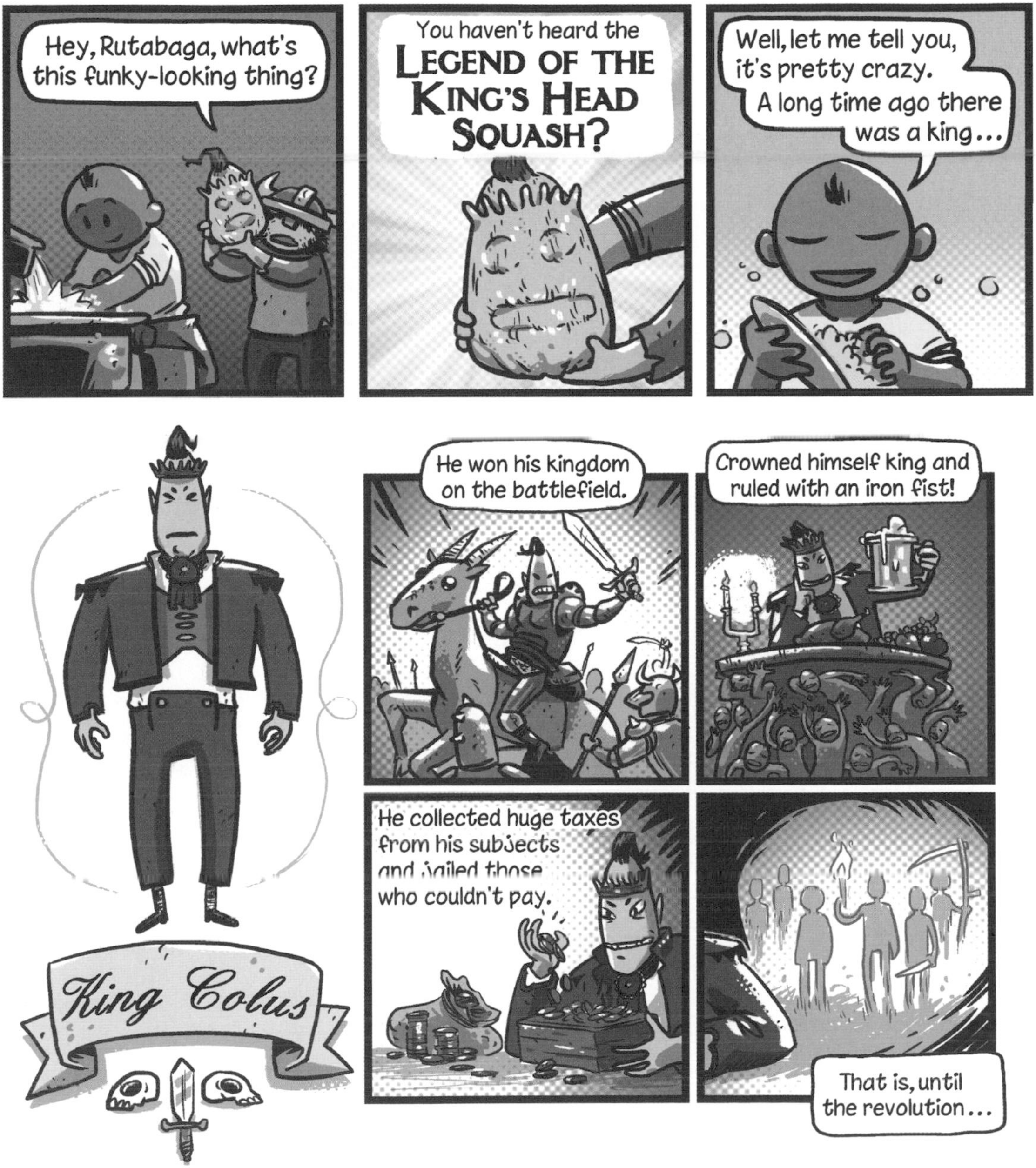

Hey, Rutabaga, what's this funky-looking thing?
You haven't heard the LEGEND OF THE KING'S HEAD SQUASH?
Well, let me tell you, it's pretty crazy.
A long time ago there was a king...
King Colus
He won his kingdom on the battlefield.
Crowned himself king and ruled with an iron fist!
He collected huge taxes from his subjects and jailed those who couldn't pay.
That is, until the revolution...

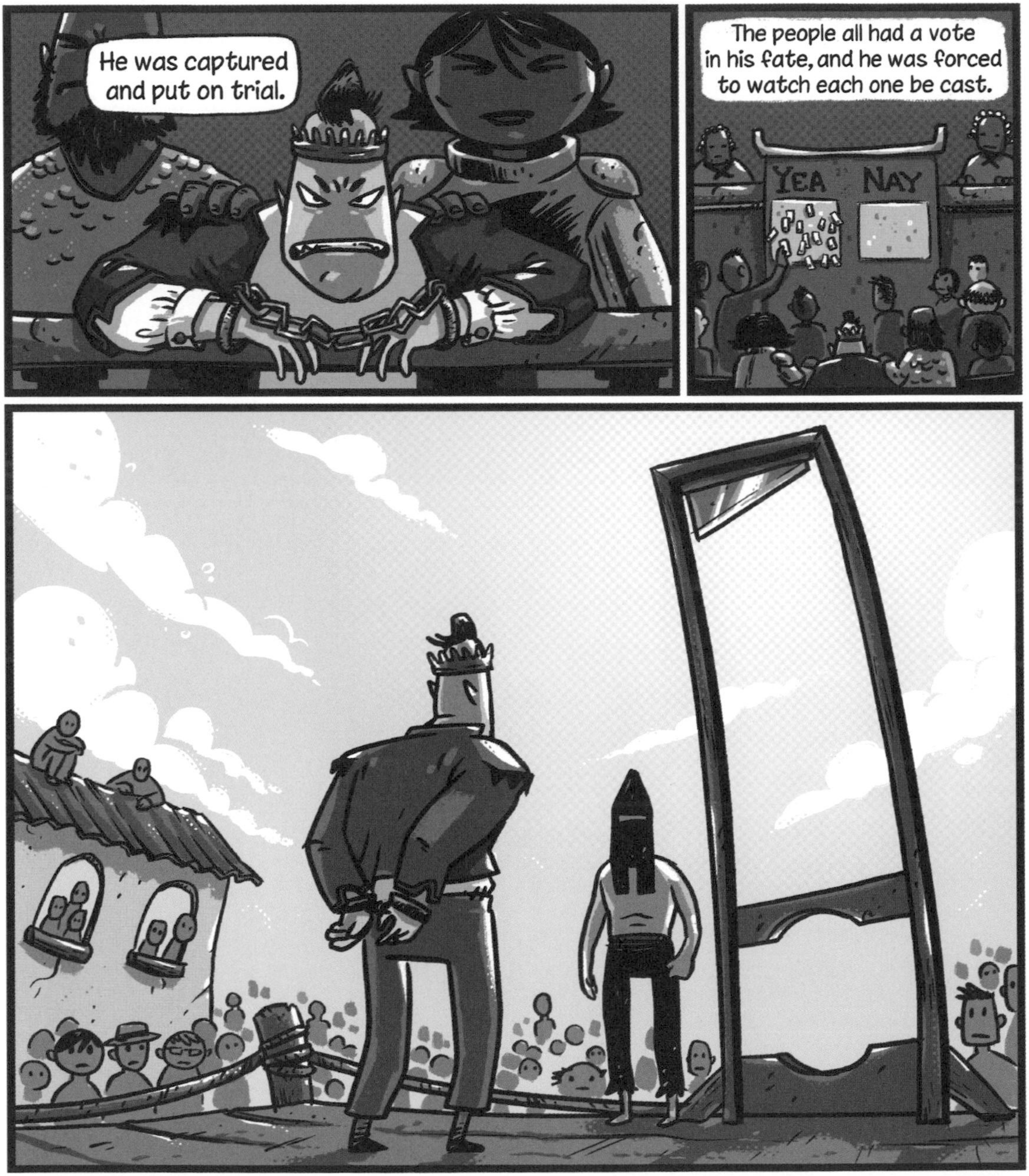
He was captured and put on trial.
The people all had a vote in his fate, and he was forced to watch each one be cast.
YEA
NAY

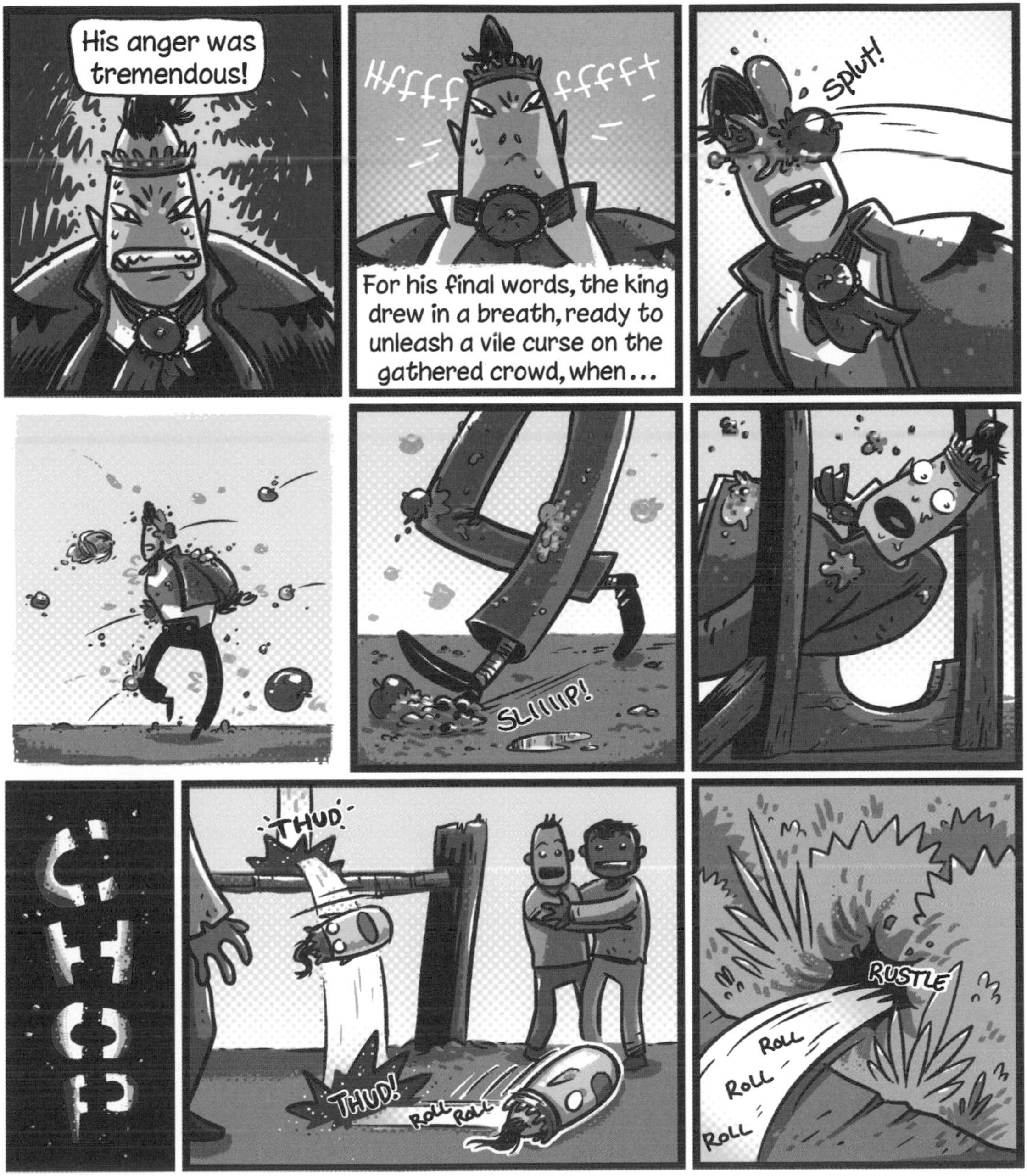
His anger was tremendous!
Hffff
fffft
For his final words, the king drew in a breath, ready to unleash a vile curse on the gathered crowd, when...
Splut!
SLIIIIP!
THUD
THUD!
ROLL
ROLL
RUSTLE
ROLL
ROLL
ROLL

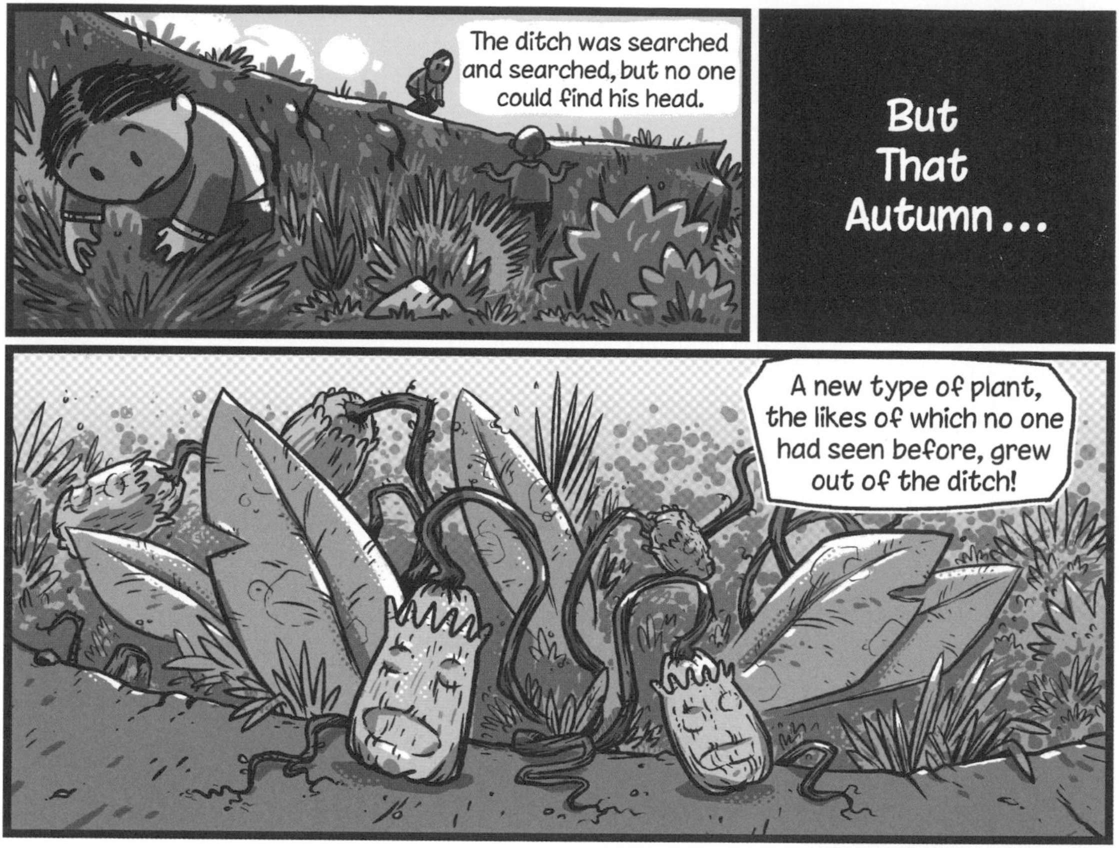
The ditch was searched and searched, but no one could find his head.
But That Autumn...
A new type of plant, the likes of which no one had seen before, grew out of the ditch!

It was delicious too!

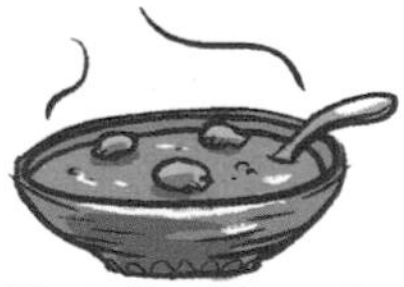

King's Head Squash Soup and Crackers

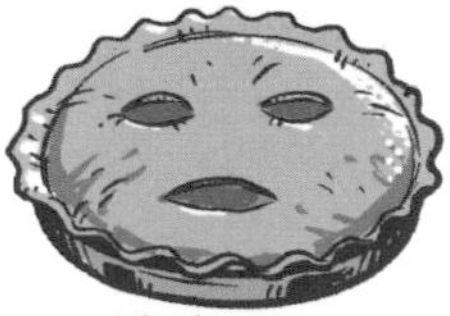

King's Head Squash Pie

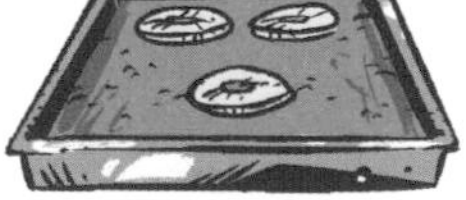

King's Head Squash Bread with Pineapple Slices

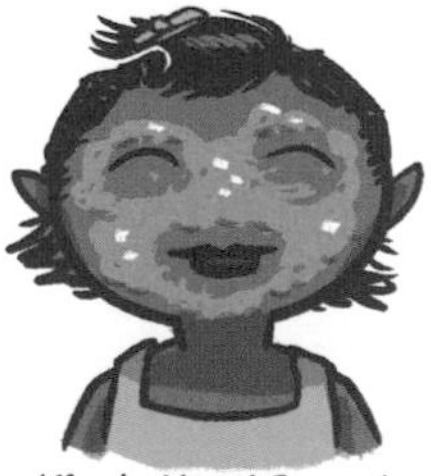

King's Head Squash Facial Scrub for Smoother Skin!

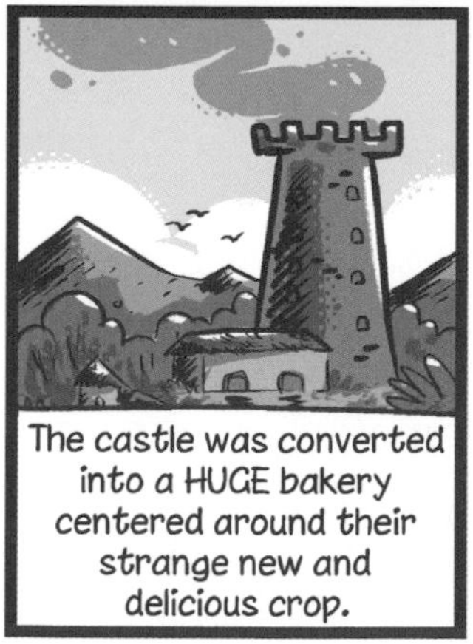
The castle was converted into a HUGE bakery centered around their strange new and delicious crop.

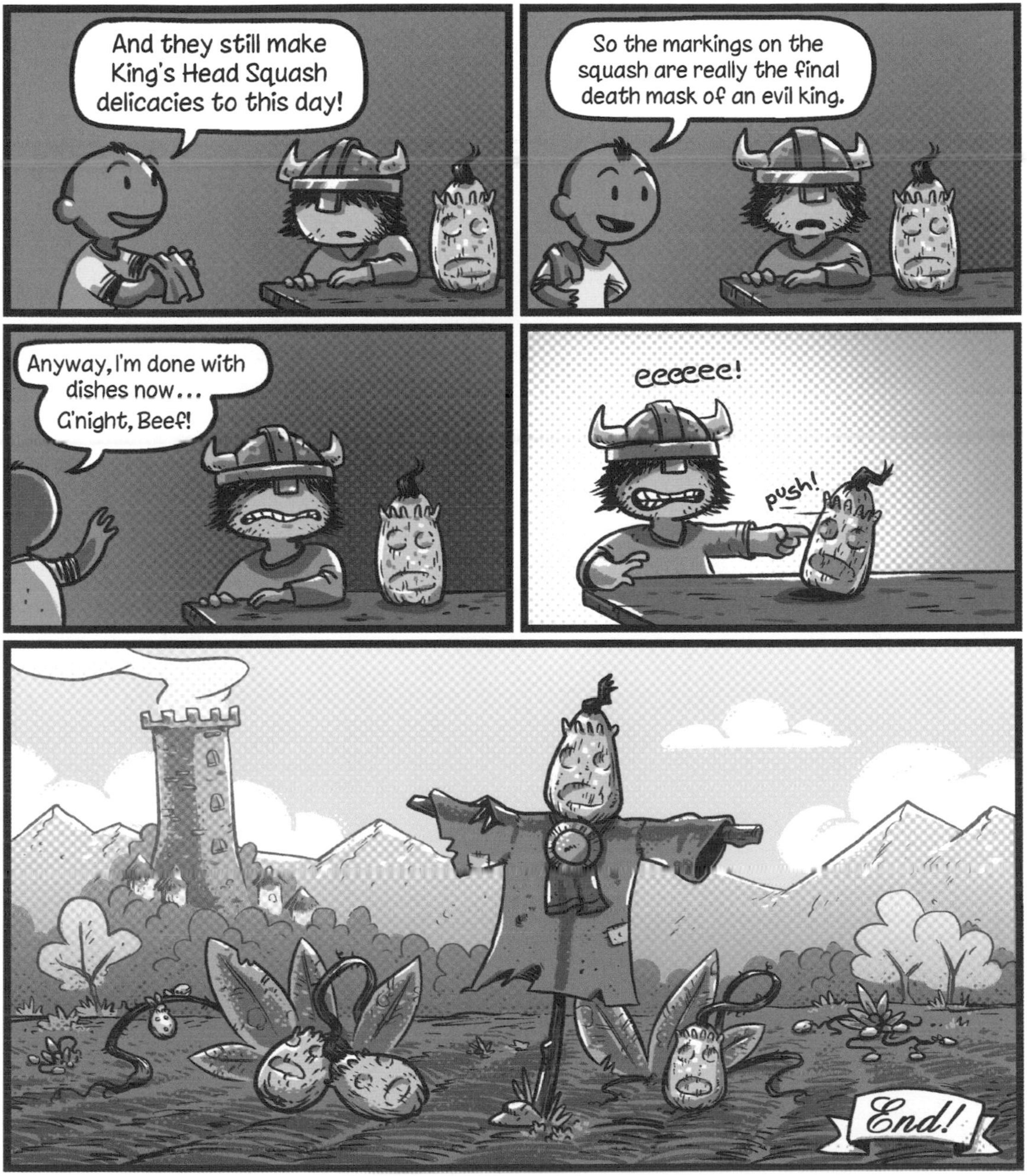
And they still make King's Head Squash delicacies to this day!
So the markings on the squash are really the final death mask of an evil king.
Anyway, I'm done with dishes now... G'night, Beef!
eeeeee!
push!
End!

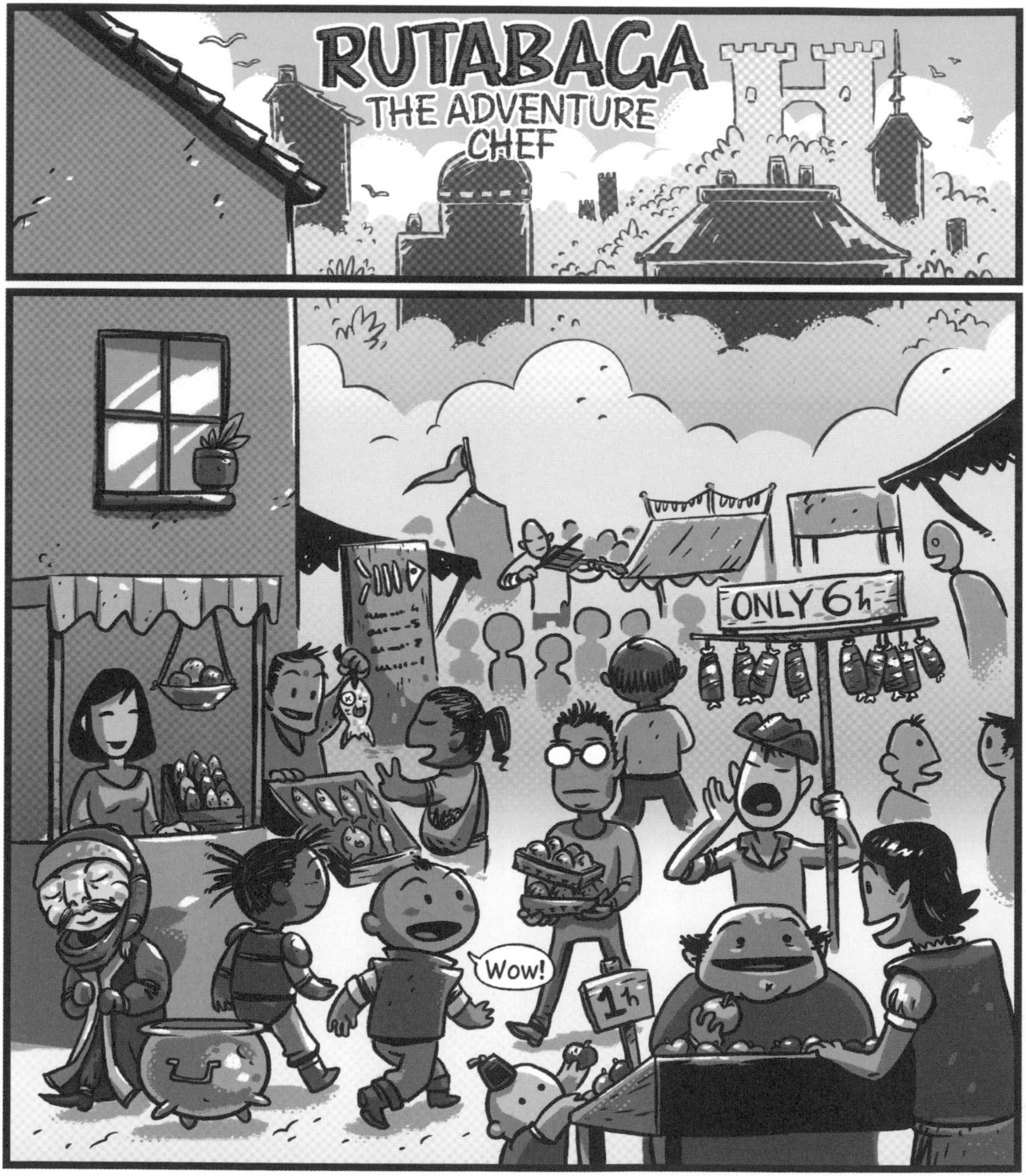
RUTABAGA
THE ADVENTURE CHEF
ONLY 6h
Wow!
1h

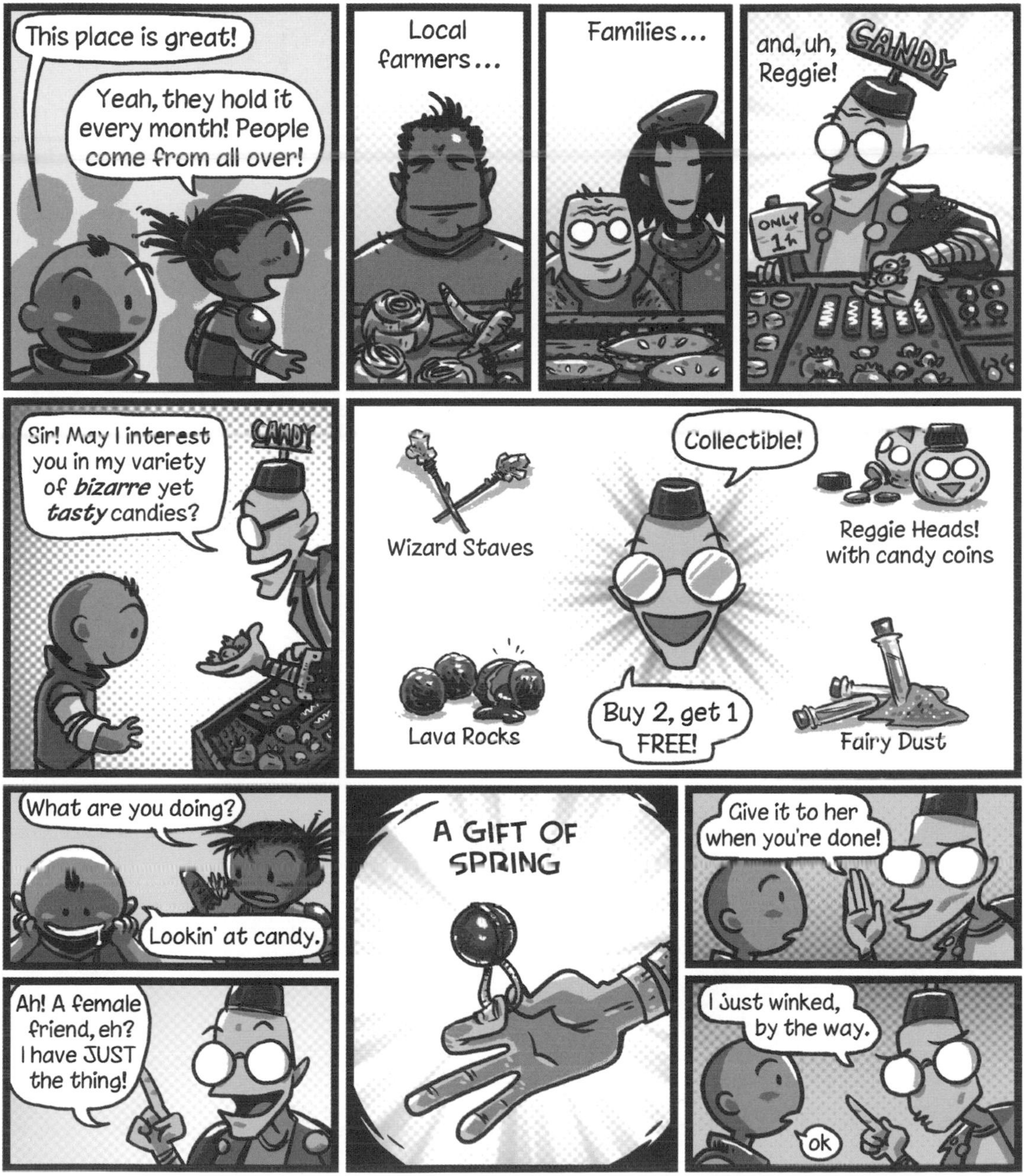
This place is great!
Yeah, they hold it every month! People come from all over!
Local farmers...
Families...
and, uh, Reggie!
CANDY
ONLY 1h
Sir! May I interest you in my variety of *bizarre* yet *tasty* candies?
CANDY
Wizard Staves
Collectible!
Reggie Heads! with candy coins
Lava Rocks
Buy 2, get 1 FREE!
Fairy Dust
What are you doing?
Lookin' at candy.
Ah! A female friend, eh? I have JUST the thing!
A GIFT OF SPRING
Give it to her when you're done!
I just winked, by the way.
ok

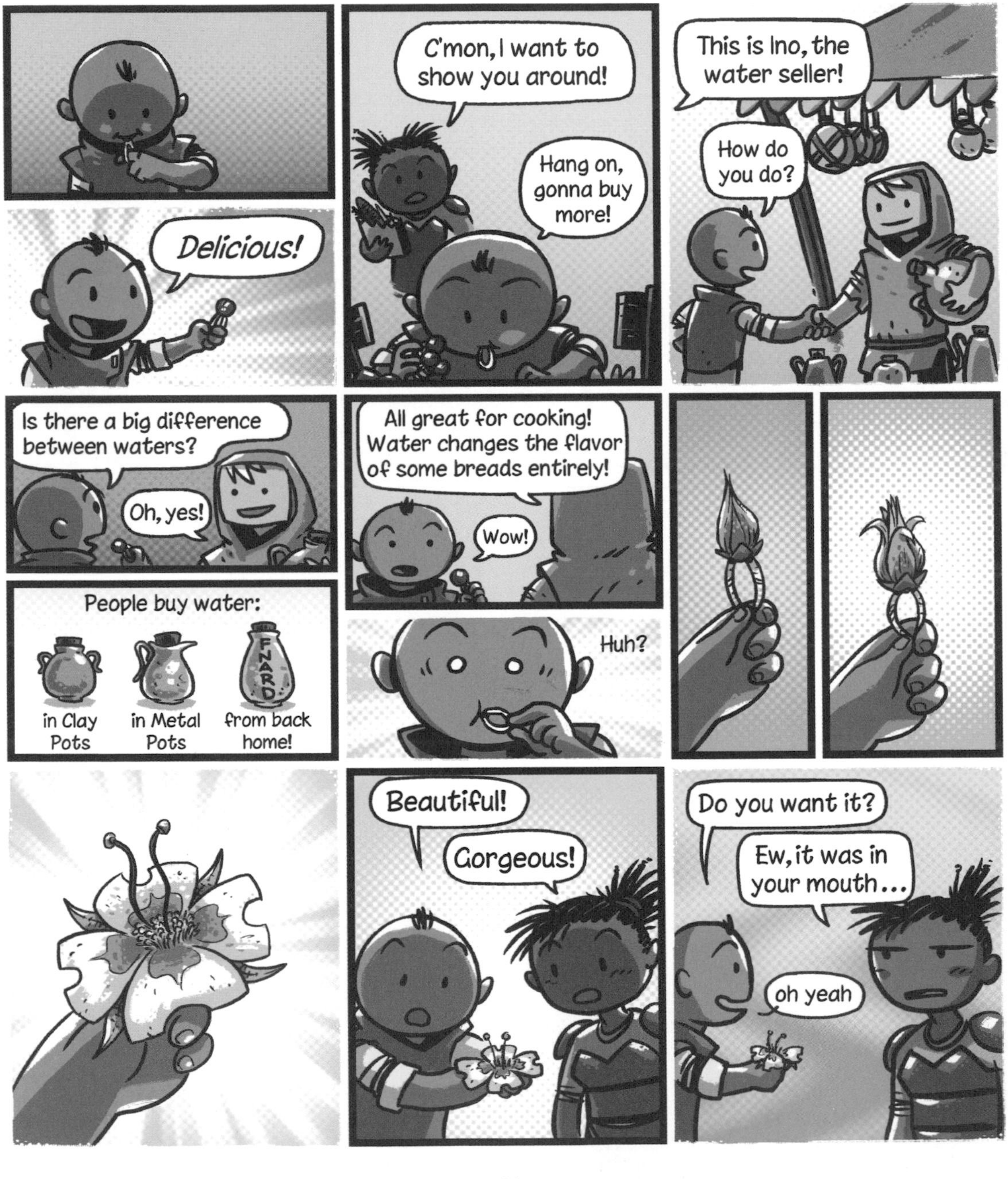
Delicious!
C'mon, I want to show you around!
Hang on, gonna buy more!
This is Ino, the water seller!
How do you do?
Is there a big difference between waters?
Oh, yes!
People buy water:
in Clay Pots
in Metal Pots
from back home!
FNARD
All great for cooking! Water changes the flavor of some breads entirely!
Wow!
Huh?
Beautiful!
Gorgeous!
Do you want it?
Ew, it was in your mouth...
oh yeah

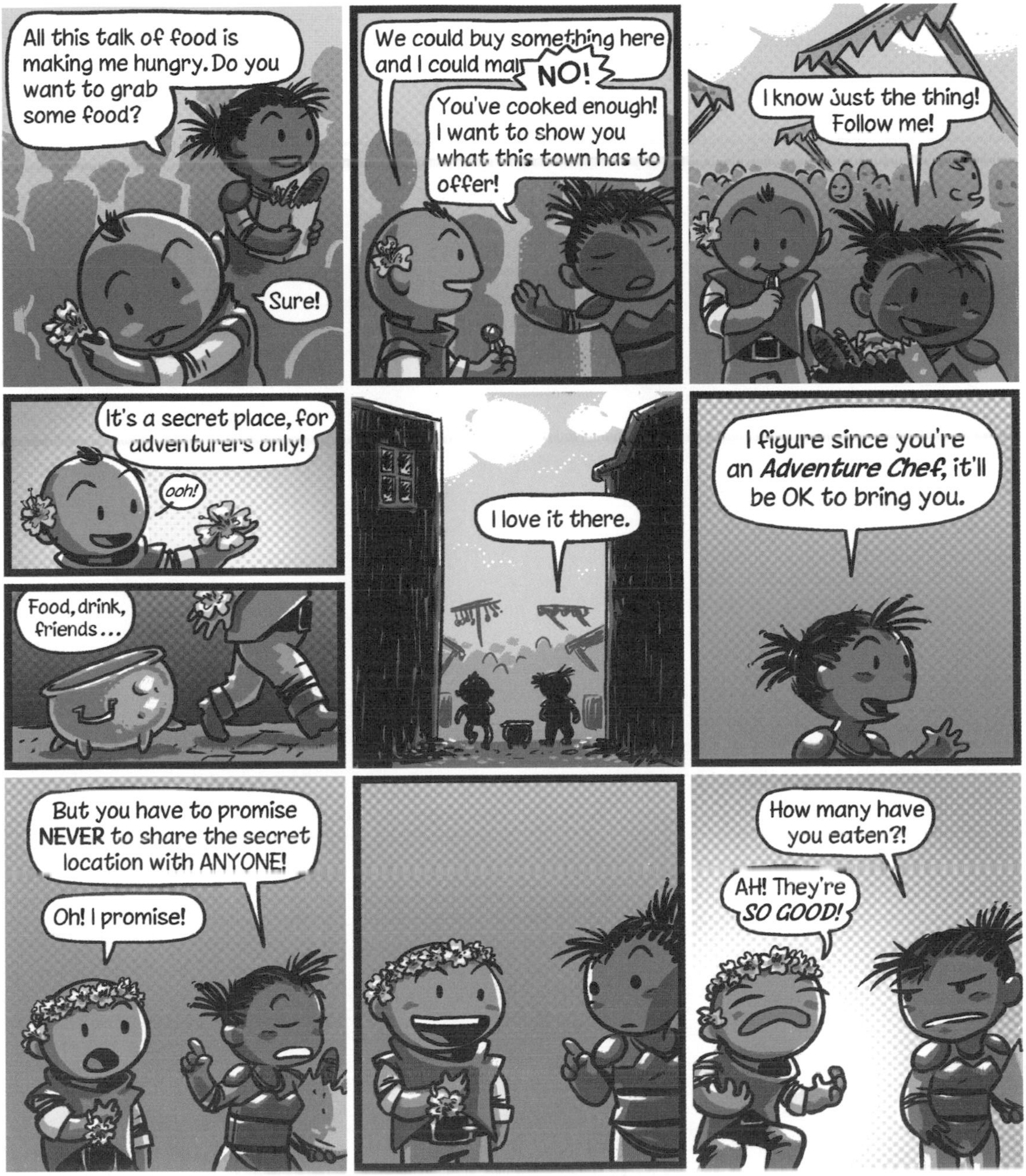
All this talk of food is making me hungry. Do you want to grab some food?
Sure!
We could buy something here and I could mal
NO!
You've cooked enough! I want to show you what this town has to offer!
I know just the thing! Follow me!
It's a secret place, for adventurers only!
ooh!
Food, drink, friends...
I love it there.
I figure since you're an *Adventure Chef*, it'll be OK to bring you.
But you have to promise **NEVER** to share the secret location with ANYONE!
Oh! I promise!
How many have you eaten?!
AH! They're *SO GOOD!*

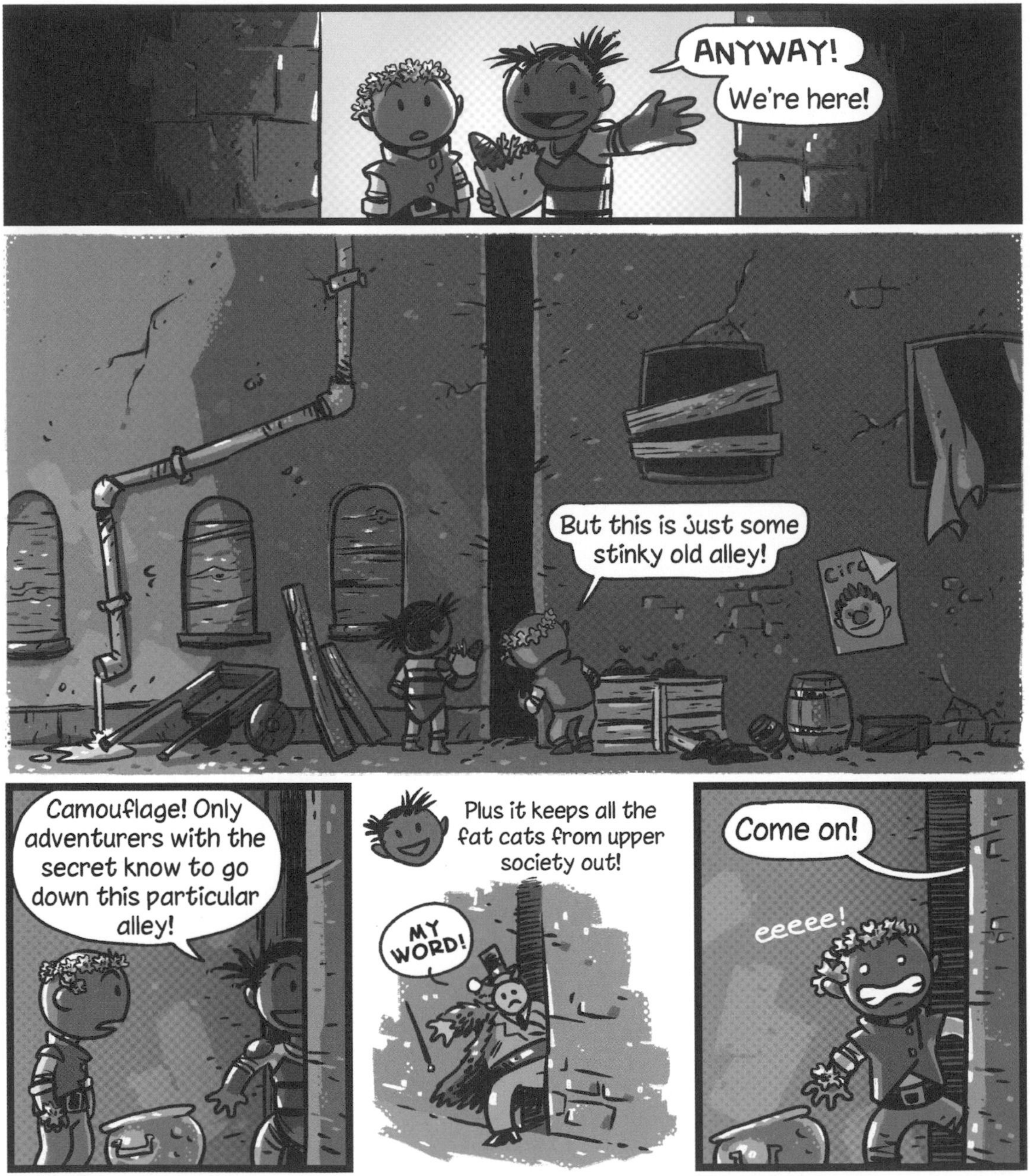
ANYWAY!
We're here!
But this is just some stinky old alley!
Circ
Camouflage! Only adventurers with the secret know to go down this particular alley!
Plus it keeps all the fat cats from upper society out!
MY WORD!
Come on!
eeeee!

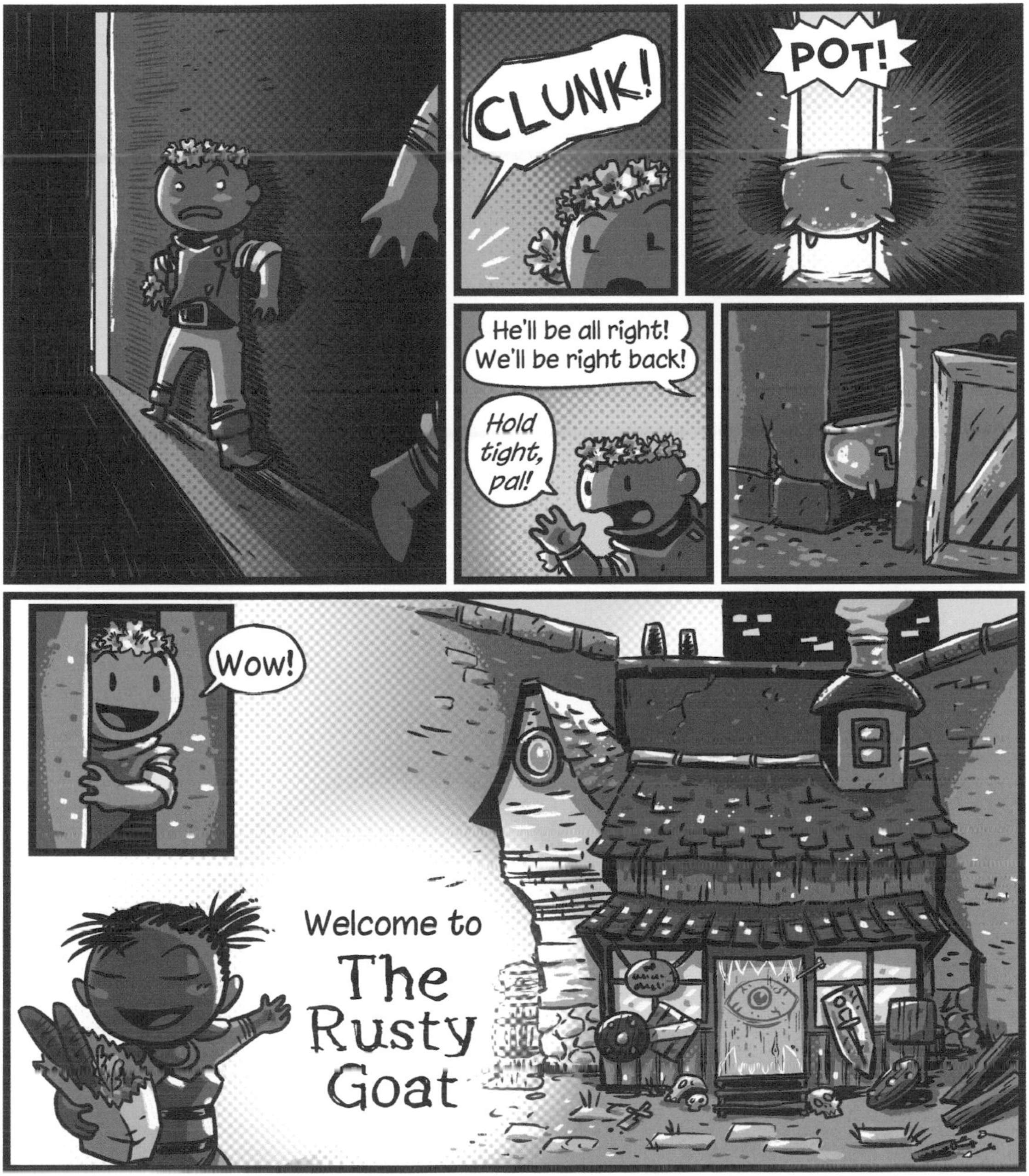
CLUNK!
POT!
He'll be all right! We'll be right back!
Hold tight, pal!
Wow!
Welcome to The Rusty Goat

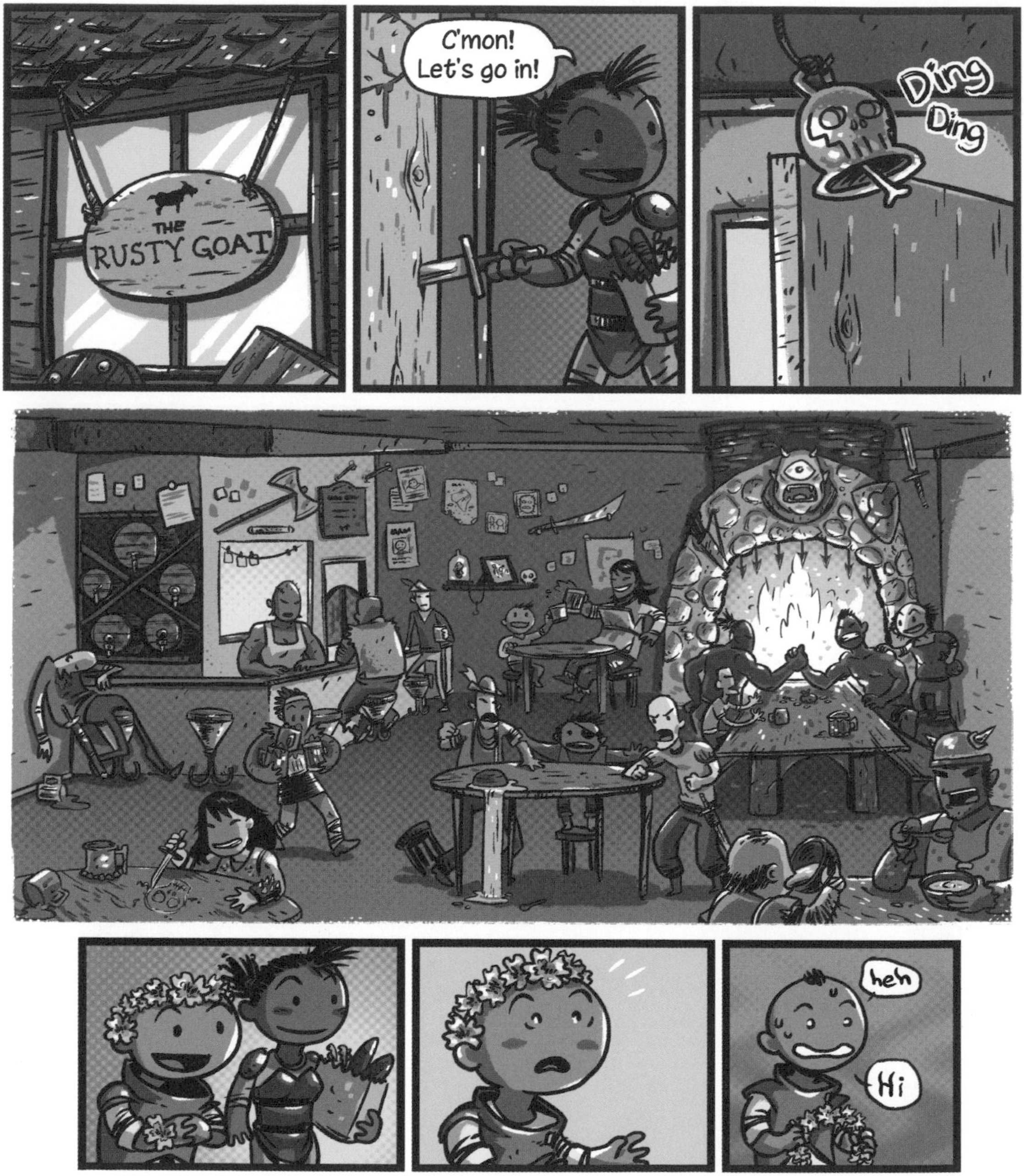
THE
RUSTY GOAT
C'mon!
Let's go in!
Ding
Ding
heh
Hi

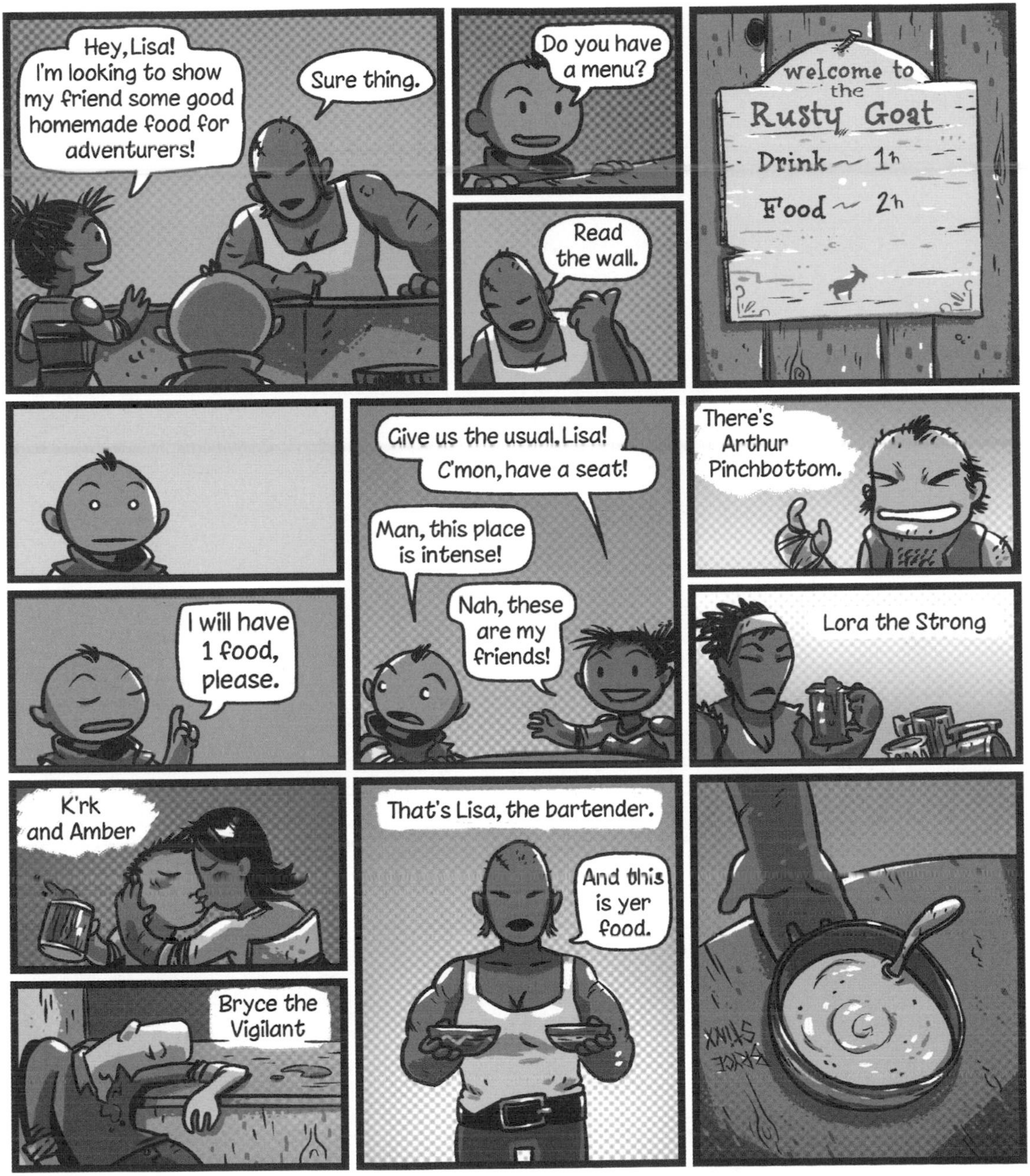

Hey, Lisa! I'm looking to show my friend some good homemade food for adventurers!
Sure thing.
Do you have a menu?
Read the wall.
welcome to the
Rusty Goat
Drink ~ 1h
Food ~ 2h
I will have 1 food, please.
Give us the usual, Lisa!
C'mon, have a seat!
Man, this place is intense!
Nah, these are my friends!
There's Arthur Pinchbottom.
Lora the Strong
K'rk and Amber
Bryce the Vigilant
That's Lisa, the bartender.
And this is yer food.

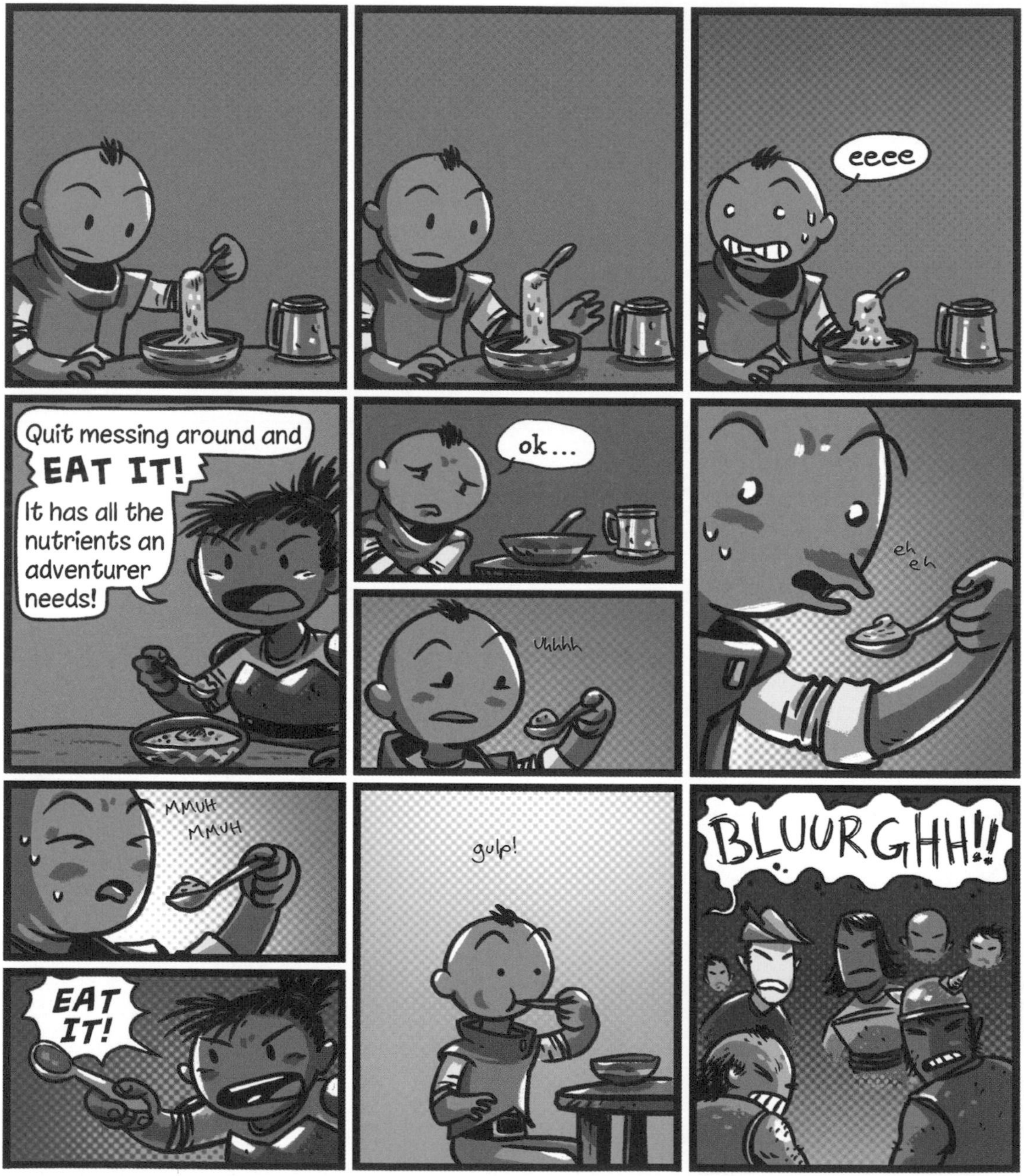
eeee
Quit messing around and EAT IT! It has all the nutrients an adventurer needs!
ok...
Uhhhh
eh eh
MMUH MMUH
EAT IT!
gulp!
BLUURGHH!!

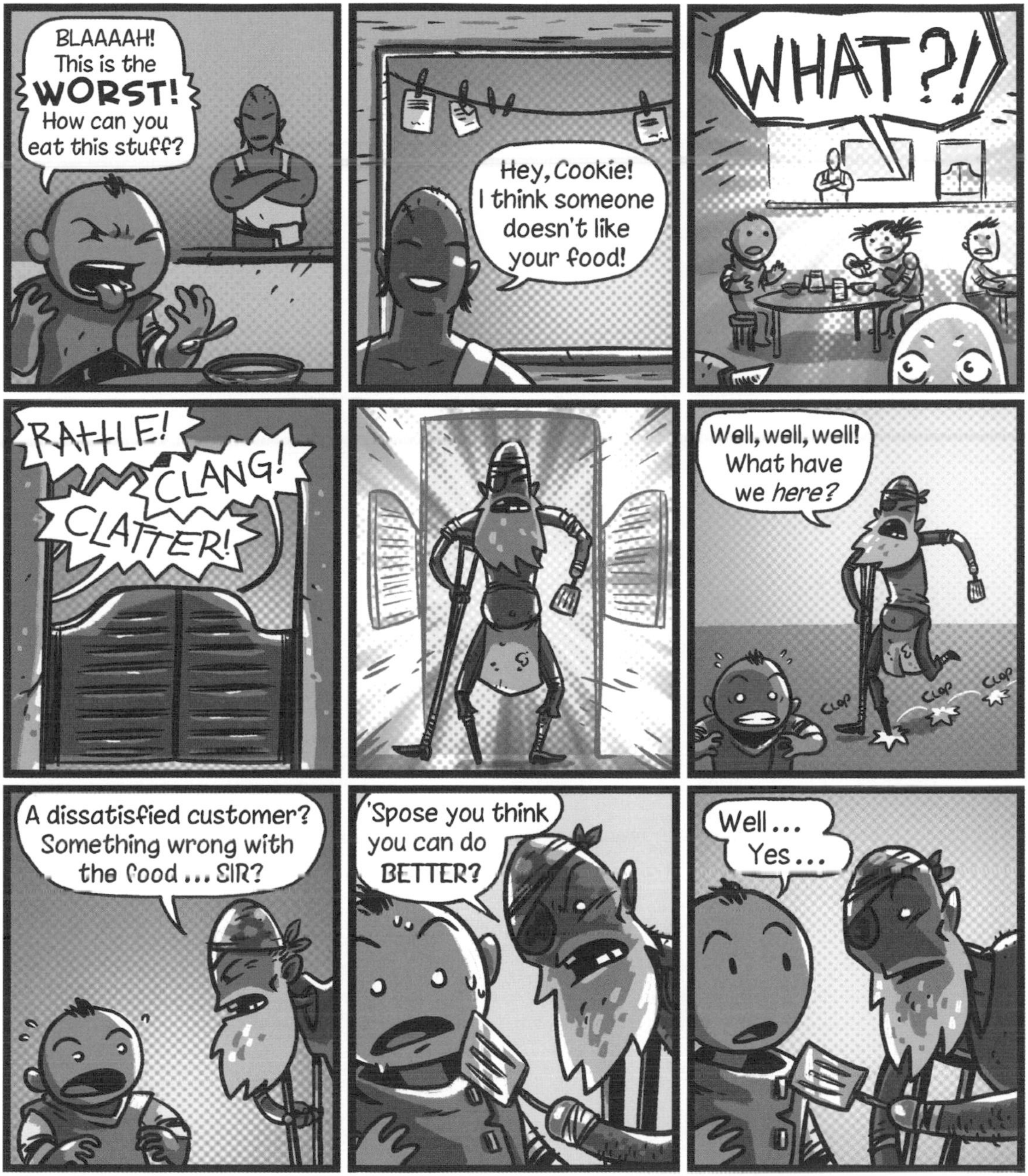
BLAAAAH! This is the WORST! How can you eat this stuff?
Hey, Cookie! I think someone doesn't like your food!
WHAT?!
RATTLE!
CLANG!
CLATTER!
Well, well, well! What have we *here*?
CLOP
CLOP
CLOP
A dissatisfied customer? Something wrong with the food ... SIR?
'Spose you think you can do BETTER?
Well ... Yes ...

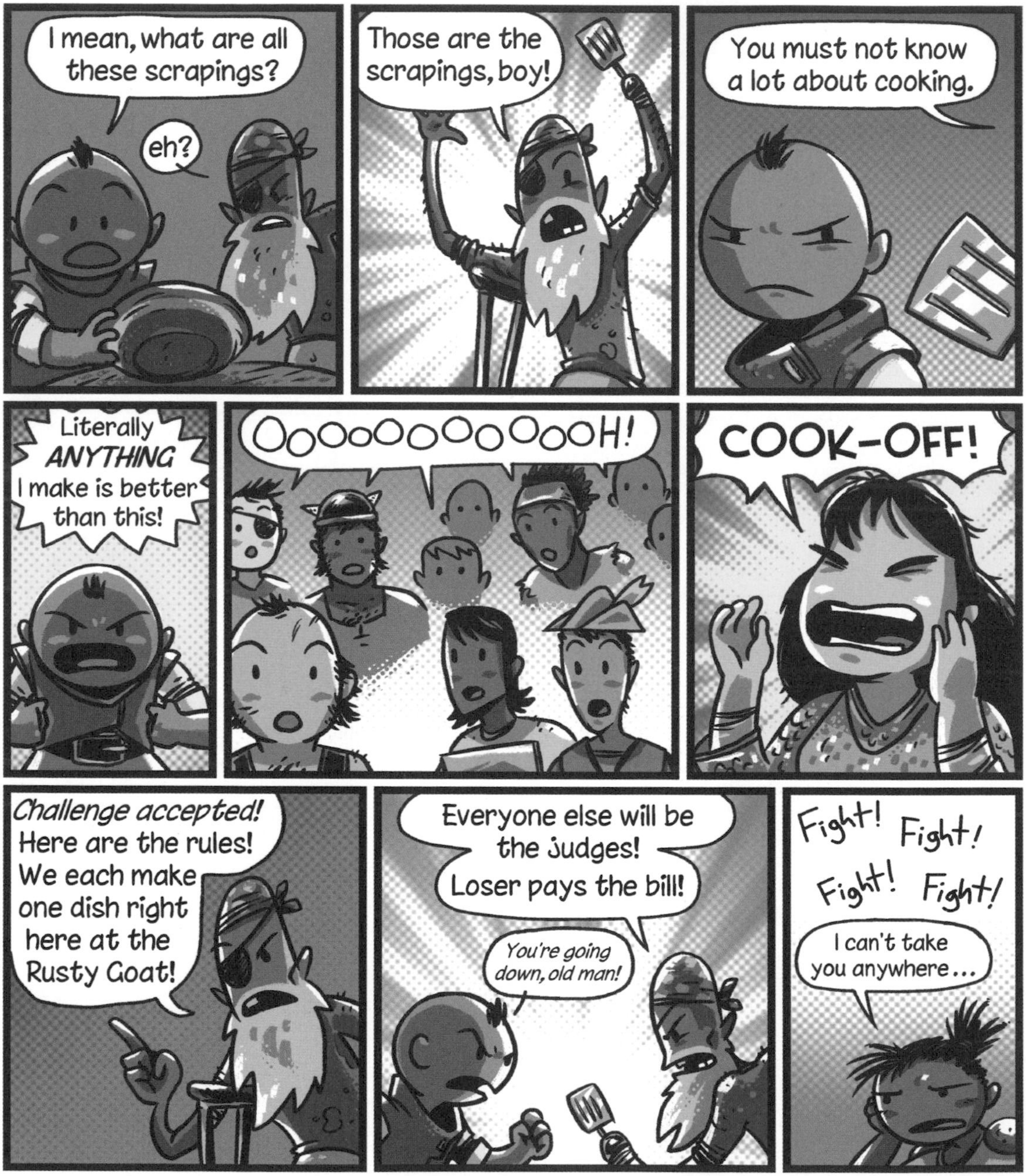
I mean, what are all these scrapings?
eh?
Those are the scrapings, boy!
You must not know a lot about cooking.
Literally ANYTHING I make is better than this!
OOOOOOOOOOOOOH!
COOK-OFF!
Challenge accepted! Here are the rules! We each make one dish right here at the Rusty Goat!
Everyone else will be the judges! Loser pays the bill!
You're going down, old man!
Fight! Fight! Fight! Fight!
I can't take you anywhere...

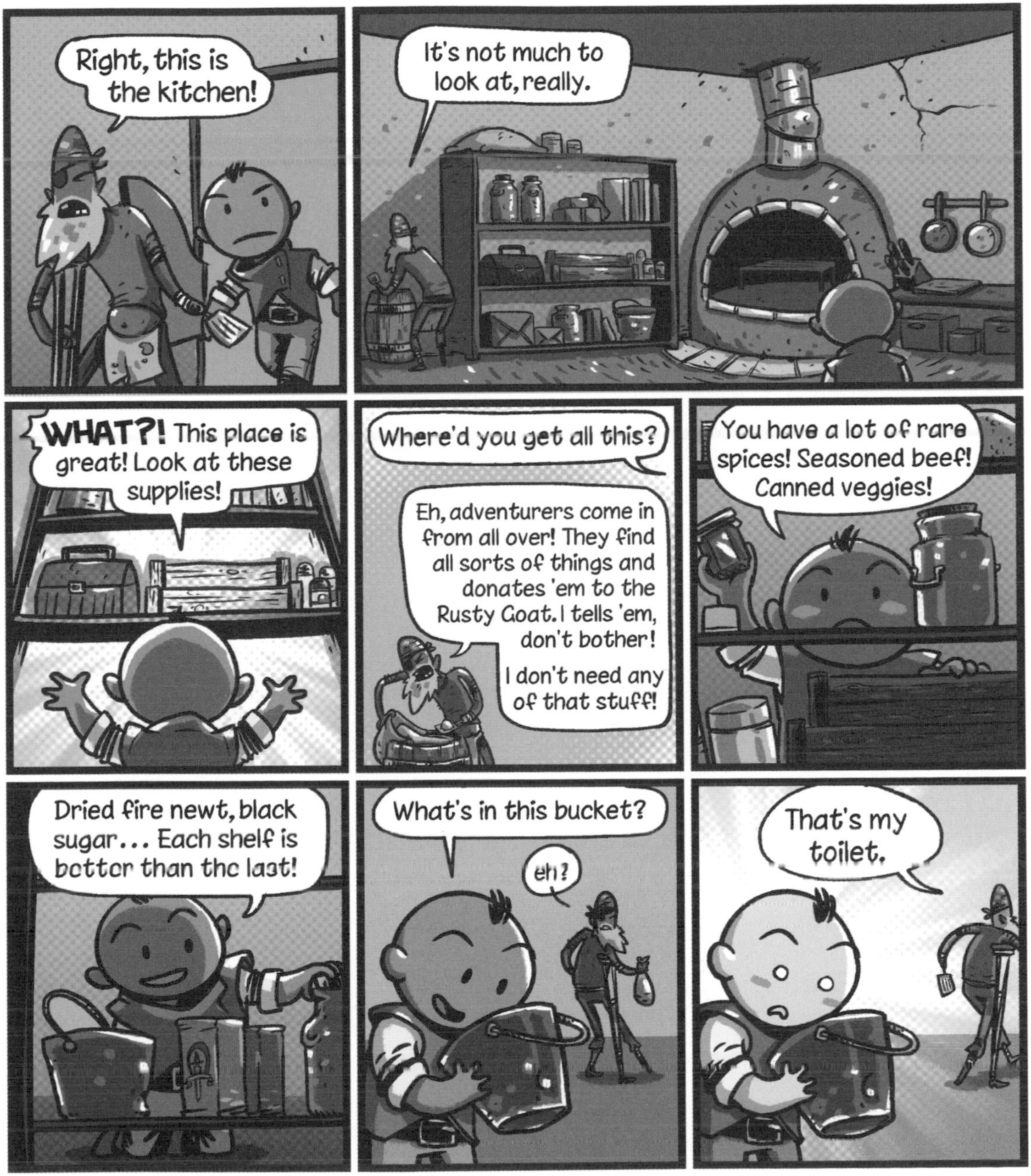
Right, this is the kitchen!
It's not much to look at, really.
WHAT?! This place is great! Look at these supplies!
Where'd you get all this?
Eh, adventurers come in from all over! They find all sorts of things and donates 'em to the Rusty Goat. I tells 'em, don't bother!
I don't need any of that stuff!
You have a lot of rare spices! Seasoned beef! Canned veggies!
Dried fire newt, black sugar... Each shelf is better than the last!
What's in this bucket?
eh?
That's my toilet.

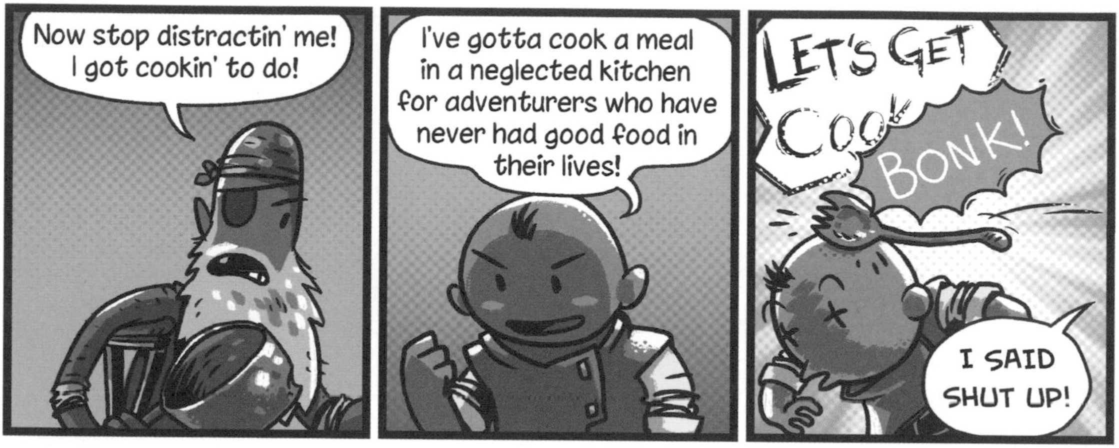
Now stop distractin' me! I got cookin' to do!
I've gotta cook a meal in a neglected kitchen for adventurers who have never had good food in their lives!
LET'S GET COO
BONK!
I SAID SHUT UP!

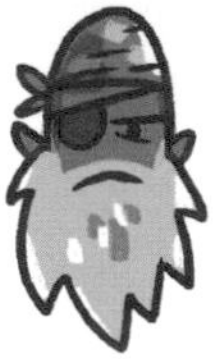

Cookin' with Cookie!

1\. 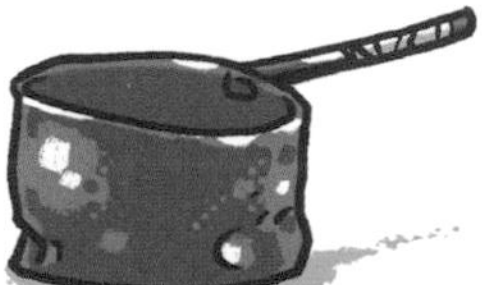

Get yerself a pot.

2\. 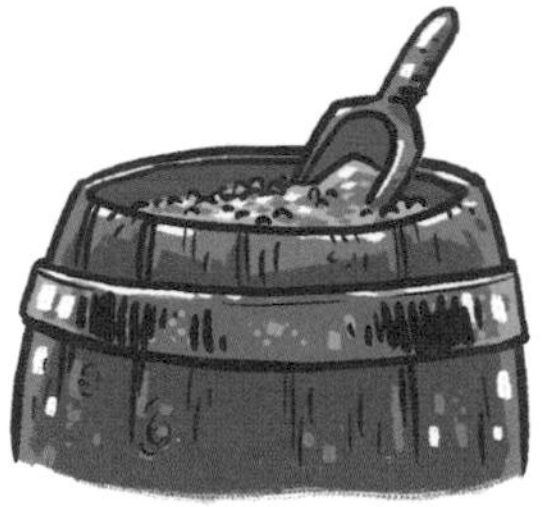

A big ol' scoop from that barrel over there.

3\. 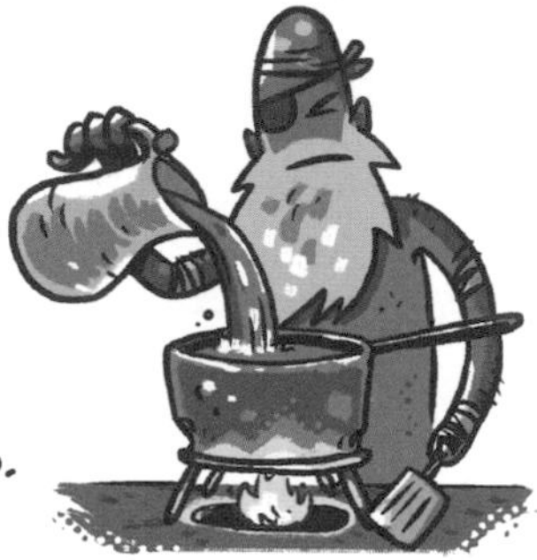

Add water and boil it until it's edible.

4\. 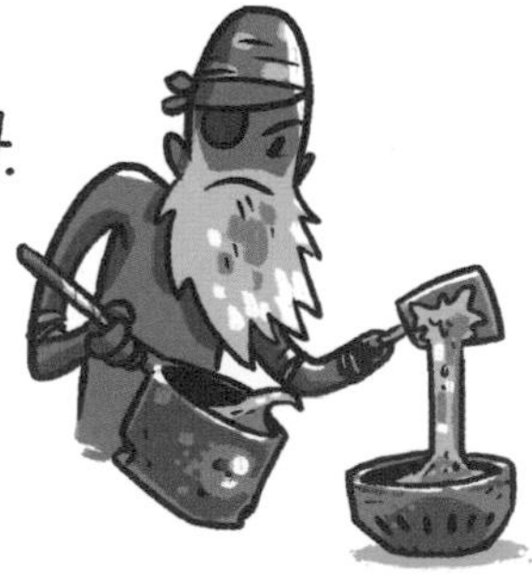

Scoop out a handful and serve hot.

You've made . . .

FOOD

(WITH SCRAPINGS)

Eat it and shut up!

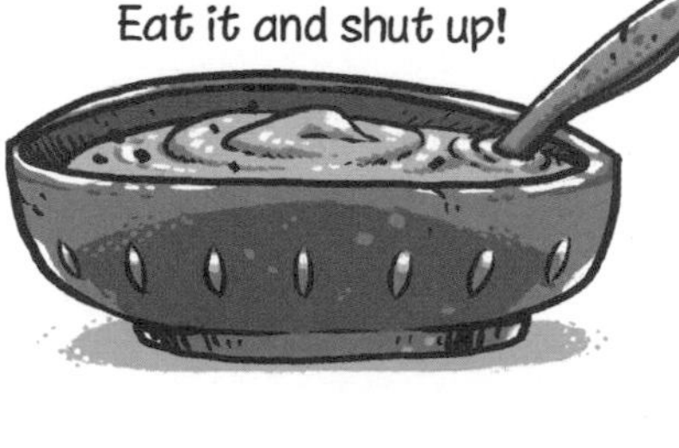

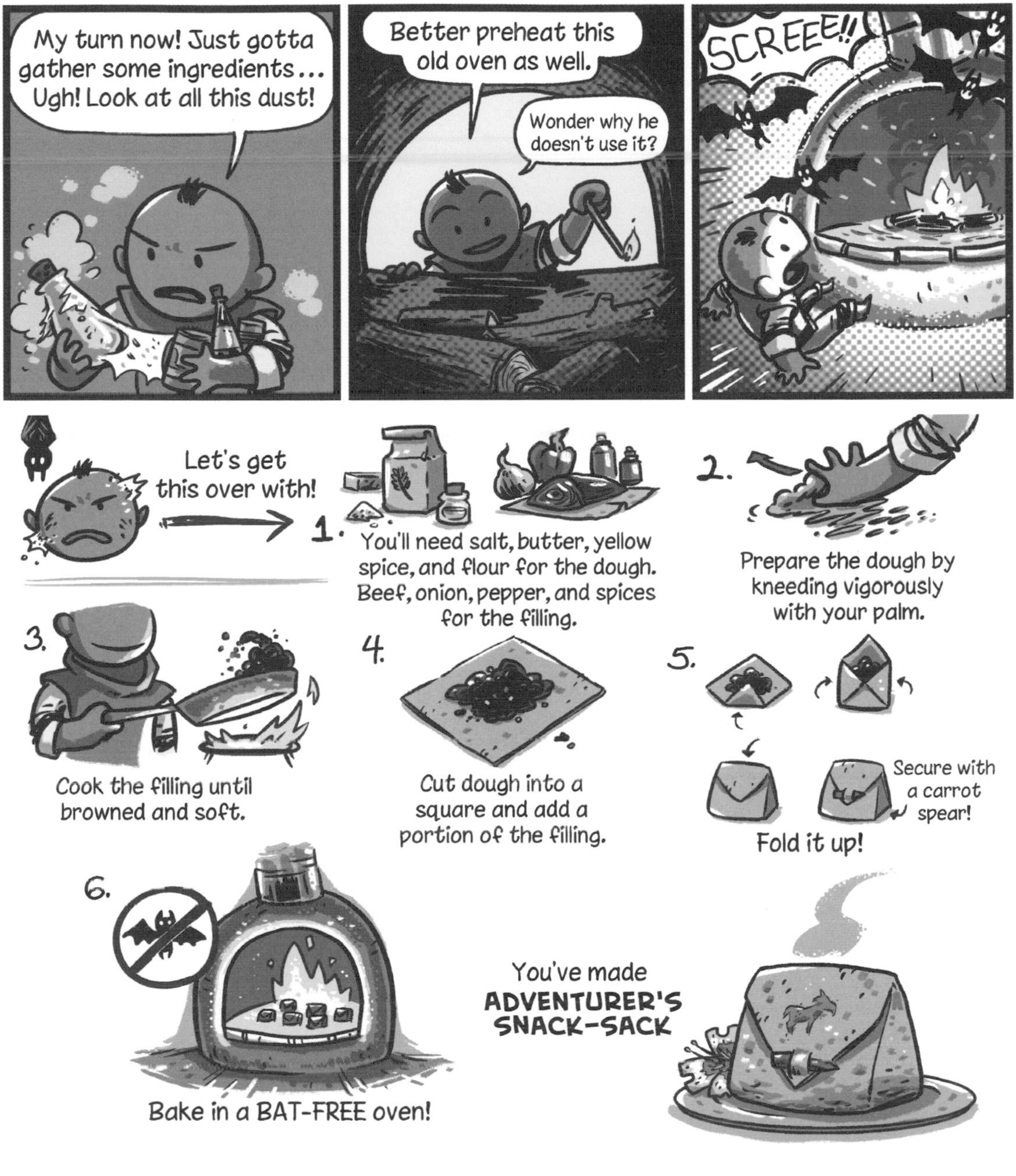
My turn now! Just gotta gather some ingredients... Ugh! Look at all this dust!
Better preheat this old oven as well.
Wonder why he doesn't use it?
SCREEE!!
Let's get this over with!
1. You'll need salt, butter, yellow spice, and flour for the dough. Beef, onion, pepper, and spices for the filling.
2. Prepare the dough by kneeding vigorously with your palm.
3. Cook the filling until browned and soft.
4. Cut dough into a square and add a portion of the filling.
5. Fold it up!
Secure with a carrot spear!
6. Bake in a BAT-FREE oven!
You've made ADVENTURER'S SNACK-SACK

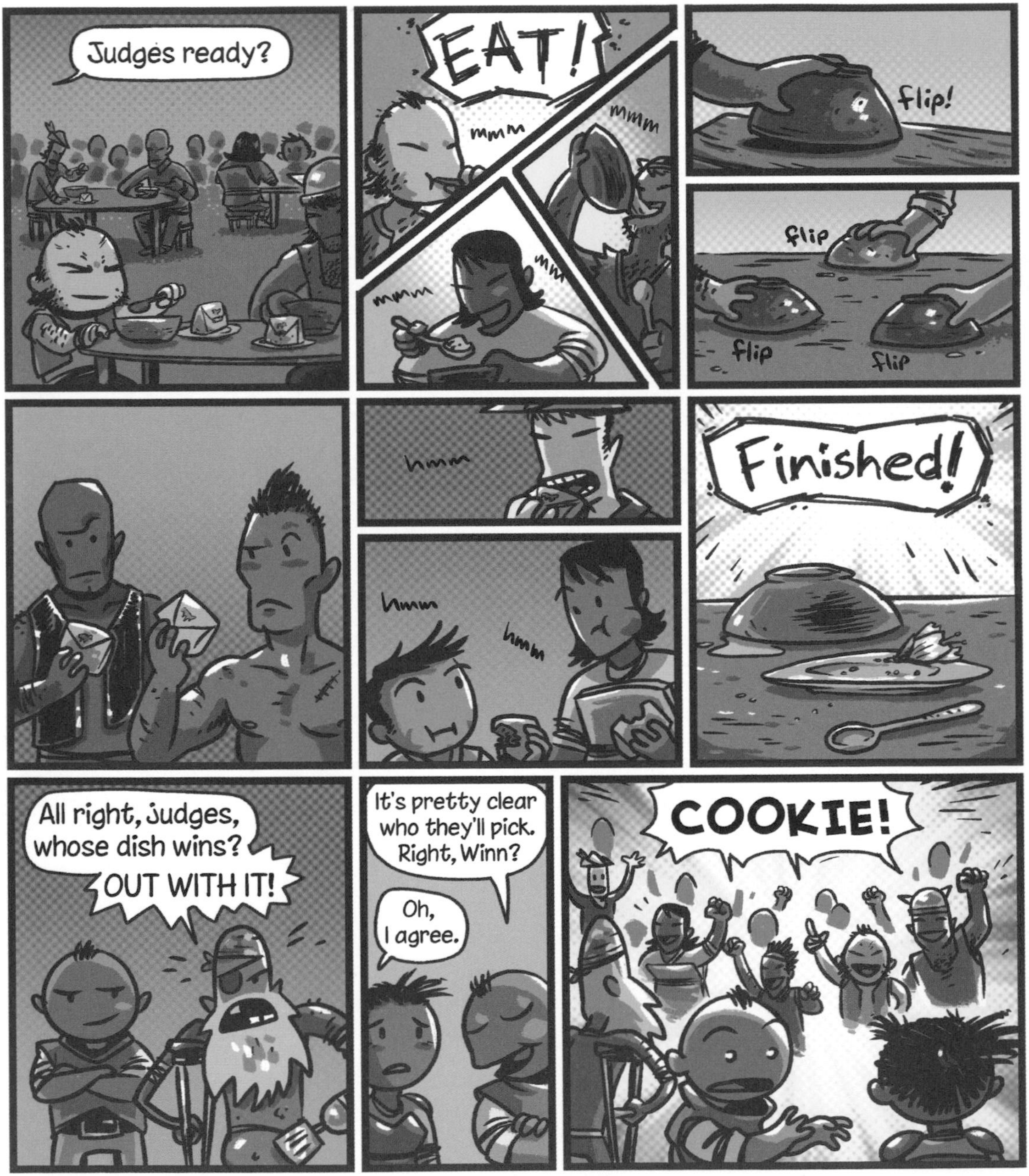
Judges ready?
EAT!
mmm
mmm
mmm
mmm
flip!
flip
flip
flip
hmm
Finished!
hmm
hmm
All right, judges, whose dish wins?
OUT WITH IT!
It's pretty clear who they'll pick. Right, Winn?
Oh, I agree.
COOKIE!

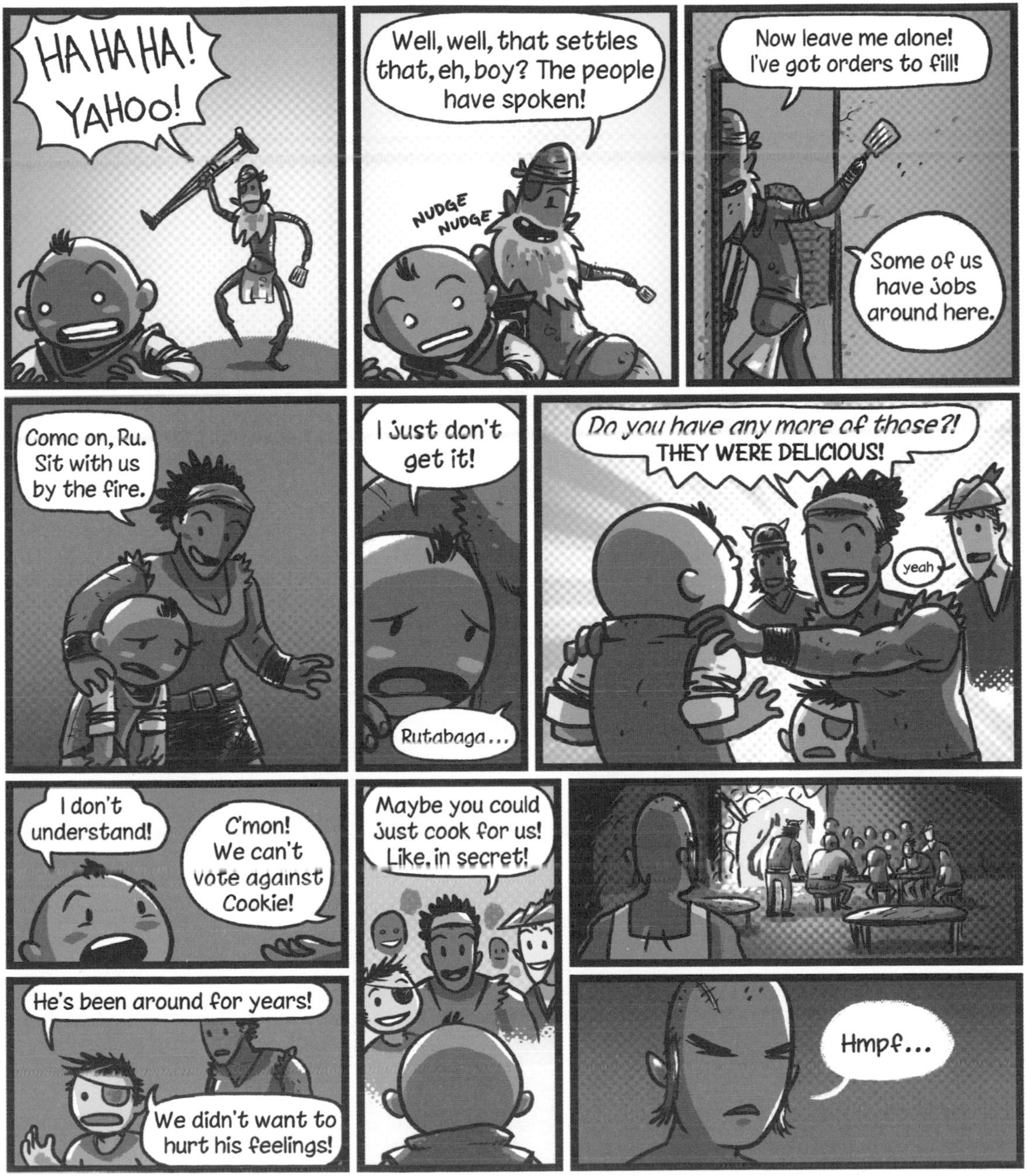
HA HA HA!
YAHOO!
Well, well, that settles that, eh, boy? The people have spoken!
NUDGE NUDGE
Now leave me alone! I've got orders to fill!
Some of us have jobs around here.
Come on, Ru. Sit with us by the fire.
I just don't get it!
Rutabaga...
Do you have any more of those?!
THEY WERE DELICIOUS!
yeah
I don't understand!
C'mon! We can't vote against Cookie!
He's been around for years!
We didn't want to hurt his feelings!
Maybe you could just cook for us! Like, in secret!
Hmpf...

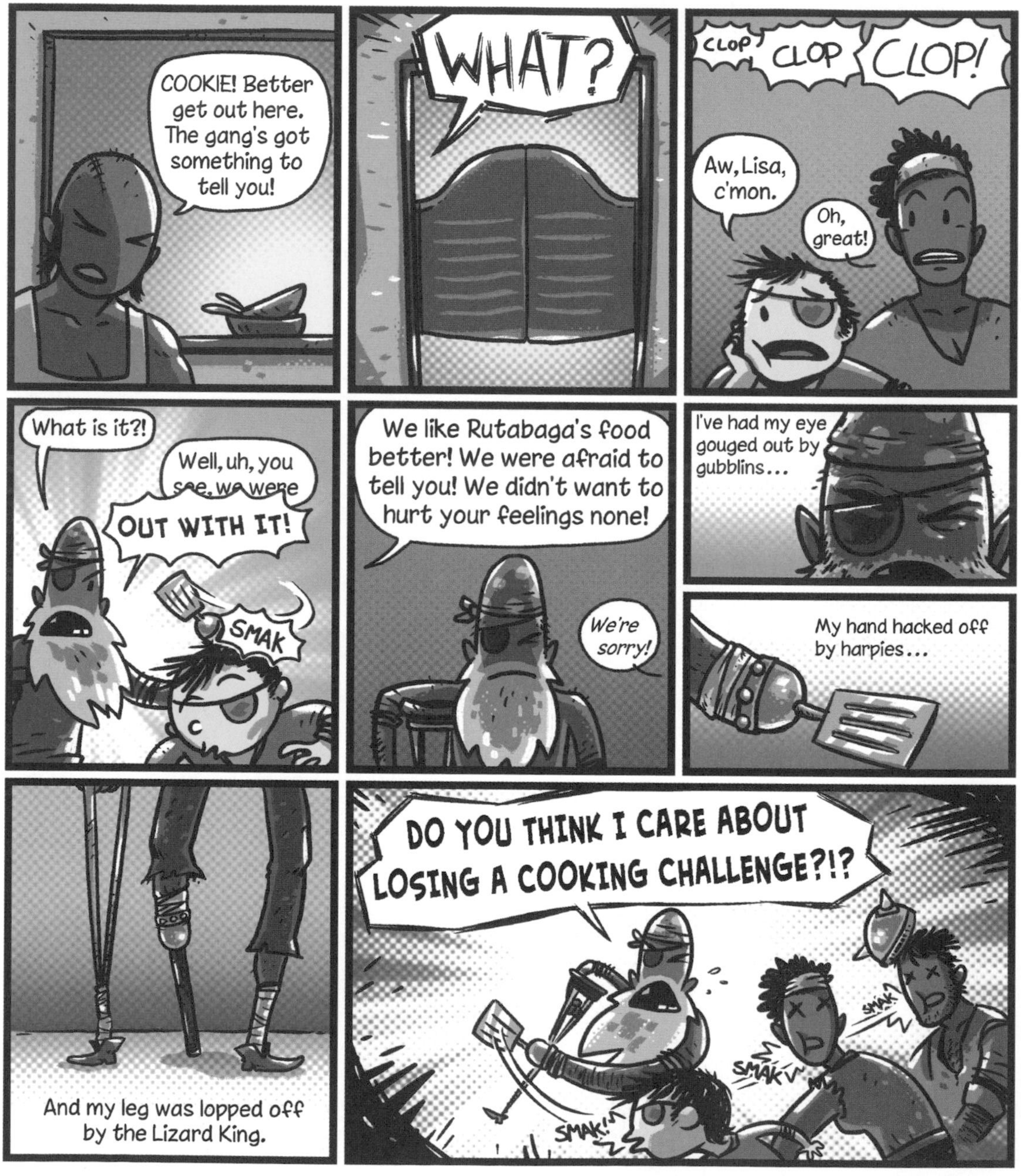
COOKIE! Better get out here. The gang's got something to tell you!
WHAT?
CLOP
CLOP
CLOP!
Aw, Lisa, c'mon.
Oh, great!
What is it?!
Well, uh, you see, we were
OUT WITH IT!
SMAK
We like Rutabaga's food better! We were afraid to tell you! We didn't want to hurt your feelings none!
We're sorry!
I've had my eye gouged out by gubblins...
My hand hacked off by harpies...
And my leg was lopped off by the Lizard King.
DO YOU THINK I CARE ABOUT LOSING A COOKING CHALLENGE?!?
SMAK!
SMAK
SMAK!

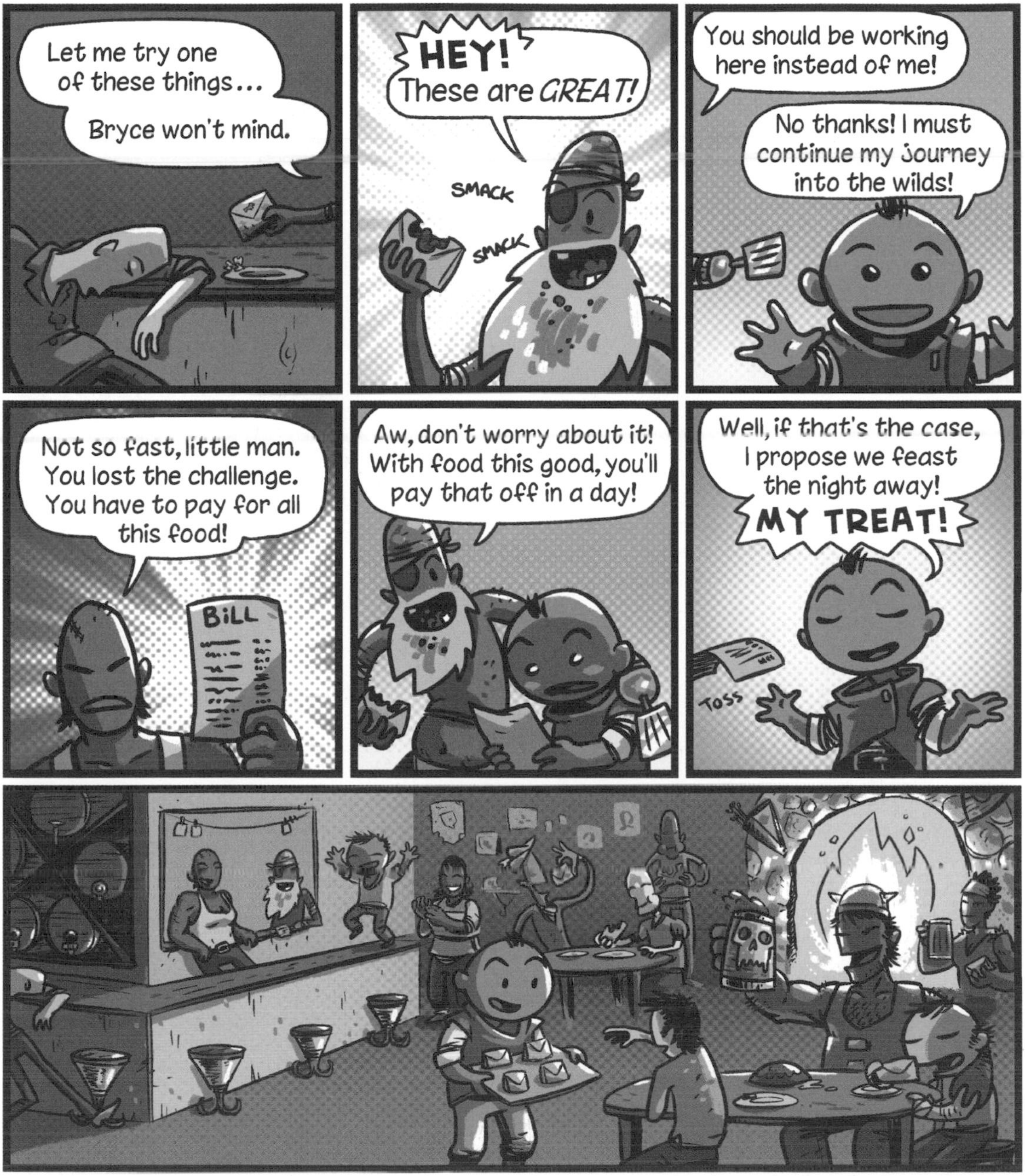
Let me try one of these things...
Bryce won't mind.
HEY!
These are GREAT!
SMACK
SMACK
You should be working here instead of me!
No thanks! I must continue my journey into the wilds!
Not so fast, little man. You lost the challenge. You have to pay for all this food!
BILL
Aw, don't worry about it! With food this good, you'll pay that off in a day!
Well, if that's the case, I propose we feast the night away!
MY TREAT!
TOSS

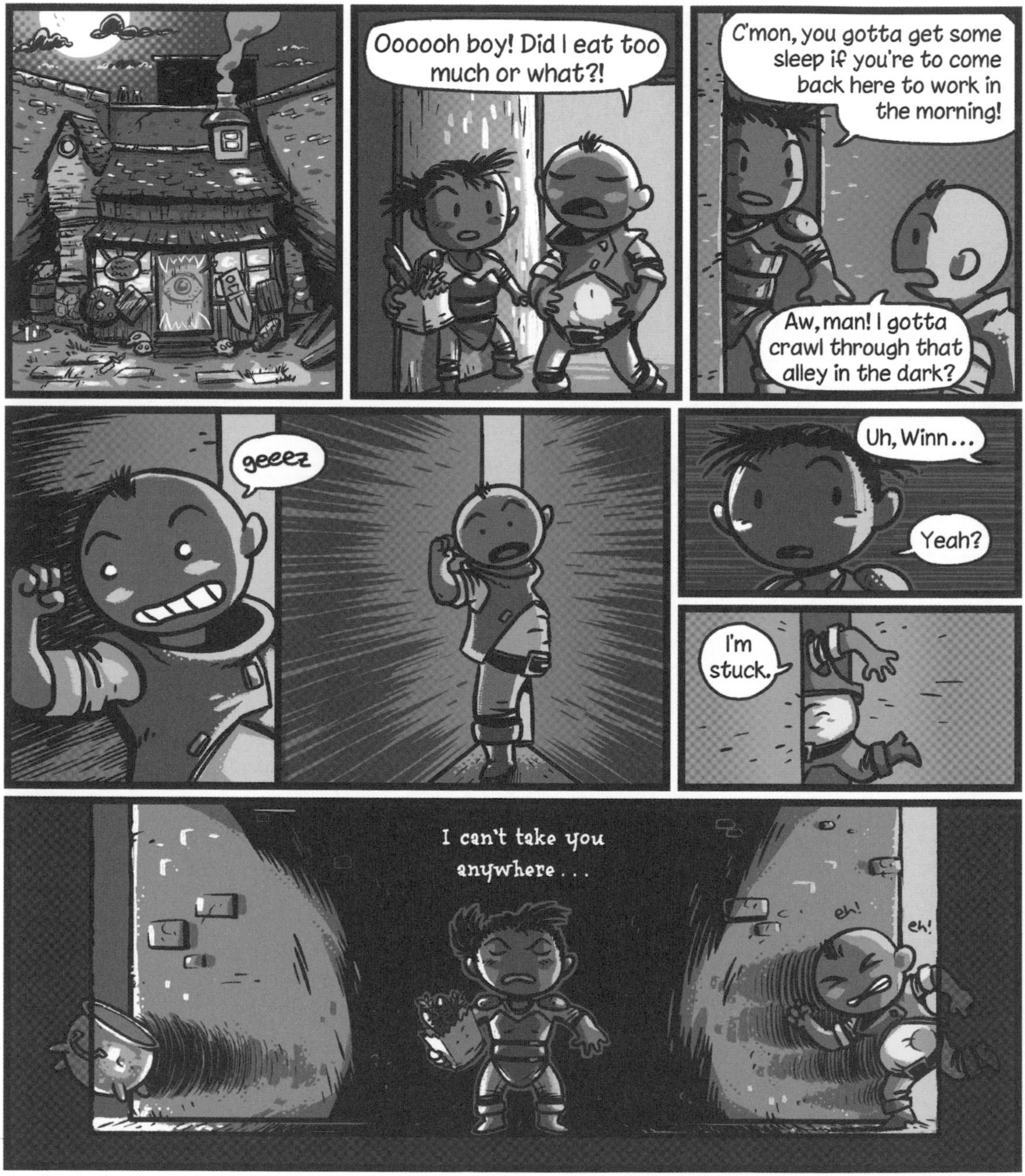

Oooooh boy! Did I eat too much or what?!
C'mon, you gotta get some sleep if you're to come back here to work in the morning!
Aw, man! I gotta crawl through that alley in the dark?
geeez
Uh, Winn...
Yeah?
I'm stuck.
I can't take you anywhere...
eh!
eh!

END OF CHAPTER THREE

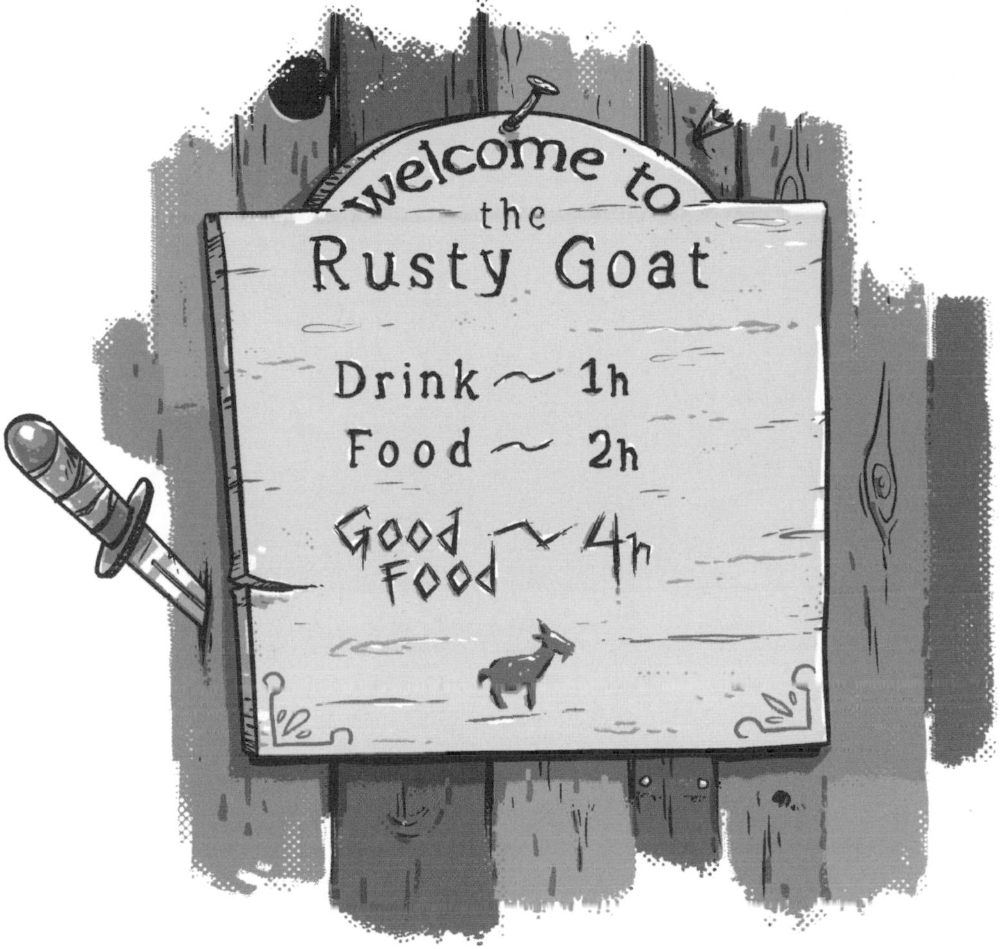
welcome to
the
Rusty Goat
Drink ~ 1h
Food ~ 2h
Good Food ~ 4h

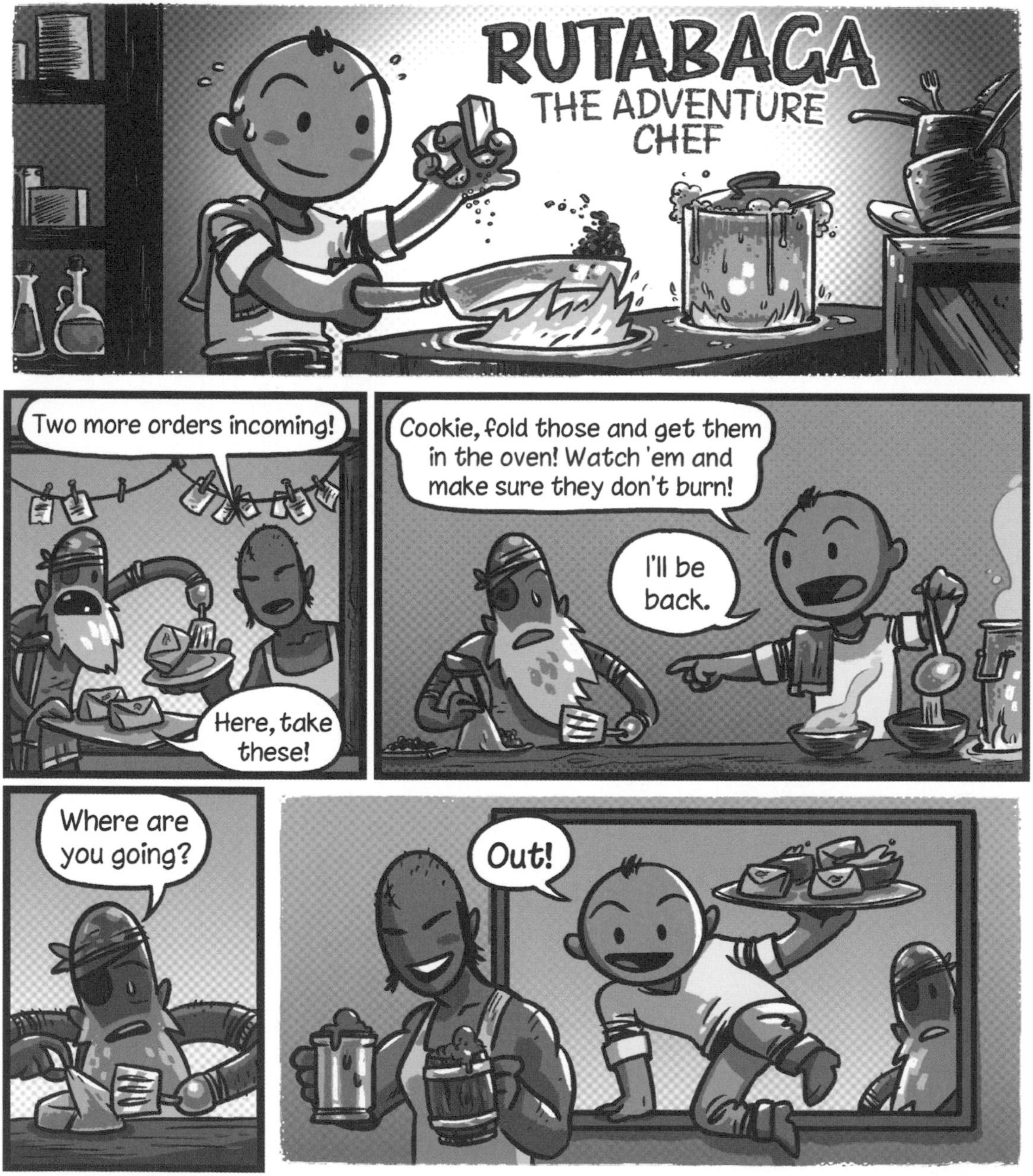
RUTABAGA
THE ADVENTURE CHEF
Two more orders incoming!
Here, take these!
Cookie, fold those and get them in the oven! Watch 'em and make sure they don't burn!
I'll be back.
Where are you going?
Out!

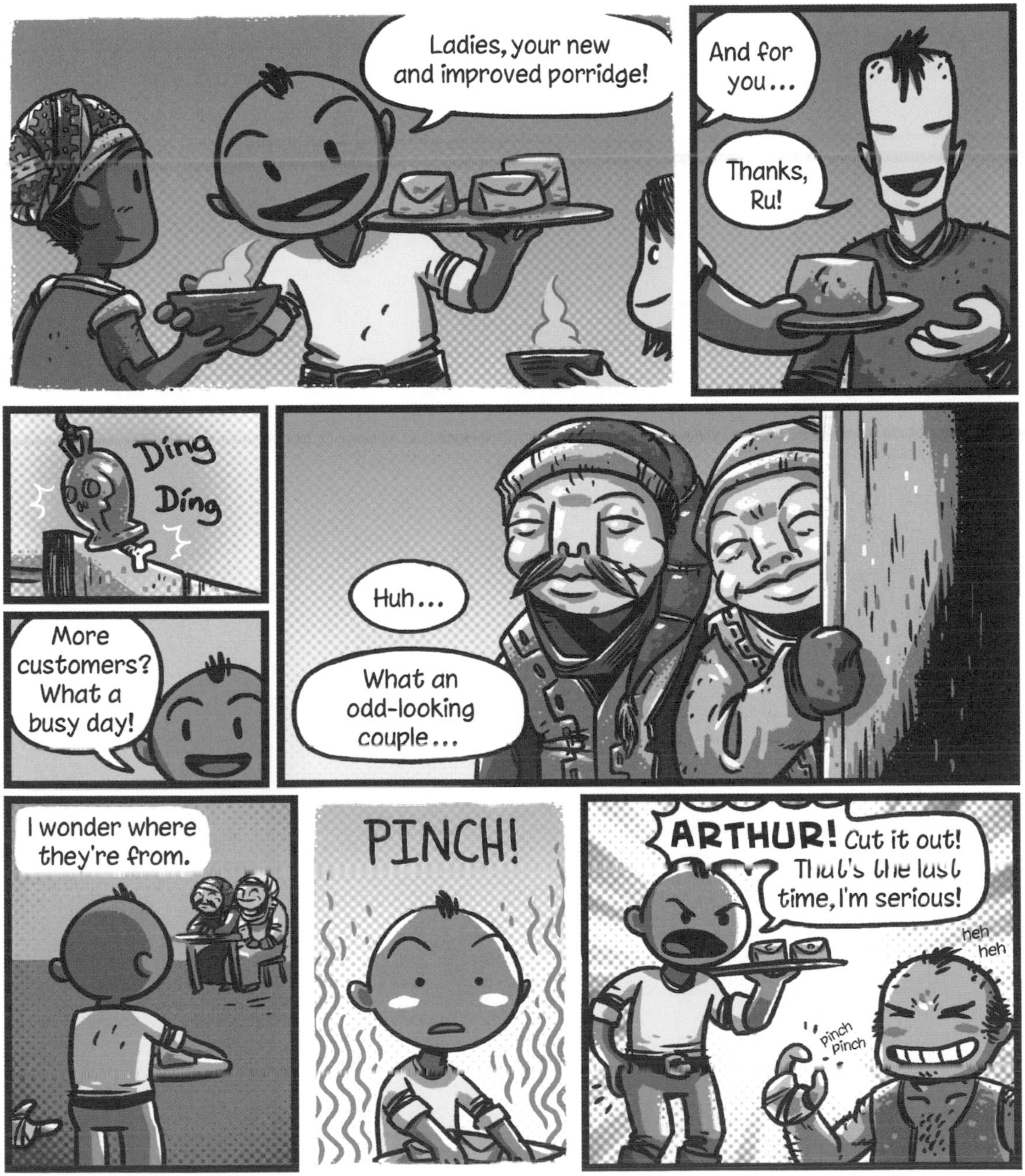
Ladies, your new and improved porridge!
And for you...
Thanks, Ru!
Ding Ding
More customers? What a busy day!
Huh...
What an odd-looking couple...
I wonder where they're from.
PINCH!
ARTHUR! Cut it out! That's the last time, I'm serious!
heh heh
pinch pinch

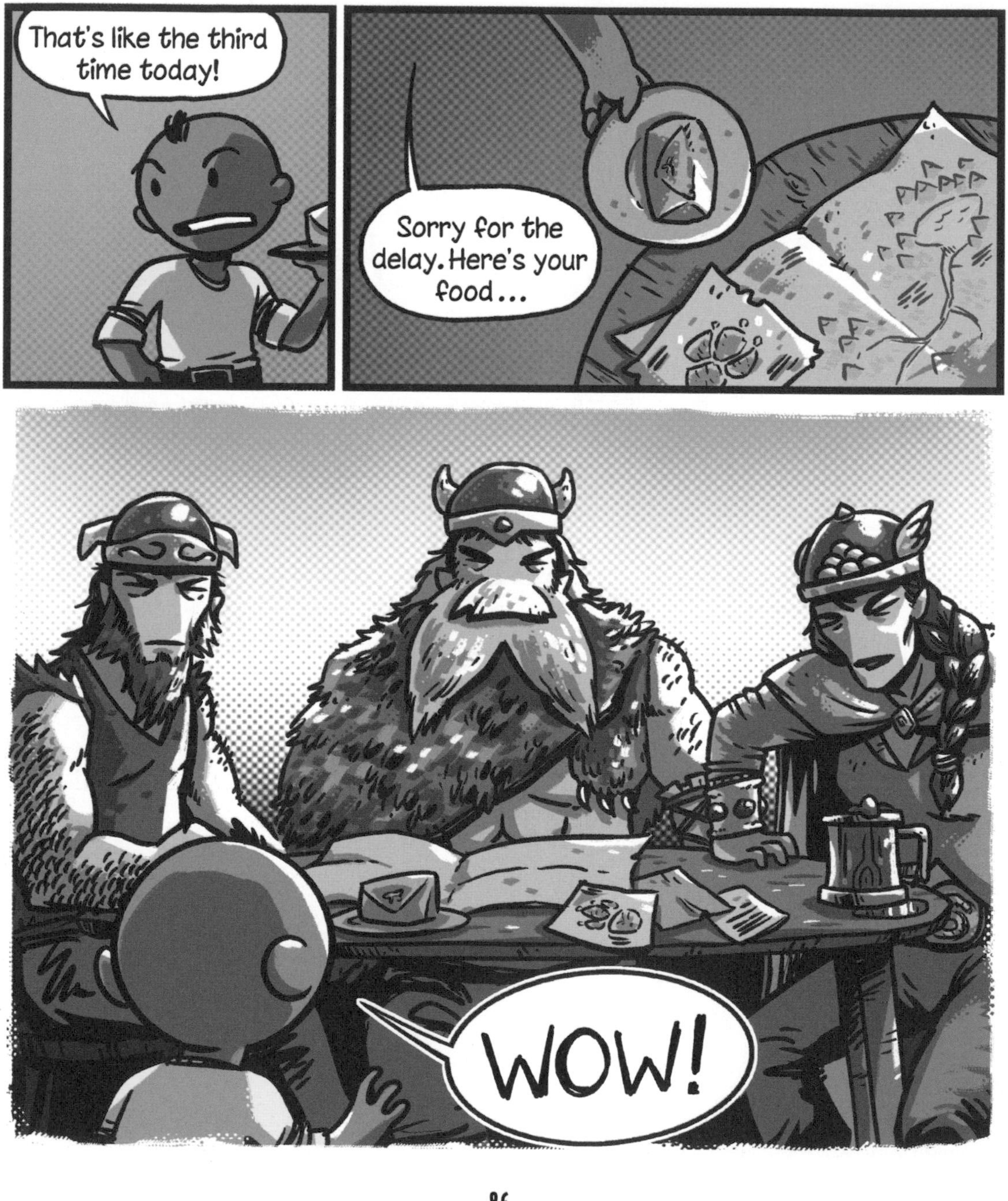
That's like the third time today!
Sorry for the delay. Here's your food...
WOW!

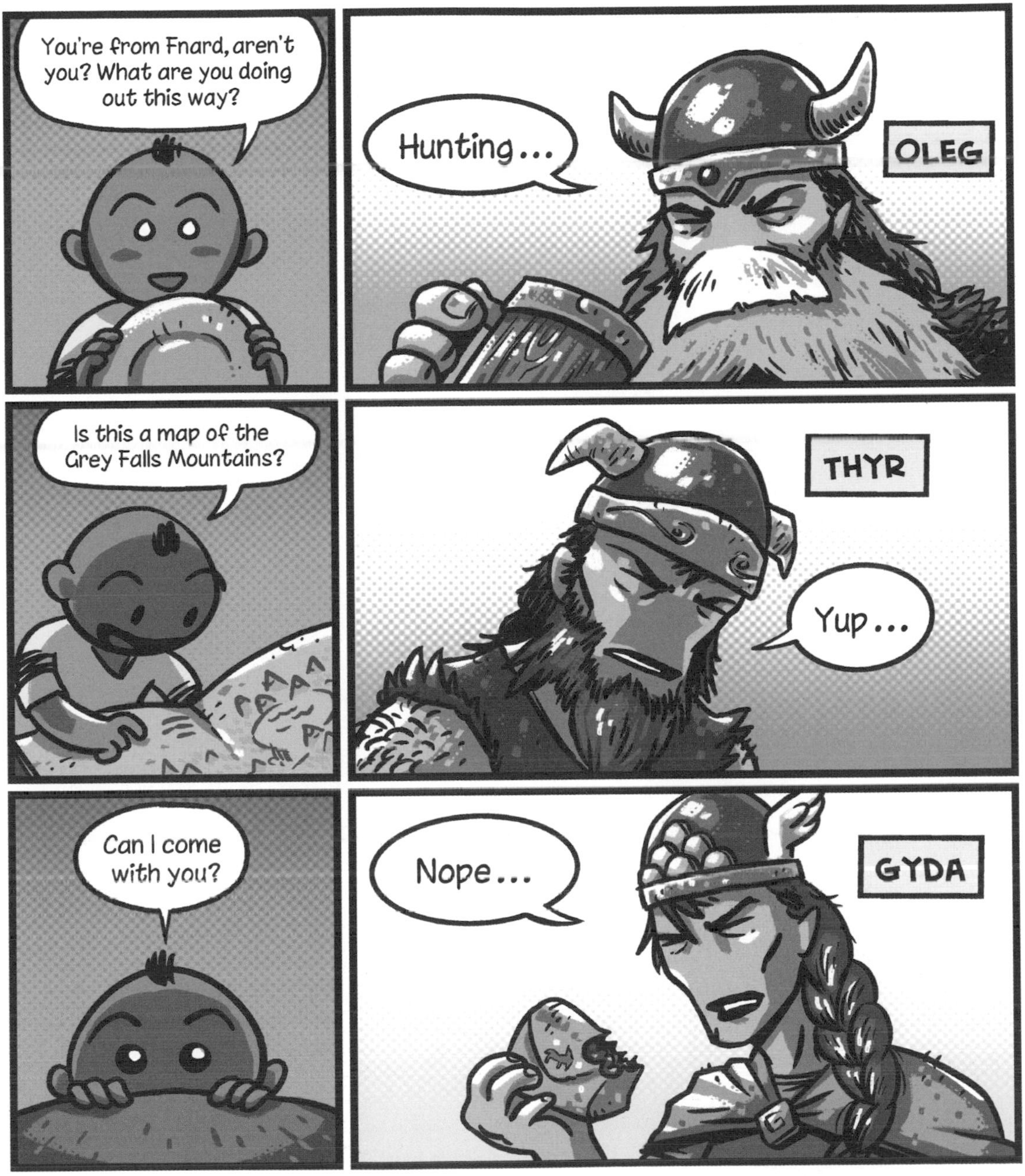
You're from Fnard, aren't you? What are you doing out this way?
Hunting...
OLEG
Is this a map of the Grey Falls Mountains?
THYR
Yup...
Can I come with you?
Nope...
GYDA

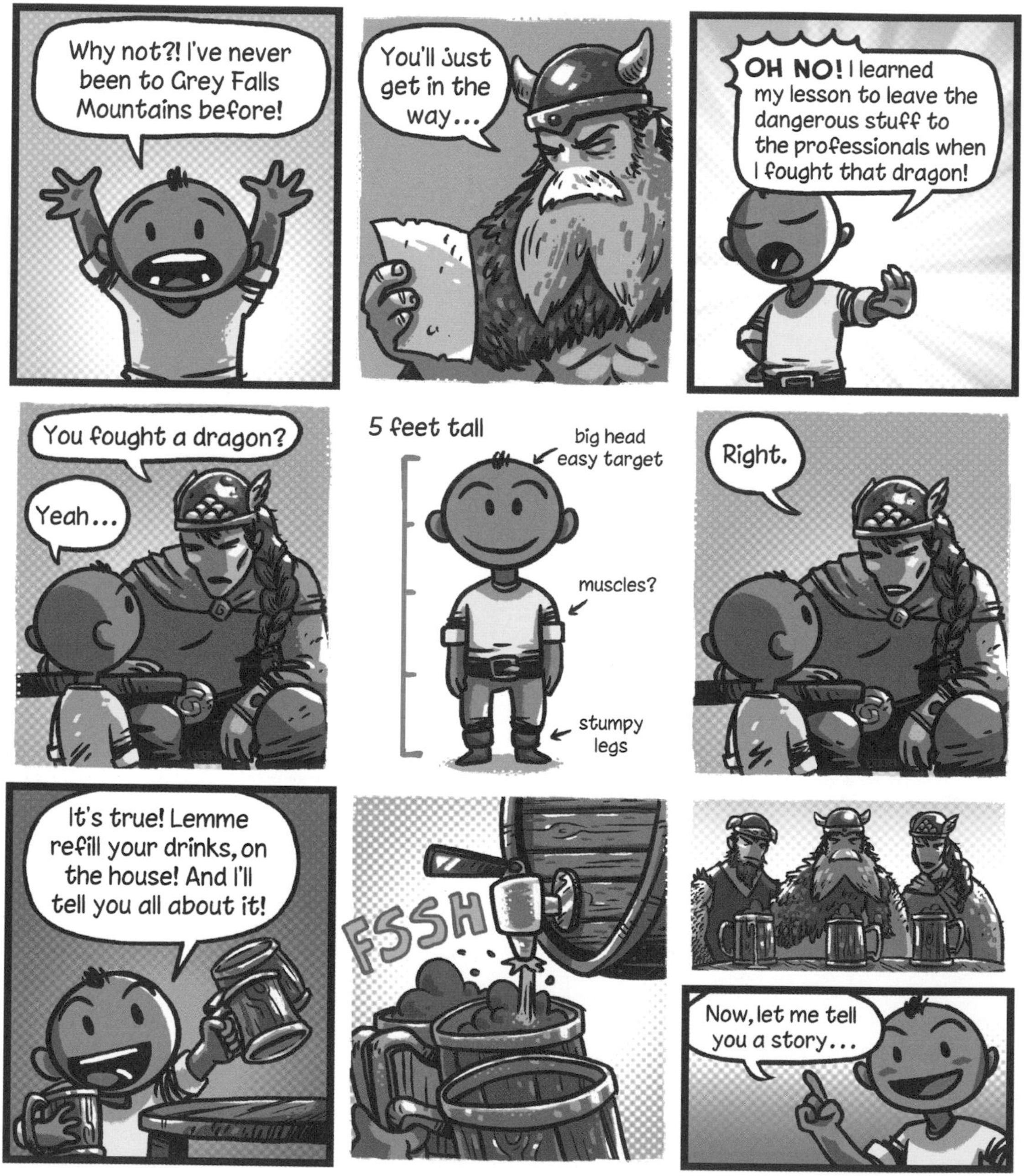
Why not?! I've never been to Grey Falls Mountains before!
You'll just get in the way...
OH NO! I learned my lesson to leave the dangerous stuff to the professionals when I fought that dragon!
You fought a dragon?
Yeah...
5 feet tall
big head easy target
muscles?
stumpy legs
Right.
It's true! Lemme refill your drinks, on the house! And I'll tell you all about it!
FSSH
Now, let me tell you a story...

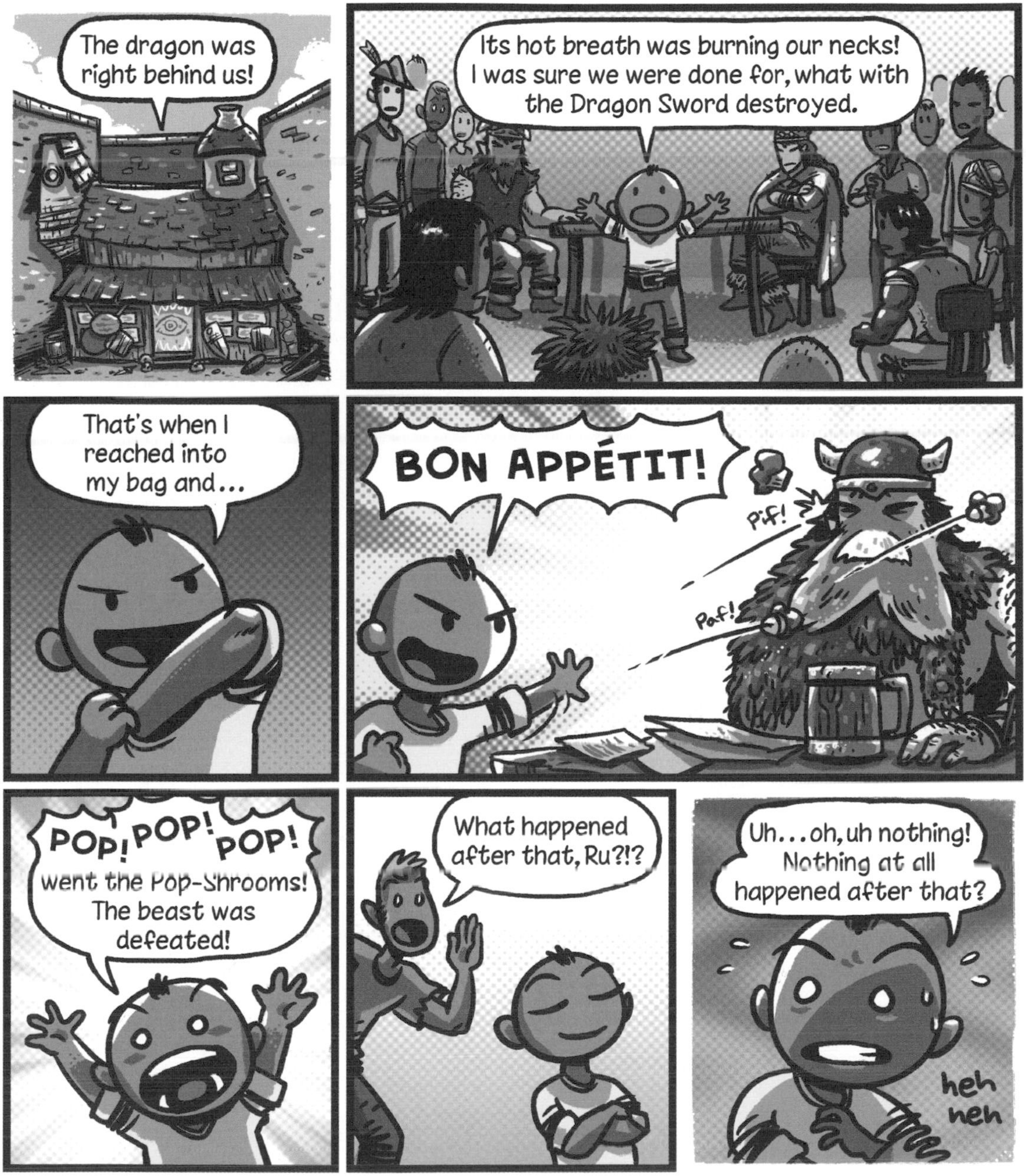
The dragon was right behind us!
Its hot breath was burning our necks! I was sure we were done for, what with the Dragon Sword destroyed.
That's when I reached into my bag and...
BON APPÉTIT!
Pif!
Paf!
POP! POP! POP!
went the Pop-Shrooms! The beast was defeated!
What happened after that, Ru?!?
Uh...oh, uh nothing! Nothing at all happened after that?
heh heh

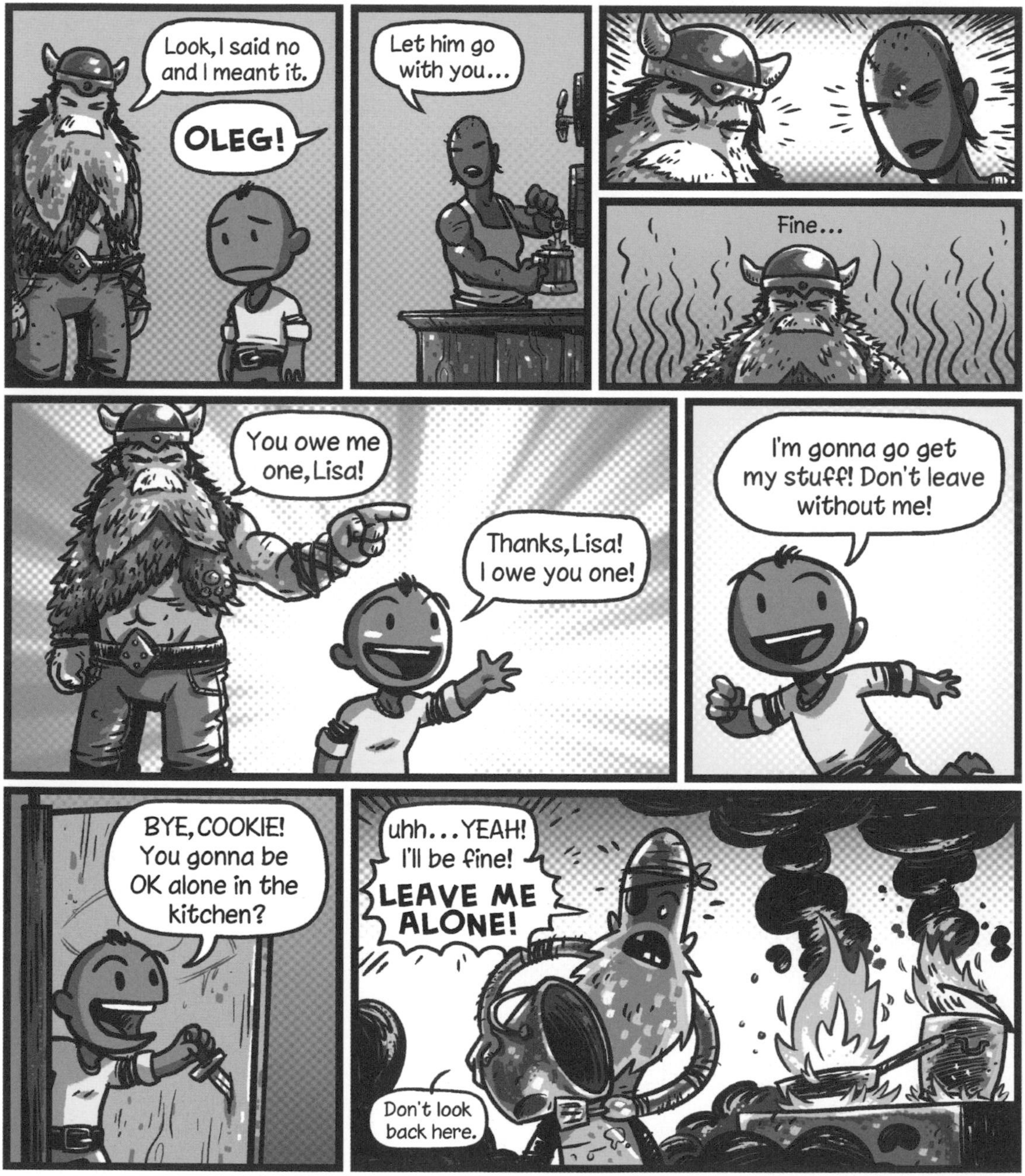
Look, I said no and I meant it.
OLEG!
Let him go with you...
Fine...
You owe me one, Lisa!
Thanks, Lisa! I owe you one!
I'm gonna go get my stuff! Don't leave without me!
BYE, COOKIE! You gonna be OK alone in the kitchen?
uhh...YEAH! I'll be fine! LEAVE ME ALONE!
Don't look back here.

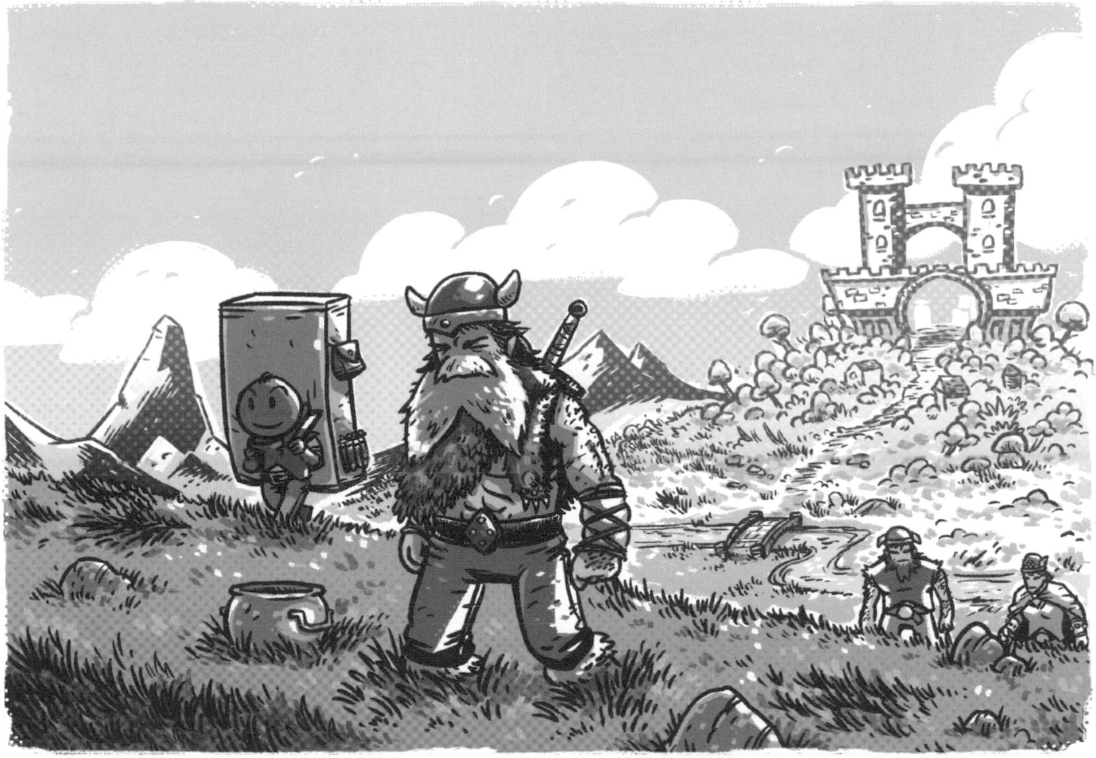

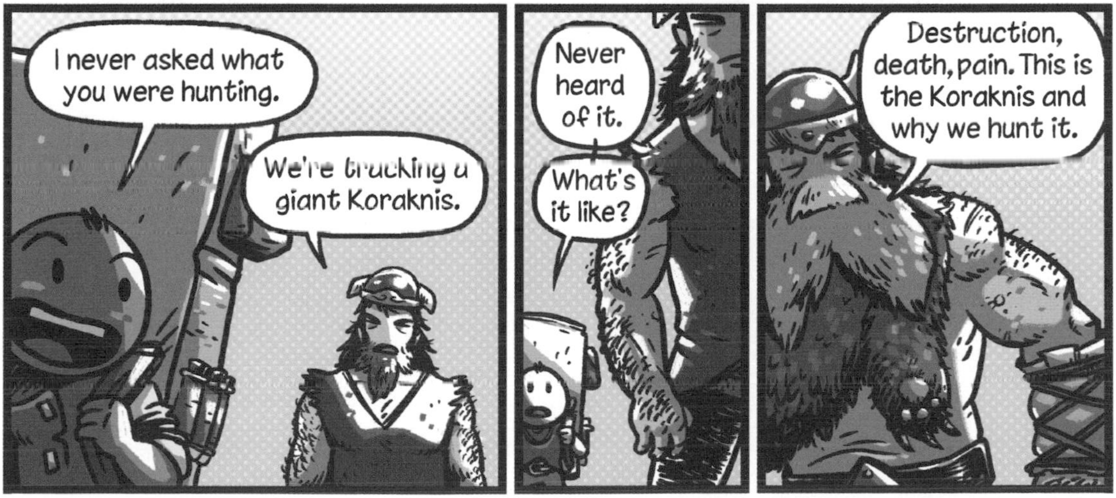
I never asked what you were hunting.
We're tracking a giant Koraknis.
Never heard of it.
What's it like?
Destruction, death, pain. This is the Koraknis and why we hunt it.

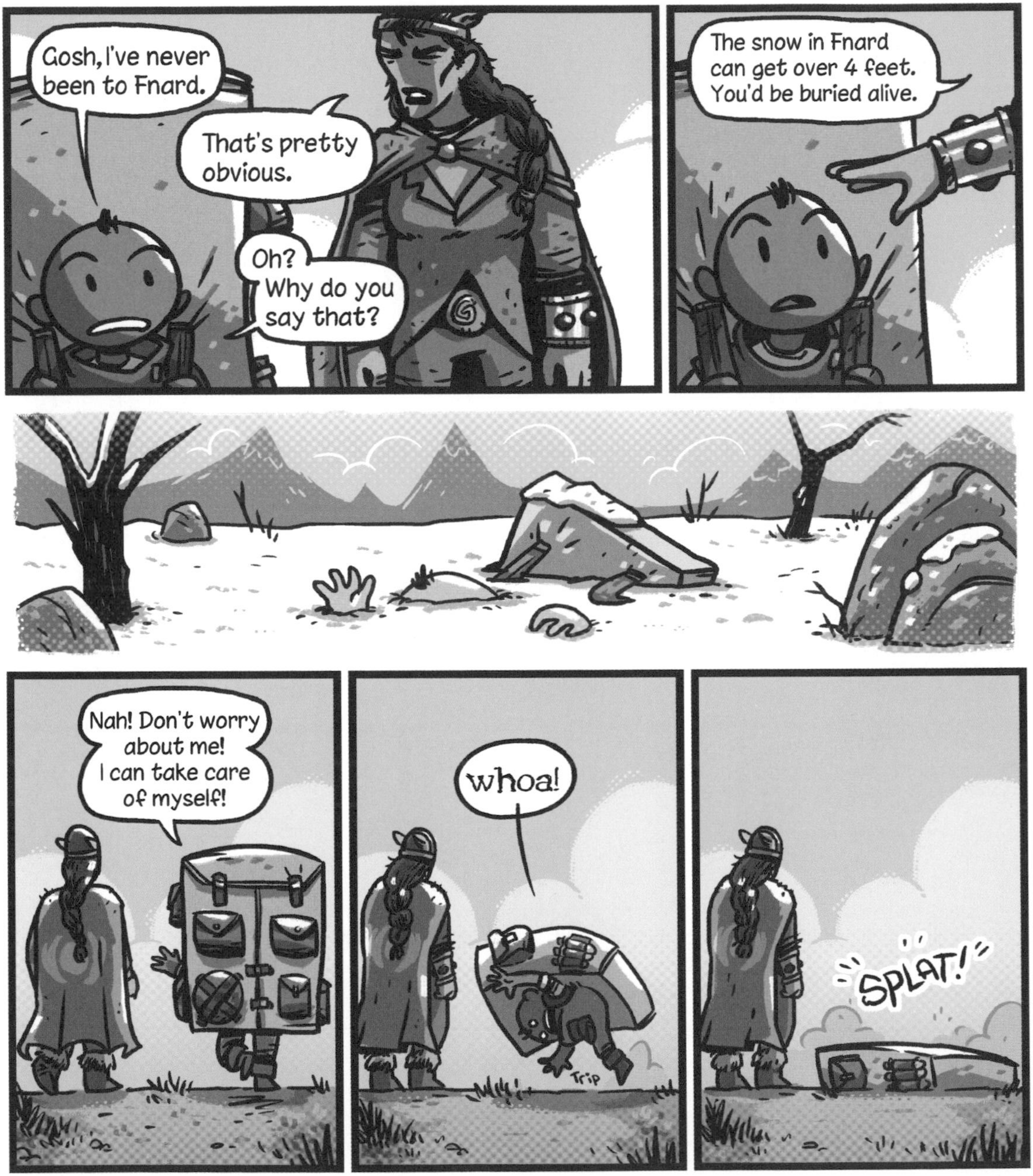
Gosh, I've never been to Fnard.
That's pretty obvious.
Oh? Why do you say that?
The snow in Fnard can get over 4 feet. You'd be buried alive.
Nah! Don't worry about me! I can take care of myself!
whoa!
Trip
SPLAT!

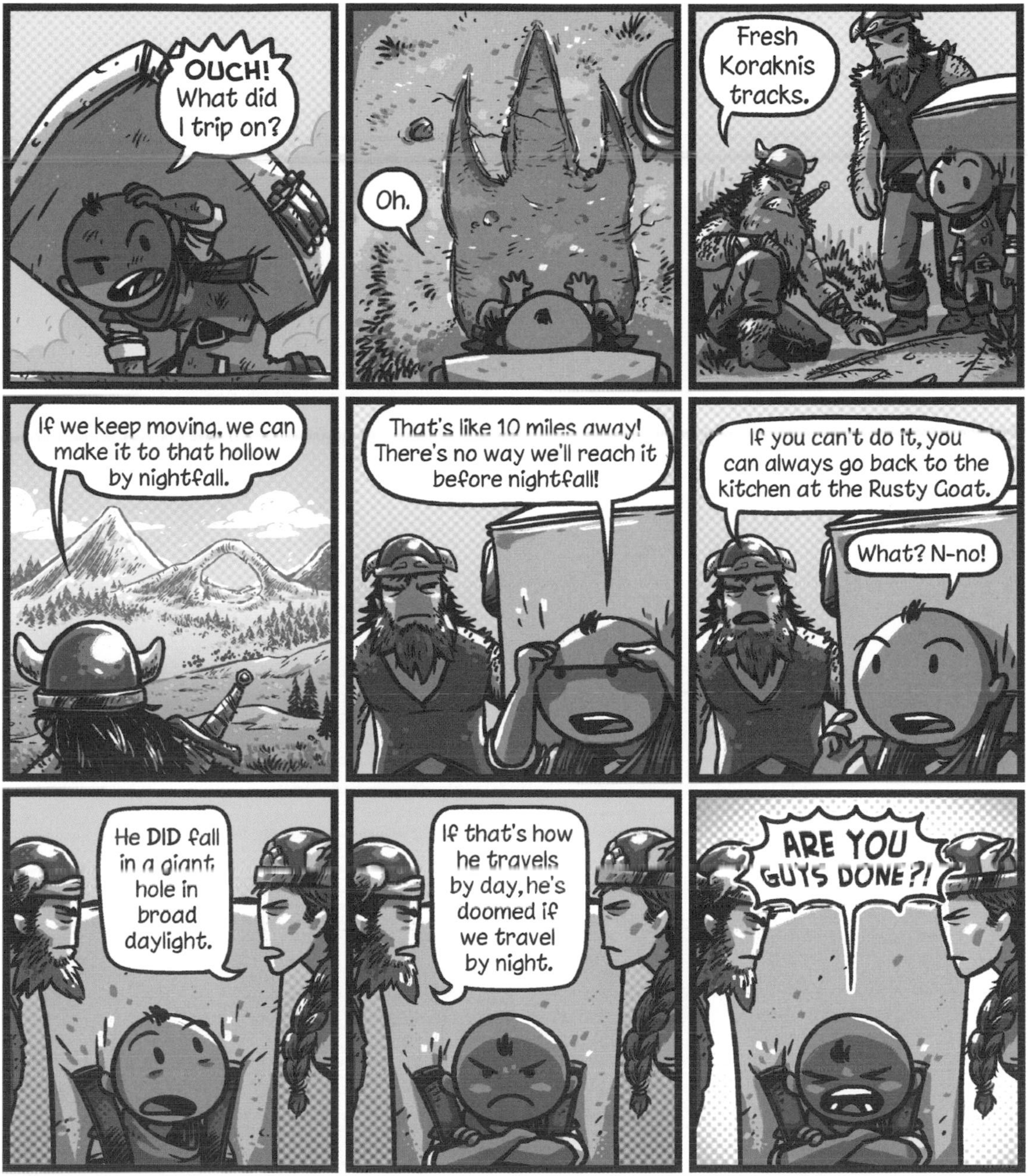
OUCH! What did I trip on?
Oh.
Fresh Koraknis tracks.
If we keep moving, we can make it to that hollow by nightfall.
That's like 10 miles away! There's no way we'll reach it before nightfall!
If you can't do it, you can always go back to the kitchen at the Rusty Goat.
What? N-no!
He DID fall in a giant hole in broad daylight.
If that's how he travels by day, he's doomed if we travel by night.
ARE YOU GUYS DONE?!

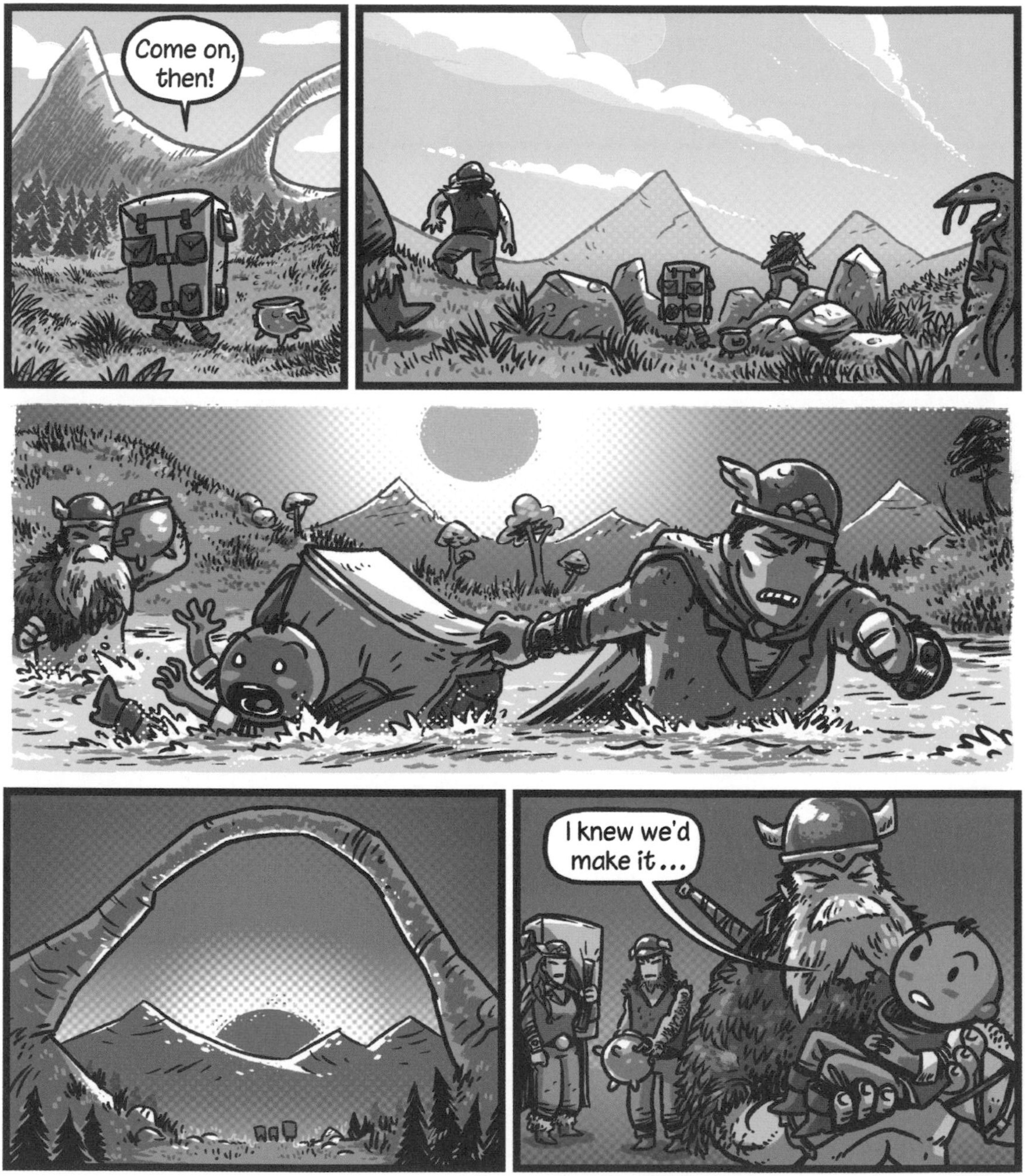
Come on, then!
I knew we'd make it...

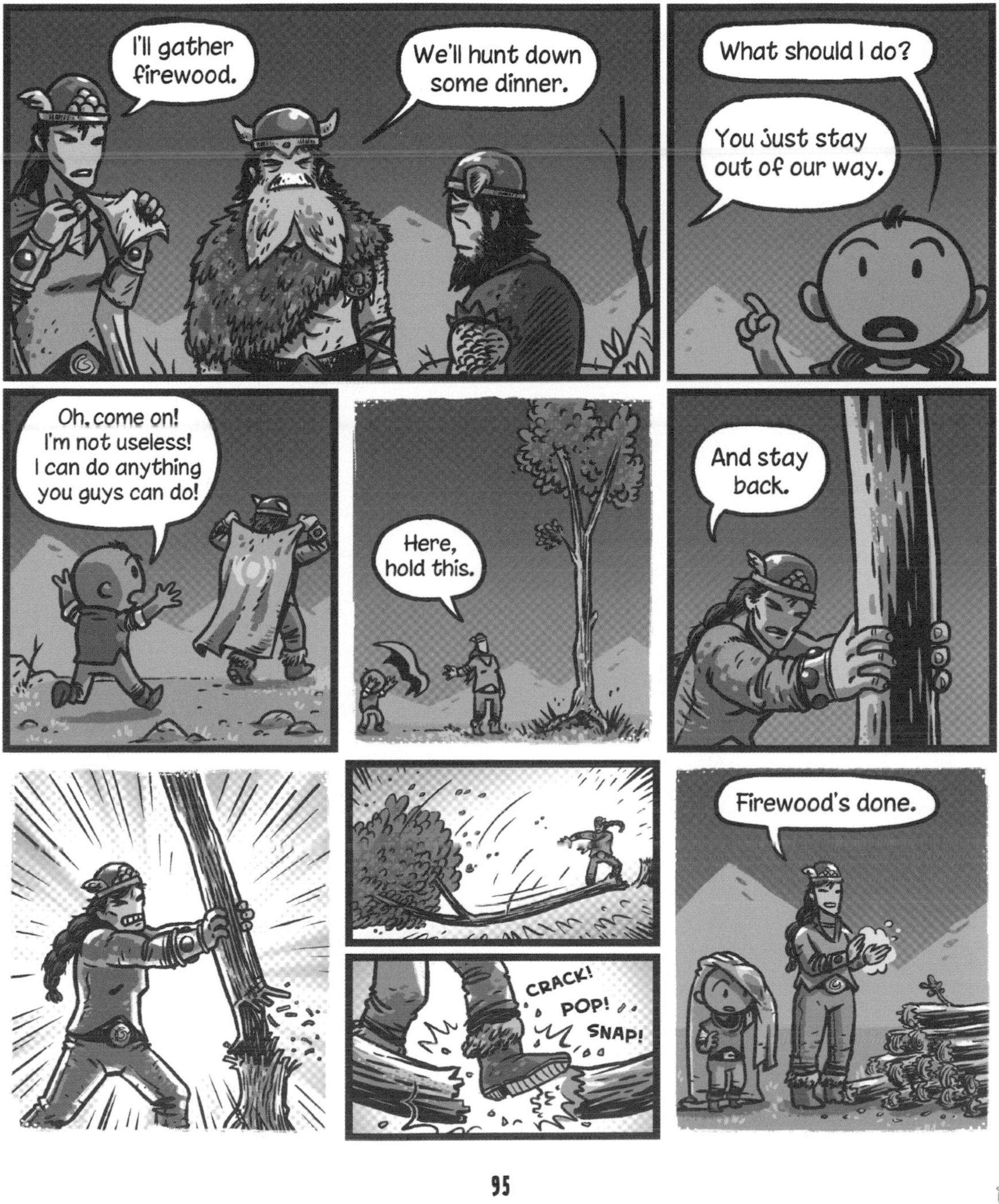
I'll gather firewood.
We'll hunt down some dinner.
What should I do?
You just stay out of our way.
Oh, come on! I'm not useless! I can do anything you guys can do!
Here, hold this.
And stay back.
CRACK!
POP!
SNAP!
Firewood's done.

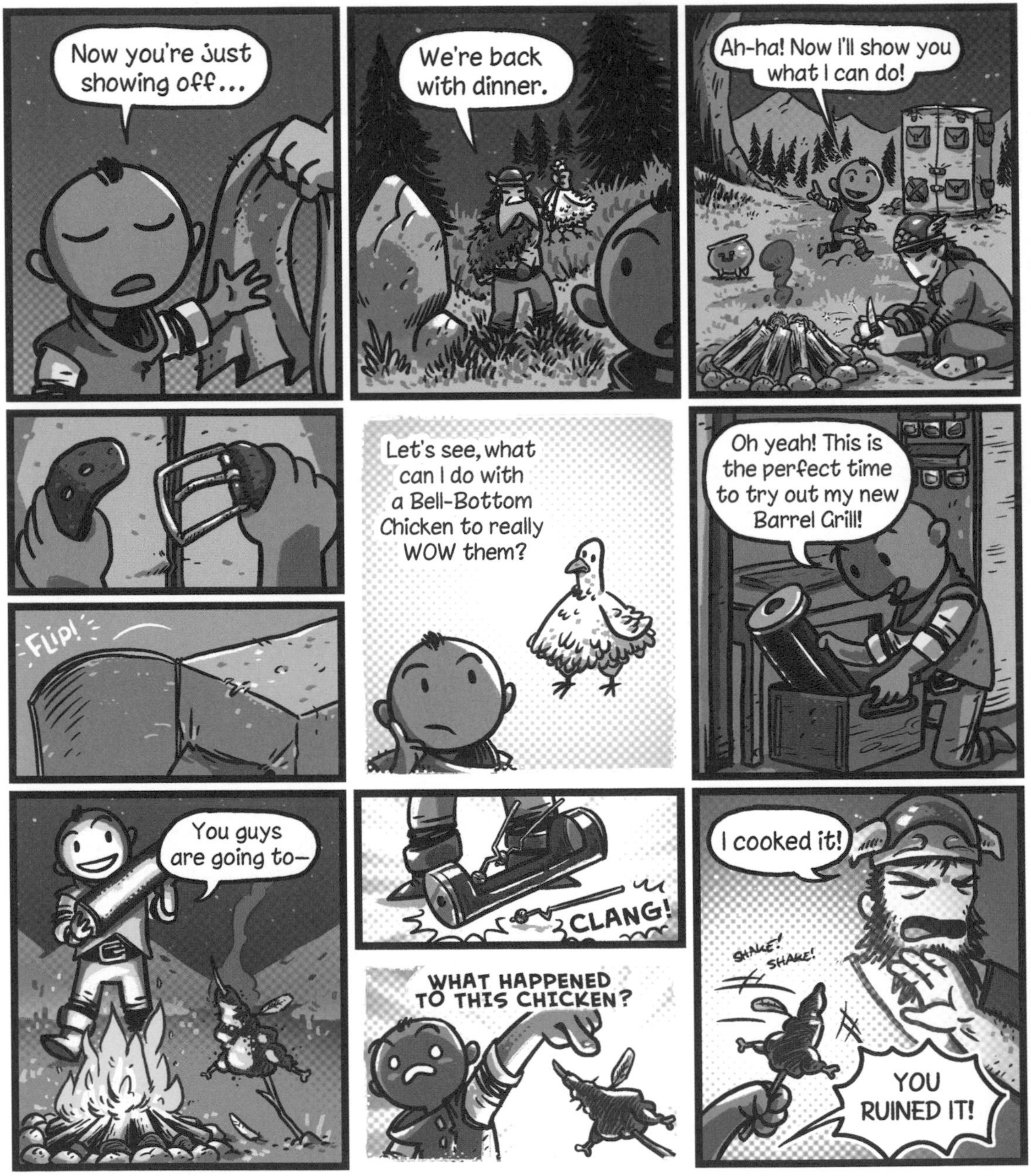
Now you're just showing off...
We're back with dinner.
Ah-ha! Now I'll show you what I can do!
FLIP!
Let's see, what can I do with a Bell-Bottom Chicken to really WOW them?
Oh yeah! This is the perfect time to try out my new Barrel Grill!
You guys are going to—
CLANG!
WHAT HAPPENED TO THIS CHICKEN?
I cooked it!
SHAKE! SHAKE!
YOU RUINED IT!

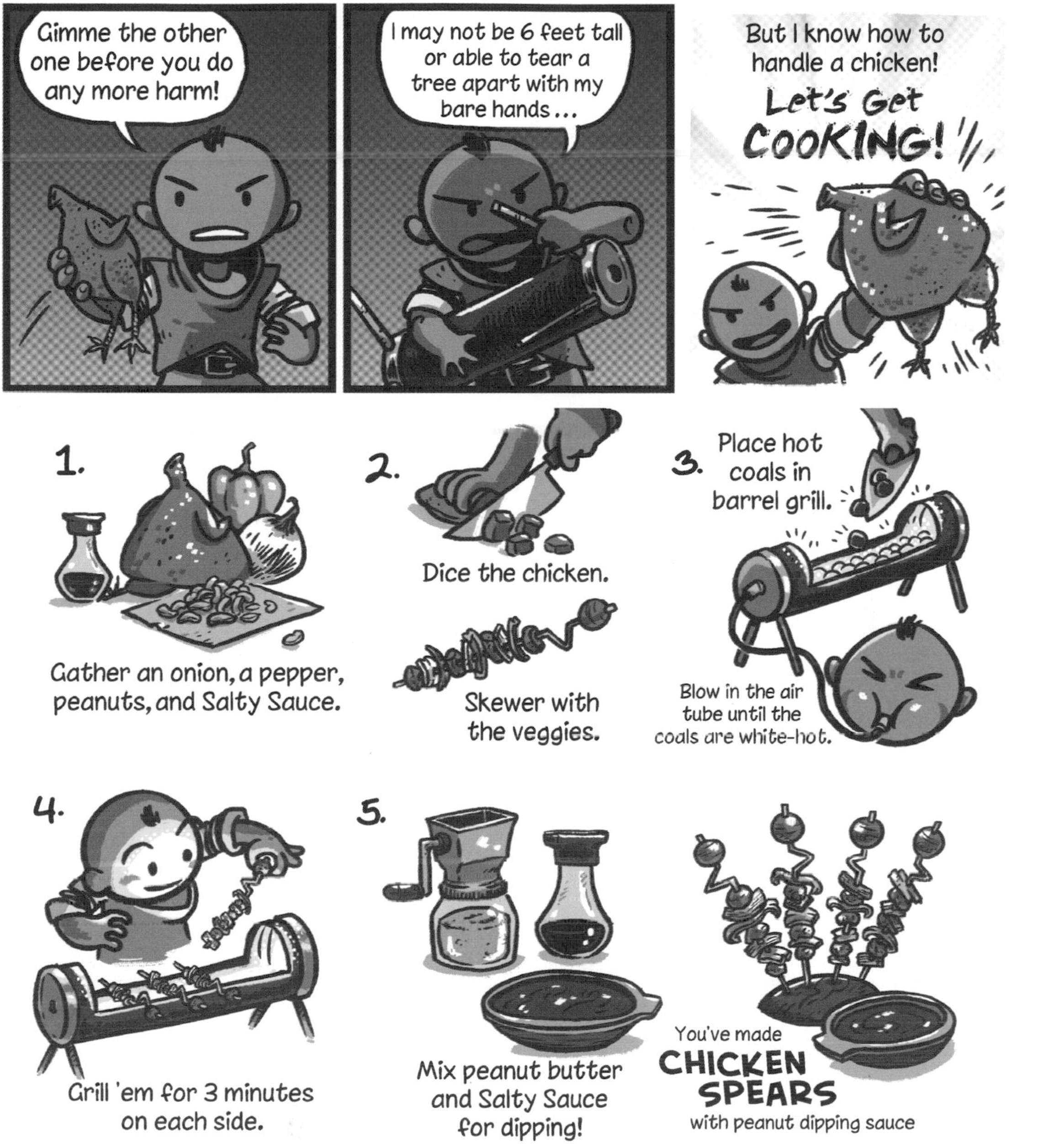
Gimme the other one before you do any more harm!
I may not be 6 feet tall or able to tear a tree apart with my bare hands...
But I know how to handle a chicken!
Let's Get COOKING!
1.
Gather an onion, a pepper, peanuts, and Salty Sauce.
2.
Dice the chicken.
Skewer with the veggies.
3.
Place hot coals in barrel grill.
Blow in the air tube until the coals are white-hot.
4.
Grill 'em for 3 minutes on each side.
5.
Mix peanut butter and Salty Sauce for dipping!
You've made CHICKEN SPEARS with peanut dipping sauce

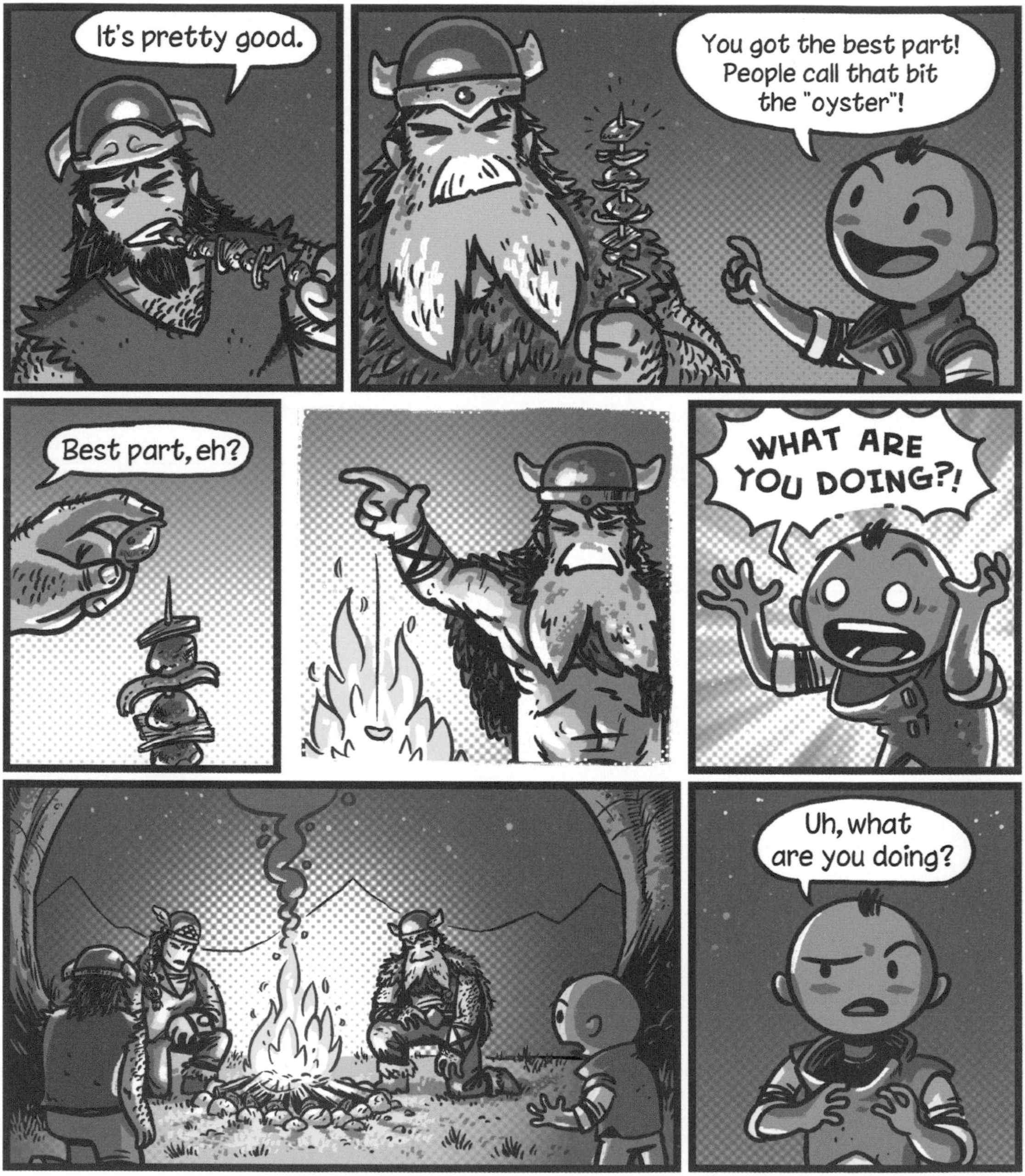

It's pretty good.
You got the best part! People call that bit the "oyster"!
Best part, eh?
WHAT ARE YOU DOING?!
Uh, what are you doing?

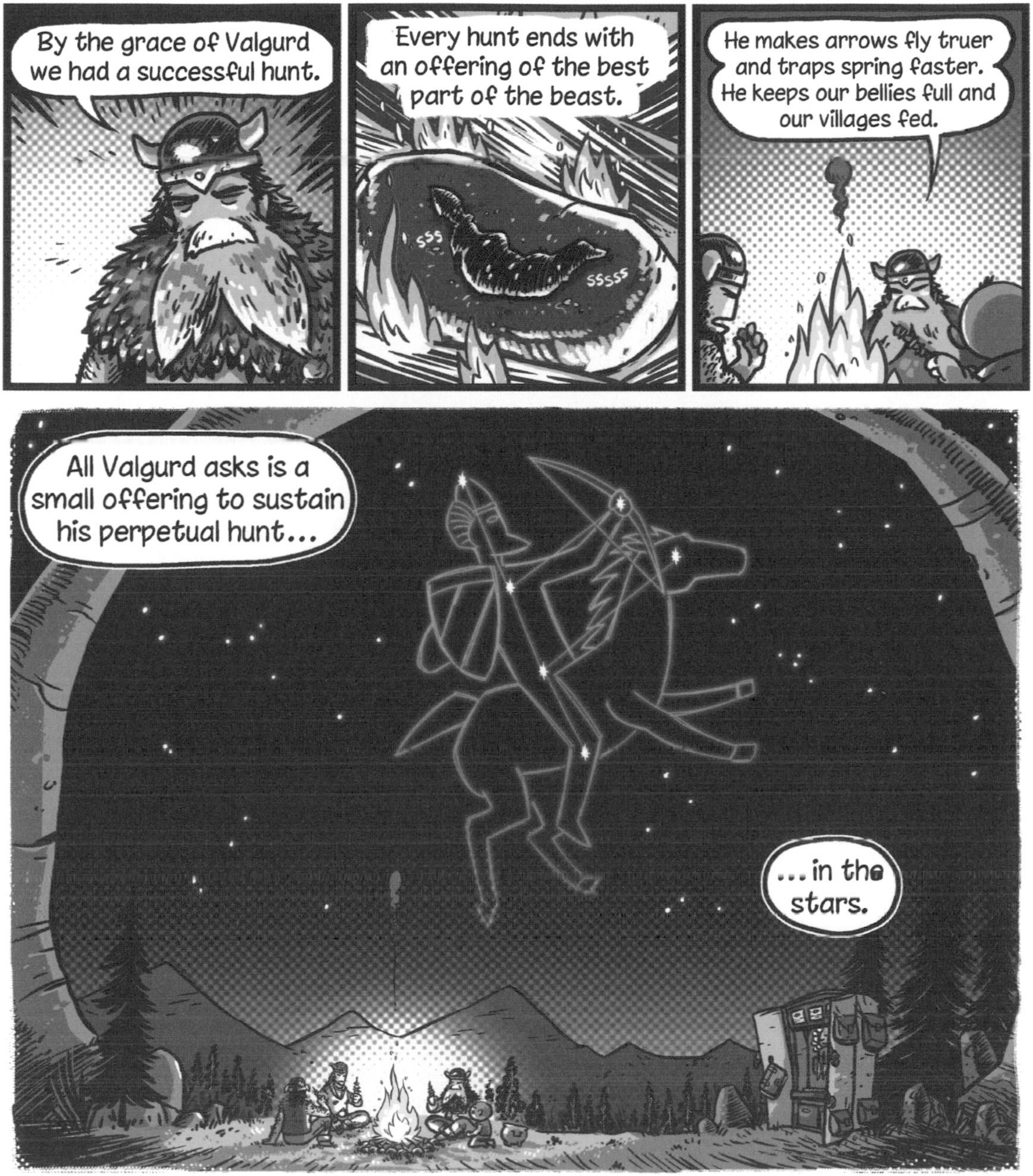
By the grace of Valgurd we had a successful hunt.
Every hunt ends with an offering of the best part of the beast.
SSS
SSSSS
He makes arrows fly truer and traps spring faster. He keeps our bellies full and our villages fed.
All Valgurd asks is a small offering to sustain his perpetual hunt...
...in the stars.

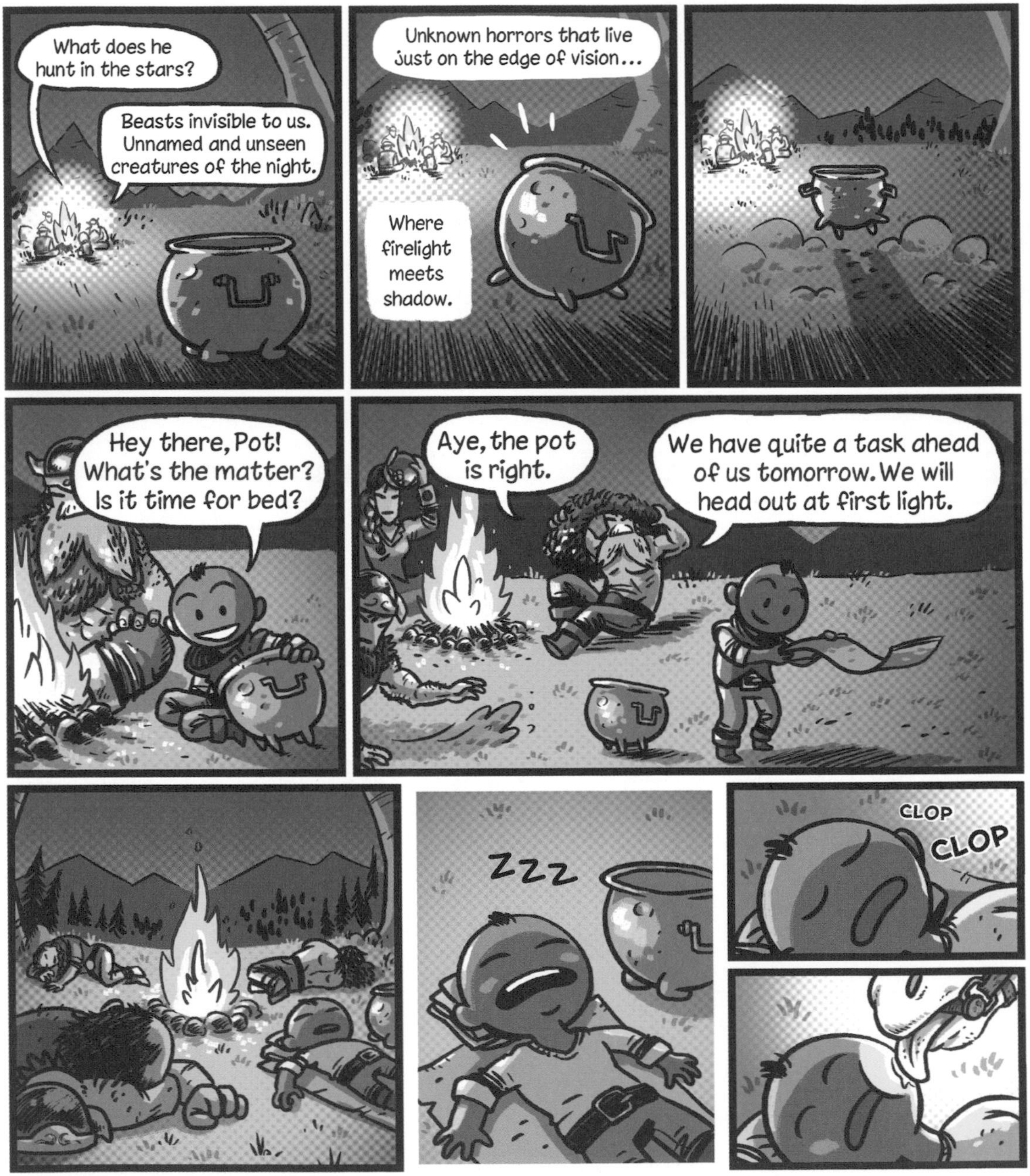
What does he hunt in the stars?
Beasts invisible to us. Unnamed and unseen creatures of the night.
Unknown horrors that live just on the edge of vision...
Where firelight meets shadow.
Hey there, Pot! What's the matter? Is it time for bed?
Aye, the pot is right.
We have quite a task ahead of us tomorrow. We will head out at first light.
ZZZ
CLOP
CLOP

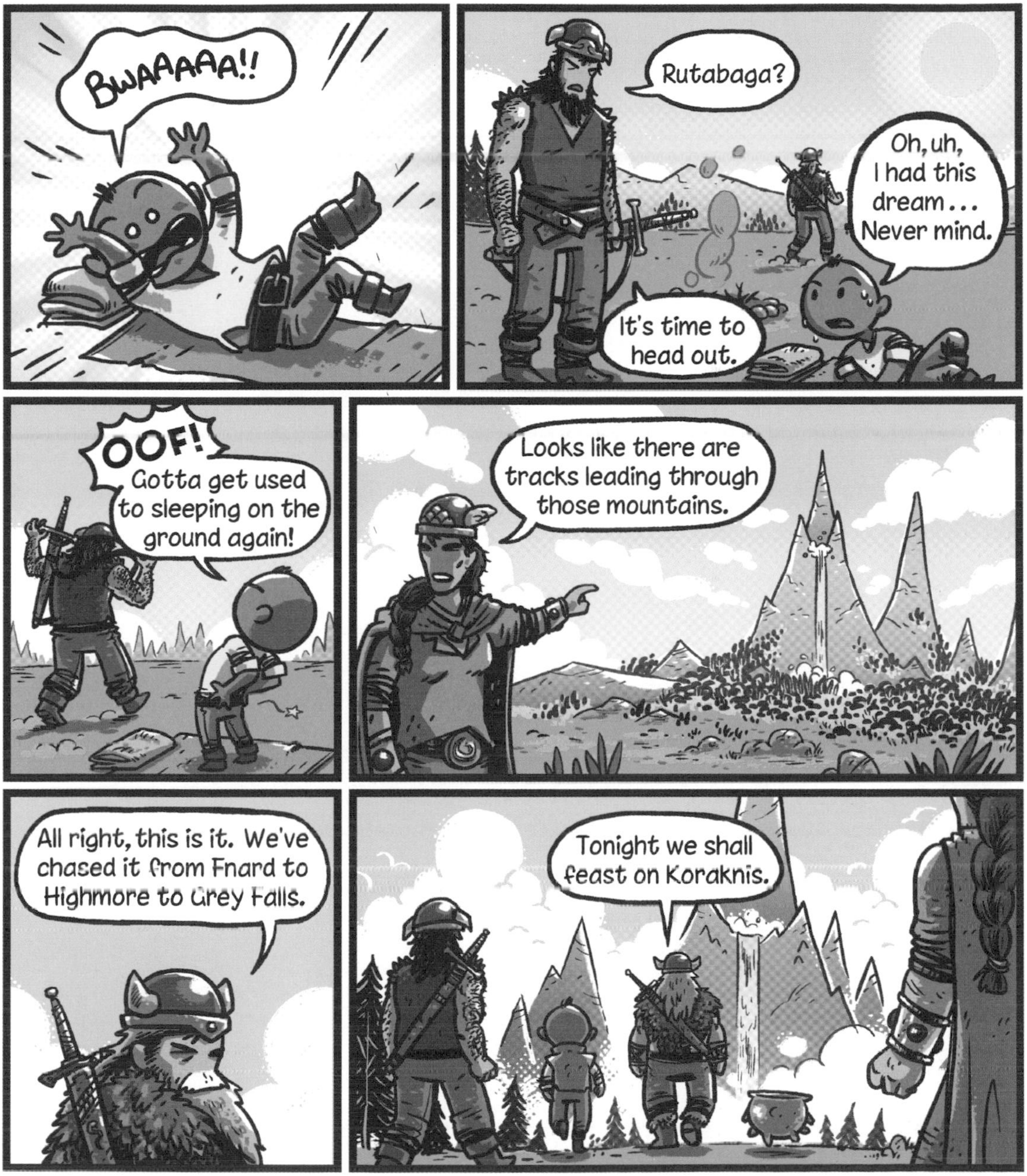
BWAAAAA!!
Rutabaga?
Oh, uh, I had this dream... Never mind.
It's time to head out.
OOF!
Gotta get used to sleeping on the ground again!
Looks like there are tracks leading through those mountains.
All right, this is it. We've chased it from Fnard to Highmore to Grey Falls.
Tonight we shall feast on Koraknis.

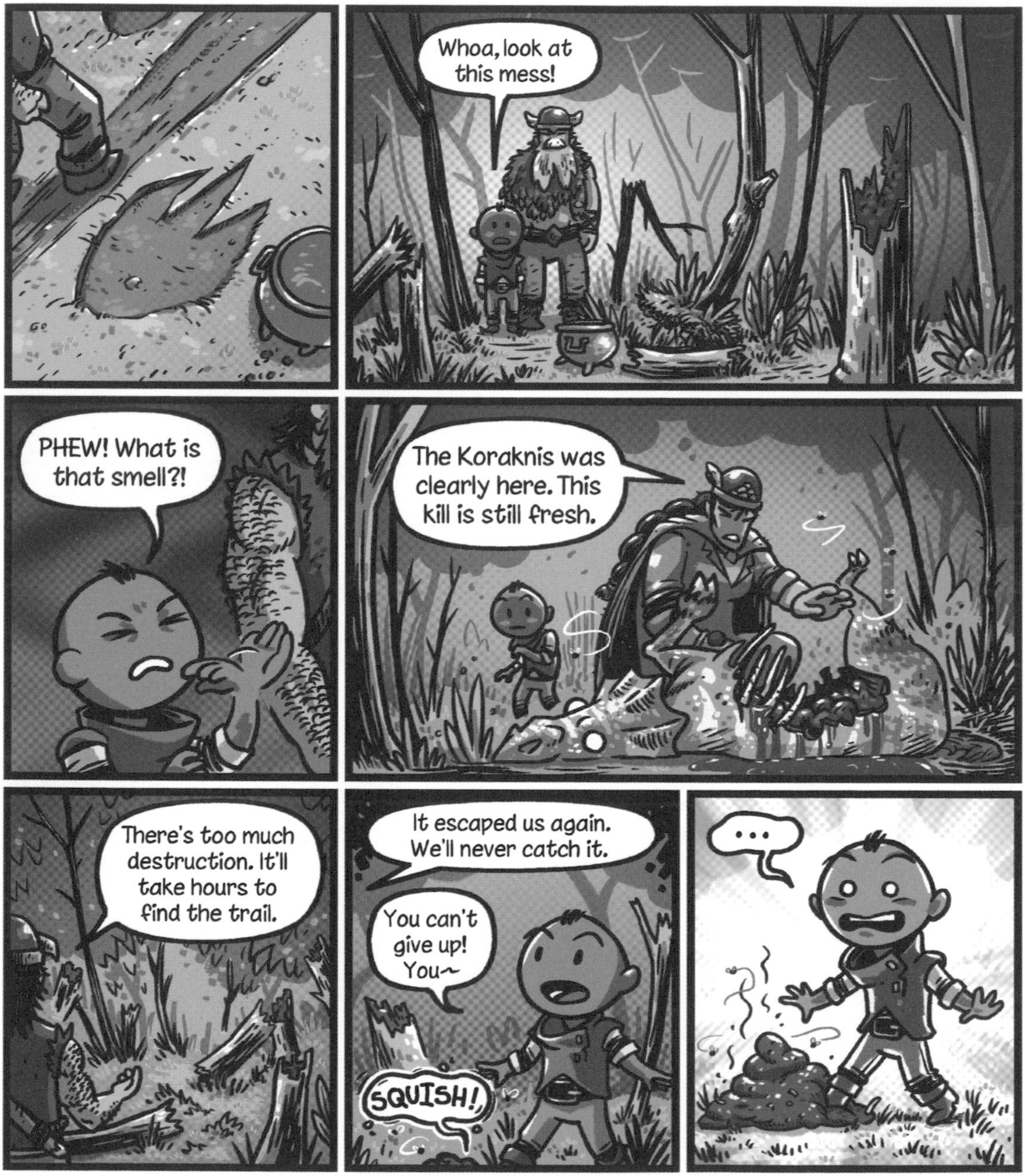

Whoa, look at this mess!
PHEW! What is that smell?!
The Koraknis was clearly here. This kill is still fresh.
There's too much destruction. It'll take hours to find the trail.
It escaped us again. We'll never catch it.
You can't give up! You~
SQUISH!
...

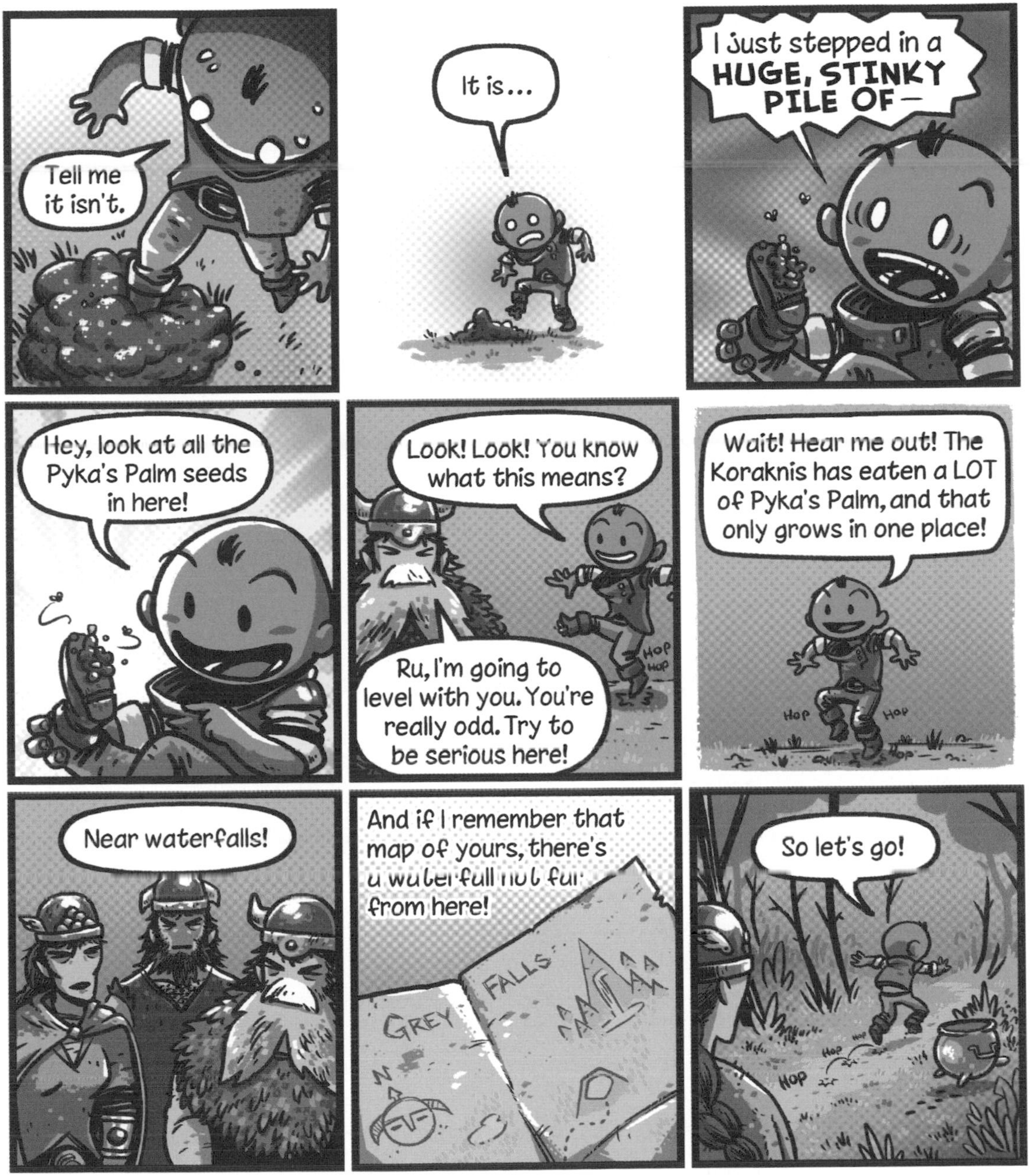
Tell me it isn't.
It is...
I just stepped in a HUGE, STINKY PILE OF—
Hey, look at all the Pyka's Palm seeds in here!
Look! Look! You know what this means?
Ru, I'm going to level with you. You're really odd. Try to be serious here!
HOP HOP
Wait! Hear me out! The Koraknis has eaten a LOT of Pyka's Palm, and that only grows in one place!
HOP HOP
Near waterfalls!
And if I remember that map of yours, there's a waterfall not far from here!
GREY
FALLS
N
So let's go!
HOP HOP HOP

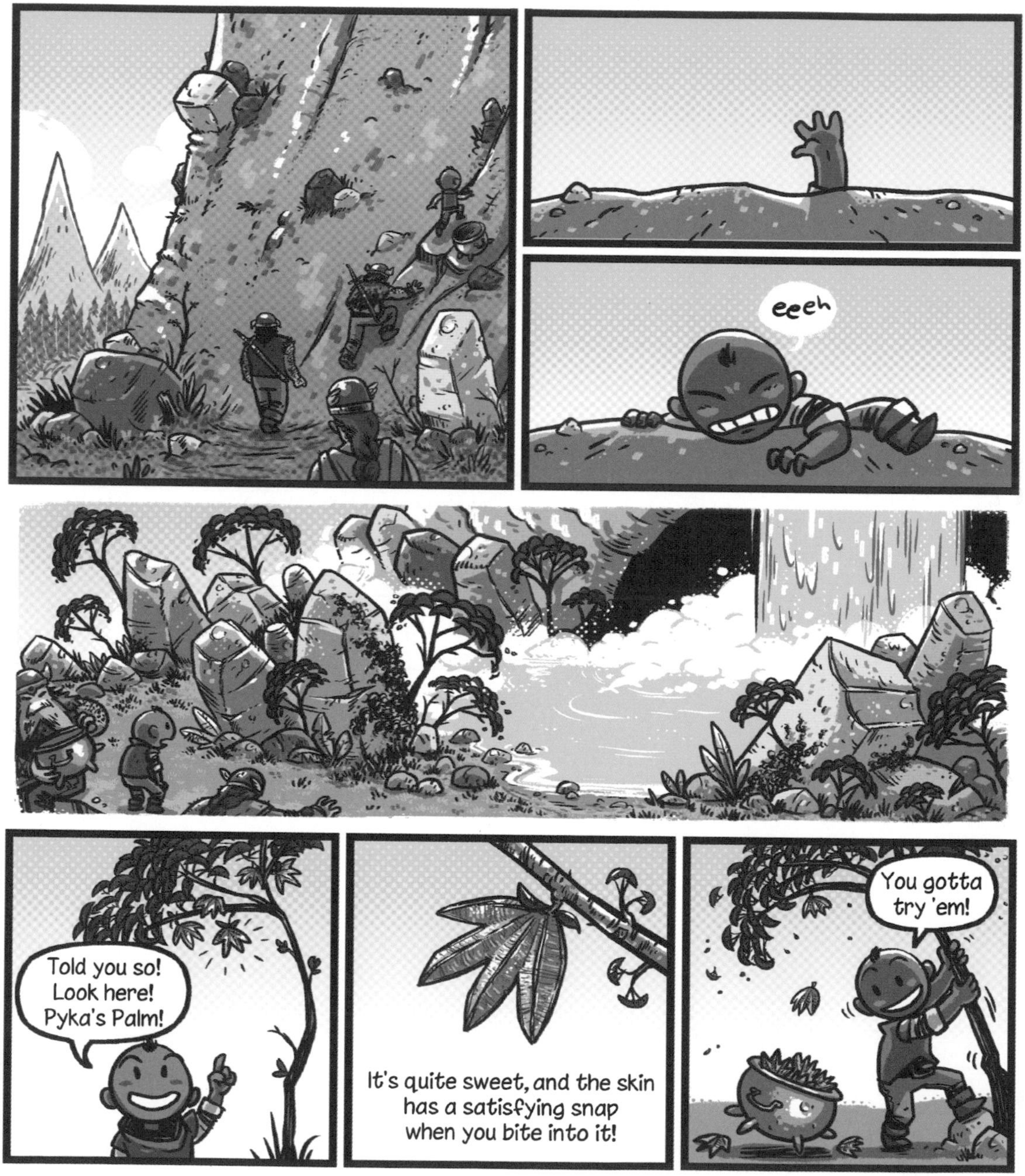
eeeh
Told you so!
Look here!
Pyka's Palm!
It's quite sweet, and the skin
has a satisfying snap
when you bite into it!
You gotta
try 'em!

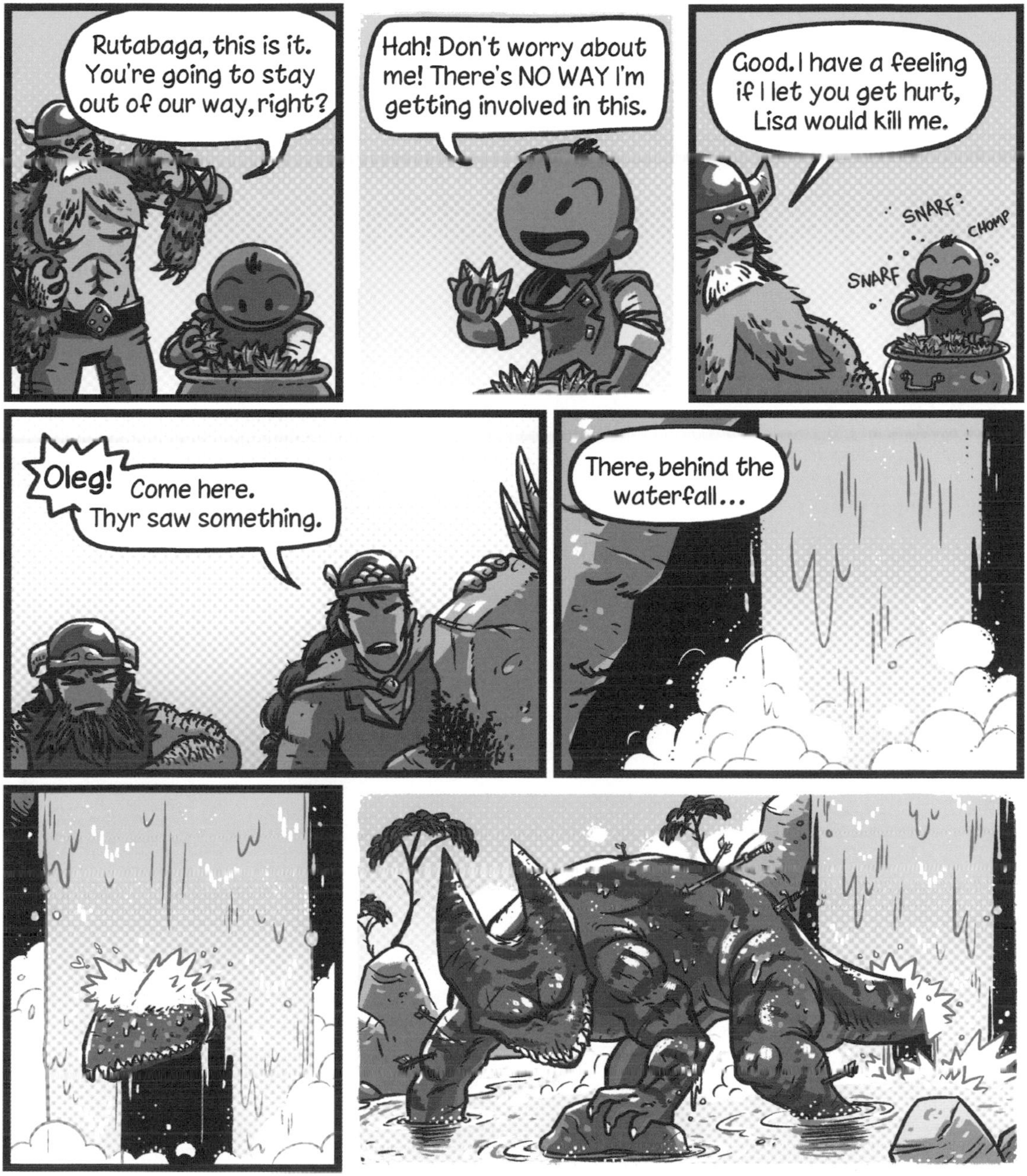
Rutabaga, this is it. You're going to stay out of our way, right?
Hah! Don't worry about me! There's NO WAY I'm getting involved in this.
Good. I have a feeling if I let you get hurt, Lisa would kill me.
SNARF
CHOMP
SNARF
Oleg! Come here. Thyr saw something.
There, behind the waterfall...

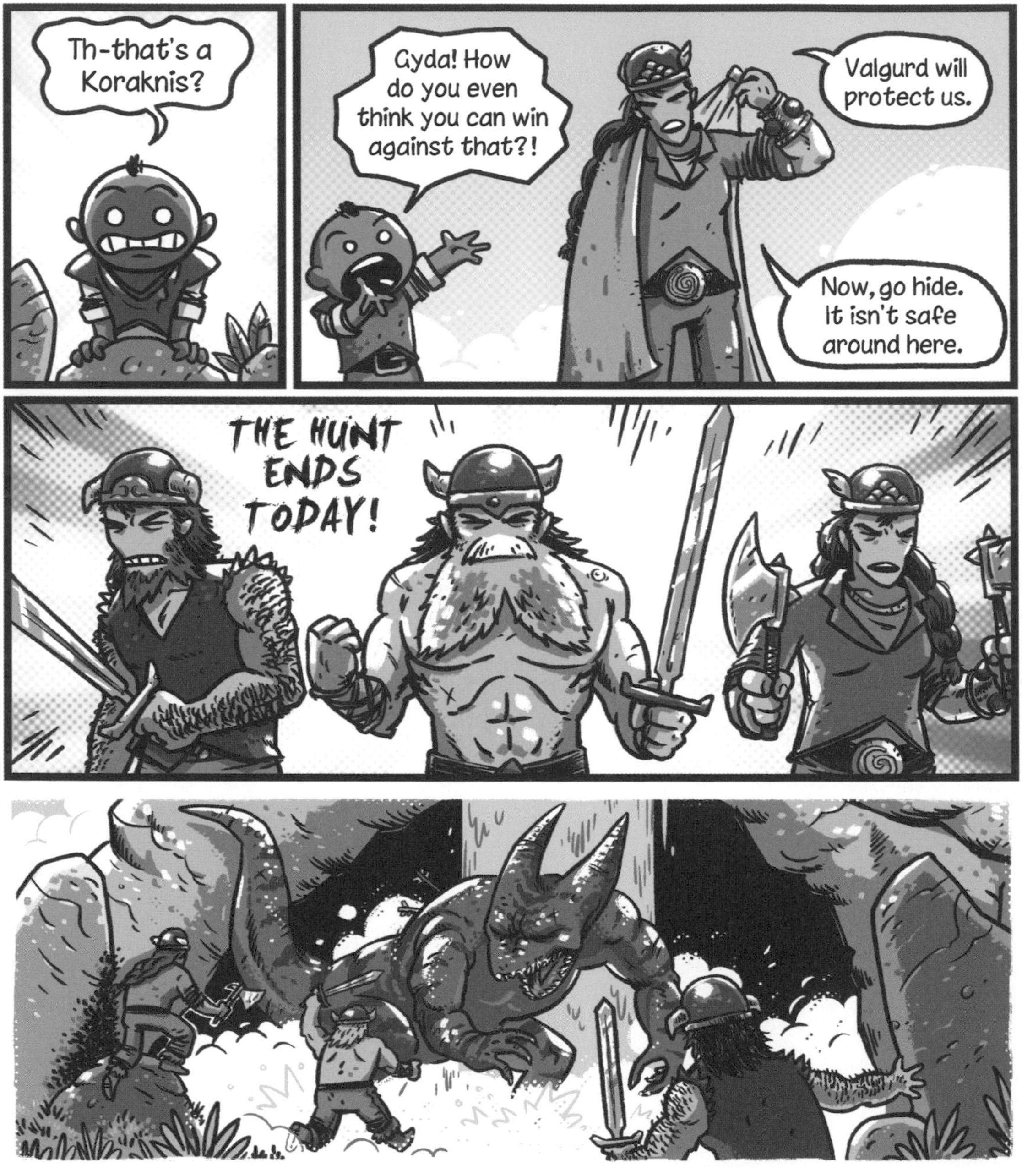
Th-that's a Koraknis?
Cyda! How do you even think you can win against that?!
Valgurd will protect us.
Now, go hide. It isn't safe around here.
THE HUNT ENDS TODAY!

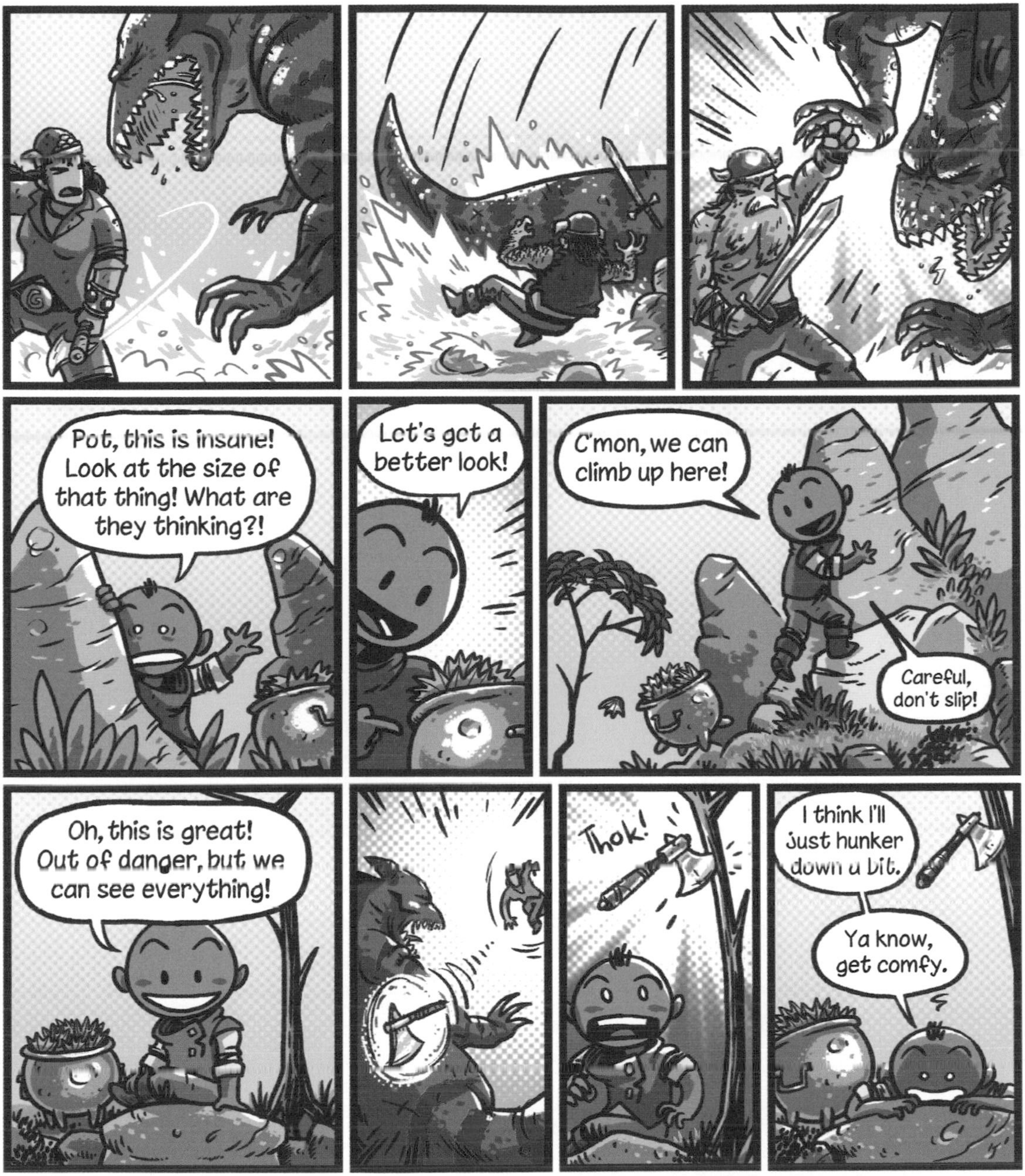
Pot, this is insane! Look at the size of that thing! What are they thinking?!
Let's get a better look!
C'mon, we can climb up here!
Careful, don't slip!
Oh, this is great! Out of danger, but we can see everything!
Thok!
I think I'll just hunker down a bit.
Ya know, get comfy.

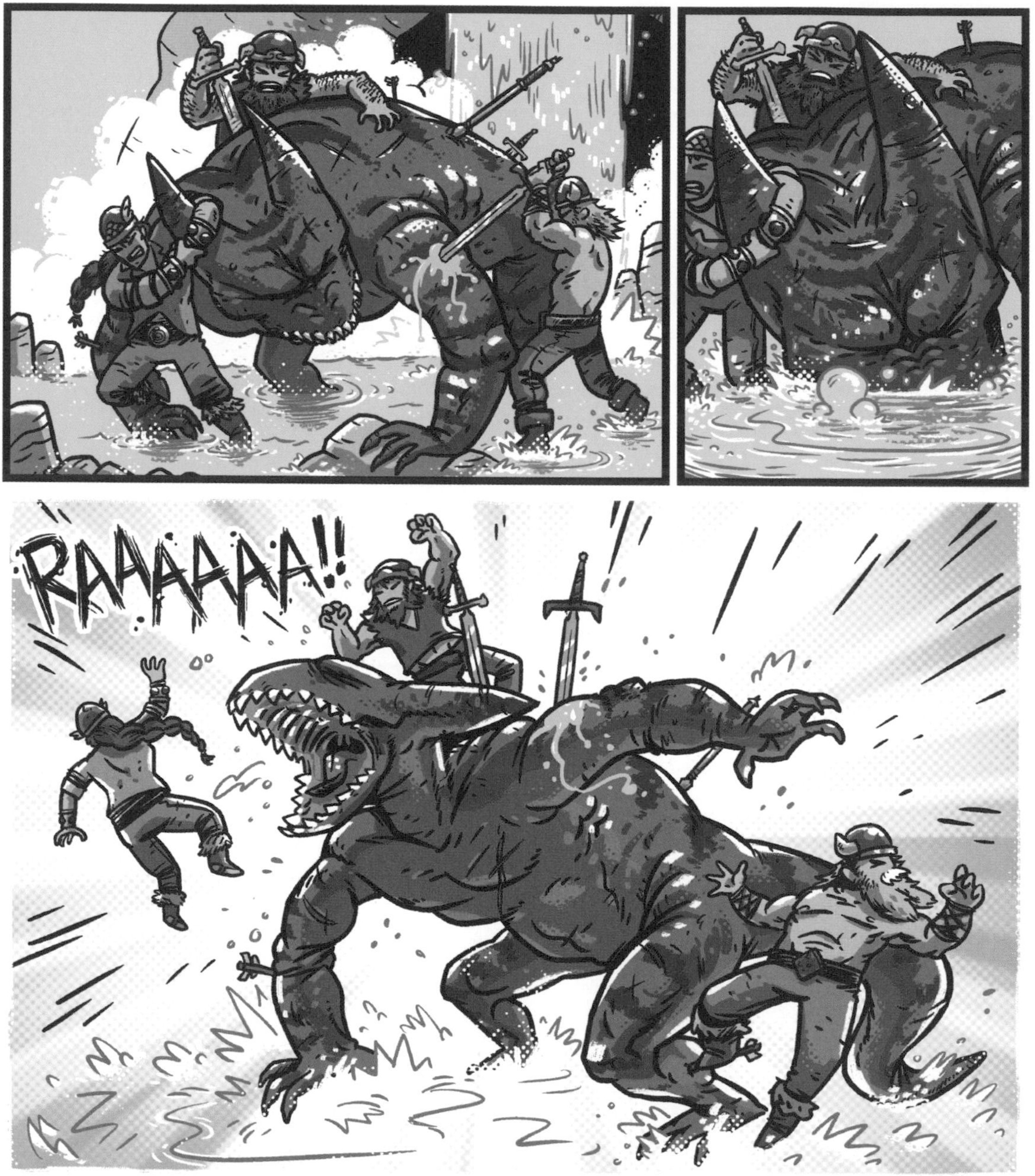
RAAAAAA!!

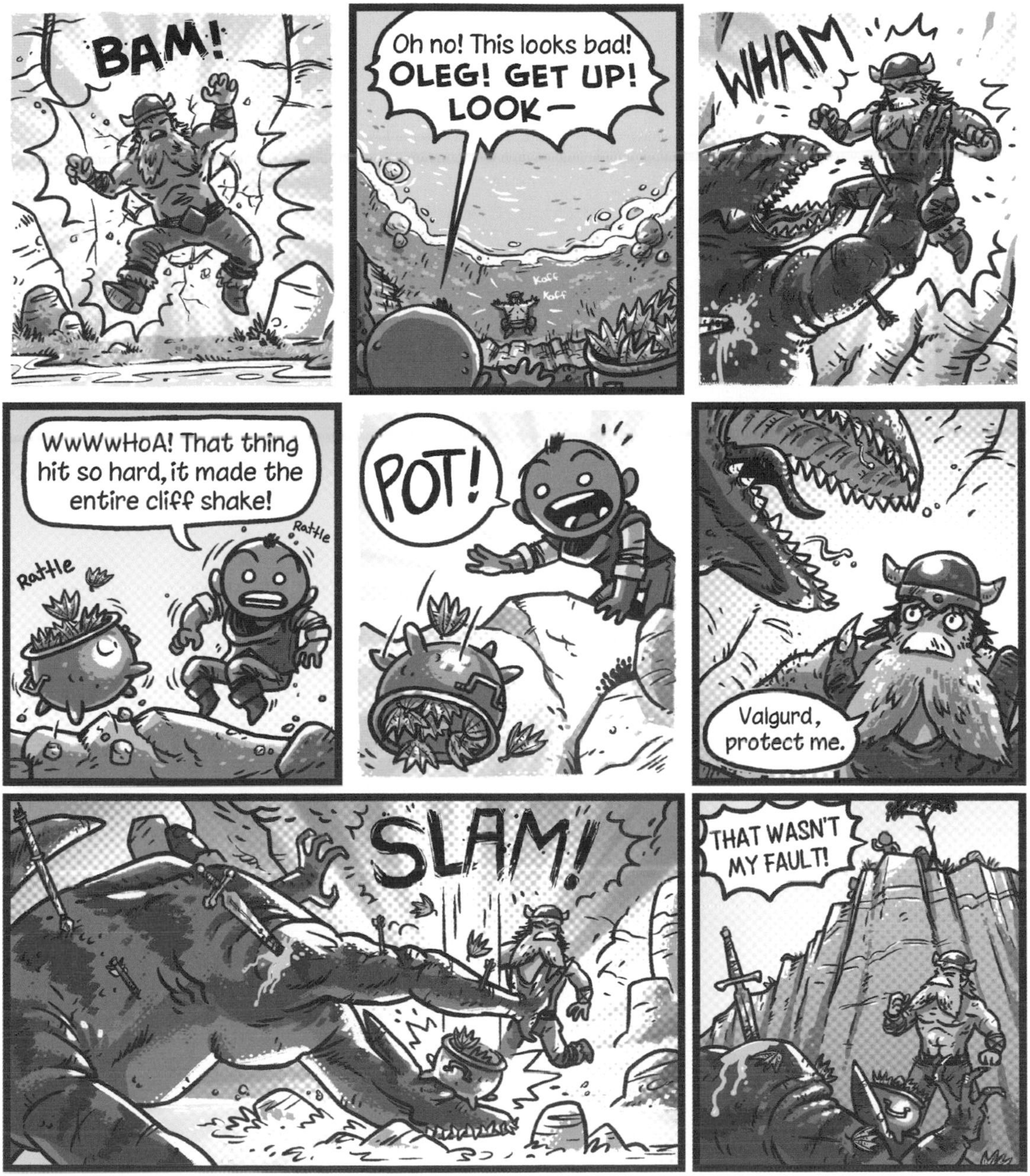
BAM!
Oh no! This looks bad! OLEG! GET UP! LOOK—
Koff Koff
WHAM
WwWwHoA! That thing hit so hard, it made the entire cliff shake!
Rattle
Rattle
POT!
Valgurd, protect me.
SLAM!
THAT WASN'T MY FAULT!

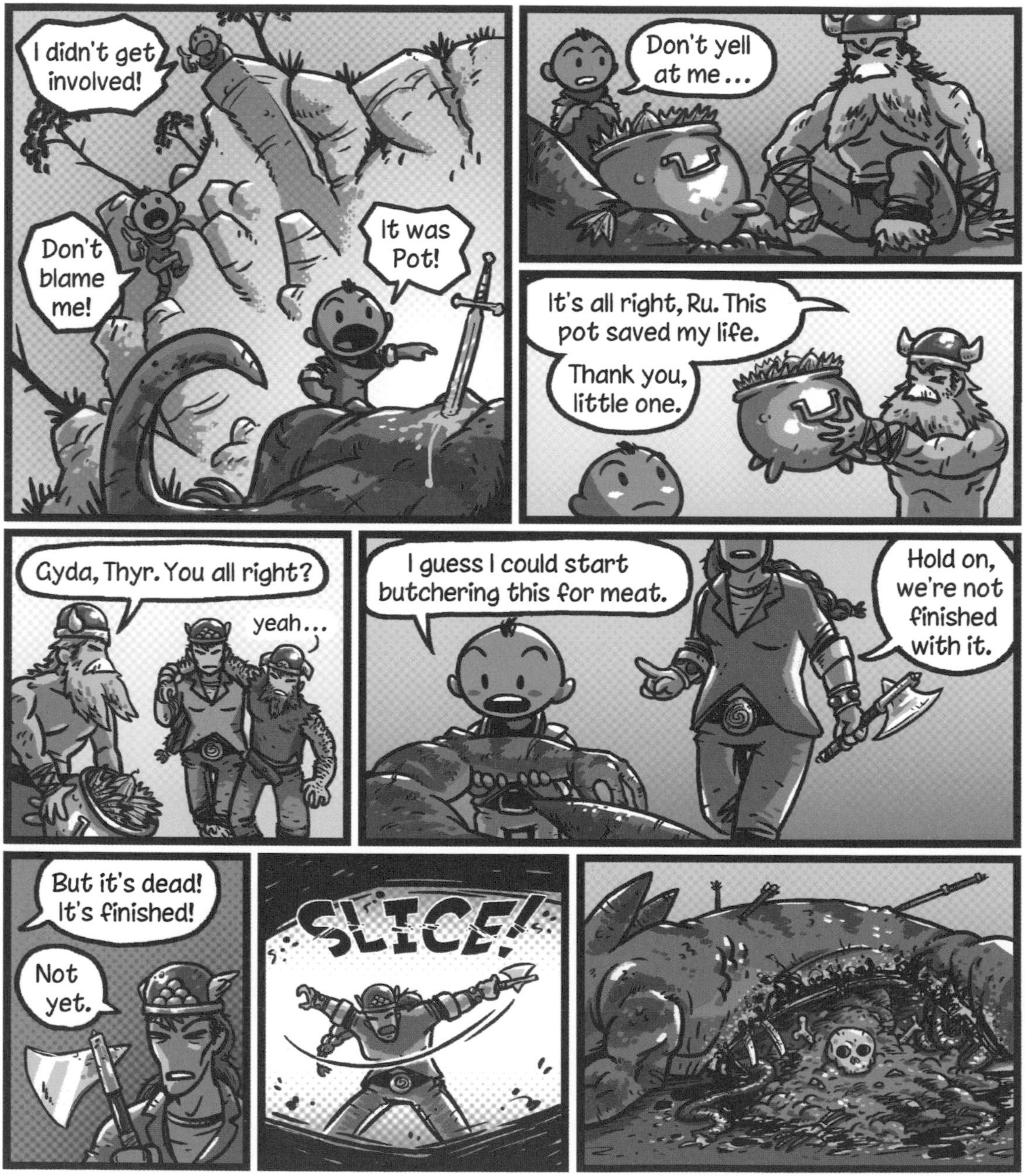
I didn't get involved!
Don't blame me!
It was Pot!
Don't yell at me...
It's all right, Ru. This pot saved my life.
Thank you, little one.
Gyda, Thyr. You all right?
yeah...
I guess I could start butchering this for meat.
Hold on, we're not finished with it.
But it's dead! It's finished!
Not yet.
SLICE!

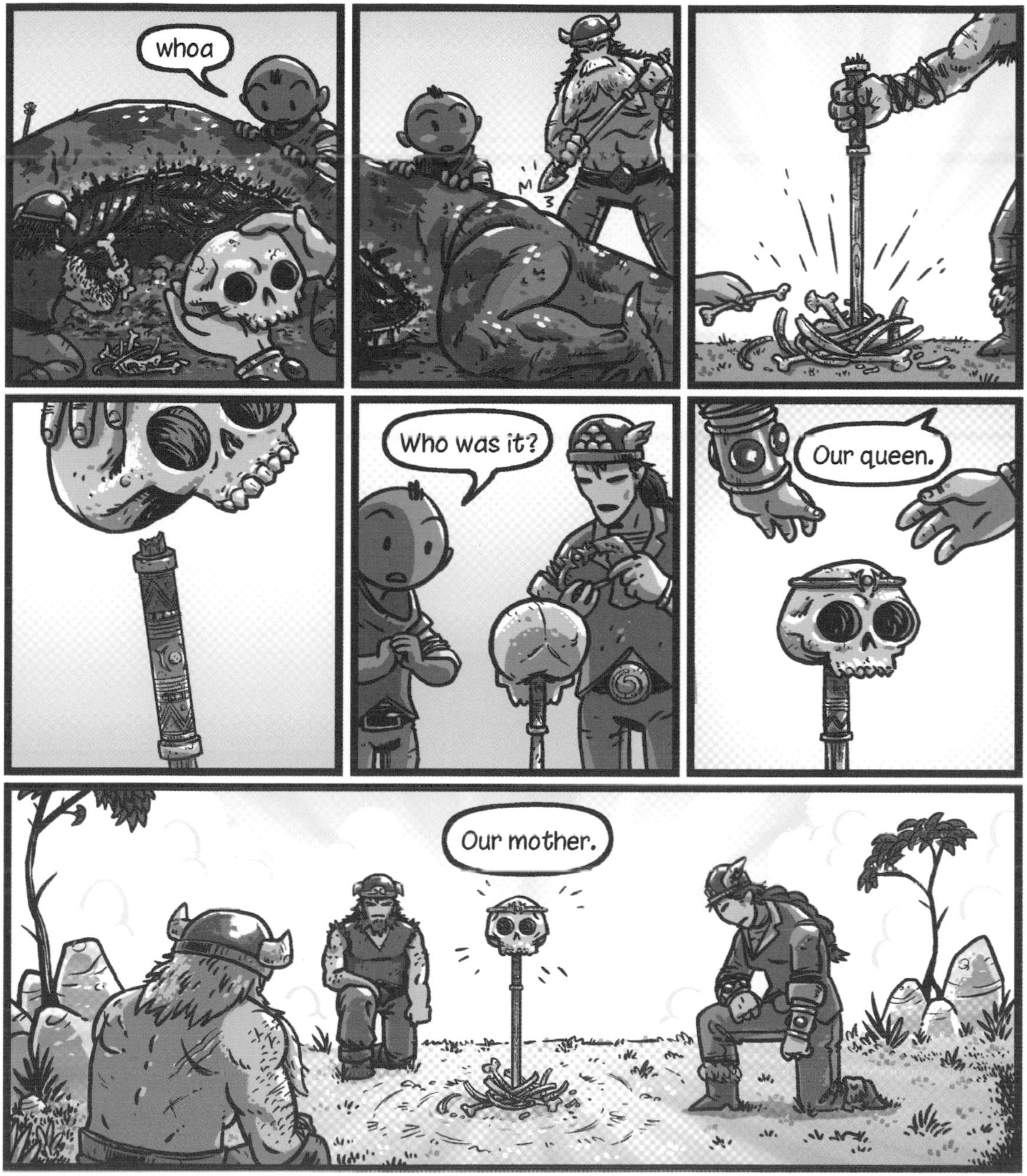
whoa
Who was it?
Our queen.
Our mother.

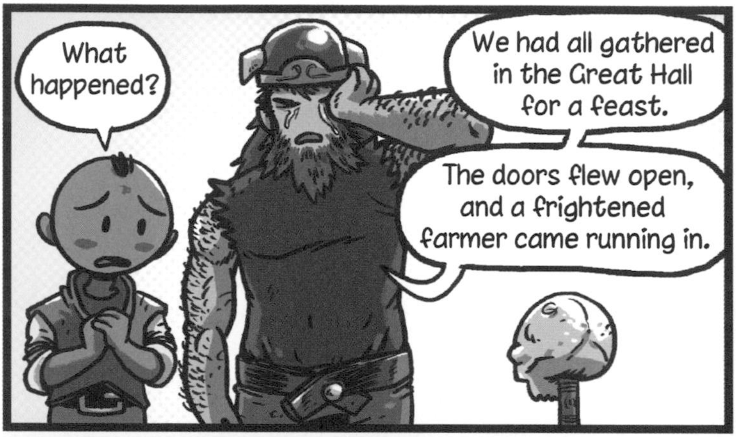
What happened?
We had all gathered in the Great Hall for a feast.
The doors flew open, and a frightened farmer came running in.

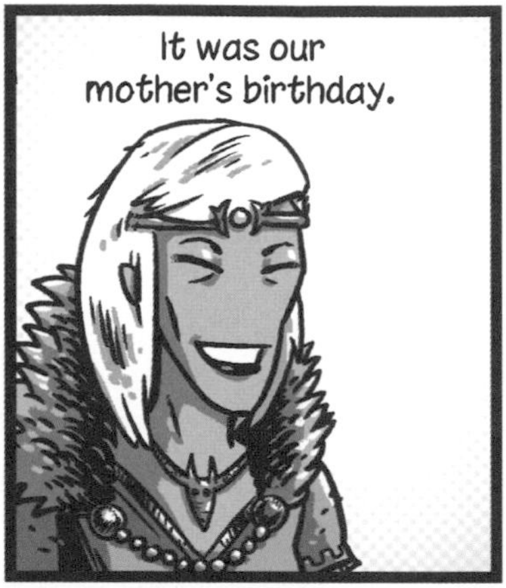
It was our mother's birthday.

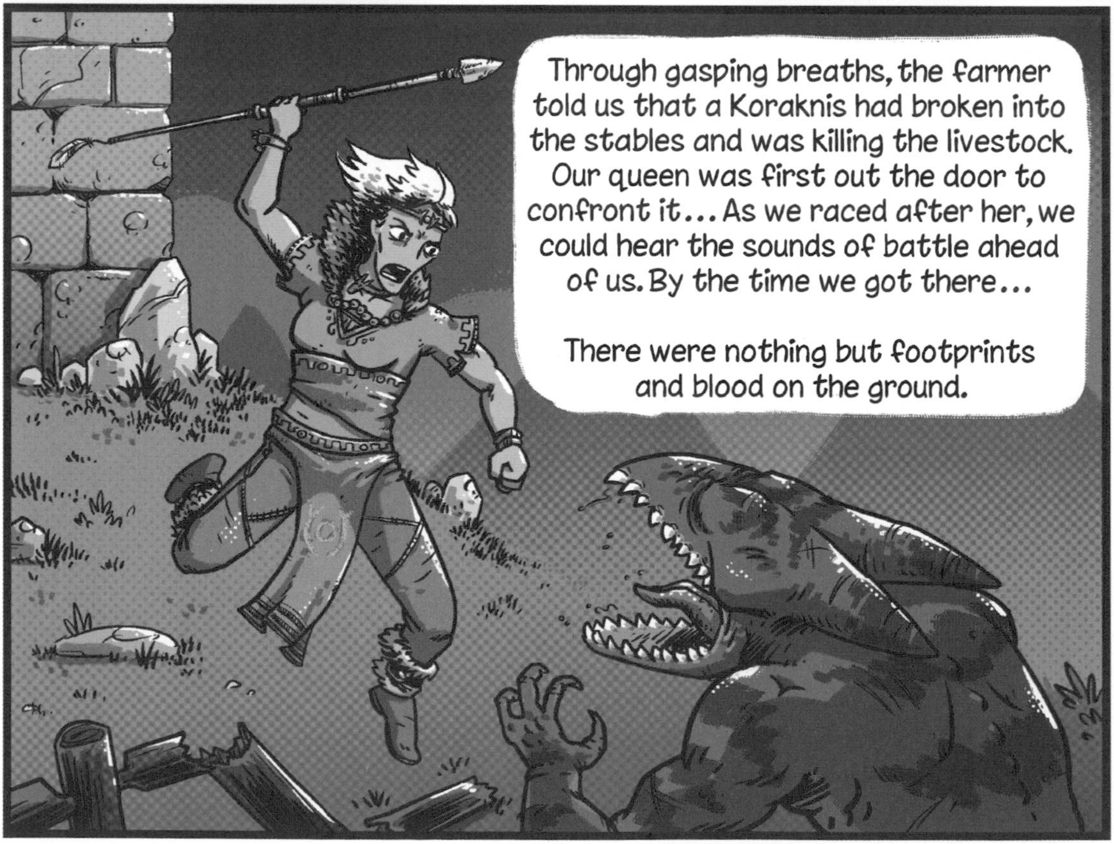
Through gasping breaths, the farmer told us that a Koraknis had broken into the stables and was killing the livestock. Our queen was first out the door to confront it... As we raced after her, we could hear the sounds of battle ahead of us. By the time we got there...
There were nothing but footprints and blood on the ground.

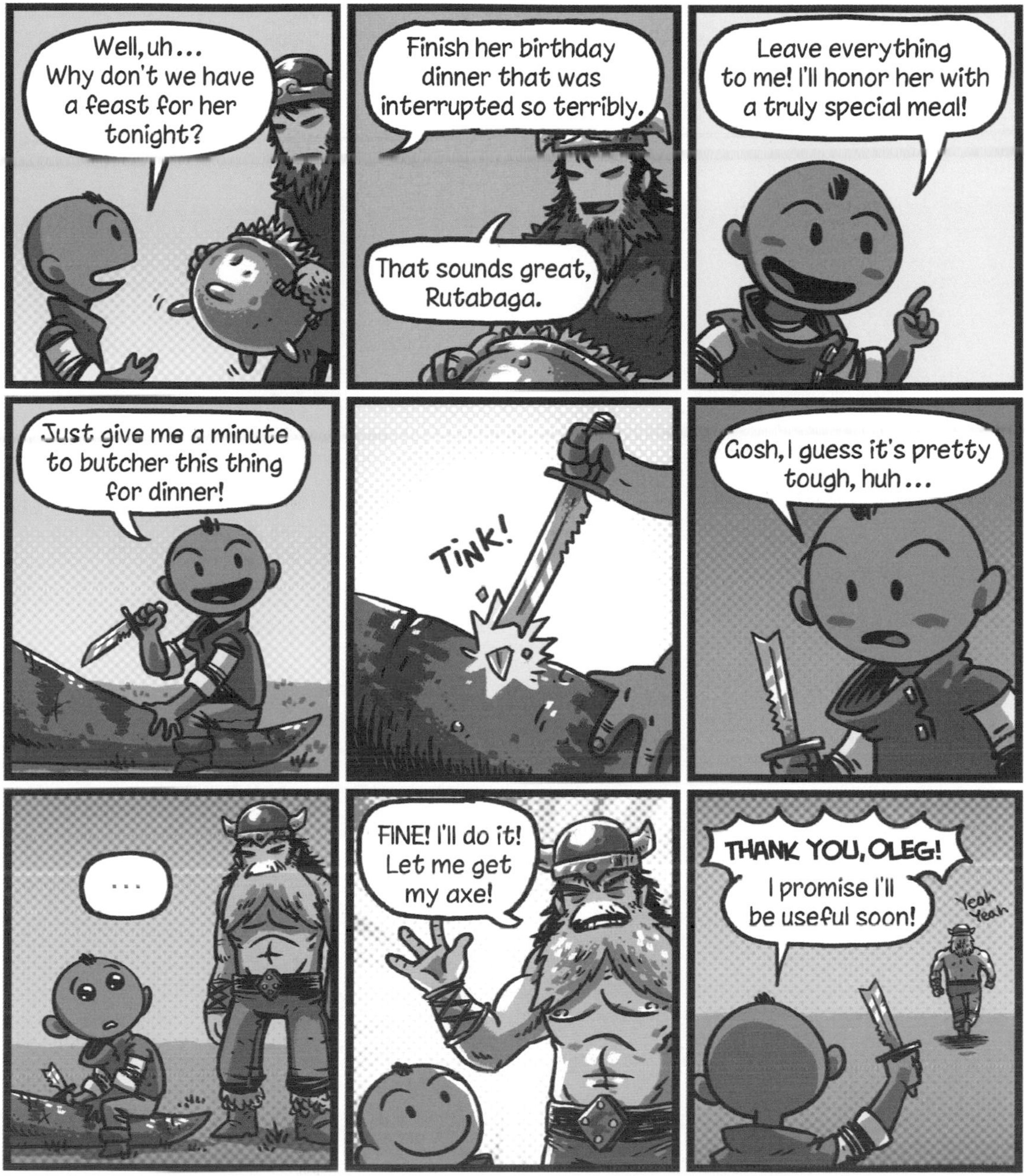
Well, uh... Why don't we have a feast for her tonight?
Finish her birthday dinner that was interrupted so terribly.
That sounds great, Rutabaga.
Leave everything to me! I'll honor her with a truly special meal!
Just give me a minute to butcher this thing for dinner!
TINK!
Gosh, I guess it's pretty tough, huh...
...
FINE! I'll do it! Let me get my axe!
THANK YOU, OLEG!
I promise I'll be useful soon!
Yeah Yeah

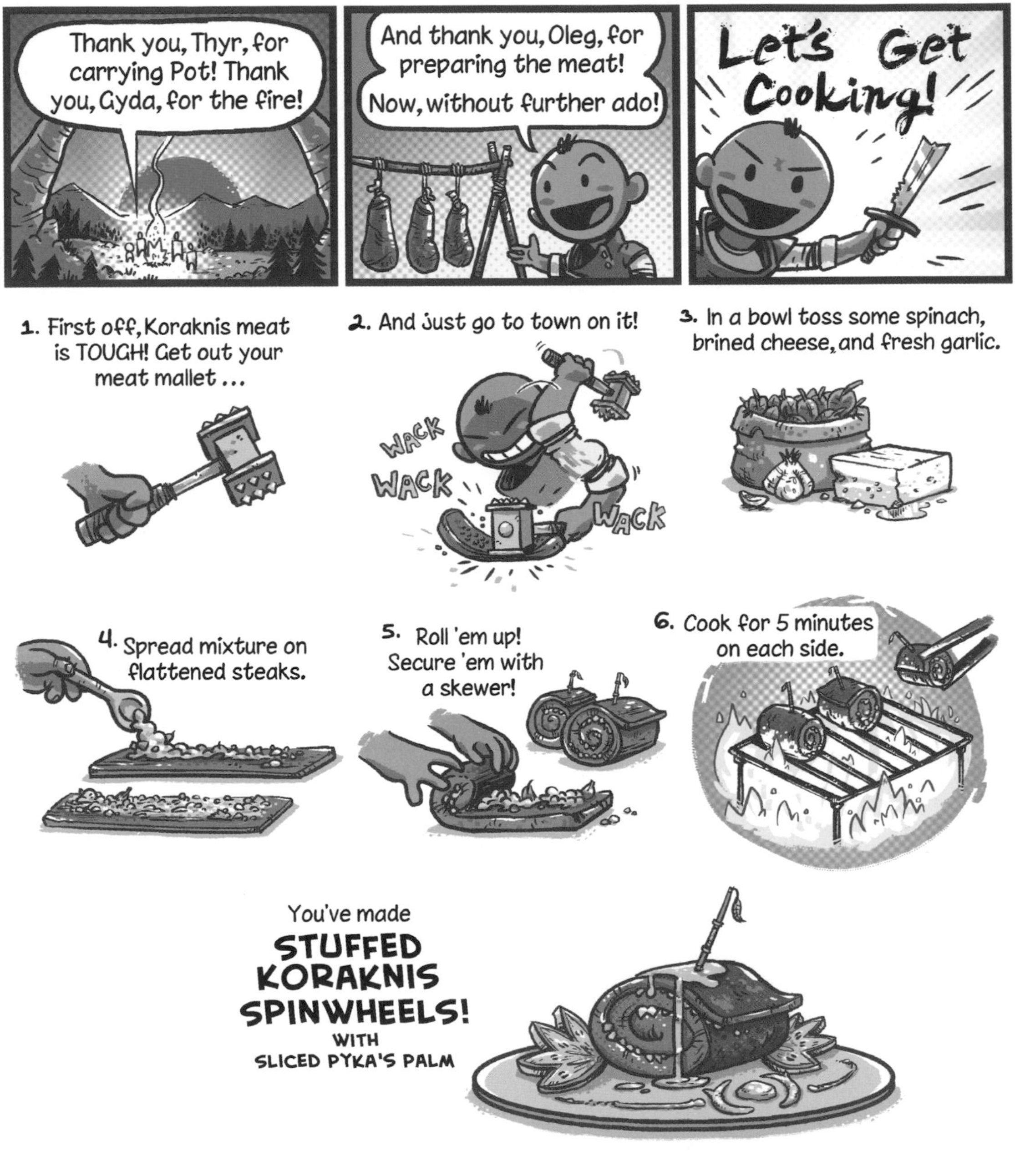

Thank you, Thyr, for carrying Pot! Thank you, Gyda, for the fire!
And thank you, Oleg, for preparing the meat!
Now, without further ado!
Let's Get Cooking!
1. First off, Koraknis meat is TOUGH! Get out your meat mallet . . .
2. And just go to town on it!
WACK
WACK
WACK
3. In a bowl toss some spinach, brined cheese, and fresh garlic.
4. Spread mixture on flattened steaks.
5. Roll 'em up! Secure 'em with a skewer!
6. Cook for 5 minutes on each side.
You've made
STUFFED KORAKNIS SPINWHEELS!
WITH
SLICED PYKA'S PALM

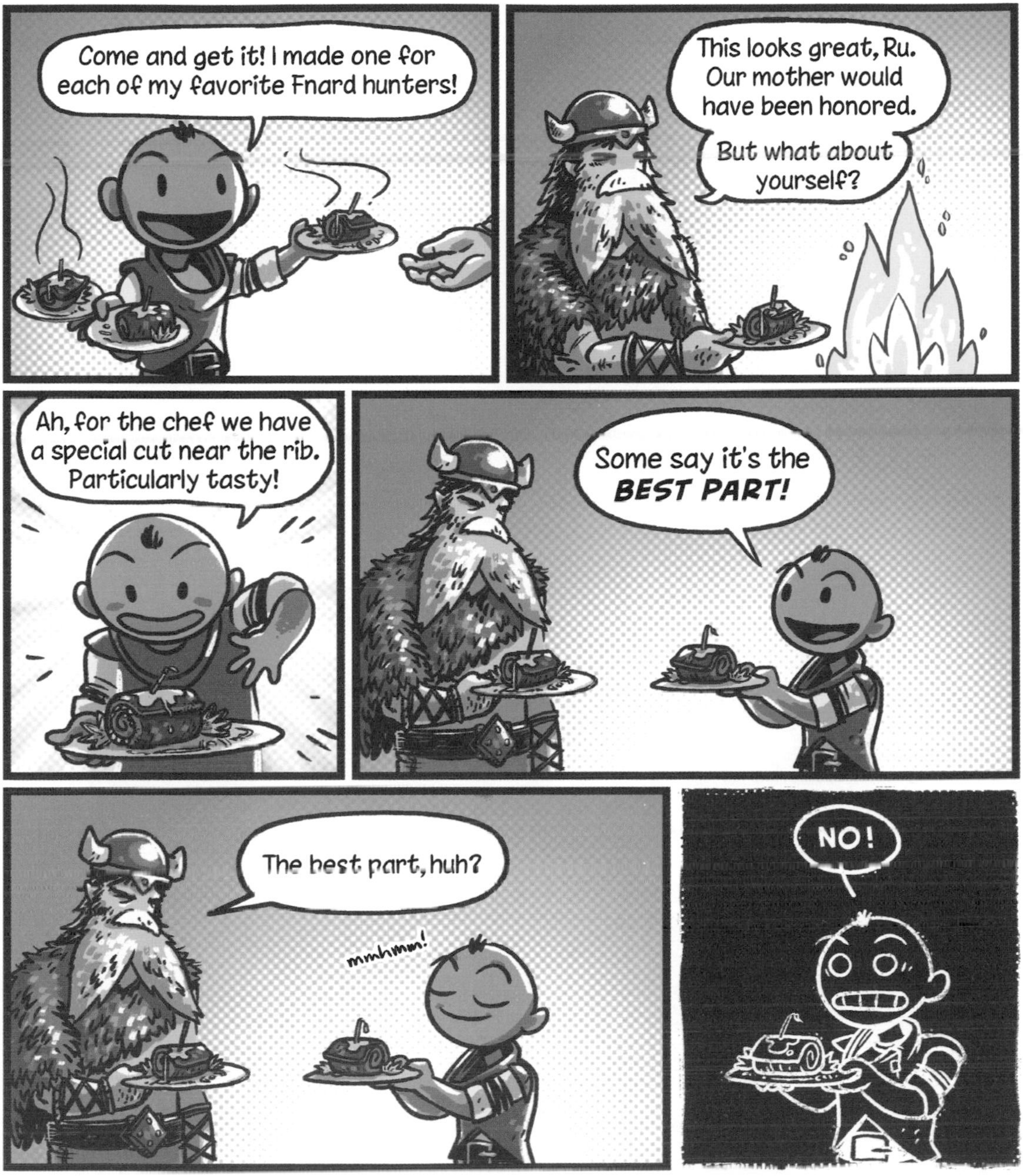
Come and get it! I made one for each of my favorite Fnard hunters!
This looks great, Ru. Our mother would have been honored.
But what about yourself?
Ah, for the chef we have a special cut near the rib. Particularly tasty!
Some say it's the **BEST PART!**
The best part, huh?
mmhmm!
NO!

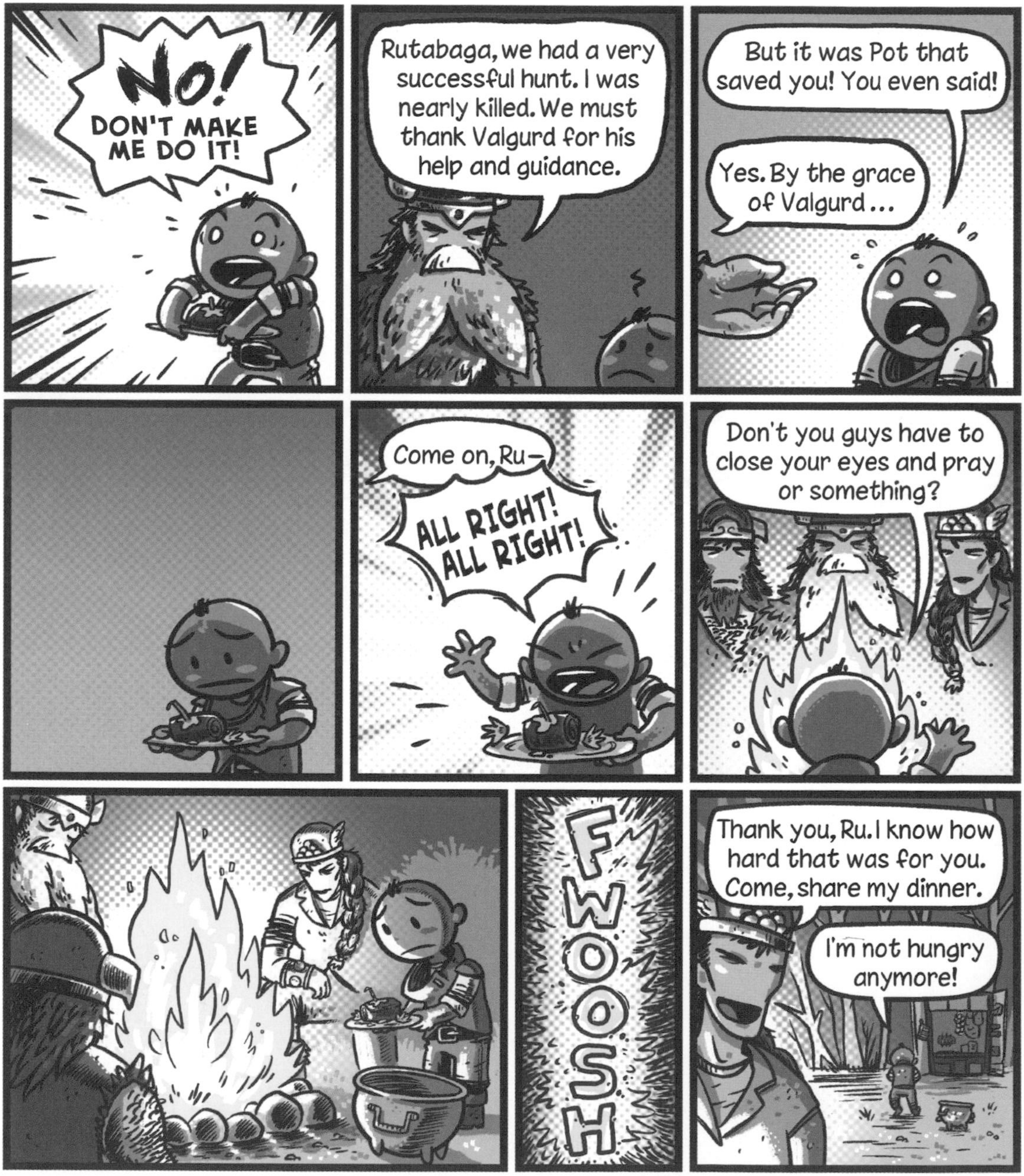
NO!
DON'T MAKE ME DO IT!
Rutabaga, we had a very successful hunt. I was nearly killed. We must thank Valgurd for his help and guidance.
But it was Pot that saved you! You even said!
Yes. By the grace of Valgurd...
Come on, Ru—
ALL RIGHT! ALL RIGHT!
Don't you guys have to close your eyes and pray or something?
FWOOSH
Thank you, Ru. I know how hard that was for you. Come, share my dinner.
I'm not hungry anymore!

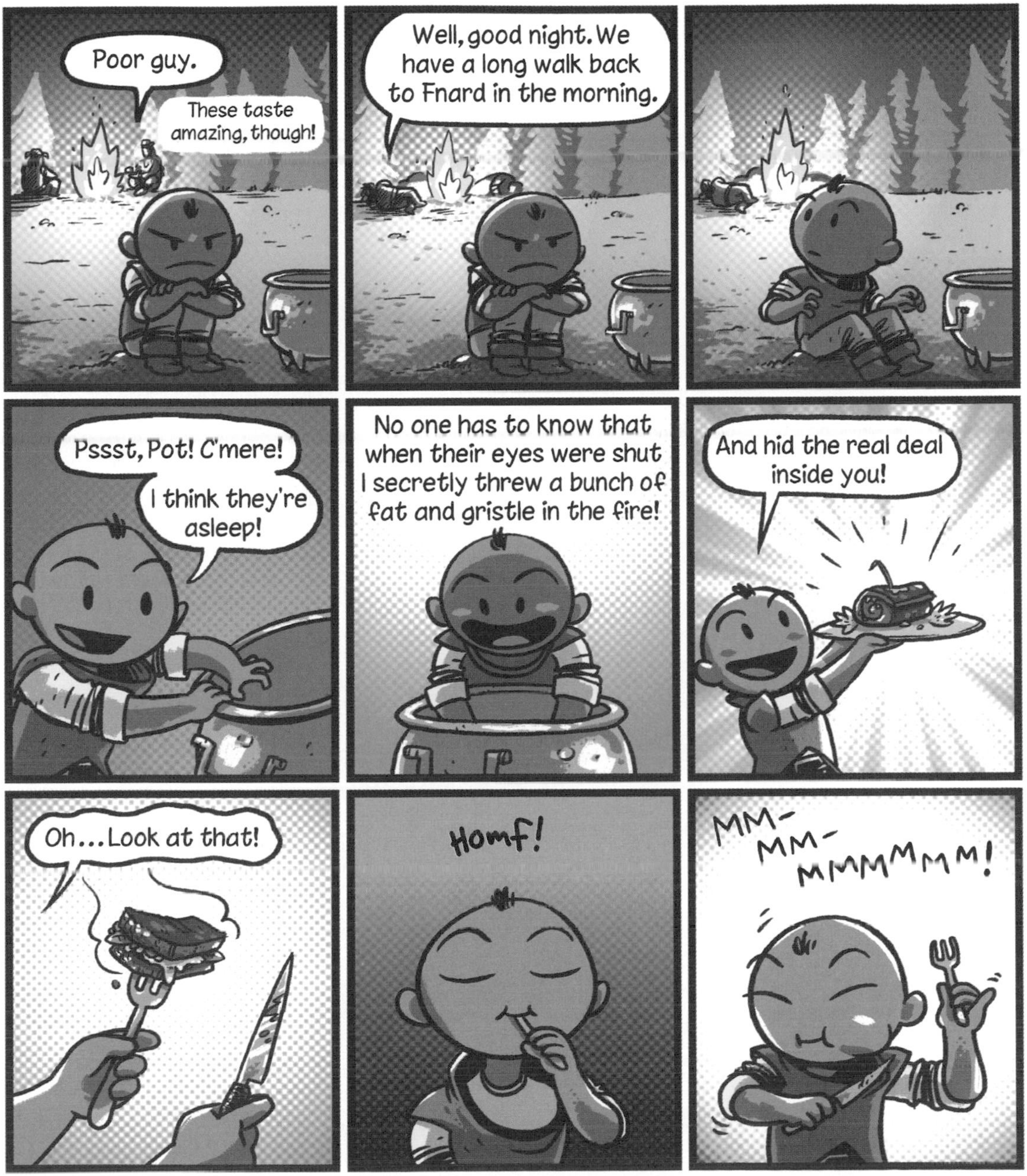
Poor guy.
These taste amazing, though!
Well, good night. We have a long walk back to Fnard in the morning.
Pssst, Pot! C'mere!
I think they're asleep!
No one has to know that when their eyes were shut I secretly threw a bunch of fat and gristle in the fire!
And hid the real deal inside you!
Oh...Look at that!
Homf!
MM-MM-MMMMMMM!

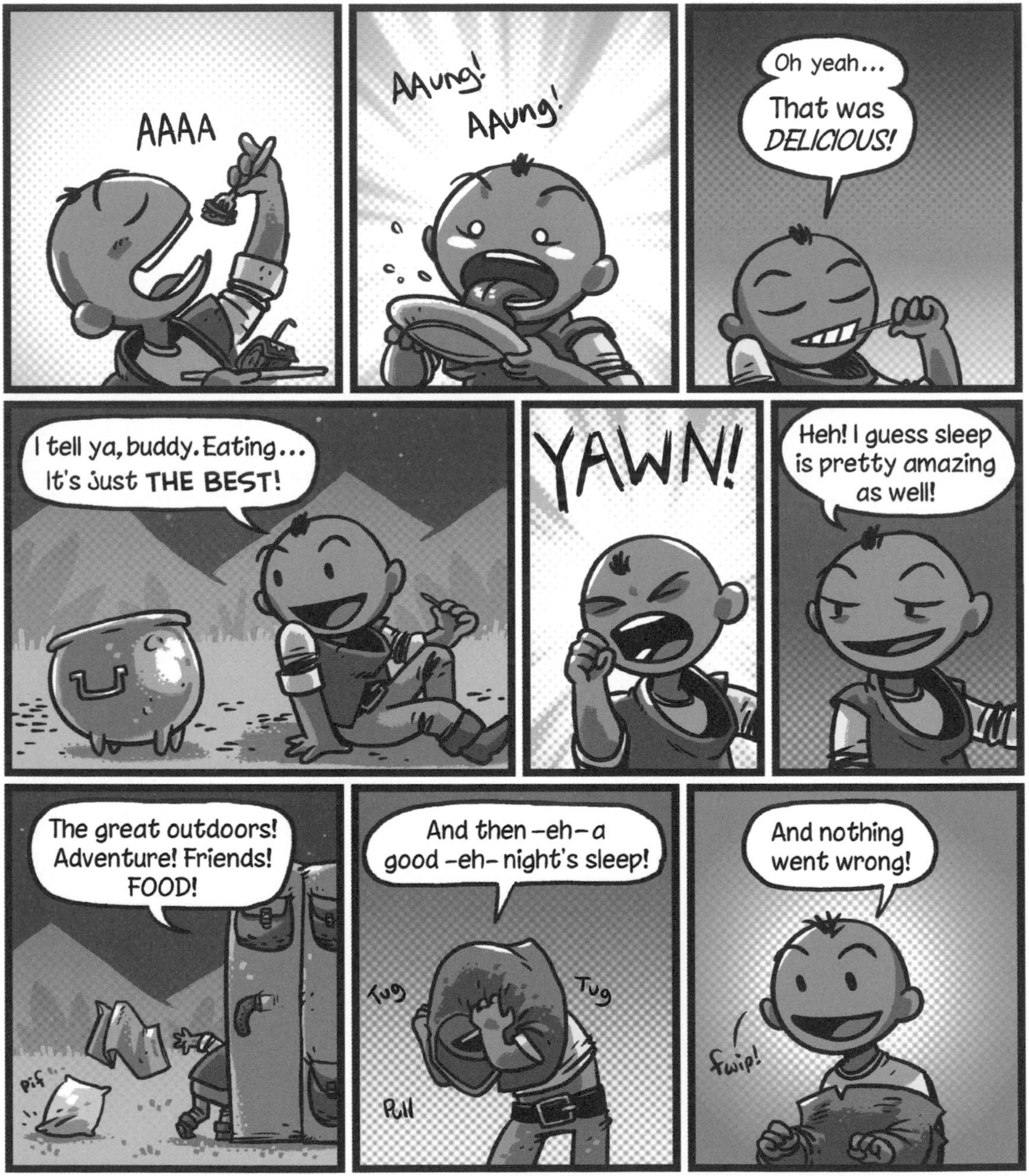
AAAA
AAung!
AAung!
Oh yeah...
That was DELICIOUS!
I tell ya, buddy. Eating... It's just THE BEST!
YAWN!
Heh! I guess sleep is pretty amazing as well!
The great outdoors! Adventure! Friends! FOOD!
Pif
And then -eh- a good -eh- night's sleep!
Tug
Tug
Pull
And nothing went wrong!
fwip!

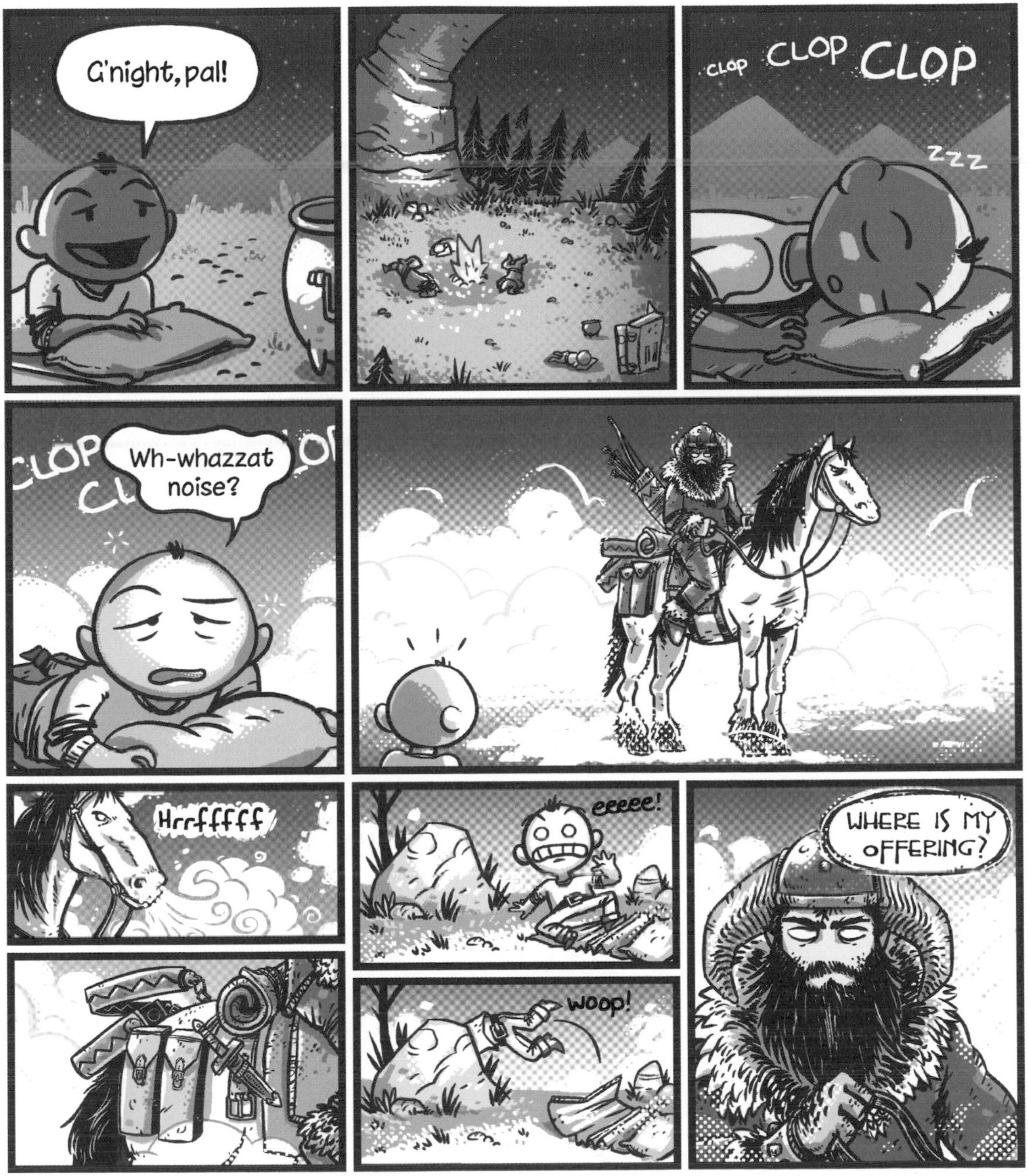
G'night, pal!
CLOP CLOP CLOP
ZZZ
CLOP
Wh-whazzat noise?
Hrrfffff
eeeee!
WHERE IS MY OFFERING?
woop!

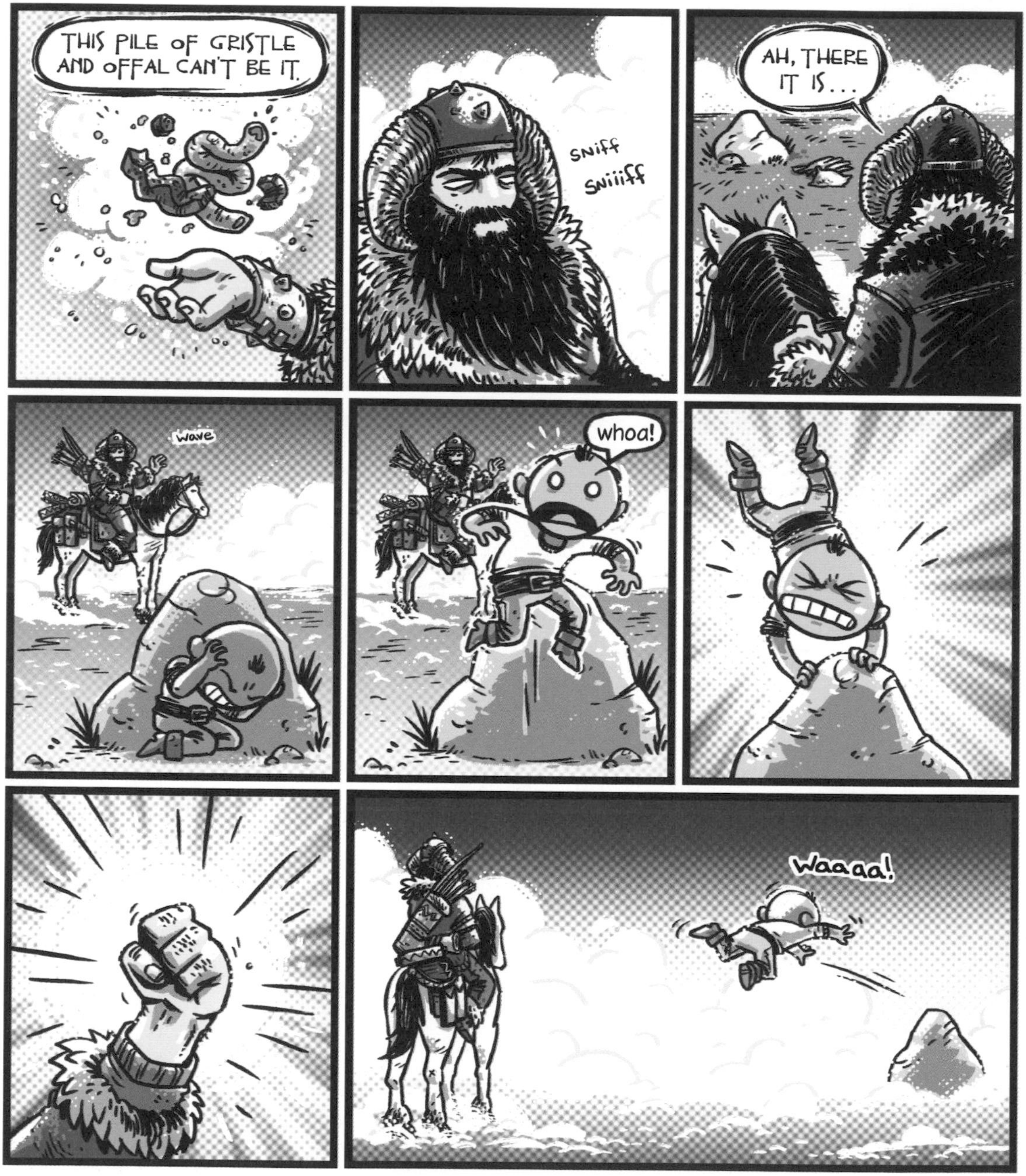
THIS PILE OF GRISTLE AND OFFAL CAN'T BE IT.
SNIFF
SNIIIFF
AH, THERE IT IS...
wave
whoa!
Waaaa!

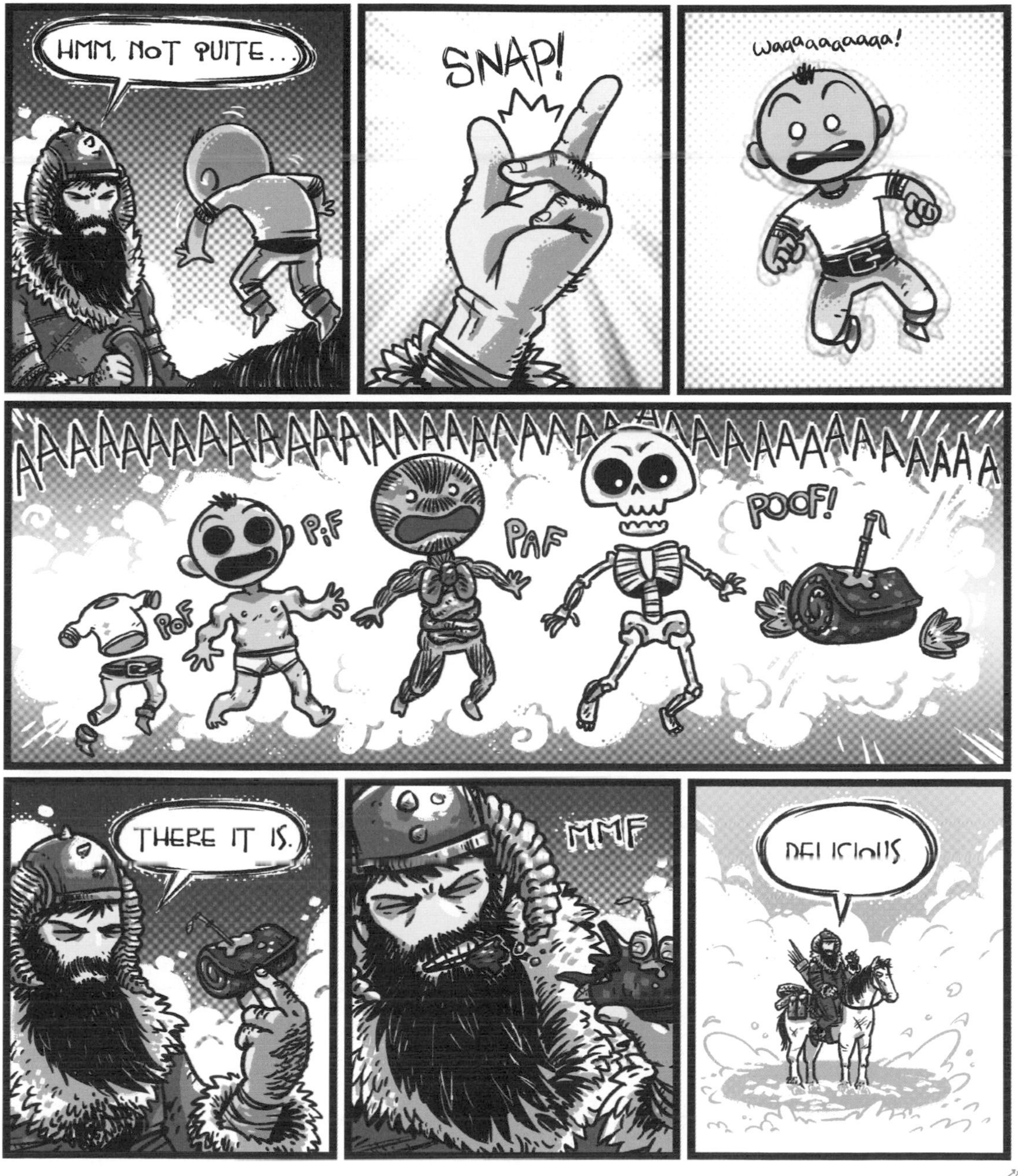
HMM, NOT QUITE...
SNAP!
Waaaaaaaaaa!
AAAAAAAAAAAAAAAAAAAAAAAAAAAAAAAAAAAAAA
PiF
PAF
POOF!
POF
THERE IT IS.
MMF
DELICIOUS

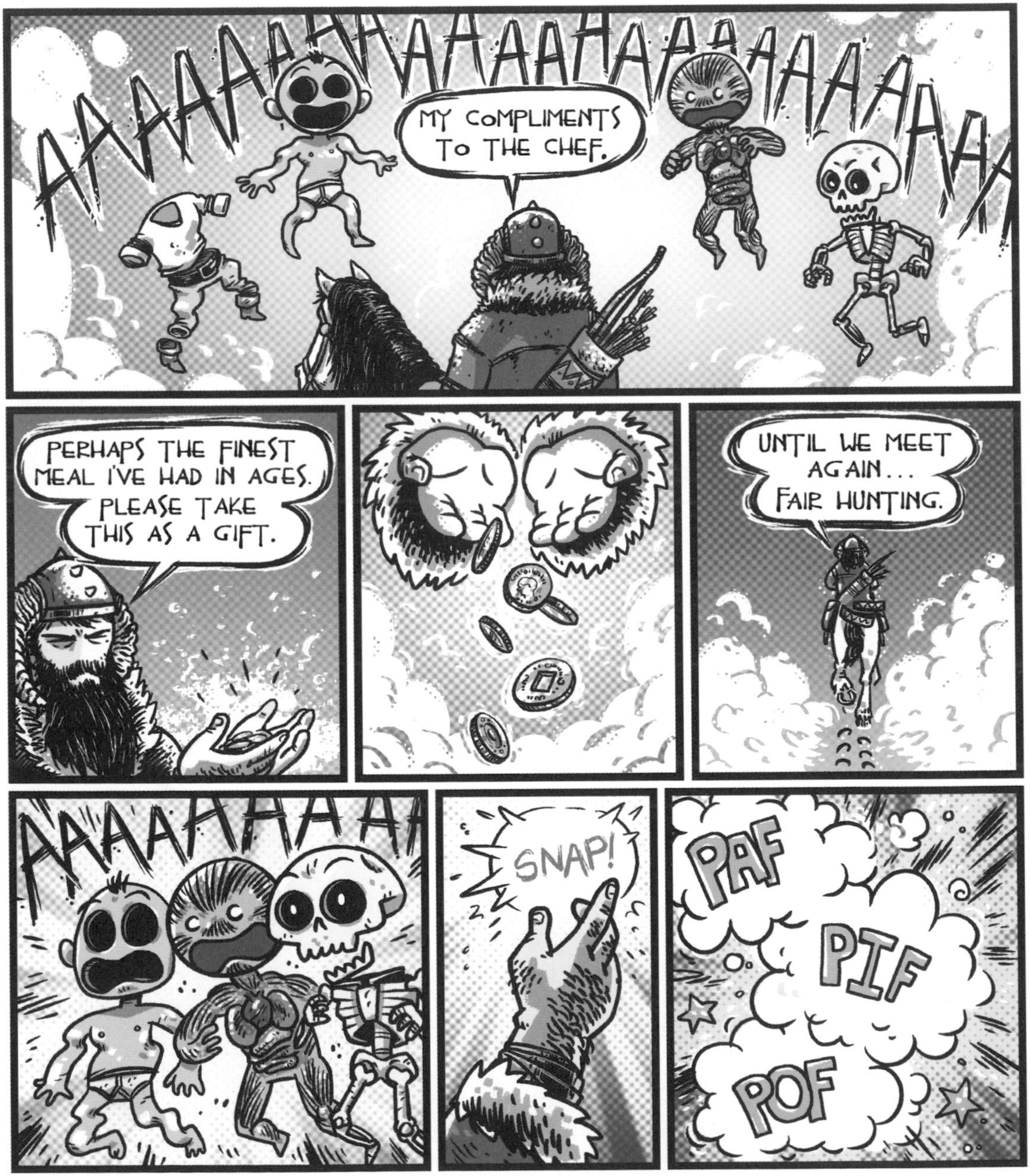
AAAAAAAAAAAAAAAAAAAAAAAAAA
MY COMPLIMENTS TO THE CHEF.
PERHAPS THE FINEST MEAL I'VE HAD IN AGES. PLEASE TAKE THIS AS A GIFT.
UNTIL WE MEET AGAIN... FAIR HUNTING.
AAAAAAAA
SNAP!
PAF
PIF
POF

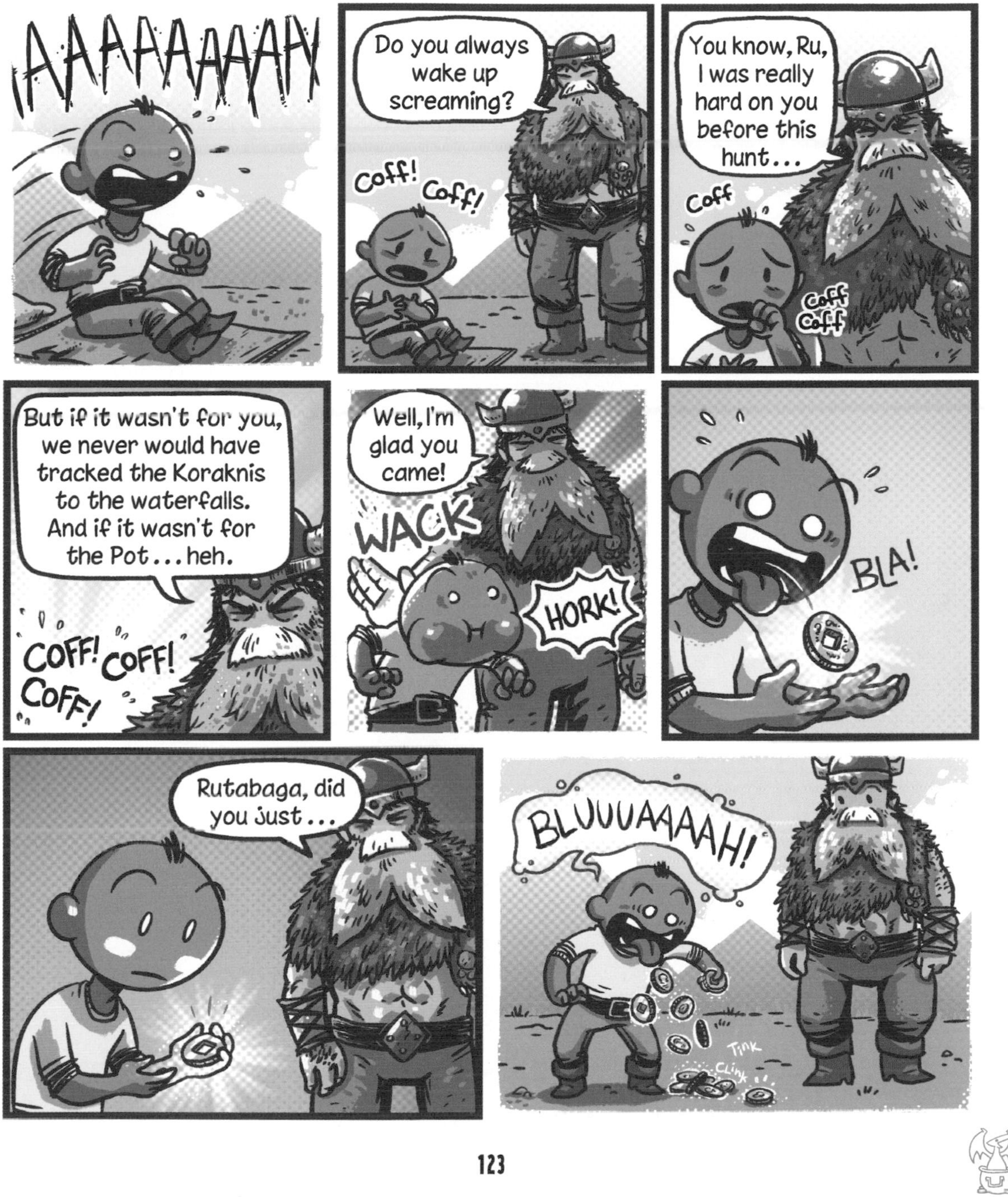
AAAAAAAAAH
Do you always wake up screaming?
Coff! Coff!
You know, Ru, I was really hard on you before this hunt...
Coff
Coff Coff
But if it wasn't for you, we never would have tracked the Koraknis to the waterfalls. And if it wasn't for the Pot... heh.
COFF! COFF! COFF!
Well, I'm glad you came!
WACK
HORK!
BLA!
Rutabaga, did you just...
BLUUUAAAAAH!
Tink
Clink

End of Chapter Four

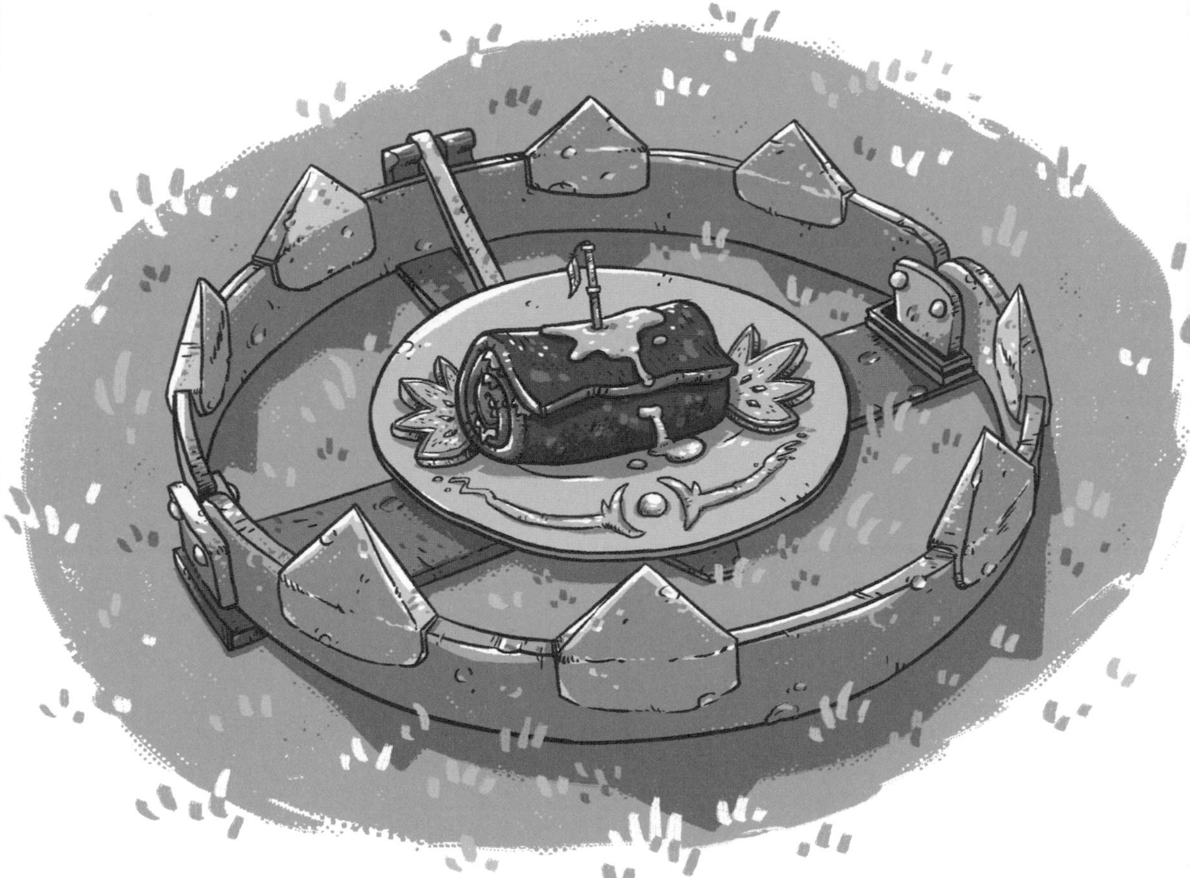

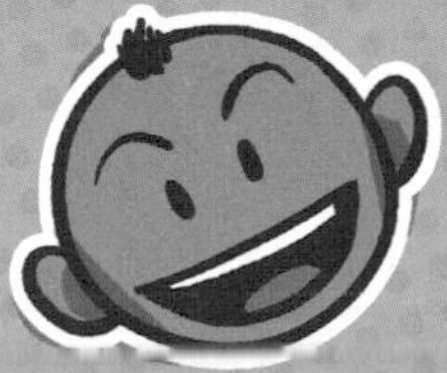

CHOCOLATE-DIPPED DRAGON CLAWS

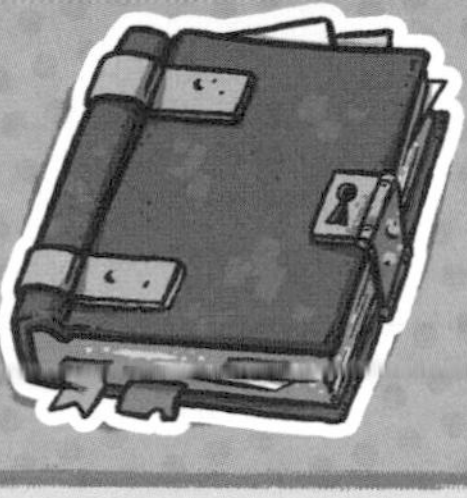

INGREDIENTS

- 2 ripe bananas
- 6 ounces melting chocolate, any color (I like to use red!)
- 2 tablespoons vegetable oil
- a box of wooden Popsicle sticks

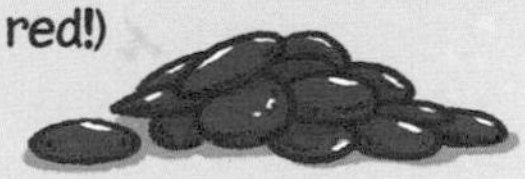

Peel the bananas and cut them in half.

Gently press a wooden Popsicle stick into the flat end of the banana.

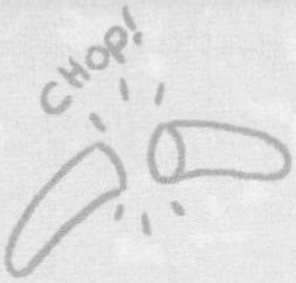
CHOP!

Place them on a baking sheet lined with parchment paper and freeze for 15 to 30 minutes.

Melt chocolate together with vegetable oil according to package instructions.

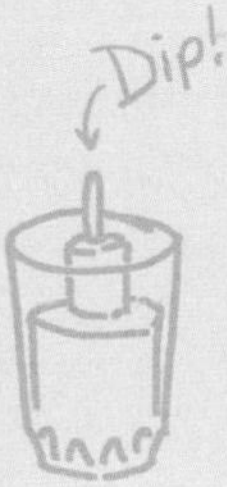
Dip!

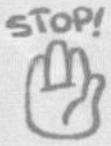
STOP!

GET AN ADULT'S HELP WHEN HEATING ANYTHING ON THE STOVE OR IN THE MICROWAVE!

Chocolate should be very smooth.

Transfer chocolate to a tall glass for easy dipping.

Take the bananas out of the freezer and dip them one at a time into the chocolate so they are almost completely covered.

Allow excess chocolate to drip off back into glass.

Place chocolate-covered bananas back on parchment after chocolate has hardened a little.

Freeze for another 15 to 30 minutes or until chocolate has hardened completely!

You have made

CHOCOLATE-DIPPED DRAGON CLAWS

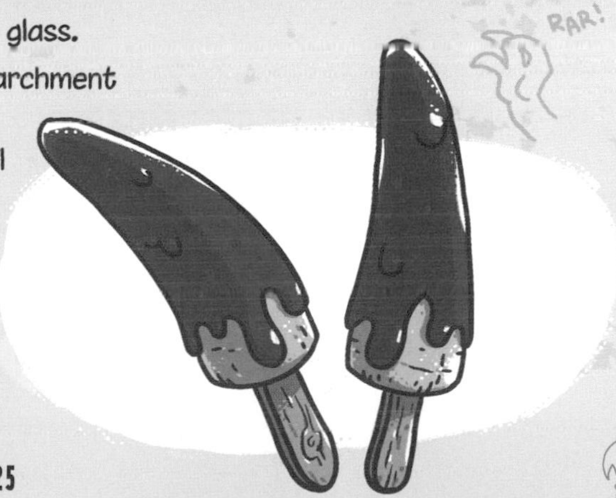
RAR!

CHOCOLATE PEANUT BUTTER POTS

INGREDIENTS

- 1/2 cup creamy peanut butter
- 1 cup powdered sugar
- 8 ounces melting chocolate
- raisins

Got a peanut allergy but still want to make this recipe? Go ahead and use a marshmallow instead of peanut butter!

-R

Dump peanut butter into a large bowl and gradually mix in powdered sugar.

This isn't really an exact science, so just keep adding sugar until the peanut butter has lost its stickiness and turned into a big doughy ball.

Refrigerate dough ball for about 10 to 15 minutes.

Tear bits off with your fingers, roll them into balls about an inch wide, and place them on a baking sheet lined with parchment paper.

After you've run out of dough, refrigerate the balls for another 20 minutes.

STOP! Melt chocolate according to package instructions.

GET AN ADULT'S HELP WHEN HEATING ANYTHING ON THE STOVE OR IN THE MICROWAVE!

Use a toothpick to pick up and dip the peanut butter balls (one at a time) into the chocolate. Allow excess to drip off.

Place back on baking sheet and press 4 raisins into the top of the chocolate.

Refrigerate one more time for 20 minutes!

When finished, pop them off the parchment paper and stand them up on the raisin feet!

You have made

CHOCOLATE PEANUT BUTTER POTS!

SO CUTE!

SO Delicious!

RUTABAGA'S PERFECT PEP POTION!

INGREDIENTS

- cranberry juice
- apple juice
- cinnamon breath mints

Yum!

CHASE BRANCH LIBRARY
17731 W. SEVEN MILE RD.
DETROIT, MI 48235
313-481-1580

Place 15 cinnamon breath mints in a plastic bag and seal it tight! Then wrap the bag in a dish towel.

Take a rolling pin or hammer and smash them to dust!

STOP! GET AN ADULT'S PERMISSION BEFORE SMASHING ANYTHING ON THEIR NICE COUNTERTOP!

WHAK

Pour 1/2 cup of cranberry juice and 1/2 cup of apple juice into a large glass.

Stir in the smashed candy dust.

Fill the glass full of ice and drink up!

You have made

PERFECT PEP POTION!

If it's too spicy, try using fewer cinnamon mints! If it's not spicy enough, add as many as you can handle!

Be wary of dragon breath!

Fwoooosh!

ERIC COLOSSAL is an artist living and working in Upstate New York. His great loves are his cats, Juju and Bear; his lovely girlfriend, Jess; and eating. He is currently working on a magic spell that lets him eat all he wants, without the unhealthy side effects. It's a work in progress.